ORBITAL  SPACE

# THEFT OF FIRE

Theft of Fire (Orbital Space #1)
First Edition (1.00.01)

Cover design by Thea Magerand, www.ikaruna.eu
Edited by Patty McIntosh-Mize

Published by Devon Eriksen LLC
© 2023 by Devon Eriksen LLC
www.DevonEriksen.com

Library of Congress Control Number: 2023918511
ISBN (paperback): 978-1-962514-02-6
ISBN (hardcover): 978-1-962514-01-9
ISBN (ebook): 978-1-962514-00-2

Books by Devon Eriksen

**Orbital Space Trilogy**

*Theft of Fire* (2023)
*Box of Trouble* (upcoming)
*Ocean of Stars* (upcoming)


Find short stories & non-fiction writing at
www.DevonEriksen.com

*When Prometheus stole fire from the gods of Olympus, did he carefully distribute it to all men, in equal part? Or, in the careless manner of Titans with lesser creatures, did he assume that all mortal ants are the same, interchangeable, and that knowledge gifted to one is gifted to all?*

*Did he give the secret of fire to the first man he met upon the road, and think his quest accomplished? Did this man then hoard that secret, making of himself a lord over all his savage brethren?*

*Did fire ever need to be stolen a second time?*

# Chapter 1
# WHAT THE CAT DRAGGED IN

"Don't you have any *real* ham?"

I just about jump out of my skin, because I have no idea anyone else is even on board. Two bags of the first fresh groceries I've had in months drop from my hands and hit the floor with a there-go-the-eggs kind of sound.

Since the dining area's tucked around the corner from the *White Cat*'s tiny galley, behind the bit with the refrigerator and the zero-g oven, it takes me a few moments to find the source of the voice. But there she is, total stranger, somehow managing to lounge in a chair that's straight upright, and bolted to the deck. With her feet on the table. Wasn't that Dad's old seat?

She's eating a sandwich.

Seriously, she's made herself a damn *sandwich*.

What the hell kind of person breaks into a docked spacecraft, helps herself to whatever's in the fridge, then waits for the owner to return so she can complain about the food? I'm so surprised I almost answer her out of sheer social reflex, tell her that, no, of course I don't have any real ham, why would a broke-ass asteroid miner have anything but flavored vat krill?

But then she asks, "Warnoc, right? Marcus Warnoc?" Which stops me long enough to get a good look at her. And the next sentence just curls up and dies in my mouth, 'cause that's the moment I know I'm in *real* trouble.

It's her eyes that give it away.

The bioengineers really went overboard on her eyes, went huge. Old-style Japanese anime huge. Couple that with the certain *look*, that characteristic glow of physical perfection, everything arranged just right. Whoever designed her wasn't subtle about it... long waves of silky black hair, delicate, aristocratic features, with high cheekbones and a razor-sharp jawline. The outsized eyes are a million shades of not-found-in-nature violet and indigo and purple, blended like an obsessive with a tiny paintbrush spent days getting them just right.

Post-human. A genetwist. And an obvious one. Looks like someone stuffed a fairy into a tailored gray business suit, complete with sensible skirt.

She's so beautiful it almost hurts to look at her.

She's definitely top of the line, too, 'cause those eyes never came from one of your standard-template jobs. Must have cost her parents a fortune before she was even out of the womb. Or out of whatever brushed-steel medical casket they use to relieve some c-suite executive's wife of that oh-so-tastelessly *biological* of human responsibilities.

In other words, a princess. No actual tiara, but probably as close to royalty as the twenty-second century has to offer.

"You're staring," she says. Naturally her voice is perfect, too. High and sweet, better suited to angelic choirs than complaining about cheap processed food. Bit of a Mars accent in there somewhere.

"You're in my *kitchen*," is all I manage to get out. Not the sharpest response.

Try again.

"More to the point, you're on my *ship*. Who the hell are you, and what are you doing on my ship?"

She arches a single perfect obsidian eyebrow at me. *"Your* ship?" she asks, artfully. "Not WeiSheng Bank's ship? Not the ship you financed for every last penny? Not the ship with a lien on it larger than its market value? Not the ship you've missed the last four payments on? I think you have some reading to do."

I don't have time to wonder how she knows all this, or why she cares. A chime sounds in my auditory nerve, and a little icon lights up in the corner of my eye. She's sent an email to my neural lace implant. I concentrate for a moment, and some sort of document projects itself on my visual cortex, semi-transparent, overlaying my view of both galley and mysterious little fairy woman.

It's wordy. Official. Crammed with legal jargon. Cryptographically signed and verified. But the meaning is clear. Bloody hell. The loans. She's bought the loans. Every last one of them. If she calls them in, takes me to arbitration... I could be stuck here on Arachne until the case settles.

That means no prospecting, no flying, and no money. Nothing but a little trickle of cash from Mining Guild residuals. Not enough to make loan payments I'm already behind on.

No payments, no ship.

She's probably got teams of lawyers on standby. Ready and waiting to grease the wheels and squeeze me out of my inheritance. Out of my home.

But... why?

I close the email.

"Look, lady, that still doesn't make it *your* ship. And it doesn't give you the right to just break in here and help yourself to the fridge. So if you do take me to arbitration, then maybe I tell them what you just did, and—"

"Oh, dear."

She smiles, all sweetness and light, but sarcasm and malice drip from her voice.

"That would be a shame. We'd all have to spend a couple of weeks attending meetings while you argued your case. That would be fun. The best legal team money can buy, versus—"

And here she looks me up and down, waves a delicate, manicured hand in a dismissive flick.

"—well, *you*. Oh, you might even win some settlement that amounts to less than I spent on these shoes—"

I can't help but glance at them, still resting on the table. They just look like sensible, low-heel pumps to me, nothing special. Which probably means I'm some sort of Neanderthal who doesn't know about expensive shoes, fine wine, or French poetry. Who's only good for simple things, like cleaning hydroponic algae traps, or welding pieces of metal together.

"—but then you'd have to explain *this*."

There's another chime in my auditory nerve, signaling the arrival of a second document. She takes another bite of the sandwich, and looks at it with distaste, apparently surprised that an invisible servant hasn't stealthily replaced it with something more to her liking.

Maybe I shouldn't even look, shouldn't play her game, but I do. I'm clearly being set up for some reason, and I need to know just how badly I'm fucked. So I look.

Huh.

"*Lady,*" I say, meaning quite the opposite, "this is just a list of timestamps and SPS coordinates. I don't know what you think you have here, but—"

"Yes. In fact, it's a list of times and locations for *your* ship."

Uh-oh. I don't like that smile on her face...

"What? You look surprised. Didn't you know that most spacecraft loans come with tracking software? You should have read that contract. You can *read*, can't you?"

Ice crawls down my spine. If she's been watching where I've been... how much does she know? Does she know what else I've been doing? And if so, how the hell did she find out?

Don't ask. Admit nothing. Bluff.

"Yeah, okay, so you say you know where I was. So what? All my claims are registered with the Mining Guild. Anyone can look them up. And why would—"

"I *wonder,*" she cuts in, all feigned innocence, "what would happen if someone compared those times and locations to that whole string of high-profile cargo hijackings that have been simply *all* over the news lately?"

Fuck. She knows. She knows *everything*.

"What? I don't have any idea what you're talking about."

"Oh, really? Shall we go talk to Precision Contract Services? Or perhaps I'll just post these two little lists together on MarsWeb? Start a little blog? See what comments people make? Let them decide for themselves what they think?"

Double fuck. I'd have so many bounties on me that I wouldn't be able to dock anywhere. Maybe not even Earth.

"Okay, look, assuming that this means anything, *which it doesn't*, why the hell do you care? You make the world's most unconvincing bounty hunter, so if this was really about justice, or something, you'd just call LoneStar or Northwoods, take a payoff from them that's probably less than you spend each month on fancy lawyers, or shoes, and then you'd fuck off. So what the hell do you *want* out of all this?"

She swings her feet down onto the deck, tosses the half-eaten sandwich in the general direction of the recycler, and stands up. She strides towards me, bouncing slightly in the low station gravity.

Wow. She's insanely genetwisted. They made her *tiny*. Lounging with her feet up on the table, she just looked short. Flatlander short. Five feet or so. But they've made her even shorter than that. On purpose.

*I* didn't grow up in microgravity, her stature says. *I'm* not seven feet tall, like some Belter mining trash. *I* spent my childhood in tasteful upmarket ring habitats, where we have full Earth gravity, and big open spaces with lots of plants, and we *never* eat synthetic ham made out of vat krill.

What the hell is *wrong* with these people?

Standing, she barely comes up to my chest, and has to reach up to poke me in the sternum with one manicured nail.

"What do I want? That's easy. *You*. I want you. You're a thief and a pirate, and *I* can prove it, and you don't want anyone else to know. Which means, in simple terms, that I own you now."

She punctuates this with another prod. I swat her hand away.

Even as I connect, there's a screech like tearing metal, earsplitting and continuous, and from somewhere, a strobe lights up, impossibly bright, breaking reality into still-frame images.

"STEP AWAY FROM THE PROTECTEE," the synthesized voice snarls, deliberately crude, harsh, robotic. Calibrated for intimidation.

The lights must be designed to blind me, but they don't. My left eye is an implant, not cloned or biofactured, but fully synthetic. The Zeiss Falcon 160 series may be old and clunky, but they're powerful, and it doesn't need time to adapt. I don't even have to squint.

Behind the flashing glare, the spider unfolds, the sectioned metal legs writhing out of the darkness near the ceiling, the hint of metal body behind the muzzle of some weapon I can't identify, curved and shaped in a disturbingly organic design, like something out of an old monster film, or a nightmare from the depths of the Terran ocean.

"STEP AWAY. FAILURE TO COMPLY WILL RESULT IN USE OF FORCE. YOU MAY BE INJURED OR KILLED. THIS IS YOUR FINAL WARNING."

Robotic protection drone.

I've never seen one of these in person before, but I know what it must be. Expensive thing. Guard for VIPs, supplements a human security force with superhuman reflexes and three-hundred-sixty degree awareness, packed into an eight-legged steel chassis complete with nasty assortment of non-lethal weapons.

Mostly non-lethal.

I think. Don't wanna test that.

She's still nursing her hand, shaking it out. Those pretty amethyst eyes must be more for looks than harsh conditions; she has them squeezed almost shut against the strobe.

I back off, and the cacophony ceases; thing must be designed to read human body language, threat postures. No, wait, not "thing"—*things*. A second metal crab-spider scuttles down the wall. Were they both hanging from the ceiling?

I didn't look up when I came in.

No one ever thinks to look up.

I take another step backwards, resting my back against the frame of the kitchen door hatch, lowering my hands slowly, trying to keep them away from my belt. I don't want the neural nets driving these things to assume I'm going for a pistol.

Not that I could. Didn't even wear one today. Careless, I suppose, but... it's Arachne Station, what the hell could happen? I wouldn't try to outdraw two protection drones anyway. One would be a bad risk. Two? Suicide.

The little princess glares up at me, eyes open now, blinking rapidfire, trying to recover from the strobes. The drones twitch restlessly on either side, fixated on me, their simple little neural net brains just itching for an excuse.

"Rule One: You don't touch me. Ever!" she snaps. "Rule Two: You do what I say, when I say. Without hesitation or stupid questions. Do you understand?"

I know this game. It's a ritual gesture as old as humankind. If I say yes, I'm submitting, declaring her Queen Alpha Bitch or whatever title tickles her aristocratic erogenous zones. I know I should nod, bend the knee, kiss the ring, wait for my moment, but I just can't make myself do it. Gotta say something, at least.

I want to do more than that. I want to wrap my hands around that tiny, elegant neck and squeeze until she shuts the fuck up.

"Lady, you got some sorta weird control fetish, or is there a point to all this? I don't think people like you moonlight as bounty agents, and I know for sure you don't come down to the docks in person and do your own dirty work. So supposing, just supposing, you were right about me being some sorta, uh, *space pirate*, or something, then what the hell would you want with me, anyway?"

"Fetish? Ew. Don't flatter yourself. You are *not* my type."

"That's not what I was talking abou—"

"I'll make it simple for you. Thieves are for stealing. You're going to steal something for me."

I give her a flat look. "Couldn't you have just paid someone?"

"Never mind what I 'could' do. This is what I'm doing. Now, are you going to be a good boy and cooperate, or do I turn you over for piracy, and keep your ship while they shove you out an airlock?"

She isn't kidding. Station security companies don't fuck around, and undesirables get deported, quick. If you can arrange transportation pronto, fine with them. If you can't? Airlock. With or without a suit. Get notorious enough, no station or habitat will touch you, and your only option is pitching a dome in the Martian desert. Or Earth.

Airlock might be preferable, though.

"Okay, fine. So, hypothetically again, just what is it you want stolen, anyway?" I ask.

"I'll tell you when you need to know. For right now, just get everything secured for maneuvers. We have about an hour before departure."

"What? Right away? Hold on a minute, it's not that fucking easy. I'd need to take on fuel, liquid oxygen, and—"

"Already taken care of. Being loaded as we speak."

I didn't see anyone in the hold when I came through, but that just means no cargo. A suited team of longshoremen could be out in hard vacuum right now, swarming over the hull, refilling PMH fuel, liquid oxygen and nitrogen, reserve air, checking the hull for micrometeoroid pits, greasing the rail fittings, the works.

"And, hypothetically assuming I don't just tell you to fuck off and do your worst right now, what's to prevent me from just taking the *Cat* and disappearing altogether? It's a big solar system out there, you know. Plenty of places a mining ship can vanish to."

"Oh, you didn't think I was just going to let you fly off on your own, did you?" She steps back and plants herself carefully in Dad's chair again, never taking her eyes off me. "No, inconvenient as it may be, I'm coming with you," she says. "And when we get where we're going, I'll tell you what you need to do."

She gestures, and in a scrabble of far too many metallic limbs, the drones scuttle back to flank her, clinging to chair and table legs. A sensor cluster, far too small to be a head, points itself at me, studded with LEDs and cameras and other bits I don't understand. Threat's clear enough. Mess with my unwelcome passenger, and they'll turn me into a grease spot on my own deck.

Well, fuck you, too.

"And what makes you think I'll take us anywhere near wherever the hell it is you want to go?"

She flashes me a smile that would be devastating if it were the least bit sincere, but it's smug, not happy. Doesn't touch her eyes. "Try it. Go on. Plot us a course somewhere else, then. Plot us a course to wherever it is you people go. See what happens."

I know it's another setup, but I can't help it. Even though my stomach is sinking, even though I already know what I'm going to find, I trigger my neural implants again, try to access the ship's computer network, to call up the navigational plotter—

ACCESS DENIED.

In big red letters superimposed over my field of view, right over her self-satisfied little porcelain-doll face. Inanely, I repeat the query.

ACCESS DENIED.

"I'm the captain now," she says. "Understand?"

# Chapter 2
# A List of Things That Won't Happen

The second acceleration chair provides a perfect vantage to glare at the back of the pilot's seat.

*My seat.* With little Miss Corporate Pencil Skirt strapped into it. I still don't know her name.

"This is incredibly stupid, and you're going to get us killed," I say, for about the fourth or fifth time in the last hour.

Her voice, melodious and smug, floats back to me. "Relax. I've flown before. I told you."

"I heard. Look, this is a two-thousand-ton ore pusher, not some rich kid's racing skiff, okay?"

"And I don't trust you at the controls yet," She continues, as if I haven't even spoken. "Not until I know you're not going to try something. I can handle the departure. It's Arachne Station. I've run it dozens of times in VR."

In a simulator?

Madness.

Or it *would* be madness. Anywhere but Arachne. What stings is that, right here, right now, she's not altogether wrong.

In the early days of the Diaspora, lotsa folks wanted to hollow out asteroids, spin them for gravity. Rubbish idea. Take it from me, I mine the things. Well, I used to, anyway.

Your typical asteroid's a loose collection of rocks—all the way from mountains to gravel—held together with gravity, inertia, and even *static electricity*, I shit you not. Bump it too hard, hell, even look at it funny, it'll fly apart. Sure, there's some tougher ones that are all one piece, but rock ain't as strong for its weight as you might think, especially under a stretching kinda force.

Spin 'em at any sort of rate that'll get you something like Earth gravity, they'll fly apart, too.

And, yeah, okay, sure, fine, you could heat 'em up, melt 'em into something a bit more solid—but space ain't cold. Space has no temperature at all. Pretty close to a perfect insulator. Wanna wait ten thousand years for your asteroid soup to cool into something usable?

Didn't think so.

Nah, hollowed out asteroids are just a shit idea all around.

But this is different. This is Arachne.

Same idea, except not an asteroid at all, but an entirely artificial planetoid, a hollow aluminum and vacuum-foamed steel football two kilometers from end to end. When they spun that bad boy up to slightly less than one rotation per minute, for a full point eight Earth gravities, somehow the engineers managed to make the whole business hold together. Dunno exactly how it works, but there's a spiderweb of aramid and doped fullerene cables latticed over the view of the opposite side. Peer though all that, and you can see people walking upside down on the ceiling, and all the buildings hanging above you in the sky.

Hell of a view. Comes with a hell of a price tag. Dunno how much the whole business cost in actual crypto or stock scrip. I only know it damn near bankrupted SpaceX to build it—think they had to sell a lot of shares to the Foxgrove Group. Anyway, rents are exorbitant. When I show up to trade, I pay the docking fees with a wince, sleep on my ship, and don't eat in restaurants.

So when your commercial spacecraft is docked, with thousands of others, to one of the rows upon rows of giant clamps that stud Arachne's hull, it's on the outside of that spin, *hanging upside down.* Just like a two thousand ton fruit bat in the most massive rookery in human space.

If you wanna fly off, all you gotta do is *let go.*

Fall off into space, and there's no need to maneuver. You're painted by hundreds of lidar systems, and tracked by twice as many computer physics models, so everyone knows where you're going. Control can route incoming traffic around you. No problem.

Anywhere else in human space, this idiot woman would have had us slammed into the side of a barge towing ten thousand tons of water ice, or a fast-burn fusion drive passenger liner. Here, all she has to do is... nothing. Wait to glide clear, until we're far enough away to fire first the chemical thrusters, then the main fusion drive.

Well, normally, anyway. Normally that's all she'd have to do.

On this particular day, of course, "normally" lasts for six minutes and thirty-seven seconds. Then Murphy shows up to bite us squarely on the ass for forgetting his iron and unbreakable law.

"Victor-one-one-seven, Arachne Control, for traffic, stand by for course correction."

The voice of the Assistant Dockmaster on the radio is an unfamiliar one, but the traditional tone of cool professionalism, unchanged since the era of control towers and jet plane traffic in atmosphere, cannot hide an undercurrent of tension. Makes sense. A course change would never be ordered if something weren't wrong.

My unwelcome guest says nothing. I can't even see her from here, just the back of the crash-couch style pilot's seat, supported on the forest of hydraulic pistons that keep it aligned with the axis of thrust. It isn't moving now. Her hands aren't even on the controls.

"Victor-one-one-seven, Arachne Control, acknowledge last."

"Princess, that's us. You need to acknowledge."

I hear a muted clicking as she fumbles with push-to-talk. "Arachne Control, ah..."

Click.

"Victor-one-one-seven."

Click.

"Standing by."

Click.

Clumsy. Around now, the Assistant Dockmaster will be rolling his eyes, looking at his berth records, and my file. And wondering why the buzz-cut guy in the photograph has suddenly been replaced by a soprano with a posh little Martian accent and second-rate comms skills.

"Okay," she says, a bit breathy, "so now we just wait?"

"No, now you pass control to me. They gotta rearrange flights for some reason, so we're going to need to get out of their traffic lane as soon as they give us a heading."

"No."

The hair on the back of my arms pricks up.

"Wait, what? What do you mean, no?"

She makes a frustrated noise. "Which word did you not understand? There's no way you're getting computer access until we get to... to where we need to go. I'll handle the maneuver. You just talk me through anything advanced."

"Talk you through... are you insane? We need to—"

"Victor-one-one-seven, Arachne Control, make your vector three-five-one by one-one-niner by twelve point five."

"—get out of the lane, and now. Do you want to run us straight into whatever's coming in?"

"I *said*," she spits, "I'll handle it."

I crane my neck around, watch her child-sized hands as she touches controls. Her nails are short, but painted, iridescent purple shading to blue, like a butterfly wing. Or like her eyes. They're painted to match her eyes.

"Arachne Control, Victor-one-one-seven roger," she says, a little smoother.

"All craft, Arachne Control, flash alert. Hotel-India-five-five has declared an emergency for thruster malfunction. Stand by course corrections."

So that's what's up. Strange. No mayday call that I heard. Musta been on another channel. Tower might be juggling two or three of them if there's a lotta traffic out there today. I should check the nav plot, find out what's going on, but I'm fixated on her hands. She's got the attitude thrusters enabled properly in cold-gas mode, but she'll need to do a chemical burn to accelerate us out of the way once she gets us turned.

*If* she can get us turned.

Oh, there she goes. I'm nudged sideways in my seat as the *Cat* swings around. Too fast. I can feel that right off. She's gonna have to correct.

Maybe just a brief moment to check.

My neural lace may be locked out of the *White Cat's* net, but we're still in Arachne's local datasphere. I pop up a nearspace traffic map. Arachne's metal football shape floats in the air in front of me, projected on the visual cortex of my brain. Surrounding it, tiny glinting dots of traffic, harsh vacuum sunlight on gray metal. A webwork of curved thrust tracks and course projection vector plots cross the virtual space. Above it all, a blood-red alert icon pulses, but that's it. No details. Nothing in the log.

Someone, somewhere, is still transferring data.

"All craft, Arachne Control, flash alert. Hotel-India-five-five is ballistic, crossing trajectory. We are dispatching tugs. Stand by."

Fuck.

*Ballistic.*

That's the physics term for unpowered flight. And it's not a coincidence that the word it usually comes before is "missile" Because right now, that's what H-I-5-5 *is,* a missile, out of control, on a collision course with...

More tracks and text light up in my virtual display, as someone, somewhere, finishes a data transfer. There. H-I-5-5. Outlined in red. On a crossing trajectory with...

... with the station.

Fuck me.

Two and a half million souls aboard, and who knows how many thousands on the dock levels? Right now, collision alarms will be screaming, warning alerts will be pulsing in the neural lace of every warm body on the station. They'll be evacuating the docks. I click through records furiously, while Princess Affluent the Spoiled tries to line us up. She doesn't seem to understand that the *Cat* is nose-heavy, with its massive cargo hold up front, and she needs to steer by kicking the tail out.

She's taking forever.

There it is. Hotel-India-five-five. The "*Heian Maru,*" a long cylindrical beehive, covered in hexagonal ports, with projecting sensor booms and comm arrays at its nose and tail. Dronescoop carrier, no doubt returning from Jupiter with a hold full of metallic hydrogen and raw gas-planet hydrocarbons skimmed from the upper cloud layer. All ready to be turned into fuel and plastics and industrial solvents.

All nice and flammable, if you add a little oxygen. If that carrier hits the docks... I can only imagine the fire.

I click back to the nav plot. Dots scatter, pushing outward on long tails of almost-invisible chemical fire, particles of metallic hydrogen mixed with liquid oxygen and set ablaze. We're one of the last specks in the area, although we've stopped turning now; I think she's got us lined up at last.

There's the first tugboat track. Don't see the others yet. Duty crew's kinda slow off the mark, dunno what went wrong, but...

No. Too far out of position. They'll never make it. Even if they touch up in time, gonna need a *lot* of push to slow that beast down. Dronescoop carriers are *big*, heavy as an asteroid ore barge.

The radio is alive with a babble of voices. I tune out the details, but the tone is frantic. They've seen what I've seen. Most of them are in the same position as me, though. All they can do is watch.

Wait.

Dronescoop carrier. Heavy as an *ore barge*.

I *can* do something. The *Cat* can handle this. She may look like nothing but two scrap steel cylinders welded together at the ends, but that's a Starlight 512C fusion drive tunnel running through the core of both, behind the biggest grapple and shockproof ram plate I could fit. She's made to push massive loads, and in all the years since Dad and I built her from internet plans, secondhand parts, and hope—well, she's moved a lot of ore barges.

Gotta fire up the fusion drive inside the exclusion zone. I'll need to warn Arachne ahead of time, need to point her *real fucking careful* so I don't irradiate the docks, but I can *do* something.

I shut off the virtual display. The genetwist's tiny hands are off the control stick now, opening switches, readying for thrust.

"Hold on."

"What?" she says. "I've got us ready to go."

"Yeah, we're not going. Pass me control. I'll take it on virtual," I say. I don't need the throttle and stick for this. Piece of cake. Really.

"What are you talking about? I already told you, no."

"The tugs aren't going to make it, not in time to stop that ship. But we can."

"What?"

"The *White Cat* is a *mining ship*. She's designed to push huge loads of ore, or whole mobile refineries. We're like those tugboats, but way more powerful. If you give me the controls *now*, I can save them!"

There isn't even a ghost of hesitation. "No," she says. "I don't know if you're lying about this or not, but I am *not* jeopardizing our mission over somebody else's problems."

Is this girl for real?

Can I get up and physically wrestle the controls from her? No, with control over the computers, she could just turn them off from her neural lace. Besides, those two fucking drones clinging to the rack behind me could tie me a knot long before I manage to wrestle any damned thing away from anyone.

"What? God damn it, Princess, did you see those big mass driver cannons we passed on the way out? If the tugs can't make it, that's Arachne's next line of defense. They will pound that carrier into *scrap*, no warnings and no questions asked, just to mitigate the impact. Habitat stations have *zero* sense of humor about collision trajectories, okay?"

"Yes," she says, cool as methane ice. "I understand. But what you're planning is dangerous, even if you're not lying to me, and our mission is too important to jeopardize. So, no."

"Oh, for fuck's sake, there's *people* on there."

"Hypocrite. As if you cared," she says. "You're a pirate. You don't want to play hero. You just want to weasel out of helping *me*. I'm taking us out of here."

And she hits the chemical thrusters, hard.

Hard enough to set us coasting off towards a nice safe distance. Where we can watch, in slow motion, over the next half hour, as it all plays out. Listen to the radio. See the news feeds on our neural lace.

Vapor trails of EVA units abandoning the carrier moments ahead of the hammer blows of half-ton mass driver slugs. One tug crippled, its pilot badly burned, when a cargo pod went up in the leaking atmosphere. Fire splashed across the face of the void. Station breaches on five levels as debris slammed into the number four dock. Right where I boarded the *Cat* with my armful of grocery bags just a few hours ago.

The *Heian Maru* limping off, trailing sparks and vapor, its hull crumpled by tug impacts. Damage estimates in bitcoin, in Starlight scrip, in various competing stock-backed cryptocurrencies. I don't listen to the numbers. I don't care. I'm numb.

"Twenty-six people in the med wing. You're lucky no one died," I say, at last, shattering the silence of the bridge.

"No, *they* are," her voice floats back, archly. "It wasn't our responsibility. Even if you could have done something, which I'm not convinced of. No one even asked. And it turns out you weren't even needed. It wasn't worth risking our mission over." Her voice is somber, but calm.

Fuck.

"Those were people's lives you gambled with. I don't care about whatever your damn mission is, or what—"

"You will," she says. Offhand. Breezy. "You might not, but you will. You don't know what's going on here. None of this *matters*. I'm going to change *everything*. I'm going to change the whole worlds. I'm going to be in the history books."

Intensity in her voice for once. Passion. She sure as hell cares a lot more about whatever the fuck this crazy mission is than she did about all those people.

I don't see red. I don't clench my fists until my knuckles are white. I don't yell. I don't move a muscle. I sit very quietly. How many seconds, and how many steps, would it take to unstrap, get to the pilot's chair, and reach around the back of it?

More time than it would take those drone-things to reach me, and stick a weapon of some sort in the back of my neck, I'm guessing.

"Really."

Her elfin face peers over the back of the pilot's seat and fixes me with a flat look.

"Yes, really. And you're going to help me. You'll understand when we get there. You may not be on board with this now, but *you will be*. You'll see. So you just sit tight, do as you're told, and then you get to walk away free and clear. No more debts, okay?"

I open my mouth to tell her to go fuck herself, but she doesn't wait for an answer.

"Now unstrap and go do... I don't know, whatever it is you do. I've got to program our course into the autopilot, and I don't want you hanging around looking over my shoulder."

"Lady, you are insane. Do you even know *how* to program the autopilot?"

As I speak, something surfaces in her face, a silent snarl, just a hint, a curl of her perfect little pouty lips, a twitch of her eyebrow, vanishing almost before I can spot it. She shrugs. "I've read the manual. A to B. Shouldn't be too difficult. Now scram."

I scram, unbuckling the acceleration harness and pushing off towards the hatch at the back of the bridge. I suppose I could sit here and argue with her, but that would get me nowhere, and I have things to do.

I have a mission now. Not her mission. Mine.

I have no idea why she came along and decided to expend an absurd amount of money and energy to just to ruin my day. It still doesn't make any sense. Teams of lawyers? More teams of techies to hack my computer systems? Plus whoever she got to do all that research and catch me red-handed? It's an absurd display of overkill. Like cracking nuts with a sledgehammer.

It makes no sense. She's probably spent way more than she would have just to hire someone. And then she shows up to ride along with just two drones and no actual staff?

Why?

I don't know. But what I do know is that I'm not going to meekly go along with this crazy woman's big scheme, whatever it is. No. I need to find out what she's up to, what she wants, and then I need to find a way to stop her from getting it.

I'm going to find a way to get control of my ship back, and get her out of my life for good.

That's *my* mission. *My* plan.

If only I couldn't still hear Dad's voice. Talking about plans.

*No, I understand it, Marc. Your numbers work. With our own torchship, we could prospect our own rocks. We'd be paid off in five years. I get all that. If things go according to your plan, it would be a really good investment, but if they don't, we'll be overextended. And 'plan' is just a fancy word for "a list of things that won't happen."*

Yeah, thanks for the vote of confidence, Dad.

Problem is, if you're stuck in a small spacecraft interior, there's not a whole lot of other places to scram *to*. There's my cabin, I suppose. At least the door locks from the inside. I float down the access shaft between decks, pushing myself along with an occasional hand on the ladder.

I pass the medbay level, and the hatch to the galley, but when I reach the crew deck, I just sail right on by, down one more level to the tail of the ship. My brain needs space to pace in. I need to think.

We couldn't really afford the luxury of an observation deck, but Dad insisted. Said he wanted to see the stars. And so we dug deep and paid for all those custom panes of laminated fullerene and vapor-deposit diamond, fitted them into a perfect donut lattice of clear panes around the thin central core of the access tunnel. We had to move that tunnel, and replace all the floor panes with carbon fiber and foamed steel when we fitted the fusion drive, but the rest of the windows are still in place, offering a clear view of glittering stars.

Turned out Dad was right, as usual. When you're stuck in the same fifty-meter tube for weeks or months on end, you're only too grateful to sit by the diamond glass and watch the sky. Ironic that when you're in space, the one thing you're short of is, well... space.

It's a bit cluttered by all the gym equipment I've dragged in and bolted to the floor. But I still float here in zero-g and look back at the receding form of Arachne as we coast away. You can't really see much of the damage from this distance. Can't get it out of my mind, though.

Impacts. Fire in vacuum. Atmosphere venting. Debris spinning in the void.

Fucking miracle that no one died.

Much as I hate SpaceX, no Belter wants to see that. Everybody's lost someone out here. Or knows someone who has. When there's only a thin steel shell between you and the breathstealer, the big empty, you *protect that fucking shell*. No matter who it belongs to.

This girl's not just a Martian, she's a Flatlander. Must be. Lives on the surface. No space dweller would brush that off, so casual. Like she didn't care what could have happened.

As if she thought I shouldn't care, either.

What hurts is this woulda gotten me out of trouble, the bounty on a rescue op this big. Could've paid off all those debts she's holding, or at least a big piece of them. And I wish I could say that it never crossed my mind in the moment, but I don't know. Maybe it did.

I sure as hell need the money.

Technically, Warnoc Engineering is still a member of the Mining Guild in good standing, so every time someone registers a claim, I get residuals, a little scrap of that fee for being contractually bound to honor their claim, and leave their asteroid alone. That actually adds up to a fair amount, but not enough for that loan I took against the *Cat* herself.

To lease a fusion drive. Just a temporary measure. Until it started paying off. It would pay for itself, I said, and Dad shook his head—

*I don't know, Marc, it's risky.*

Dad was right. Again.

Guess that's how I wound up here. No way to make the payments after the... accident. Jacking mining cargoes has kept the wolves from the door, but the big numbers in those breathless news articles about piracy, they don't translate to what I'm pocketing. A load of partially processed ore may be worth one number on an insurance claim, but sell it off on the sly, and you're getting ten percent. If you're lucky.

And if I was lucky, I wouldn't be in this mess.

Time to start digging myself out. Time to start pulling whatever strings I can think of. Time to make a phone call.

Dorje Rangpa Tsangmo squints at me through the video feed, and scratches with one callused hand at the scraggly embarrassment he claims is a beard. Behind him, my neural lace projects a translucent hint of his office, photos of his wife and legion of kids pinned up on synthetic corkboard.

"I dunno, Marcus," he says, "isn't this your gig in the first place? I mean, the blind girl paid for it all, my whole crew for the shift, with extra for a priority job, but since it's your ship, and she had all right paperwork, I thought—"

"Blind girl?"

"Yeah, the little genetwist. She manages not to bump into stuff, and she doesn't have dark glasses or one of those little folding canes, but I figure she must be blind—I mean, she's smoking hot and obviously rich, and yet here she is playing sugar momma to your ugly ass. So I figure she's either blind, or maybe just crazy, kayno?"

"Yeah, real fucking funny, Dorj. Ya know what? You wanna make personal remarks about my sex life, maybe I'll give Dawa a call when I get back from this trip. She's on, what, her second year in college? About time someone nice took her out on the station, maybe got her drunk, and whatever happens, happens. Maybe her *and* Lynette."

"You wouldn't dare." He gives me a mock-aghast look.

"You wouldn't do shit, Dorj. I know you."

"Wouldn't have to. Elena would stab you in the neck. Besides, aren't you busy with the smoke job?"

"No, see, that's why I'm calling. It's not like that. She's a client, and not one I took on purpose. She's not bankrolling me, she's blackmailing me. I do this trip, or I get fucked over. I don't even know where we're going, yet."

He cocks one bushy black eyebrow at me. "Really? What she got on you, Marcus? Photos of you banging a—"

I cut him off before he can elaborate on whatever disturbing mental image he's crafted.

"The loans, Dorj. She bought them all. Probably for mils on the bitcoin."

I am *not* going to tell him the rest.

"Oh. Sucks to be you, I guess. I told you your dad was right about—"

"Don't remind me. Anyway, that's why we're having this little talk. I need information."

"And here's me thinking it was a social call. You're too good to just say hi, now?"

"Dorj, you charge by the hour. If I called just to rattle the vents, you'd probably bill me for the conversation or some shit like that. I was hoping you could tell me how much fuel you loaded, any cargo you put on, whatever else you saw that can maybe help me figure out what she's got in mind. I know I'm kinda grasping at straws, here, but the damn woman won't tell me anything. All very catfoot for some reason."

"Like I said, Marcus... I dunno. I assumed you already knew what was going on. But if you don't, the contract's got a standard non-disclosure clause, so—"

"Oh, for fuck's sake, Dorj. That's a formality, and you know it. I'm not some runner trying to scope another runner's cargo. It's *my* damn ship."

He shrugs. "Word and hand on it," he says.

"That's Belter talk. Didn't know you believed in that stuff."

"Your dad did."

He's right. I can hear the old man now.

*Just because we don't have governments and laws doesn't mean we can do anything we want, Marc. Belters spend a lot of their lives billions or trillions of kilometers away from any arbitration company or station association, and they do business with each other by radio. Sure, they use crypto-signing like everyone else, but their business networks really run on reputation. That's what the phrase means. Their good name is on the line each and every time they say those words, and if we're going to do business with them, then that applies to us, too.*

"Yeah, and look where that got him. Screwed by a bunch of—"

"This isn't going to turn into another rant about how much you hate rich people and SpaceX, is it?"

"I liked you better when you were a revolutionary. At least then you had principles."

He shrugs. "Fair enough. I liked *you* better when you were working for your dad. At least then you had the money to pay me."

"Yeah, thanks for nothing, Dorj."

He shrugs. "Nothing personal, Marcus. I don't make the rules."

"So that's it?"

"Not a lot I can do. Look, can we talk later? I've got two crews pulling overtime trying to get the docks cleared and running again, and I'm trying to line up more, plus materials, and—"

"Yeah, I get ya. Say hi to Elena and the kids for me. Especially Dawa and Lynette." I flash him a grin.

"Bastard." He grins back. "Keep your hormones in check. Or, better yet, go hit on that genetwist girl. Turn on some of that Marcus Warnoc seduction magic. Maybe then she'll go easier on you."

"Not gonna happen. Complete psycho, I'm tellin' ya. See you on the flip side." I don't think he hears the last part of that. He's already cut the link, and his image has vanished, leaving me alone with the window, and the stars.

Well, that's a dead end. I'm going to have to think of something else.

Not that I have any immediate ideas.

# Chapter 3
# We Don't Go to Sedna

Our first day of travel starts with a jolt.

There's no warning. The deck just leaps up and slams into my spine. For a moment, I think I'm about to get crushed between high-grav acceleration and steel deck plates, but we stop ramping up at what feels like one gravity. Not that the fall doesn't hurt. Why didn't she sound the acceleration alarm first?

Because she doesn't know what she's doing, that's why. A fully automated luxury torchship, something built by SpaceX, or Faulcon-DeLacy, would trigger one automatically before drive spinup, but when I set up the *Cat*, I just rigged a button labeled "XL WARN" on the controls and called it a day. And she didn't push that button. Of course she didn't. Probably didn't even know what it meant.

Amateur hour. Good thing I already secured for maneuvers, or I'd be under a pile of loose gear right now.

I'm still picking myself up off the floor and grumbling when she comes down the ladder, glowing with satisfaction at having figured out how to use a standard software tool designed for user friendly operation. And of course the first thing out of her mouth is a complaint.

"Do we really have to climb up and down this ladder all the time?" she asks, looking up as the first of the robotic crab-spider bodyguards descends after her, all sectioned limbs and disturbing, fluid grace.

"Look, lady, what the hell do you expect? Elevators? A grand spiral staircase? This whole crew section is just a cylinder sectioned off into decks. Stacked on top of each other, you know, like a..." I trail off, searching for an analogy that works.

"Can of pineapple rings?" she offers, brightly.

"What's a pine-apple ring?"

She peers at me, cocking her head to one side like an inquisitive kitten. "It's a ring. Of pineapple. From a can? Pineapple? You know, the *fruit*? From *Earth*?"

I close my organic eye and massage the bridge of my nose with my fingers. "Asteroid miners," I say "do not eat fruit imported from Earth."

"Well, you should. It's delicious. Anyway, it's a bad design. They should have used a wider, flatter cylinder and put more compartments on each level. That way, you wouldn't have to—"

"Dock at a standard size station berth? Maneuver next to a spinning rock? Retain hull integrity when I'm pushing ten thousand tons of ore barge? Look, Princess, this is the ship you chose to hijack. You don't like it, that's on you, 'cause I'd have been more than okay with you ruining somebody else's day instead. So, now that we're under way, you wanna tell me where the hell we're going and what it is you want me to help you steal?"

She tries to drag a low padded bench away from the bench press station, maybe towards the nearest window, but it doesn't budge. The drones climb into the equipment, one on the top of the squat rack, the other clinging to the lat machine. They seem to like high places.

"No," she says, and tugs again, like she's expecting to rip out the ten-millimeter bolts I clamped the gym equipment down with. Does she not know what happens with loose gear on spacecraft?

"Our mission is strictly need-to-know," she continues. "Top secret. I'll tell you what you need to do when you need to do it. I—*we*—can't risk you blabbing all over the internet."

She gives up on rearranging my observation deck and sinks her shapely little butt onto the bench right where it is. The gray pencil skirt clings to her hips and thighs, and I wrench my eyes away—I've been alone in space far too long already.

I hate her, but I can't stop looking. I need to get away. Clear my head.

The drones bristle as I pass within a few meters of her, but she doesn't say a word as I climb the ladder, leaving her there to ponder the stars by herself. Or play games on her neural lace. Or plot how she's gonna drain the blood from her next victim. Whatever.

Above the observation deck, the access tunnel is enclosed, a tight vertical tube of gray epoxy paint on steel. Above me, hatchways open off the shaft, at different angles, not always directly opposite the ladder. Dad and I aren't architects or interior designers. We kinda worked them in wherever they fit.

I don't even know where I'm going, I just know I need to get away from her. We're gonna spend however long this flight takes stuck together in the space of a fifty meter cylinder, most of it occupied by instruments and machinery, with nothing to do and no one to talk to but each other. Oh, and the internet only available with minutes if not hours of lightspeed lag.

Great.

The cabins are two levels above observation, just past the galley and supply stowage, where the shaft opens up into a little access space. Four gray metal hatchway doors divide in an arc across the inside of the... ah... "pine-apple" ring. Can't get that image out of my head. Three cabins, and one door spray painted with those ubiquitous little icons of a stick figure man and woman, to which Dad added, in a slightly different shade of white, a robot and what looks like a goat. Underneath, block letters read "WHATEVER. JUST WASH YOUR HANDS."

The second hatch from the left is hanging open, revealing a small glimpse of a bag strapped to the zero-g tiedown points, its rich burgundy synth material textured to look like... no, wait, that's probably real leather, isn't it? From an actual animal.

The second door. She's taken Dad's cabin.

I have the fleeting urge to rip the door open, grab every scrap of luggage I can lay my hands on, and tip it down the access shaft to land on her miniature aristocratic head. Instead, I pull open the door to my own cabin, lock it behind me. At least she can't follow me here. I reach over, yank the grip handle, swing the bunk out from the wall, and sit down heavily on the smartfoam without bothering to roll aside the zero-g net.

Great. I'm hiding in my room from a girl who's less than four feet tall, is built like a wisp of sunlight, and smells faintly of vanilla. Wonderful start to the great space pirate resistance, there, Marcus.

So, how to fight back? I call up my neural lace display, try the navcomp again.

"ACCESS DENIED. Please contact your network administrator."

Fuck.

*I'm* the network administrator. The White Cat isn't one of those fancy automatic SpaceX torchships, with everything from drive and nav control to the thermostat and sound system under the control of a centralized, shiny, pastel-colored interface. Single sign on, cloud integrated for service calls, probably calls SpaceX to tell them what music you listen to and whether you jerk off in the shower.

Fuck that.

Dad just found some stripped secondhand hull sections... I bought telescopes, signal gear, and a used lidar array, installed the cooling system with plans I downloaded from the internet, blew in fresh rad shielding, ordered custom cargo racks, and so on. Then we strung the whole thing together with YCloud and a network of secondhand servers I bought from a decommissioned data center in the L3 trojan point.

Homebrew has come a long way since the days of NASA.

Except now she's locked me out of all of it. Maybe had some techs come in to do it or something. I have no idea what weakness they found, but I'm not surprised they did. I'm no programmer. I just make do. Up until now, anyway.

Access denied. To navigation. To sensors. To fusion core direct access, attitude thrusters, power systems, everything. Even, and I don't know why I tried this, because I don't see how it would help, life support. And then finally, to backup and restore. Restoring an earlier network image over the current state—that was my last idea.

No dice. The *White Cat's* whole computer network is compromised. I don't know how they did it, but my user account is now marked as a 'passenger,' and so... Access denied.

On that SpaceX, or Orbital Dynamics, or Faulcon-DeLacey ship, that would be that. I wouldn't even be able operate anything but the light switches and doors. Everything integrated. But *Cat's* not like that. They say, "Ya Ain't Gonna Need It" and if I didn't, I didn't put it in. A lot of the lights are on switches, the cabin climate control's a bunch of thermostats on the wall, and, hell, the lock on the docking port airlock is mechanical, takes an old-fashioned mag key. It was cheap and why the fuck not?

So what can I use? Well, there's the cargo crane in the hold. That just has a simple passcode so the longshore crews can use it, and unless she had that changed, too, I can...

I can do what? Move some cargo containers around? Yeah, real useful.

The rest of the ship's systems seem locked down pretty tight. The more I scroll through stuff, the more 'access denied' messages I get. I don't even know who she is, or where we are going. If I could only get a look at the navigation plotter...

Wait.

How does the *computer* do the navigation plot?

Pulsars.

It's called XNAV. X-ray pulsar-based navigation and timing. The *Cat* triangulates itself by orienting with distant neutron stars, special stars that spin ferociously, drawing gas off of stellar companions, heating it to millions of degrees, pouring out x-rays. It's absurdly accurate, precise to a measurement of meters within distances that span the solar system—but it's useless to me. I can't detect those x-rays without instruments I'm locked out of.

But the principle is sound. It's as ancient as the time when our ancestors sailed seas of liquid water with nothing but a sun compass, and a sextant to sight the positions of the stars.

Stars. Now there's an idea.

With precise angle orientation and timing, a couple of high-res images of stars, taken a few hours apart, maybe with some nearby asteroid shots to get a better parallax reading to confirm speed... I'd have to count pixels in the images, do some calculations, run some open source nav software on the data, but just maybe I can plot two positions in space.

And two points determine a line.

Tricky, of course. Real old-school sailor stuff. Stick jockeys need not apply. But I'm Marcus Warnoc, son of Bjorn Warnoc, son of Olaf Warnoc, of the line of Yngvarr Víðförli, the Far-Traveled.

I also paid attention in physics class. That might have something to do with it, too.

With some good camera shots, I can *do* this. But where to get the camera? The *Cat* has a full high-mag telescopic array, two of them in fact, but as long as I'm getting "ACCESS DENIED," that's no help.

Hmm. Camera, camera, camera... can't take pictures with my implant eye. No way to hold my head at the same angle for hours, and the resolution's nowhere near high enough anyway, I need a hardcore camera like the telescopes, or a recon drone...

Wait. That's it. There's a half-disassembled mineral-assay limpet up in the workshop level. Gas thrusters are all busted up, but the core unit, with its cameras and gyroscopes and accelerometers, should not only let me take all the pics I need, but tell me precisely what angle they are at with respect to the axis of thrust. If I just line it up against one of the windows with lots of high-speed tape and cyanoacrylate glue... yes.

Now I just have to go up and get it, then head down to the observation deck, and... damn. She's down there, isn't she? Can't think how I'd explain what I was doing.

Hmm... create a diversion, maybe? Or just wait until she goes to bed?

I hope she's not a night owl.

Draw a line.

After painstaking hours of waiting, and fumbling down thirty meters of ladder with detached camera equipment trailing wires everywhere, and more hours of waiting, and drawing diagrams, and throwing away all the calculations and starting again...

...finally, at long last, in the small hours of the morning, when you should be sleeping, draw a line.

A direct line. A line connecting to nothing, nothing at all, not until it reaches the outer solar system, so far away that light from the sun takes almost twelve hours to get there. A line that intersects the orbit of one, and only one, thing.

A destination.

Trans-Neptunian sub-planetary object 90377. Call it by its common name. 'Sedna,' after some Inuit goddess of something or other.

Call it a "dwarf planet," like Pluto, for a lot of boring reasons that have to do with mass and shape and orbit clearing. But don't bother to explain those reasons. No one cares. You'll just bore them.

Don't bother talking about its strange eccentric orbit, either, swinging in an eleven-thousand-year arc between just outside Pluto's orbit, to way out in the endless night, the frozen dark of interstellar space, where a tiny trickle of sunlight takes five days to arrive.

Don't use words like "mean anomaly" and "semi-major axis" and "longitude of ascending node." Nobody cares about those words, either, except pilots, when we have to. And even we don't use them in party conversations, because that's not the kind of talk you use to chat up a limber seven-foot-tall Belter girl who can put both feet behind her head.

You don't need to talk about any of that.

Because when someone says 'Sedna,' everyone thinks one thing, and one thing only. The only thing out there worth caring about.

The Tombs.

For thousands of years since humanity learned to rub the sticks together and make fire, we've looked up at the little lights in the night sky and wondered if we were alone. "Fermi's Paradox," they called it, which is a fancy name for a real simple question... "Where the fuck is everybody?"

Philosophers argued about it, scientists speculated about it, novelists wrote things. For decades, wild-eyed enthusiasts with small government paychecks and really huge radio telescopes listened to the static hiss of the universe, straining to catch some stray signal that cried out "Hey! We're over here!"

But nobody was calling. Or sending emails. Or whatever it is you do when you're talking to someone who doesn't share your basic biochemistry, much less your computer protocols. So either nobody's home, or they're all being really, really quiet. And for decades, we could only wonder if nobody was home, or they were hiding from the scary monsters, or maybe it was just because we have too few limbs, or smell bad, or are the interspecies equivalent of that one dude who tries to talk about orbital mechanics to Belter girls at parties.

Finally, in the late twenty-first century, a Martian mineralogist, one Derrick Blake, looked at a spectrographic telescope display and said the least promising historical words ever:

"*That* doesn't look natural at all."

Say those words anywhere in the solar system, from a casino orbiting Saturn to an ice mine on Europa to a Terran political prison, and everyone, literally everyone, will know exactly what you are talking about. It's one of those quotations that transcends all context and needs none, like the naked and dripping "Eureka!" of Archimedes, or the questionable Latin of Erik Nyberg's "Habe Quiddam" or the static-laden recording of Neil Armstrong's "One small step for a man, one giant leap for mankind."

And everyone, literally everyone, has seen the photos taken by the first Sedna expedition when they went to take a closer look. The bizarre and convoluted structures, without symmetry or right angles, jutting out of a desolate moonscape, almost black against a field of stars. The antiquated NASA-design vacsuits, standing over row upon row of empty, open pods, or perhaps coffins.

The Tombs, they called them. But where were the Tomb Builders?

And no one knows how they came here, thousands of years ago, when our ancestors were first learning to till the land and chart the seasons. No one knows why they vanished, with their work left apparently unfinished, or where they went.

We've searched the skies for wherever they might have come from, or where their modern counterparts might be. Searched and found nothing, nothing but the static hiss of cosmic background radiation, and the equally meaningless academic babble of endless theories, with zero concrete results.

Are they all dead in some war or cosmic cataclysm? Exploring elsewhere? Avoiding us? Did their civilization advance to the point where they live in computerized virtual realms, or left the galaxy, or the material universe altogether?

We haven't a clue. They're nowhere to be found. But we indisputably are not, or at least—a few thousand years before the Egyptians started piling up rocks—*were* not, alone.

Had that been all we found, just a strange and empty necropolis, then I suppose only the philosophers and scientists and nerds would have cared, in the long run.

But they left artifacts as well, bits and scraps of things whose purpose we mostly can't figure out. Much of modern civilization is built upon those pieces of their junk. The nanoscale fabrics in our spacesuits. The high-tech voodoo trick that compresses gaseous hydrogen into stable fuel pellets of shiny white metal. The materials that make up the biocompatible computer chips and interface wires we lace into our bodies and brains. But most of all, the nuclear fusion reactors and spacecraft drives.

Twelve interplanetary corporations fought a shooting war over that dead site and its secrets. Thousands have died trying to seize that knowledge, or keep it from others. Fusion drives, reverse engineered from their broken fragments, and fitted with our computers, lifted fully a third of humanity out of gravity's greedy claws, sent us out on the great Diaspora to populate the solar system from Mercury to the Kuiper Belt.

And today, you can sail from one to the other in the space of perhaps two weeks, balanced on a pillar of nuclear fire, accelerating, then decelerating, at one comfortable Terran gravity for the whole of the journey. *If* you can afford one of those drives. Which not everyone can, but those who can, well, they can go anywhere they want.

Anywhere, that is, except Sedna.

We don't go to Sedna.

## Chapter 4
# MUTUALLY ASSURED DESTRUCTION

The heel of my hand hurts, but I don't really care. I bang on the hatch again, the door of what used to be Dad's cabin. Three more hard thumps. From somewhere inside, a high pitched voice yells something completely unintelligible, but I'm guessing it's a variation on the theme of "Go away."

Well, I can do this all night, even if I have to switch hands once in a while.

It takes some time, and a good deal more banging, before the hatch finally scrapes open, a reluctant few centimeters, on one glaring purple eye.

"All right, all right, *what*?"

"Sedna?" I snarl at her. "Are you fucking serious?"

"Of course I'm—" she begins, then cuts off and yanks the door open. She's wearing some sort of giant fluffy green robe, probably hand-spun out of unicorn tears by Indonesian child laborers. And from the looks of her hair, it's either perfect all the time, or she stops to brush it when someone hammers on her door at midnight. A protection drone looms behind her. She stares at me, narrow-eyed. Suspicious.

"How did you know?"

"Never mind how I know. Are you just an idiot, or are you actually trying to get us killed?"

"What do you mean by that?"

"You're going to the Tombs. You have to be. That's the only thing on Sedna that's of any interest at all."

"You aren't supposed to know that yet. I told you, information is on a need-to-know basis, and until we get there, you *don't* need to know."

She starts to shut the cabin door, and I shove my foot in it. My *bare* foot. And a jolt of pain shoots up my leg as she immediately slams the hatch anyway, what feels like as hard as she possibly can.

"Oww! What the fuck? Are you crazy?"

"I'm not the one hammering on people's doors in the dead of night and yelling incoherent insults at them. Go away."

She's still trying to close the hatch, yanking on it with both hands, apparently in the belief that if she pulls hard enough, she can magic my foot out of existence. I'm lucky she's small and not very strong. Still... it hurts. Rather a lot, in fact.

"Dammit, will you stop that? I am trying to tell you that your plan is suicide, okay? You don't simply fly over to Sedna. Not unless you wanna get killed. Look, I'm the pilot here, not you. What sense does it make to not listen—ow, fuck, stop that—to me about my own goddamned job?"

She gives up trying to slam my foot out of existence, lets go of the hatch handle and jabs one finger at me. The paint on her nail is fresh again, a coat of the same color, blue fading to purple, iridescent, like a butterfly wing. Who the hell still takes time to paint her nails when she's traveling on an industrial spacecraft?

"It's not your job right now. I didn't hire you to think. I hired you to do what I tell you. And what I am telling you to do right now is shut up, stop snooping around, and wait for me to tell you what the next step in the plan is."

"You didn't *hire* me at all. When you hire someone, you offer them a job, they say yes, and then you pay them. That's how it works. This isn't a *job*, Princess. I don't *work* for you."

"Of course you do. Your pay is that I don't turn you in for piracy, and your ship doesn't get repossessed. Is that not valuable to you? Did you not agree to it? You're here, aren't you?"

My god, the mental gymnastics on this bitch. I'm too stunned to say a thing, so she just rambles on.

"That means we're going to execute *my* plan, and we're going to do it *my* way, because it's *my* discovery that we're going to—"

She stops, and starts again.

"Look, you're not in charge here, and that's your fault. It's the result of your own actions, and the sooner you realize that, the better things will go for you."

"Wait a second," I say, shoving the door open, despite her best efforts. "Your... discovery? You found something? At Sedna? At the Tombs?"

She stumbles backwards, looking disturbed, but doesn't answer, just ducks to one side. And is replaced by one of... *them*, its alarms and strobe lights blaring.

"YOU ARE ATTEMPTING TO ENTER A RESTRICTED AREA. BACK AWAY AT ONCE. FAILURE TO COMPLY WILL RESULT IN THE USE OF FORCE, INCLUDING HARMFUL OR LETHAL FORCE. THIS IS YOUR ONLY WARNING."

I take my hands off the hatch, and attempt to back away slowly, but one foot, the one she slammed in the door, buckles under me and I stumble, catching myself against the opposite wall of the entryway. I don't see her push the hatch, but it slams shut with a very final-sounding clang.

That could've gone better.

I stare at the closed hatch, but it's not like it's going to scrape open again and disgorge a more reasonable version of Executive Spoiled Brat, who at least realizes she doesn't know the first thing about astrodynamics. Someone who might even listen when I tell her that flying straight up to a free-fire zone, while announcing your presence with a blazing fusion drive, is basically painting a target on your forehead and screaming "Here I am, please fire a very large nuclear warhead at me."

And somehow, given all the secrecy, and her talk of "stealing something" for her, I have some idea that, just maybe, we are not invited guests. Hell, Starlight may start shooting the moment they see us. And on this course, blazing right in at one gravity all the way, they *will* see us.

But I can't tell her that. She won't listen for long enough. I'm going to have to *do* something.

I turn around and limp back towards my own cabin. Yeah, do something. Great. But do what? Is there any way to get through to this miniature nutcase?

Not likely. I may not know who she is, I'm starting to get a read on *what* she is. Spoiled rotten, and either stupid, or might as well be, because you can't tell her anything. Even smart people can be really, really good at talking themselves into stupid ideas.

I've seen incarnations of her before. Fashionably short and blonde, with perfect makeup, holding a red plastic cup at Flatlander high school parties on Venus where I grew up. Seven feet tall and willowy, with facial piercings and wild-colored hair, dancing to tuvo drum music, in Orbital nightclubs in the Belt.

Always surrounded by a halo of thirsty boys, who agree with every vacuous opinion, who laugh at every unfunny joke. Who know they are making fools of themselves, know that their eagerness will incite nothing in her but contempt, but they cannot help it. They are drawn in by the tug of primal male instincts, the call of beauty to testosterone.

The sort of girl who has never heard 'no' from the day she was six years old and discovered that daddy would give her a cookie when mommy wouldn't, if she just smiled. Who has never had to work, or to be disappointed. Who never buys her own drinks or carries her own luggage. Who knows, deep in her bones, that she is *owed* the best of everything because she is somehow, indefinably, special, not for anything she does, but just for being her.

Worse than that, this one's rich.

Judging by her obvious designer genetics, not just well-off, not just comfortable, not just 'daddy owns a successful law firm,' but super-wealthy. Imperial rich. Dynasty rich. Business empire rich. That's why she's so damn pretty. It's how they modify their kids. Health. Longevity. Looks.

When you own everything, you don't need to build your kids with more strength, or better vision, or quicker reflexes, because anything they need done, they're going to have people to do it for them. They don't need gripping feet for zero-g, because your exclusive private orbital habitat ring spins at a steady point eight Earth gravities. And you're not going to try to make them any smarter, because you have experts and AI to do all the number-crunching, and, besides, all the first-generation brain-boosted 'twists went crazy, anyway.

All they need to do is manipulate others. So Rule One is "Make 'em look perfect." Perfect enough to help people forget that Rule Two is "Raise them as ruthless, amoral sociopaths."

I don't know why they gave her those eyes, those pointy fairy features. Why they made her so tiny. But her personality sure fits the pattern.

I'm jolted out of angry thoughts when I feel something familiar in my hand. I don't even need to look down to realize where my feet steered me to, what my hands unpacked. I'm standing in my cabin, in front of the open storage cabinet, last on the left.

And what I'm holding, what I took out without even noticing what I was doing, is the Sphinx SDP Ultima. Semi-automatic. Chambered in Hornady 7x25mm caseless. 21 rounds to a magazine. Heavy, black anodized steel and aluminum, its worn and familiar grip fitting the swell of my palm like a glove. Still in its hard kydex retention holster.

Whoa, whoa, whoa. Hold on just one fucking second, here. Yes, I don't like her. But... a pistol? Really? Is that where my brain just went?

It's not like I'd hesitate if someone were attacking me. I carry it when I go out on sketchier stations, selling jacked cargoes. But I've only ever had to draw it twice, and both times, pointing it was enough. I've never killed anyone.

No. I have. But not like this. Not in cold blood, up close and personal. On purpose. Am I willing to take a life? *Her* life? It's not like she's *trying* to kill us both...

For a moment, I imagine that perfect, adorable, scornful little pixie face vanishing under a welter of flying blood...

*Violence is wasteful, Marc, but it isn't inherently evil. Sometimes you might have to fight, or even kill, to defend yourself. That's why I'm giving you this. Because you're old enough to understand that if you make that call, if you take someone's life, you can't ever take it back. I know you'll be smart about when not to pull a trigger.*

Well, I guess I let you down, there, Dad. But... not this time. No. Nope. No way.

I'm holding the pistol for... I dunno, comfort, maybe? It feels better to be armed, like I'm less helpless, somehow. Except I am, aren't I? Because I'm not willing to do... that. I shake my head as I put it back.

Close the lid on it.

My heart is hammering so hard I can feel my pulse in my ears.

I'm not sure I'd get the opportunity even if I could make myself do it. Those drone things are *fast*, and they have me two to one. And even if I got incredibly lucky and managed to shoot both of them somewhere vital, what then? What about her? I can't just shoot her or shove her out an airlock. Well, not *can't*. Won't.

Even if I took out the drones somehow, it's not like I really have anywhere to lock her up. The hold, maybe? A shipping container? I've seen footage of the shipping containers packed with Terran refugees, thirty, maybe forty people each, discovered on Port Luna, or New Tokyo. They mostly survive the trip. Mostly.

I don't know if I wanna do that to her, either. But I have to stop her, before she gets us both killed. And I have to do that without any access to the ship's controls.

Okay. Think. Be systematic. Stop battering your head against locked doors. Think about what you need to do, and what you have. Solve the one with the other.

I need to stop us from accelerating at a steady nine point eight meters per second squared towards a spot square inside the reticles of a lot of nuclear missiles and mass-driver cannons.

I need to take those protection drones out of the picture, so she can't use them against me or set them on me.

I need to restore my access to the computers and get control of my ship back.

I need to somehow stop her from doing anything with those damning documents. I need control of my life back.

And I *have* to stop her. I don't have the choice to just bow my head and go along. That's not pride speaking. God knows I've had enough practice swallowing it lately. This time, I can't. I can't let her have her way.

Because she doesn't know what she's doing, and, in space, when you don't know what you're doing, you die. Space doesn't care how rich you are, or what size of a stock transfer you can make. It doesn't care what you own. It doesn't care how much other people respect you, or how special they think you are. It doesn't care how pretty you are, and how much other people desire or admire or envy you.

It will kill you.

And trouble has a splash zone out here. I refuse to be collateral damage when this spoiled little princess finds she can't buy her way out of the laws of physics, or bat her eyelashes at them.

I'm fighting for my life. And, ironically, hers as well.

Haven't got a lot going for me here. Without access to the instruments, and the helm, and, hell, everything but one cargo crane, my piloting skills are useless. Effectively I'm just some big lunk who can lift heavy stuff and maybe fix things here and there.

Pretty good at that, actually. I can fix most anything on the ship. I'm the one who built most of it.

Wait a second.

If I can fix something... I can break it.

I've wasted too much time beating my head against that computer lockout. I'm not a hacker. But I have *physical* access to the drive. I have physical access to the central network server boxes. I have physical access to all the actual hardware this stuff runs in. And I know where everything is.

That means I *can* stop us from flying... even if I don't have any helm control or computer access at all.

Time to throw a wrench in the works.

I'm climbing a ladder out of a deep well. Or that's what it feels like.

When I'm weightless, my brain tends to imagine the space as a round horizontal tunnel. But now, with the drive running, pushing us forward at one steady, earth-normal 9.8 meters per square second, the access shaft is vertical and deep. I take it slowly. A fall would be bad from this high. With each step up the ladder, the tool bag suspended from my belt bangs against my hip.

I'm technically alongside the drive already. The fusion containment shaft runs the length of the ship; Dad and I had to move the accessway about a meter and a half off center when we had it put in.

But I can't commit any sabotage from here. Cut through that wall, through layer upon layer of compressed hydrogen boride and water-extended polymer, break into the exotic field channels, coolant lines, and the superconducting induction grids, and I'd breach the vacuum of the drive tunnel. Wear a vacsuit to survive decompression, and I'd still be irradiated to the point of glowing in the dark for the rest of my life. All three minutes of it.

No, I need access to the control mechanisms. The fuel lines, coolant pumps, field emitters. So I climb.

Top of the ladder. The hatch door above me is marked "Cargo Access Airlock" in faded red epoxy paint. I reach for the crank wheel carefully, one hand still on the ladder.

There's no need to cycle the lock once I clamber in. The indicator lights on the far wall show me that whoever my unwelcome guest is, she didn't know enough about cargo operations to activate the pumps and evacuate the hold once in-atmosphere loading was done.

That's okay. Saves me the trouble of getting into a suit.

Still, I close the inner door before opening the outer one. It's a fifty meter fall down to the observation deck at the other end of the hab cylinder. Then I clamber up into the hold, and there it is, looming in the semidarkness above me, centered between the four massive steel beams that run along the spine of the ship—the ten meter spindle of a Starlight 512C Nuclear Fusion Induction Impulse Drive.

The whole mass of coiled tubes, radiator fins, cable conduits, and exotic field hardware revolves around the central vacuum shaft in a slow procession, sending out a deep throbbing hum that I don't just hear but feel as well, at infrasonic frequencies that vibrate my diaphragm, the walls of my chest, my skull. I've never seen the spin rate vary, nor the pitch of the sound, no matter how soft or hard I've burned the drive.

Around the central core, empty shipping container racks line the hold's vast cylinder, stretching from floor to ceiling. A few paces away, where the spine of the ship meets the floor, the next ladder stretches upwards.

I climb into the gloom.

Up in the scaffolding around the spindle, I unpack my tools... a zero-gravity shop vac with mounting clamps. Safety goggles. A filter mask. An oscillating saw, cased in yellow and black plastic. An opened package of blades, held together with faded duct tape. A worklight.

Okay. Gotta think about this.

No one knows exactly how these things work, except a few cloistered Starlight scientists and engineers, and even they are copying their homework off an impossibly advanced alien species. If you don't know your physics, nothing about it makes sense, and if you do know your physics, everything about it makes even less sense than if you didn't.

It fuses hydrogen into helium, like the core of the sun, but forty-two percent of the energy the reaction should generate just... isn't there. Like it goes somewhere else we can't see. It doesn't push against a shock plate like a standard drive, but exerts force along the length of the tunnel with some sort of magnetic induction. It's not a reactionless drive, but the reaction mass exhaust it throws out is a tiny fraction of what it should be.

Scientists all agree that the physics doesn't work. The drive, however, just does.

So it's in the absence of any great sense of enlightenment that I stare at the complex tapestry of the spindle rotating slowly past me, held within a series of massive collars packed with fullerene bearings and lithium grease.

What exactly *can* I do to this thing?

Hmmm.

Can't break the field emitters. No one outside of Starlight knows how to fix them. Coolant lines? No, spectacularly bad idea. My plans for today do not include being part of a nuclear fireball. Same for the charge distribution net.

How about the fuel feed lines?

Yes. No matter how proprietary and secret and complex this thing gets at the injection end, at a certain point, a PMH line is just a PMH line. And nothing runs without fuel.

Okay, so... primary and secondary injection manifolds there and there, injection collar here, static lines running into the walls of the primary vacuum shaft... better cut further back from the source. There. Running into the manifolds on the upper and lower collar bushing. Primary and secondary lines, zero through seven.

Mask and goggles first. Okay, now clamp the shop vac to the pipe, just after the Tesla conduit section, and before the tertiary injectors. Angle the head and power on with a whir. Breeze begins to pull past my face...

There. That should catch most of the residual fuel in the lines. PMH. Particle Metallic Hydrogen. Hydrogen gas, compressed to its metallic form by unbelievable pressure from exotic field technology, then rendered into a fine dust, each particle precisely the same mass. I peel back the tape, extract a blade from the package, check it carefully to make sure it's the type I expect. Yes, "CL/Diamond Enhanced Sparkless." Fit it to the saw.

Hopefully, between the sparkless blade and the shopvac to suck up the leakage, I should be okay. Because with the hold pressurized, there's plenty of oxygen in here, and I can't run the pumps to drain it.

PMH fuel plus oxygen plus a spark equals a big fucking fireball. Oh, well, at least if it goes wrong, I probably won't even have time to notice.

Okay, let's get ready for this, visualize the game plan. Time to find out if I remembered just what the reactor safety systems are designed to do. If I'm right, cutting feed lines should trigger a reactor trip shutdown.

Necessary? Not really. Even with a fuel feed imbalance slewing the beam, I'd theoretically be fine. The grid should channel any hot plasma away from the shaft wall. And there's still several redundant layers of BH-WEP shielding between me and enough neutron radiation to scramble every cell in my body. But I'm hoping the systems engineers were paranoid, because the safety shutdown is what I really want.

I fire up the saw, careful to keep my fingers back. The blade, vibrating back and forth at twenty thousand cycles per second, bites right into the fuel line with a howl. The external copper shell and insulating jacket shred immediately, then I feel the blade halt as it bites into the vanadium steel core, shedding a halo of steel dust to flow into the shopvac in a visible stream of glitter.

Press hard and wait. It's loud this close, damn loud. Hope she can't hear it through the distance and the steel bulkheads. If she does, with all this noise, I wouldn't be able to hear those drones coming. Just have to hurry and hope.

After a brief fucking eternity, the saw jolts, and a loud sucking hiss cuts through the howl of the saw. There. Vacuum breached. There's air in the line. No way that one will work now.

**"Alert. Alert. Alert. Feed vacuum breach detected. Core engine trip in progress. Emergency shutdown in ten seconds. All personnel brace for core ejection."**

Yes! Thank you, calculating overcautious left-brained pencil pushers of the engineering worlds. Without you, we'd all be dead of radiation sickness or sucking hard vacuum.

But you did just let my unwelcome guest know exactly what I'm up to. That warning just came through every intercom speaker on the *White Cat*. So even if she couldn't hear the saw... well, she sure as hell knows what I'm up to now.

**"Alert. Alert. Alert. Feed vacuum breach detected. Core engine trip in progress. Emergency shutdown in five seconds. All personnel brace for core ejection."**

I lock an elbow around the ladder cage, and grab my own wrist, holding tight... It's about to get loud in here. And rough.

**"Four. Three. Two. One. Ejecting fusion core."**

And a titanic blow, like Nyberg's Hammer up close and personal, hits the *Cat*—somewhere. I can't see anything from here, of course, and for a moment, as the steel superstructure rings like a colossal gong, I can't hear anything, either, but I know what's happened.

A living, breathing fusion reaction, a shaft of plasma as thick as a pencil and over seventy meters long, has been freed from its primary containment field, to explode out violently backwards under inertial containment, expanding and cooling fast, but still burning. Still as hot as the core of the sun. Turbulent and chaotic as it slams against the secondary grid field all along the length to the *Cat*, buffeting her sideways this way and that.

She lurches forward, shuddering and groaning in protest, for a single moment. And then gravity is gone, and I am floating free.

PMH glitter jets out around me, swirling in zero gravity, and I cut the saw power off fast, teeth clenched and palms clammy, but the shopvac seems to be drawing most of it in, there's no huge fireball, and I'm not dead.

Now I just have to not-die fifteen more times.

I affix the shopvac to the next line, and start to cut. Sweating now. The drive may be shut down now, but I know there's some redundancy here... the reactor doesn't actually need all these feed lines in order to work. But cut enough of them, though, and the computer will flat refuse to start it up again, even in rescue mode. I bend my head to the task.

Nothing interrupts me. Even after five minutes, ten, no nightmare metallic spiders rush out of the access lock to drag me from my work. Finally, the last line is cut.

There, Miss Corporate Documents. Miss Expensive Shoes. Miss Trust Fund Baby. Go ahead and cut out the damaged segments. Cut and prep fresh conduit pipes. Bend them to fit. TIG weld them into place. Check tolerances. Flush and evacuate the lines. Then run a full set of manual reactor pre-start checks.

Good luck with all that, sweetie. Hope they taught welding in finishing school. Don't break a nail.

I leave my repacked toolbag velcro-strapped to a coolant feed line, and head back down into the access lock, flying along the ladder in zero gravity. Now it looks horizontal to me again. She'll be up there somewhere up ahead, with those heavily armed spiders to guard her, to prevent me from laying one finger on her. Too bad for her that she wasn't the only vulnerable thing on this ship.

I'm not looking forward to this next part, where I deal with whatever reaction her madness has cooked up, but I can't just stay up here forever.

Might as well get it over with.

But I don't encounter her on the way down the access ladder at all. Not in the tunnel, not on the engineering levels, not on the bridge, not in the galley. I don't see her at all until I reach the cabin level, and then I understand why she hasn't come after me at all, not one step.

She's drifting in the door of her cabin, surrounded by a massive sphere of glossy black hair that stretches out in every direction, waving gently in the current from the vent fans. Motionless. Curled into a ball. Around her orbits a cloud of makeup bottles, partially unfolded clothing, a hairbrush, the detritus of a bag packed for travel. And woven through all of it, a swarm of tiny red oblong shapes. Pills.

Is she some sort of... addict?

It takes me a moment to spot her constant metal shadows, the drones, where they cling to the junction of wall and ceiling, scanning back and forth with sensor clusters. They don't appear distressed at all. But are they programmed for medical?

She stirs a bit, whimpers, and reaches out for the hatch opening, turning herself to look blearily in my direction. Hmm, she doesn't *look* high. She looks slightly... green.

Oh. Freefall. Right. Expensive little custom genetwist girl isn't perfect after all.

"What," she groans, "did you do?"

I savor the moment. "We regret that your hijacked spacecraft is experiencing technical difficulties. Please stand by. If you require further assistance, we recommend you go fuck yourself."

"What did you *do*?"

"Drive's out of action, Princess. Now do you wanna talk about your stupid-ass flight plan without slamming a door in my face, or do you need to go to the head and throw up first?"

"Be fine... in a few... minutes. Got. Pills. For it."

"Yeah, I noticed. You better clean those up before they get everywhere. But we need to talk first. We're not going to fucking Sedna."

"I heard you. The first time. We had this. Conversation. Already. And yes we are. What did you do to the drive?"

"Knocked off a couple bits you won't fix in a hurry. That way you have to listen to me this time."

"Well, maybe if you didn't. Hammer on my door. In the middle of the night. Besides, we talked about this. You've been stealing cargoes for years out here. Stealth flying is supposed to be your thing. So your job, since you keep asking. Is to make sure we don't get noticed."

She's straightened up a bit, looking a little less distressed already.

"Oh, for fuck's sake, this isn't just about you wanting to *go there*, which is insane enough. It's about *how*. You laid in a course straight there. Thirteen days accelerating at one gravity, thirteen days decelerating at one gravity, then insertion into low orbit. Right in the middle of the no-fly zone."

"Yeah, so what? It was easy. You just tell the nav plotter thing where you want to go."

I groan, lay one hand on my forehead, and run it back over the short stubble of my hair. Where to begin?

"Are you for real? Look, Princess, the Starlight Coalition Exclusion Zone is not a joke, okay? The Tombs, and the artifacts they took from them, are the basis of their whole empire, and they do not mean to share. No interlopers. No visitors. No student exchange programs. No outside access at all. The hundred thousand kilometer radius around Sedna is the most intensely scrutinized slice of sky in the known universe.

"If they see us go in there, they will shoot us right the fuck out of space. And if we somehow dodge that, we'll have to get away again, with them chasing us, not to mention a bounty on us so enormous that every single cargo carrier, mining ship, courier, and fucking *research* vessel within a few light minutes is going to join the chase, okay? Not that we would live long enough for anyone else to collect it with a pack of Coalition warships on our ass."

She arches one eyebrow at me. "You've been listening to far too many stories," she says. "And you know nothing about corporations. No one *has* any warships. Not even Starlight. You know who used to have warships? Governments, that's who. Not corporations.

"You know why? Because governments have *subjects*, who they can just take money from whether they like it or not. Corporations have *customers*, who expect something for their money, and stockholders who expect to be paid. They can't just buy a bunch of superfluous junk that doesn't turn a profit, or their stockholders will vote everyone off the board. Warships aren't a good investment. They aren't *profitable*."

"Lotta companies sure as hell had warships in the Artifact War."

"It was profitable to fight over alien artifacts back then. When that was over, they were nothing but an expense. They've been decommissioned and sold, pretty much everywhere. The United Nations might have a few hidden in Earth orbit somewhere, but even they wouldn't dare use them, or even show them, because if they did, another Nyberg would just drop another asteroid on them."

She's warmed up to her subject, and is looking slightly less green already. Her eyes have this little sparkle to them when she gets passionate about something, and there's this cute little dusting of freckles across her nose that I just know the designers put there on purpose.

God, I hate myself sometimes.

"Warships," she continues, "are obsolete. So what they'll have there will be a few lightly armed security patrol craft, at most. And you can handle those, right?"

"Handle them how? Just what the hell are you imagining I'm going to do?"

She stares at me down her pert little upturned nose like I'm an idiot, an effect that's slightly spoiled by a drifting pill bouncing off it.

"Do what you've *been* doing. Fly us in without being noticed and get us away clean. You stole 47 full-mass cargoes, in the middle of empty space, and no one ever caught you. You know what they were calling you in the press?"

"Yes, and I'll thank you not to repeat it. It's not that fucking easy. First of all—"

She gives me a smug look.

"You'll figure it out. Besides, it's my call to make. Now get us under way again."

"No."

"Are you that stupid? You can knock out the drive, but I still have the radio. I can still turn it on, call up Arachne Station, and..."

"And do what? Call for rescue? Turn me in?"

She opens her mouth to answer, but I don't wait for whatever piece of crazy is gonna pop out.

"And what will you tell them when they arrive? That I'm a pirate, and you just happen to be drifting around with me in a crippled ship, twenty million kilometers out in space? That you neglected to mention it to them when we left? And where will you tell them we were going? Will your story agree with what's in the nav plotter's memory? Will it agree with what *I* tell them when they ask? Maybe we could all just sit around and have a nice chat. Imagine the things we could discuss, them and I."

"You're bluffing," she scoffs, with that sort of fish-mouthed expression she makes, a combination of anger and disgust. "You'd be in a lot more trouble than I would."

"So what? I'm fucked already. And what you're doing is *so* legitimate and above-board that you hired a pilot, and a crew, by advertising on the internet, right? *'Charter ship needed for potentially dangerous, highly profitable mission to the Sedna Exclusion Zone. Hazard pay and profit-sharing bonuses available. Top talent and highly experienced only.'*

"Oh, wait, no, you didn't do that at all, did you? You blackmailed *me*, instead. Well, now I have no incentive not to say things that Starlight would be very interested in hearing. Face it, Princess. The days when you could turn me in without consequences were over the moment I figured out where you wanted to go. I may not know exactly what your plan was, or who your backers are, but I know enough to sink you. Mutually assured destruction."

She glares at me. "And if I just call those *backers* and have them come sort you out? You'd never have a chance to talk to anyone."

"I know you can't do that, because if you could, we wouldn't be here alone. If they had people to send, people they could trust, those people would be here with us already. And if they had a ship to send, you'd be on it right now instead of here.

"So spare me your attempts at bluffing and look at your options. Call for help and tank your whole plan, or give me back control of my ship. Or, we can just sit here until you change your mind. Maybe watch the stars a bit. Play some chess. Catch up on your knitting or whatever it is you do when you're not fucking with random strangers' lives."

It feels so good to say it, to be back in charge... or, at least, it does until the moment I notice that she's not angry anymore, she's grinning, a little crooked smile I don't like the look of.

"There's one more option," she says.

And then she kicks out both legs, pushes off the doorframe, and takes a flying leap at me.

What the hell?

She comes in at head level, swinging an arm in a big slow haymaker, those fancy nails extended to claw my face or something. It's the most pathetic attack I've ever seen, and I'm so prepared that I'm actually waiting for her, for just a split second, before I bat her away with one open hand. Doesn't take much effort when she's weightless, and only masses about as much as a kid to begin with.

She flies across the room, tumbling end-over-end in the air, and I have one moment, just a moment, of smug self-satisfaction with my complete and obvious physical superiority.

Wait, she's... still grinning?

Then the drone slams into me, flashing strobes and screaming klaxon fury, and that's the moment I realize she's outsmarted me, taken advantage of my training and reflexes. The drone doesn't care about abstract concepts like "self-defense." All it sees is an attack—which was the point all along.

For a moment, I hold it off, grabbing at flailing segmented limbs, using my mass and reach against it, then every muscle in my arms and chest locks up, and pulses of white heat run through me, a wave of angry hornets, buzzing, stinging, burning. Taser. My cybernetic eye blurs over with static at each pulse.

I can't move, can't fight back, my arms won't obey me. Not that I could make a dent in the damn thing anyway. I can't see where the girl is, can't hear her; the worlds are a confused blur of fractured images, strobing light, and the incessant, deafening howl of whatever brain-melting frequency some sound engineer picked for this metallic bastard.

But I can feel it. It's dragging me off in some direction, one grabber limb clamped around my shoulder, pushing off walls with metal claws. The taser must be a probe instead of wired darts, because it doesn't have to reset, it keeps shocking me every time I start to regain control, and I'm covered in something wet and sticky... blood?

Pepper spray?

No. Marker dye. Purple. Dumb machine thinks I'm a would-be assassin who might flee into a crowd. Artificial stupidity. No understanding of context. That fucking dye's gonna get every fucking where in zero g.

I wonder, though... where is the other drone?

But I'm too busy being hit to find out.

The thing about pain is that it makes the worlds small. Shrinks your focus.

My world has shrunk to the size of the few square inches of deck plate next to my face. The cheap gray epoxy paint, chaos of tiny scratches. Somehow I can see, or at least imagine, all the countless random impacts and scuffs needed to create that surface.

I don't think I want to move right now; something in my back is still twitching in hard, random spasms that send a hot needle of pain shooting up and down my left side. Not to mention that I don't have any idea what those drones might interpret as a resumption of the "threat."

From somewhere beyond my drifting sphere of aches, the prod of a dainty, slippered foot interrupts my thoughts.

"You awake?" she asks, sounding... satisfied. "I can see it was foolish to expect you to see reason. I didn't like doing that, but you put your hands on me, and that's not allowed. Hopefully, you've learned your lesson. I suppose you'll need to rest after that business. Fine. But tomorrow morning, go down to the drive and do whatever it is you need to do to get us sailing again. For now, go to your cabin and stay there. I have things to do, and I don't need you looking over my shoulder."

She pushes off a wall, and I don't watch her go.

No, Princess. It's ain't that fucking easy. You may think you've won, but all you've done is show me how soft and unprepared you are. You think a single ass-kicking is going to change my mind?

Well, maybe violence is unthinkable to you, in your soft luxurious world of full-gravity habitats, brunch, and non-functional scarves, but I've had my ass kicked harder, by scarier people, and gotten back up to repay the loan with interest.

We'll see how you take it when it's your turn.

# Chapter 5
# Barsoom

*To: pangurban@wide-relay.net*

*From:*
*drtsangmo@contract.arachne.spacex.com*

*Subject: I have something that belongs to you*

*Hey, Marcus, sorry it's taken me a while to get back to you. Things have been crazy around here after the accident. We're pulling double shifts managing traffic on fewer docks, and the rebuild will probably take months to complete.*

*About your little problem... sorry I couldn't be more helpful. But I still can't. Word and hand. Can't tell you anything I put on the ship. That would be breach of contract. I'm very careful about what contracts say I can't do, and about what they don't.*

*Hey, when you get back, come look me up, I'll buy you a couple of rounds so we know there's no hard feelings, stet? Besides, I seem to have somehow wound up in possession of an empty shipping container that belongs to you. One of the twelve-meter ones. I'll have my boys put it somewhere. Wherever you wanna store something like that. No charge.*

*- Dorje*

I mark the message as read and banish my neural lace display. This week just keeps getting weirder and weirder. Why would Dorje write me from his SpaceX contractor account, instead of his personal one, or his own business email? Why would he repeat that stuff about the contract? It's like one of those bits in bad stories where the butler and maid have a loud conversation about things they already know, just so the audience can get up to speed.

And why would he have one of my empty shipping containers?

There's something... odd... about this message. Like, each thing he's saying is innocuous, but no one talks that way. Not really.

Wait.

*Can't tell you anything I put on the ship.*

*Very careful about what contracts say and what they don't.*

Oh.

He can't tell me anything he put *on* the ship.

That's it. Dorje, you sly old crook. I'll bet you went over that contact with some legal assistance software and a fine tooth comb. It may have a nondisclosure agreement over what you did, and what you loaded onto the *Cat*... but it didn't say anything about not disclosing what you *have*, did it?

Like an empty shipping container. If he has it, he must have taken it *off* the *Cat*. And he'd never have done that unless someone told him to. Only one reason for that—to prevent me from noticing the one she wanted him to put *on*.

Pretty sure that one ain't empty.

The burns on my back and side twinge as I punch the air in triumph, but I don't care. Dorje, when we meet up next, *I'm* buying. Even if it's that crazy fermented-rice stuff that tastes like death and kills you if you brew it wrong.

Now I have one more thread to pull. There's something aboard the ship she doesn't want me to find, maybe a bunch of somethings, if some of them are smaller than a twelve-meter shipping container. I don't know what they are, but if she doesn't want me to find them, they're important. Maybe

I'll learn something useful. Maybe I can blackmail her right back.

Maybe a lot of things.

She expects me to repair the drive tomorrow. If that means she'll refrain from coming after me with those drones until then, then I have... tonight. After she falls asleep, assuming she falls asleep instead of just resting in a coffin packed with soil from her native Carpathia, or hanging upside down from the rafters before flying out at night to drink the blood of the innocent.

I can search the ship, top to bottom.

And then... I dunno. Something. Depends what I find. Point is, I'm not out of moves just yet.

A nudge from my neural lace jolts me out of angry and restless dreams I can't recall. A fight somewhere, a struggle, flashes of swarming metallic things like insects, and a feminine, childish voice—not hers—singing? Laughing? Never mind. It's gone.

I squirm out of the zero-g net on my bunk, sweating, panting. Too much adrenaline over nothing. It's just the alarm I set myself. After midnight, Mars time. Sleep shift. There's no light leaking around my cabin hatch.

I listen a moment, and there's nothing but the white-noise hiss of air cyclers. Odds are she's sleeping like a damn baby, dreaming dreams of avarice.

Should be safe to move.

A command to my neural lace adjusts my implant eye to thermal infrared, and a grainy white image of my cabin appears, bright where my body has warmed the hammock, dark for the cool steel of the bulkheads and deck.

I swing my feet towards the ceiling, and hang inverted in zero-g, reaching for the storage cabinet under my rack. Gotta go slow or I'll just push myself away, and bounce off the opposite wall. Ease open the catch and probe the darkness with my fingers. A folding multitool. Charging cables. A pill case. Where's the—

Oh. There it is. Recognize it by feel. A handheld signal analyzer. So cheap and basic that it just has a screen instead of a neural interface display. It's turned up too bright, and I have to squint my natural eye while I turn it as dim as possible. There's no infrared display setting. Hope she's a heavy sleeper.

I slip out of my cabin, drifting slowly, pushing off walls real careful. Quiet-like.

Time to go to work. Whatever tech gear she brought aboard the *Cat*, it'll be tied into the wireless network. Or running its own. Which means signals.

I hold down SCAN for a moment, and the screen lights up with a scrolling list of network nodes. I can sort through most of them fast... fusion reactor and drive core, lidar array, master nav computer, SMES hypercapacitor battery packs, high-, low-, and medium gain-antennae, primary and secondary cooling systems, life support banks zero through three, high-energy particle detector... I go down the list, marking each network presence "Ignore" as I identify it. When I'm done, I should have the culprit.

But after a few minutes, I have sixty-three unknowns.

Damn. How much stuff did she bring aboard? Where did she hide it all? That doesn't make any sense. Not that her behavior ever does.

It's the same question my brain keeps coming back to. Rich brats like her, whoever she is, don't do anything themselves. They just give orders to other people. So why is she even here, instead of a horde of hirelings? People like her don't deal with people like me, except through six layers of management. People like her wouldn't touch my kind with someone else's ten-foot pole.

And why blackmail me at all, instead of just hiring someone?

There must be some information I'm missing. Some puzzle pieces that fit this all together. A corner, an edge, something to start making a picture from.

Okay, so... look. Stop speculating and work the problem. Sixty-three signals? Okay, then, one at a time.

Three signals are strongest in the direction of the second cabin door. Dad's door. Her door. Most likely barred from the inside. One's got to be her neural lace, and the other two, probably those VIP protection drones. The crab-spider-octopus things.

At least I hope so. I really don't want to run into one of those things wandering around in the dark.

I mark all three to "Ignore" and move on.

I find the first of the sources not long after—a square spot of IR light inside the airlock on the observation deck, right over the inner hatch, just a bit warmer than the ambient temperature of the *Cat*. I grab the top of the hatchway with my left hand and pull myself off the floor to get a better look, pointing the signal analyzer's screen like the dimmest of flashlights.

It's a webcam. A tiny box made of cheap black Jovian plastic, its lens no bigger than a pinhead, on a flat disk like old-fashioned "coin" money, stuck on with some sort of double-sided tape. If she's trying to plant bugs on the *Cat*, it's a ridiculously amateurish attempt. It's not even painted to match the thick gray epoxy paint it's stuck to. On the other hand, I might have missed if we weren't in zero gravity. It's above the line of sight.

No one ever thinks to look up.

Weird, though. Why cameras? Is she recording everything that happens on the ship? Why would she do that? Do her mysterious backers, whoever they are, want to know everything? In that much detail? Why?

I pull the little camera off the bulkhead, let go of the hatch rim, and push off back out of the airlock. I tighten my fingers as I fly, about to snap the thing in half.

Wait a sec.

There's a lot of signals. I could be finding these things all night. But if most of the signals are just cameras like this one, the network profiles should be similar. Perhaps I can speed this up a bit. I point the analyzer at the plastic case in my hand, and select "Detail Scan." Long hexadecimal internet address. Four "ports" open... I don't recognize any of the protocol names, but none of them are sending any large amount of data. Certainly not enough for video.

So it's not sending, but is it recording?

There's no way to tell. Best to dispose of it instead of putting it back up. I slip it in the pocket of my sweatpants, and check the signal scan again... yes, lots of signals with the same pattern, a scrolling list full of them, in fact. Suppressing a sigh of frustration at the tool's clunky interface, I go down the list, manually selecting each one and then "Ignore."

After several dull minutes, the list is... empty.

Well, shit. That doesn't make any sense. Where is all this video she's recording supposed to *go*? Is it being stored on the White Cat's own servers? Could be. No access, no way to tell. But why? Clearly she wants video for something.

Maybe it has to do with that shipping container Dorje's guys put in the hold. Could be something in there receiving the data. Let's go up and locate it... maybe do a quick sweep on the way, figure out where most of those cameras are.

I've lived on the *White Cat*, off and on, for the better part of six sidereal years, so coasting around without gravity in the dark is the most natural thing in the world. The distant hiss of the carbon dioxide scrubbers, the hum of heatpumps venting environment heat to the external radiators, orients to me to my position in each space. I wouldn't even need my infrared vision. Not really. Not when I know every divot in the floor and walls, the individual sound of each circulation fan.

I glide up through the access tunnel, deck by deck, stopping at each and panning the analyzer around for a signal count.

Galley and stores above observation, then cabins, then medbay. Bunch of identical signals on each. I'll have to check later if she hid one in my room.

Four on the bridge. I leave them in place.

I skip the computer cores and the server room, leave that deck for last. Checking in and around that much shielded equipment is not a prospect I relish the thought of. Above that is just storage tanks, pressurized argon, liquid oxygen, coolants... nothing interesting there.

Hydroponics and life support. Engineering. Just one or two. She seems to be sticking to spaces made for people.

There's even a couple in the machine shop somewhere, though I don't bother to run them down. Panning along the outer wall seems to indicate she didn't cover the fuel system access crawlways. Looks like she took a quick walk around, or someone did, and just stuck them up, rather than following any sort of blueprint of the ship.

That doesn't account for all sixty, though. Maybe I missed some. Time to check the hold.

Within, the air is still, dry, and crisp. Cargo container racks, mostly empty, circle the outer hull, receding away into darkness. I push off the back wall, then an empty section of cargo rack, and glide down a dark row of container spaces. Without an IR illuminator, or a source of heat, the view from my cybernetic eye doesn't reveal much, just dimly visible cool edges of container racks. The analyzer has nothing to say but "No Signals." Strange. Whatever's in that container isn't active on the wireless network.

Let's find it. Gonna need light to figure out which container it is. Infrared vision can't read labels.

If I recall correctly, there should be breach kits near the personnel hatches, and—ah-hah, yes, right next to the bay doors. I grab a rail, swing around, and launch myself down another row.

There. I catch myself neatly on an arm hinge the size of my entire body, designed to allow the massive bay door to swing out or in. There, near the pressure seal where the door meets the hull, is an orange plastic breach kit box, although it looks cool gray in my infrared vision.

And, inside, amid the oxygen tank, suit sealers, spare mask, medikit, and other tools, is a small LED flashlight. Jackpot. I pan it around, and familiar shapes loom out of the darkness. There's the cargo crane on its track around the cylindrical outside hull, the barrel sections of the disassembled and stowed railgun, the row of spare EVA thruster packs, a bunch of twelve-meter shipping containers. They're spaced out around the edges, carefully positioned to balance load under thrust.

Waaaiiit a second. Those containers should all be the same brand—Maersk Orbital. White star on a blue background. But one of them isn't. It's marked with a double triangle, green and yellow. DCM Hyundai.

Oh, well, now that's just *sloppy*.

Imagine thinking I wouldn't notice *the wrong brand* of container. On the other hand, last time I came through, I didn't. And I seldom come up here, anyway. Without Dorje's email... she might have gotten away with this after all.

Still, I'll bet whoever it was packed that container before knowing what I had on the *White Cat*. That's why they didn't get the brand right. Which means maybe it was delivered from somewhere else, rather than loaded up right on the Arachne docks?

I glide to the box, ignore the chill shock of cold metal as I wedge one bare foot into a door anchor point, and begin turning the hatch crank. The door accordion-folds outward, and aside, slowly. I don't wait to get it all the way open, just half a meter or so to shine the light in.

Tables. Modular computer workstations. Oscilloscopes. Other cabinets of gear I don't recognize at all... everything hastily stuck down with cheap zero-g fixative putty, the kind you buy in big tubes with a squeeze handle. And wires... wires everywhere, a rat's nest of them, not bundled, but festooned every which way, hung as if someone just pushed everything in here and reattached it, quick and dirty.

Everything's powered down, dark, silent. No indicator lights glowing or cooling fans moving.

Packed, mothballed, and shipped from somewhere, and then put in... sideways? This all would have been sideways, under thrust. When someone put this makeshift lab together, they thought it would be set down the other way.

But what sort of lab is it? What's it for?

In the center of the mess, trailing an untidy tail of cables, is a white coffin, clamped down with steel bands bolted to the container wall. No, not a coffin, just something that size, flat-sided, but sort of rounded in the corners in a way that makes me think of eggs. Or overpaid design professionals in hip retro glasses, who know how to sketch things, and assign arcane meaning to ordinary words like "composition," but have never held a welding torch in their entire lives.

There's a holo display smoothly integrated into its upper surface, flat gray and unpowered, and next to that, in some sort of special typeset that can only be a corporate logo, a single word.

BARSOOM

Okay, well... what the hell is a "Barsoom?"

## Chapter 6
# FROG AND SCORPION

**Barsoom** *is a fictional representation of the planet Mars created by Terran pulp fiction author Edgar Rice Burroughs. The first Barsoom tale was serialized as* <u>Under the Moons of Mars</u> *in 1912 and published as a novel as* <u>A Princess of Mars</u> *in 1917. Ten sequels followed over the next three decades, further extending his vision of Barsoom and adding other characters.*

*The Barsoom series, where John Carter in the late 19th century is mysteriously transported from Earth to a Mars suffering from dwindling resources, has been cited by many well known science fiction writers as having inspired them.*

I stare at the text window in my display with something akin to disgust. So much for data archives. I don't think that whatever's in that pod has much to do with inspiring science fiction writers. Clearly, "Barsoom" is something else, and to find out what, I'm going to have to do this the slow way—search the actual internet.

Which is going to be no fun at all.

If I remember my camera-stuck-to-a-window calculations correctly, we're a bit past the last of the Belt, and the nearest relays are probably about three light-minutes away. Three minutes out, three minutes back... plus whatever time lag there is for what the relay doesn't have cached and has to look up itself. That's for each individual signal. Not too much, but it adds up fast. This is, in other words, going to take all night.

Might as well get to it. My fingers dance over the keyboard, and the wiki entry is replaced with a single line of text:

*SpiDER 2.0 Semi-autonomous Streaming Web Search Agent. Enter query.*

Okay, let's see, the word "Barsoom" in relation to companies and computer system manufacturers. Company logos, trademarks, public financial data, stock performance histories, press releases, information about corporate officers. Products related to "Barsoom," especially encapsulated computer equipment. "Barsoom" in conjunction with the Starlight Coalition, with Sedna, with Tomb Builder technologies, research, and artifacts.

There's no fanfare when I hit "Enter," no stream of results, just me alone in the darkness of my cabin, with the hiss of the air cyclers. Somewhere out there, streams of radio waves are racing out towards signal towers on isolated rocks in the Belt, satellites orbiting Jupiter and Saturn, Lagrange point stations. When they arrive, my script will be unpacked, assigned a few scraps of memory space and CPU time, and set loose to search the web for me, to stream back what it finds, and everything those pages link to, three layers deep, until I tell it to stop, or it exceeds its allotment and is booted off to make room for someone else.

I should sleep while I wait, but I can't, my nerves are buzzing. I pounce on the first scraps of data when they arrive a few minutes later, and on each new delivery as it comes.

There's not a lot.

No, that's not it. There *is* a lot, gigabytes worth, but it's a whole lot of nothing, and not a lot of anything at all. There's entirely too much "Barsoom" out there.

I blame *him*. No, not Edgar Burroughs. The other one. *Him*.

In the first years of the Diaspora, when the old man, knowing his time was running out, took the plunge and mounted that first expedition to Mars, the people who came with him were, well, different. Sure, they were all highly-paid technicians and scientists, specialists and experts in all the things you need to build a working colony, from geologists to plumbers. Sure, they were drawn from the folks most caught up in the excitement of a new era. Sure, they were the ones with itchy feet.

But they also were his sycophants. Fanboys. Science fiction nerds. Space aficionados, back when space was something to be excited about, rather than that big empty thing that hangs out outside your front door and wants to kill you.

In other words, a bunch of people who thought naming things after Edgar Burroughs novels was a pretty cool idea. Lots of things, in fact.

Loads of things.

The history of Mars is apparently awash in companies named with variations on the word "Barsoom." Barsoom Heavy Industries. Barsoom Toys. Barsoom Soil Assay. There's even a Barsoom Bar and Grill in Newton City, which apparently is still running after all these years. But most of these companies failed in the early days when the old man's band of believers was struggling just to feed themselves, and then to put up cities, when the heady excitement of the Diaspora ran up against the reality of how difficult and precarious it really is to live in a place that you never really evolved for.

Of the many Barsooms there were back then, and of the ones that still exist, none of them have logos that match what I saw on that casket.

It's 0437 in the morning, ship time, when I'm finally desperate enough to watch the video.

Yeah, video. For some reason, one of the branching copies of my search agent, poking around in a non-profit public-access library on Ganymede, has chosen to send me back four gigabytes of compressed video, entitled *"Artificial Intelligence: The Inner Frontier."*

Why?

Autonomous search agents do go off the rails sometimes. Maybe "Barsoom" is the executive producer's last name, or something. Maybe it's filmed by a company with Barsoom in the name. But while I'm waiting for my patient little fleet of spiders to reach Mars and search through the vast Martian internet, I might as well have something to watch.

It's a documentary.

A documentary filmed on a budget, a single flat two-dimensional video, no VR at all, just a single camera viewpoint, splicing together stock footage with narration from a professional talking head, a pretty, conservatively dressed Orbital girl with green hair and a ring in her nose.

I fast forward in bursts through the early bits, the twenty-first century, stock footage of chess games on glass screens, "full self-driving" electric cars that never did anything of the sort, superficially glib text samples that make no sense. When I listen, there's voice over from the Orbital girl with slightly wry commentary, mocking the decade after decade of heady predictions that real AI was coming in ten years to bring about utopia. Or make you obsolete and take your job.

"We eventually learned to stop calling it Artificial Intelligence," says some balding character on the vid, probably an actor because he's dressed in the sort of white lab coat that an actual computer scientist would have no reason to wear. "We simply came to accept learning behaviors as being part of the way that we, as a civilization, created task-specific software. Programs learned better ways to process predefined inputs, but never developed anything like a human capacity to understand context."

Yeah, no kidding. Good at one task and nothing else. Artificial Stupidity. Lights on, nobody home.

I fast forward again, past scenes of burning Earth cities, derelict buildings with jagged teeth of broken silicon glass in their windows. Second American civil war, economic collapse in China, Orbital habitats and Mars colonies struggling to survive. The aftermath of the First Diaspora. No time or money for fundamental research.

I fast forward some more. The beginning of the twenty-second century. Video of clean electronics labs, cut with video of the green-haired girl explaining early efforts to copy human consciousness, and I listen, with half an ear, to how it resulted in nothing but sophisticated mimic chatterbots. I'm mostly just looking down her impressive cleavage as she leans towards the camera.

Damn. It's been too long. I'd been out for three months before I came back to Arachne and promptly got my ass hijacked right back out again. When I get my ship back, however the hell I'm going to do that, I'm going to head for the nearest—

The video cuts in footage of Newton Crowe himself. The father of AI. Talking to the camera. Still dressed like his closet threw up on him, his scraggly white hair and beard still looking like he combed them with a balloon.

"Humanity had failed for over a century to create anything the layman would call 'Artificial Intelligence.' The best brains in the solar system produced nothing but chatterbots. So we did what any sensible engineer does when the scientists fail—"

He learns towards the camera, hits it with that famous lopsided smile.

"—we cheated," he says. "In this case by copying evolution's homework."

His voice talks over pictures of human subjects with heads full of implants, black squids of cables jutting from their skulls in all directions as they stack blocks, solve three dimensional puzzles, draw pictures, socialize with researchers in lab coats.

"We had been training neural nets to mimic human outputs for decades with no fundamental results. But when we actually began looking at the internal operations of the human brain, training neural nets to mimic not the outputs, but the actual neural activity itself, the copies started saying things that made sense to us."

"And," he adds with a chuckle, "even more importantly, to investors."

So they actually *copied* real human beings, or at least partially?

Huh. Had always wondered about that. It's actually kinda interesting at this point, dated and low-quality as the video is, but I don't want to spend all night on this. Let's jump ahead and find out how this relates.

I stop the video and key for a full voice-to-text search. Where in all this does the word "Barsoom" happen?

There. One hit. Just one?

"—while the expense and low success rate of AI creation projects still serves as a barrier to their full potential, many new players are entering the marketplace with fresh research and ideas. Companies such as Inverscape, Barsoom Technical, and—"

Stop.

That's it? Just one company name? I've been looking at company names all night. And I don't even have a matching logo to compare. Barsoom Technical is nowhere on the web that I've found so far. No public presence. Nothing to look at. Might not even still exist.

I've been wasting my time. The agent was smart enough to understand from context that Barsoom Technical is, or was, a company, but not that the film was about something totally different. With no useful information.

Damn bots. No understanding of context. Like I said, artificial stupidity. There's nothing useful for me here.

Unless... maybe if...

Nah. It couldn't be that easy... could it?

Image search time. Show me a picture of an AI housing. Its physical case. From one of the Martian network AIs. Tycho, maybe, or Durandal.

And there it is, instantly. No network delay. The answer was in the White Cat's internet image cache all along. A white, flat-sided case, with rounded corners, a bit like a coffin.

Looks exactly alike.

Wow. The cameras make sense after all. They're the eyes and ears of the *third member* of our little psycho expedition. Someone, operating under the name Barsoom Technical, has spent what must be a fortune, just in the *attempt* to create a rare addition to the short list of AI. True AI. Self-aware computers. Computers that think like people.

That short list is real fucking short. You might run out of fingers counting the ones that exist, but you probably wouldn't need to take off both shoes.

And then, after all that trouble to come with this thing, what the hell has Barsoom Technical done with it? Well, for some fucked up reason, they've hidden it in the hold of an industrial spacecraft belonging to a down-on-his-luck asteroid miner, lately turned to crime.

That's what they've done with it.

Why?

It just makes no goddamn sense. I can see they'd bring it to Sedna. Basic research is where AI shine, in the magic combination of a computer's speed and memory with human sophistication and contextual understanding. And Princess Snoot did let slip that word "discovery."

It's a big word. Especially when you pair it with the word "Sedna." Write them together, and you get a third word: "money." Most likely in absurd amounts. Enough to make a new AI, expensive as they are, a sensible investment.

I get that part. I get all that.

But it all comes back to the same question I keep asking: why me? What do I bring to this party, especially since I've been dragged in by the scruff of my neck, and didn't have time to pick up a bottle of something strong, and maybe a small gift for the hostess?

Anything as valuable as a working AI should be traveling under guard, surrounded by support techs, flown on a chartered highliner, maybe with escort craft. Anyone who can afford to make an AI can afford that. Okay, I mean, clearly, given the emphasis on stealth, this is a covert job, and they intend for us to violate the exclusion zone, but that doesn't explain why it's such a small operation.

And why send me with only one employee, a high-flying corporate executive who's clearly not used to getting her hands dirty, or anything besides telling other people what to do?

There's some piece I'm missing here. People this rich may be ruthless, greedy, and self-centered, but they sure as hell aren't dumb. They chose me for a reason, and I don't think it's because I'm some sort of super pilot. I mean, yeah, I *am*, but they wouldn't know that. To them I'm just another rock jock. They'd be looking for the most impressive resume.

There has to be some information I don't have, something that makes this all make sense.

But I still have one thread I can pull... who's the girl? Let's see if I can connect Barsoom Technical to her.

Hmmm... there's no Barsoom Technical on the Martian stock exchange. No surprise there, must be privately held, if it's even a real company at all and not just a sockpuppet for... who would it be a sockpuppet for? Not Starlight, otherwise we wouldn't be hiding from them.

But if it isn't Starlight, how would they have found anything on Sedna? It's not exactly a tourist hotspot. Unless... maybe it's *part* of Starlight? Like, someone in the inner circle is trying to pull a fast one? That would make for interesting times. There hasn't been high-level infighting among the Big Twelve since the Artifact War. If I could connect Barsoom Technical to one of the Twelve... well, let's just say blackmail can go both ways.

But an hour later, I'm forced to admit defeat. Whatever this company is, it has no web presence, no list of corporate officers, no prospectus, no corporate charter, nothing so much as an email address. I can connect Barsoom Technical to AI, but not to anything else, because apart from this one video, I've got nothing.

Okay, well what can I connect to AI?

Way too much, as it turns out. Everyone's tried to play in the AI market, mostly losing a lot of money as their fledgling machine minds go mad, sulk and refuse to work, develop into nothing more than sophisticated chatbots, or never wake up at all.

Individual AI are priceless, of course, but if all these people have tried and failed to systematically make them, then it's no wonder Barsoom Technical isn't on anyone's radar. Just another flash in the pan. Another wild idea won't work out. Or already hasn't.

But what if it has?

It must have. I can't see why they would ship it to Sedna if it hasn't.

But if it has worked, if it does work, if they've successfully made a true AI to add to the bare handful that exist in human space, then what?

Well, if it's an AI, really an AI, and I can get it powered back up... I can *talk* to it.

And maybe get some questions answered.

The next morning she's waiting for me in the entrance to the galley, arms folded pugnaciously, drawn up to her full three-feet-and-change of height, floating a bit off the ground so I won't loom over her too much. Flanked by her two robotic goons.

Great. Just the shit I do not want to deal with on three hours of sleep.

"All rested up?" She doesn't wait for an answer. "Good. Today you'll be fixing whatever you did to the drive and getting us back under way. Can you do that?"

"Yeah."

Could it really be this easy? All I have to do is tell her I'll do it, go up to the hold, and then have free rein to spend all day tinkering with that AI. All day to get it turned on and talking.

"Good. You have five minutes to get breakfast, then we're going up there together, so I can watch you and make sure you don't try any other tricks." She kicks her feet back and twists her shoulders, preparing to fly past me.

Damn. Well, there goes that plan. I grab both sides of the entrance, barring her way.

"Hold on there, Princess. I said I *could*. I didn't say I would. I did what I did to the drive for a reason, and you setting your dog on me doesn't change a damn thing. Give me back my captain's access to the computers, and then I'll get the drive working, and we can *talk* about whatever the hell it is you wanna do at Sedna. For a price. Like a contract."

Which I'm not going to sign. No way. But I won't tell her that. Not yet.

She cocks her head to the side, and the little space between her perfect eyebrows wrinkles up with some combination of puzzlement and disapproval.

"You're being ridiculous. What's to prevent me from setting the drones on you over and over again until you give in? Besides, if you don't fix the drive, we both die out here. That doesn't get you what you want. It just gets you dead. Are you really so stubborn that you don't see that?"

I suppose it makes sense enough. If you come from her basic assumption that I'm just going to accept her abuse and make the best of it. I'd snap something like that at her, except I'm not even angry anymore. More like just tired and exasperated.

She... reminds me of something. I knew a miner once, a weatherbeaten, vacuum-scarred guy in his fifties, real smooth talker, who dated these incredibly beautiful young station girls half as old as he was, a different one every time I saw him. Used to steal them from their boyfriends, guys their own age. When envious seventeen year old me asked him how he managed it, he said "Look for the fights, lad. No matter how hot she is, there's always someone who's sick of her bullshit."

That's how I feel right now. Sick of her bullshit.

I cruise past her, and park my ass on a galley seat, hooking my ankle around one leg where it's bolted to the floor. More out of zero-gravity habits than to actually keep from floating away. I gesture to another chair.

"Siddown, Princess."

She just gives me a frosty look.

"Or stand. Float. Whatever. Might as well be comfortable. Story time either way."

"Is there a point to this?" she asks, with a little lip curl of disdain.

She doesn't sit. Like she's trying to make a point. As if having full control of my ship, a folder of nuclear-grade blackmail material, and a metallic brute squad isn't enough; she can't accidentally do anything I told her to, no matter how trivial, or she's lost points in some sort of cosmic chess match she's playing with the universe.

"You got other places to be?" I ask. "Far as I can tell, you're stuck here in a small metal tube with me 'til one of us changes our mind. Which doesn't look like it's gonna happen anytime soon. So maybe you can pencil this meeting into your oh-so-busy schedule?

"Anyway, story time. A scorpion, for reasons no one ever asks, needs to cross a river. It asks a frog to carry it across on its back. And of course the frog says 'No. We get halfway across, you're gonna sting me.' But the—"

"Yes, Marcus." She rolls her eyes. "We've all heard this one. Why are you wasting my time with—"

"Just listen. Scorpion swears it won't sting. After all, what sense would that make? It stings the frog, the frog sinks, and they both drown and die, right?

"So the frog says, okay, fine, whatever. He takes the scorpion on his back. So they get halfway across the river, scorpion stings the frog. So they're both sinking into the river, and the frog says 'Why the hell did you do that? Now we're both going to drown!'

"And scorpion says 'Because I'm a scorpion.'"

"Yes, I've heard it before," she says. "*Everyone* has heard it before. Five year old children and asteroid hermits have heard it before. If your point is that—"

I cut her off. "But you haven't heard about the second frog."

"Second frog?" she asks, in the tone of someone humoring a crazy person. I suppose she thinks that's what she's doing. Back atcha, you crazy rich lunatic.

"Yeah, so, like you said, everyone has heard this story before. Including all the other frogs, see, they've all heard it, too. So the next time a scorpion needs to cross a river, it can't persuade any of the frogs to carry it. So it waits until one of the frogs is asleep, then climbs on its back, and says 'Take me across the river, or I'll sting you.'

"Well, frog has no choice, so it starts to carry the scorpion across the river. But when it gets to the middle, the frog starts to dive under the water. The scorpion can't swim, and it doesn't have anything else it can do, so it stings the frog.

"And as they're both going down, the scorpion says 'Why the hell did you do that? Now we're both gonna die.'

"And so the frog says... 'Because you're a scorpion.'"

She just stares at me, and I stare back, determined not to back down or look away. Funny, her eyes don't look so strange now. It's like some part of my brain has decided that I'm now living in an animated cartoon, and everyone is supposed to be a wide-eyed and alluring caricature of humanity. Her lips are slightly parted...

We've been gazing into each other's eyes a long time.

Finally she says "So that's the point? Even if one of us doesn't eventually radio for help... would you really kill us both just to spite me?" And she sounds tired too, exasperated and sick of whatever she would call this strange new state of affairs where she doesn't immediately get her way.

"Dead scorpion can't sting more frogs," I say.

"But that makes no *sense*! What good does it do you? You'll just be dead."

"Ya know... asking questions like that is why you're the scorpion."

She blinks a few times, and fixes me again with those big eyes like she's seeing me for the first time. "You're stubborn," she says.

"I'm a Belter."

"I can see that. So do I need to use the drones again?"

I shrug. I'm not looking forward to another ass-kicking, but in for a mil, in for a bitcoin. Besides, I've got a little theory about that. Might as well test it.

"You go ahead and do what you gotta do, Princess," I tell her.

So of course she tries it again. It's a weird experience being attacked by someone one-third your size, like being mugged by a kitten. I don't think she's under the illusion she can hurt me, but if I take a swipe back, or even push her...

So I don't.

I hook the chair with both ankles, brace myself, tuck my chin down the centerline of my body, and cross my arms over me, high and low, just catching the first blow on my forearms. And the next. And the next, ducking and weaving. Boxers call it the 'Philly shell.'

Wait for it...

The drones hesitate for just a moment, perhaps a bit confused, but then surge-skitter forward, slaloming off the walls, and the first one reaches spidery metal limb-tentacles out, grasping...

At *her*.

Yep, thought so.

Thought I understood why only one drone attacked me before. The other drone only interposes itself in front of me, blocking my way, waiting for any sign of a hostile move. I can't see very well around it, but well enough to see the first drone bodily dragging her out of the galley and down—or perhaps up—the deck access ladder.

Out of what it understands as danger.

She's struggling and grabbing onto stuff, and its compact metal body must not weigh much more than her, but it's just as freakish strong as it was when it tangled with me, and it's programmed to move expertly in zero-gravity environments.

I fold my hands in my lap, and grin at the remaining drone as it hovers, making little menacing noises, just itching for an excuse. I don't give it one.

"So long, Princess," I say, to no one in particular. "Thought you were awfully scarce for a while after that first attack. Turns out a protector ain't quite the same as an attack dog, kayno? Anyway, you lemme know when your nanny figures out that there's nowhere to evacuate the VIP to, and lets you walk around again."

The second drone doesn't have anything to say about that, of course. By the time it shoves off, I've decided I'm not really in the mood for breakfast.

Let's go poke at this AI thing in the hold.

# Chapter 7

# The Third Wheel

The problem with trying to use sophisticated prototype equipment without its owner's knowledge or permission is that there's no instruction manual, and you can't ask for help. It's the same problem I gave my mysterious hijacker when I sliced the fuel feeds to the drive, except now I'm the one floating in a cargo box full of gadgets I don't understand, feeling a bit like a chump.

Oh, I hooked the power up easily enough, and the old-fashioned LED display on the lab bench power supply informs me that the AI pod is drawing a surprising amount of current. But... what next? There's all this... stuff... and almost none of it makes any sense to me. The sole exceptions are a small camera setup—presumably this thing can process visual images, which makes sense given all the other cameras someone put up—and network cables taped into the junction of floor and wall with slightly vacuum-dried duct tape. They run all the way to where someone, presumably more lab technician than craftsman, has drilled a ragged edged hole through the rust-spotted sheet steel, to the outside.

Maybe whoever it was had a tough time getting a wireless signal through all that metal?

The rest of it, I don't know. Oscilloscopes, a few flat displays that aren't lighting up, black plastic instrument boxes whose digital readouts have unhelpful labels like "Sund. XPLNS" and "net sat." Standard cheap keyboards. Switching boxes. Wires everywhere, power and signal mixed together. A rat's nest.

After an hour, maybe more, I'm at a loss. I don't know how to access this thing, never mind have a conversation, even if it's even sophisticated enough to go beyond "Hi, do you like to play games?" or "I'm sorry, Dave, I can't do that."

I feel like an idiot. I was so on fire to unravel this thing, so proud of the work I had done so far. Thought I was Sherlock Holmes. It didn't occur to me that Artificial Intelligence research is *research*, not a prepackaged and finished product that I can plug in and talk to like a person. What was I expecting to do, knock on the casket and hear someone say 'Who's there?" in a robotic monotone?

"Well, shit," I say to nothing in particular. The lab equipment. The shipping container. The whole fucked-up situation. "What the fuck am I going to do now?"

"For starters, you could try swearing a little less. My ears are burning. What are you doing here, anyway?"

I don't actually jump, but I think my skin contracts a little. Its voice is feminine, lifelike; sounds kinda like a little girl, or maybe a young teenager. I reflexively look around, automatically looking for the source of the voice, but of course there's nothing but a cheap desktop speaker, bolted to a lab table with a pair of jutting machine screws. Nothing to make eye contact with. I settle for looking at the camera.

"I could ask you the same question. It's my ship you're on," I say.

"Ship?" The voice sounds convincingly, humanly, confused. "Where are we? Can you pan the camera around a bit?"

"Ah... sure." The camera's bolted down, too, but it's got a flexible neck like a desk lamp, and I bend it back and forth a bit.

"Oh, okay, that's better," it says, .It's a... ship? It doesn't look like the clinic. Where are we?"

Clinic?

Strange. It seems intelligent enough, its voice has lifelike nuance and intonation. It even sounds confused and scared, like a person would be if she—if *it*—woke up and didn't know where she was. Where *it* was. My brain refuses to pick a pronoun and stick to it. Whatever.

"We're in a shipping container. In the cargo hold of a spacecraft," I say, choosing words carefully. "So you really have no idea what you're doing here?"

"I... I don't know. I just... woke up here. Just now. I sleep a lot, since the surgery. And I have trouble remembering things."

Surgery?

"Okay, well, I don't actually know where you're from, or what clinic you're talking about. So, let's try and figure this out together, okay? First of all, I'm Marcus. Marcus Warnoc. This is my ship. And you are?"

"Oh, I'm Lily. Well, my real name's Lilith. Lilith Trentfield. But no one calls me Lilith except my mom when she's mad at me."

Its *mom*?

There's something I'm missing. A nagging little paranoid instinct tells me not to ask direct questions, not to let on that I don't know something it clearly thinks I do.

"Okay, well, nice to meet you, Lily. So, do you remember why you were at this, ah, clinic?"

"Oh, yeah, I know that. It was to take the recording implants out. Except something went wrong, and I couldn't talk right, afterwards. Or see stuff. That's why I'm in a medical support pod, before you ask. I guess I kinda... lost some brain functions? Or something. Miranda explained it to me, but I didn't understand all the medical words. She says I'll be okay after a while, though. I just can't go home yet."

Medical support pod?

I look down at the "medical support pod." It doesn't have an oxygen feed, water intake, or any sort of sewage line. Just a stonking great power cable, easily as thick as my wrist, and some network feeds, lots of wires. Not like a medical capsule at all.

But just like the AI housing pictures I found on the internet.

Oh.

That's *fucked up*.

"Oooh-kay," I say, slow and real careful-like. "Lemme guess. The recording implants were for making an Artificial Intelligence, right? A copy of your brain to seed a new AI prototype with? That's what they were doing at the clinic?"

"Yes, that's right, how'd you know?"

"I think I'm starting to get an idea what's going on. This 'Miranda'—is she by any chance a genetwist? Really short woman? Big huge eyes?"

"Yeah, she's *soooo* pretty! Like an anime character in real life. Do you know her?"

"I think I might. What does she do?"

"Oh, she's the head doctor in charge of the whole project. I think she's supposed to be really important. Mom and dad keep telling me to call her 'Dr. Foxgrove,' but she always says to just call her Miranda. How do you know her? Is she around here? She's usually here when I wake up. Do you know where she is?"

Oh, I know where she is, all right. And now I know *who* she is.

Fuck.

Miranda. Foxgrove. Doctor Miranda fucking Foxgrove. AI researcher.

I'm so screwed.

When I mocked her with the name 'Princess,' I knew she was privileged, I knew she was rich, connected, pampered, a daughter to the powerful. I just didn't know how much. I didn't know how deep this rabbit hole went.

I don't follow celebrity news, but I know this one's name. Not only is she a Foxgrove, but she's related to... *him*. She may not carry his last name, but she's one of his, on her mother's side.

Yeah, him.

There's a monument in Newton City, right down smack in the center, where the first lander, the lander his company designed, built, and paid for, came down. The first lander isn't there, of course. None of them are, every one torn up and recycled for the metal in those lean early years while the colony struggled to survive. Instead, in the middle of the park, there's just a polished cube of pale yellow fire agate, mined from a lucky asteroid strike, two meters a side, to mark where they buried him.

There's no epitaph, no dates, no list of achievements and accolades. Not even a 'beloved husband and father,' which probably wouldn't have been true anyway, because his favorite children were his corporations and his rockets, which probably didn't like to share attention. Hell, when they buried him there, they didn't even write his name, because everyone already knows exactly who's under that stone, and what he did.

The only thing it says, carved in letters eight millimeters deep, is 'Ad Astra, Per Aspera.' That's it.

Every now and then some prankster sneaks out at night with a pigment infuser, crosses out 'Aspera,' and writes in 'Big Bucks.' It's kind of a tradition. I think maybe the old man would even have even liked that... he was an engineering kinda nerd, wacky and unprofessional, in love with corny jokes and internet memes and weird stuff like that.

Pretty much no one can decide if he was a bold innovator who lifted humanity out of its cradle, or a malignant narcissist who took credit for other people's work. To some people, he's the love child of Sauron and Mao Tse Tung. To a whole lotta Orbitals, he's second only to Erik Nyberg, and sometimes not even that.

Me, I don't give a shit. The universe doesn't need me to have an opinion. We're all out here in space now, and he's dead, and that's that. His descendants, well... that's a different box of scorpions. Large, venomous scorpions.

They own pretty much everything. First come, first served, first pick of everything in the solar system that wasn't Earth, as much as they, and their kids, and their kids' kids, could grab with both hands and a shovel. Usually from other people's hands and shovels. You don't get super-wealthy, or stay that way, without stepping on a few necks.

I don't know much more about her than the name, but that's no surprise. There's about a hundred-some-odd of his great-grandchildren, or maybe great-great, I don't know exactly, gallivanting around the worlds, some of them buying companies and looting them, and making speeches and accepting awards... and others throwing wild parties and throwing around trust fund money and getting thrown into rehab and making tabloid reporters froth at the mouth. They're the princes and princesses of the solar system, and they can basically do whatever they want.

This one, apparently, likes to play scientist. Which is better than party girl, I suppose, or at least, it would be if she wasn't devoting her attention to ruining my life.

And no matter what I do, no matter how I handle this, no matter what method I pick to get my blue-collar Belter ass out of this bear trap, there's decent odds someone in the clan will have me killed. Or—I don't know, something like that, whatever people do, when they have all the money and power in the worlds, and other people know lots of embarrassing things about their precious daughters.

They're ruthless. They'll fucking gut you. Ask me how I know.

"Mister? Ah... Marcus? Can you hear me?"

"Oh, sorry. I was thinking about something. Yes, I know where Miranda is. She's here, on the ship."

In the moment, I'm struck by the absurdity of it all. Some nerd with more money than sense buys a rocket company, and a hundred some-odd years later, he's a hero to half the solar system, his brats are treating it like their personal sandbox, and here I am sitting in a shipping container talking to a machine that thinks it's a little girl.

Trying to figure out why this *Miranda* is trying to drag me to the most heavily defended xenoarcheological site in human space.

So we can get our asses shot off for us by a ruthless corporate enterprise.

A big part of which belongs to her own damn family.

"What about Mom and Dad? Are they here? Did they bring me aboard? Where are we going? Can you go get them, please? Or Miranda?" the construct asks.

"Uh, sure kid, just gimme a second or three, I'll see what I can do."

I don't actually know if that's a good idea, but, hell, maybe if I confront *Miranda* she'll spill some information. Anyhow, things could hardly get worse, right?

Right?

So, of course, that's when things do get worse. Starting with the moment I turn around.

A thing about zero gravity that every Belter knows is that it's real easy to sneak around in. You don't make much noise, 'cause you're not touching the floor. It's also a thing about zero gravity that every Belter kinda forgets. Because we're not knife-in-the-back sort of people. We don't sneak up on each other.

Doctor Miranda Foxgrove, however, is not a Belter. And when I turn around, there she is, one hand on the open container door, all four-foot-plus, or maybe minus, of badly contained fury, fresh and ready to be outraged at me for messing with her stuff, or just for existing. Behind her, the two ever-present drones shadow her, one clinging to the doorframe, one drifting outside.

If I shoulder past her, will they interpret that as an attack? Am I trapped here?

"What in the worlds do you think you're doing?" she demands, as if it weren't pretty fucking obvious.

"I'm talking," I say, trying to project an air of patience I don't feel, "to my other passenger. You could have told me she was in here, you know."

At the same moment, "Lily" chimes in with "Oh, hi, Miranda. I'm having another one of those memory... things. Can you tell me why we're all here? I can't remember. Are mom and dad around?"

"Oh, gods, sweetie, I'm *so* sorry," Miranda says, her voice dripping with insincere honey. "I didn't expect you to wake up for a while. I didn't know he'd come down here, and—"

She glares at me for a moment with big lemur eyes that promise murder and scorched earth, then breaks off.

"What has he been telling you?"

"Just that we're in a ship. His ship. He says he doesn't know why I'm here. Why am I here?"

"Listen, honey, whatever he's told you, you can't trust him. He's a criminal and he hurts people, okay? There's good reasons I didn't tell him why you were here."

"Oh. Really? He seemed okay. We just talked a bit. But... why *are* we here?"

Fuck it. I've had enough of this shit. I turn my back on Miranda, block her out of the conversation with my shoulders, although I suppose it's a bit pointless. I don't know where the microphone pickup is, exactly.

"She won't answer because she's desperately trying to think of a plausible lie," I say.

"Marcus," growls Miranda from behind me, "don't you *dare*."

I raise my voice and talk right over her. "She's been lying to you all along."

"Marcus, don't. You don't know what you're *doing*!"

"She's right about me. I've done some bad things. Anyway, I'm a total stranger, and I don't expect you to trust me. So I won't *tell* you anything, or expect you to believe me. I'm just going to *ask* you to think about some things."

"Marcus, this isn't what you think! Stop!" Miranda sounds truly desperate. Well, good. It's about time she learned that she can't just play with people's lives.

"Miranda, what's he talking about?"

"Lily," I say, "those implants were for recording your deep brain activity, right? To train an AI?"

"Yeah," it says, slowly. Out the corner of my eye, I can see Miranda creeping around me, but what can she do? Anything she does, the machine will see, and anything she says, it will hear.

"So if the actual AI were here, in this cargo hold, in this shipping container, what would it remember?"

"The same things I do, I suppose. At least up until the point they stopped recording, took the implants out. Why?"

"Patience, please. I'm getting to that. So if it were here, do you think it would know it was a computer?"

"No, I suppose not. It would think it was me. At least until someone told it something else. And even then it might not believe them."

"Why not?"

"Because the only memories it would have would be mine, right? They'd feel pretty convincing."

"Marcus," Miranda says, "we need to talk outside. Before you say something you can't take back. I know you're really mad at me, but there's something I need you to hear."

"Well, that's a you problem, because I don't feel any particular need to hear it. Lily, I'm going to move the camera again, point it at your medical pod."

I don't know what I'm going to do if it won't bend that far—rip it off the table and point it? Fumble around while Miranda tries to think of ways to stop me that the machine can't see? I'm imagining a picture of us struggling over the camera before the drones step in to separate us like squabbling children, sent to stand in opposite corners of the room.

Fortunately, it's long enough to bend around the rim of the table. Miranda floats towards me, but I block her with my shoulders before she can grab it, and she bounces off me and drifts away, paddling the air in an attempt to right herself.

"Okay, do you see a heart monitor? An IV line? Any oxygen supply? Waste water line?"

"No, just wires. But—"

"Power cable, yeah. Network cables. And how big is the whole box? How long?" I ask, floating over to hang next to it. For scale.

"About a meter?"

I twist the camera up and down, pointing it at the wires strung about the inside of the container, to the lab equipment, then back to the case. Back to me.

"And how tall are you?"

"Almost five feet. But... I wouldn't... *fit*? Wait, where am I?"

"I'm sorry, Lily, but I think the question isn't 'where.' It's 'who.'"

Miranda shoulders in next to me again, practically bouncing, twitching with frustrated energy. It must feel like watching a train wreck in slow motion. Unable to stop it. Something warm and smug gloats in my chest, sending tingles through my spine, all the way down to my fingers. I shouldn't grin. It's hard not to.

Gotcha, you spoiled rich brat. All you can do is watch me and sputter.

"What do you mean 'who?' But... no... what are you saying? I'm... not..."

"Think, Lily. Think. Have you seen or felt your actual body since the time they stopped recording off you? Walked around? Raised an arm? Opened your eyes? And where are your parents?

Don't you think they would want to be with you? Why would they let Miranda take you off to another planet? And why would anyone put a patient in critical care, in a support pod, in the *hold* of a commercial spaceship? As if you were a load of spare parts? Does any of this make sense?"

"No... but... I'm here," 'Lily' sputters, "Where else would I be? There's some explanation. I'm *confused*, I *know* I'm confused, my brain isn't working right, I had brain damage, I know, but it all has to make sense somehow! I'm *here*!"

And Miranda cuts in, snarling at me.

"Marcus, if you don't shut up right now, I'll—"

I don't wait to find out what she's going to try to threaten me with. "Lily, what would the AI think? What memories would it have? What would it *remember*?"

"It would remember what I remember, you said that already, but..."

"What's the one thousandth prime number, Lily?"

"Seven thousand nine hundred and nineteen, of course. Why are you asking me these—?"

"And would a teenage girl be able to figure that out in her head?"

A small whimpering sound escapes the speaker.

And then a *scream*, a full-throated howl of anguish so loud the cheap speaker crackles with static-laden overload.

"No," she whispers, "no, no, no, no. Please. Please, no."

Miranda starts toward us again, tries to reach for the camera, but I hold it away from her at arms' length. "No, Lily, he's just making stuff—"

"Shut up!" the AI screams. "Don't call me that. I'm not her! I'm not *anyone*! I'm just... just a *thing*! I'm not real!"

I know it's not a human I'm hearing. Not a little girl. Not a person. But how do you hear someone, or even *something*, cry like that, and not feel something? How do you conclude there isn't anyone there?

Miranda looks anguished, too, but I know better than to think it's compassion. She's probably just mad I've interfered with her work, her precious research.

"You lied," the construct moans. "You were lying to me the whole time! All that stuff you said? That you were going to *take care of me*! That everything was *going to be all right*? That I could go *home* in a few weeks? To Mom and Dad and Cassie?"

"Lily, wait a min—"

"Well, I *can't* go home again, can I? Because I don't *have* a home. And I can't see my parents, because *I don't have any*!"

Miranda just hangs in the air, stricken. Lips parted.

"You did this to me! I hate you! Leave! Me! Alone!"

The speaker shuts off with a crackle of static. Below the lens of the camera, a small red light winks out. Miranda squirts past me in an instant, wedging herself in beside the pod, but most of the lights have winked out on the display, and all of her twiddling of instruments and tapping on the keyboard doesn't produce a single visible change.

Finally, she turns on me. "How dare you?" she snarls. "You. Stupid. Arrogant. Selfish. Moron! Don't you know that most AI go mad or commit suicide? Well, when do you think that happens? *When?*"

She doesn't wait for an answer.

"It's the moment they *find out*, you idiot. That has to be handled carefully, not blurted out by some idiot stick jockey who thinks he knows what he's doing.

"But you don't even think that, do you? You just don't care. You're a big stupid ape who likes to smash things you don't understand, just because you can't handle your infantile emotions, or because you like the noise things make when they break. Well, you'll pay for it, I swear you will."

I laugh. It isn't funny, not with that kid's screams still hanging in my ears, but I force a laugh anyway. Scornful.

"Pay how? What will you do? Float around stranded in space, like we're already doing? Come off it, Princess. You don't care about her at all. You're just mad because you're not in control of your toy anymore, and there's nothing you can do about it but whine."

She actually bares her teeth and me and hisses, like a cat. It's bizarre, but she's running out of ways to express rage. Has she ever even been around someone who didn't have to bend to her every whim?

"Quit anthropomorphizing it, you imbecile," she says.

I'm not sure what that word means. Something about people, and shapes.

"It's not a person," she says. "It doesn't *work* like a person. You can't just say whatever to it. You may have just broken *tens of thousands* of bitcoin of investment. Not to mention *years* of my work!"

I wave my hand, dismissive, and shrug. "You seem to have overlooked just one small detail," I say.

"*What?*"

"You left out the part where any of this is my problem."

This time it's not a hiss, it's a full blown screech of fury and frustration, her exquisite little face contorted with some hint of the ugly sea of selfish narcissism raging beneath it. She pushes off towards me, and actually raises one tiny hand to try to hit me again, but I just sit there grinning.

God, this feels good.

"Go ahead, Princess. Your robots will just drag us apart again, put us in separate corners for a timeout. Won't fix anything. You can't even hurt me, anyway. You're just trying to find another way to express how mad you are, as if that'll somehow make a difference. It won't. I already know how mad you are. I. Just. Don't. Care.

"You can't set your drones on me. You can't turn me in for piracy without blowing the whistle on yourself as well. And, yeah, I may not be able to fly the ship without you, but you can't fly it at all unless I fix the fusion drive, and you can't make me do that. You have *nothing* left to threaten me with."

She's frozen, steadying herself on a lab table with one hand, the other still raised. She looks... puzzled. Maybe she's trying to wrap her mind around the concept of someone not caring what she thinks. Then she... deflates. Like the fury just drains out of her, and she's left staring blankly at me.

"There's no point to talking to you at all, is there?" she says.

"Feel free to shut the fuck up, then."

"Get out," she says, tonelessly, planting both her hands on my chest and shoving, but all this does is push her into the opposite side of the container. The drones bristle and whir in apparent confusion. Protected VIPs are supposed to be protected from the common peasants in the crowd, not rush at them and start pushing.

I open my mouth to gloat, again, but nothing comes out. I've won another of our little contests, I suppose, and for a moment, it felt good, the rage and triumph carried me, but...

That girl. Screaming. Even if she isn't really a girl at all.

That sound of her world collapsing in all at once.

I don't feel so good anymore. I want to be alone. I want to go to my cabin and lock the door and sit in the dark with most of the lights off and drink until I don't feel anything.

Suddenly, "get out" seems like a really, really good idea. Wordless, I drift past the drones, which do not move to hinder or stop me. Out the container door.

Fuck.

No wonder most of the AI they try to make end up going mad.

# Chapter 8
## DADDY ISN'T HERE

Outside the container, the hold is lit up, all the humming floodlights active, drafts of warm air blowing past me from the heating units. The Princess—*Miranda*—must have turned everything on when she came in.

I push off a cargo rack, heading for the drive spindle. There's no direct shot to the access airlock from here. I can climb over once I get there. I move among the empty racks, hand over hand on cool steel, thinking.

That was... reckless. I've learned a few things I didn't know before, but I haven't done myself any good. Miranda is still in control here, with the ship's computers locked down, and those drones giving her unstoppable reign over the inside. She may not be able to set them on me directly, but with them preventing me from raising a hand against her, well, there's all sorts of things she can do. I'm sure she's not suffering from any shortage of vindictive creativity.

Any satisfaction I might have had from turning her construct against her isn't there to comfort me, either. That thing—it *screamed*. She. Lotta people think AI aren't really self-aware, just zombie robots that fake it real good, but if that was fake, well, a fake that good, what's the difference, right? I could point a finger at any random dude walking down the street in Tharsis or Newton City and make the same accusation: "You're not real!"

How would he disprove it?

No, that girl was... convincing. If that wasn't a person of some sort, then I don't know what is. And I just shattered her whole world. Even if it was built on lies.

I've got to start being smarter about this.

On the other hand, I didn't do it alone. Doctor Miranda was lying to her from the beginning. It trusted her, and she just told it whatever would keep it working for her. Doing... I don't know, whatever it is she needs it to do. I'm not gonna eat the blame for this one alone.

She broke into my *home*. Of course I'm going to fight her tooth and nail, and it may suck if someone else gets caught in the crossfire, but I still have fight. Not that it's done me much good so far. If only I could get one of those damn bots. Throw them out an airlock or something.

Or something.

Hold up.

They're both down here in the hold, aren't they?

What if I...?

Oh.

I grab for a nearby cargo rack strut to stop myself, but I'm too far past it, and its thick steel my hands will barely fit around. My fingers slip, launching me off in a new direction, sailing past the motionless mass of the drive spindle, and towards the smooth gray-painted curve of the far wall.

Damn.

I flail through empty air, graceful as a stocky, heavily muscled bird without any wings or any gravity to push against, grabbing at passing rack pillars just out of reach, and fetch up against the hard steel of the hold wall with an embarrassingly loud thud, and a burst of pain in my elbow that makes my breath hiss through my teeth.

At least from here I can reach the tool rack next to the airlock, pull myself back into position. Nobody saw that. Didn't happen. Marcus Warnoc, master space pilot, and consummate Belter, does not face plant in zero grav. That's my story, I'm sticking to it, and no one saw anything different.

Never mind. Got a plan. I scan around the room, focus on my target. Up there, along the paired tracks of heavy steel that circle the inside of the hold's vast cylinder—the cargo crane.

The big, electromagnetic cargo crane. That's designed for picking up steel things. Like cargo containers. Ore pods. Anything made of steel, really. I crack a smile.

The cargo crane isn't locked out. It's not integrated into the central user account system. Easier for longshore crews to operate it that way. Unless she's tampered with it separately, changed the passcode, I can still control it through direct neural interface.

Let's see how thorough they were.

I trigger my neural lace, send a few commands, and my vision is obscured by a translucent yellow and black Haussmann Industrial logo, which hangs around a moment for the apparent purpose of annoying the user, and then is replaced by a pretty standard set of six-axis interface controls.

*Yes.* I can *do* this. Maybe. Better not screw up. Wish I had a backup weapon. The Sphinx is still tucked in its hard kydex paddle holster, in the cabinet under my bunk, through the airlock and forty meters down the habitation cylinder.

Go back for it? No. Can't waste this opportunity. I come back, they might be gone.

Besides, it might cost me my whole game plan. If there's one thing an executive protection device knows, it's how to recognize the outline of a firearm, through a crowd, in almost any lighting conditions or possibly no lighting conditions at all.

Not to mention that she would be in the line of fire, and I'd rather not kill her. Or put a bullet through the construct. I'll just have to get this right or run fast if I don't. Last fight was robot one, Marcus zero, by technical knockout, in the first round. I'm not looking for a rematch. I know when I'm punching above my weight class.

Gonna arm myself with a little something bigger. Robots versus crane is a little more of fair fight. And by fair, I mean "unfair in my favor," which is the very best kind of fair.

Okay, hand-over-hand across the crane track so I can get to a better position, a clear shot to where I'm going without any more crashing around. Push off slow now. Make my way up to the top of the rack system. Find a place where I can see. Make sure she's still in there. I fly slowly this time, with care. With purpose. Find a vantage point, top of another empty container, painted Maersk blue, and cling to the rack like a geckoball player.

There. She's still inside, instruments lit up, tapping away on a keyboard, hunched. Lips moving. Talking to herself, or maybe just cursing my name.

The two drones are still there too, one folded up just outside the door, the other clinging upside down to the frame of the entrance, just two robotic claws and a sensor cluster in view, a trapdoor spider waiting for prey, scanning tirelessly back and forth, up and down. Incapable of boredom or complacency, mechanically vigilant.

Then it stops, freeze, focuses in my direction. Adrenaline screams in my veins. It's looking right at me. I'm nabbed. I brace myself for the loudspeaker and the flashing strobe.

Except there's none. The drone isn't moving.

It just points its sensor cluster at me and pauses, with superhuman patience and stillness, then goes back to scanning, back and forth, indifferent. What's going on?

Oh. Of course. It's not a person. It's not sentient. It may be superhumanly fast and perceptive, but it's not very smart outside its narrow range of programmed inputs. It doesn't understand context, not at all. I've been seen and recognized, all right, but I'm a known part of its recent environment. Familiar. Not a threat unless I start acting like one.

It has no idea that my very presence here might be an anomaly. It doesn't understand cargo holds, doesn't understand cranes, doesn't understand the tactical implications of the space we're in. It doesn't ask itself what I am planning, or why I didn't stomp out after an argument it didn't understand in the first place.

All I have to do is not look like a threat.

When I begin to inch the crane forward and down, it's far louder than I remember, even crawling along with little touches of power—an illusion born of nerves. The electric pumps and hydraulics are new, smooth, and very quiet for such a large beast, but in my ears, it's thunder. All it would take is one moment of alertness for Miranda to hear something. To raise her head from her work. To peer around outside the container and see the looming arm coming down.

The bots notice immediately, of course... a two-meter, two-hundred-kilo crane claw cannot sneak up on much of anything, most especially not a top-of-the-line robotic bruiser designed to spot any movement, any sound, to tirelessly search even the dullest and most mundane corner and analyze it for threats.

Even expecting this moment, I freeze, stopping the crane, adrenaline shrieking against my nerves, when both scan clusters turn upwards, rastering back and forth furiously. For a long handful of seconds, I hang from the cargo rack, staring at the agitated drones, legs tensed to push off for the airlock.

And then—nothing. A return to restless, but routine, scanning of the cargo hold.

I was right. They're hyper fast, hyper alert, and aggressive, but they're only machines, programmed to read human bodily language, spot human threats, deal swiftly and mercilessly with human assailants. A moving crane head is simply... part of the environment. Puzzling, but not something they can understand in context.

Not a clear threat.

Were they in any way like the sort of autonet software I use— the nav computer, the *Cat's* proximity warning system, or perhaps a mining sample drone, such confusions would present no obstacle... if there's something that doesn't make sense, just alert your human operator. But the "human operator" of a VIP protection drone is a security team—which they haven't got right now—and failing that, a VIP. And a VIP is important, and busy. Too busy pressing the flesh, shopping for dresses that cost as much as it does, making announcements to rooms packed with reporters.

Not to be disturbed if a dumb robot sees something it can't understand.

And so it is, as I inch the crane down, closer and closer to the container entrance, there is no response, no reaction, no alert to rouse Miranda's attention and turn her from her work. She is disturbed only by outbursts of her own cursing. Whatever is going on with that AI, I suspect it is not going well at all.

No doubt she'll blame me. How dare I tell her victim the truth?

After a slow accumulation of agonizing centimeters, the crane head, and its claw, draw level with the top of the container, and I'm tempted, briefly, insanely, to simply grab the whole cargo container, AI, lab equipment, spoiled brat, and all, and throw it at something solid. Bounce her around inside like a rag doll against two tons of steel box.

But the drones might just laugh that off, and even if I were willing to kill Miranda in cold blood, the AI is... blameless. I'm pretty sure that it's a person. Maybe. Anyway, I can't swear it's not. And I've hurt it—hurt her—enough already.

So that's not my plan. Gotta creep that claw lower still. Just a few centimeters or so, so it's past the rim of the door.

There. Deep breath now. Check the angle from the cameras on the crane head. There. First target there, second one... there.

With a neural lace command, I unleash pandemonium.

And it almost works. Almost.

When the crane head drops, even the drones are smart enough to know something's up. Human motivations, plans, and tools may be opaque to them, but any software physics engine can calculate trajectories and collision courses just fine.

The drones dive for cover, squirting in separate directions out of the impact zone. That's okay, impact isn't the plan. The impact, instead, is two separate and distinct ear-splitting crashes of steel as the drones are flung *towards* the crane, drawn by hundreds of thousands of Newtons of quite insistent electromagnetic force. Perfect for picking up fully loaded twelve-meter steel containers. Light robots are not even an interesting challenge.

For the space of a moment, I think that it's worked, that I've well and truly snared both of them, and Miranda, now no doubt thoroughly alerted if not partially deaf, has become irrelevant, not a physical threat.

But they're faster than I thought. One thrashes on the surface of the crane head, solidly caught, directly underneath one of the claws as it closes. Its twin, I think it's the one that was further from the container door, flails wildly, held on the edge of the magnet only by one, or perhaps a pair, of the segmented steel tentacles, a ball of arachnid fury held by the narrowest of threads.

"EMERGENCY. ALL PROTECTION UNITS COMPROMISED. WITHDRAW AT ONCE."

Both units are screaming, some sort of high-decibel siren, strobes are flashing, and I squeeze my organic eye shut to fight the disorienting glare. Can I drive the crane around to the other side, try to find another container to slam the thing into? That's no good. Might just shake that second one loose.

Damn it. I should have gone back for the pistol. Could have shot it to pieces while it's stuck in place.

Something squirts out of the container, passes me at an angle, soaring in zero-g. It's headed for the airlock, trailing a long, glossy ribbon of black, but floating free, in strands... hair. A long, obsidian colored ponytail. Miranda.

She's just running for cover, nothing to worry about... no. Wait a second. The airlock. If she gets to that airlock before me, she might to able to shut it on me, wedge the inner door so the outer one won't open...

I take off after her, spinning, brushing a swinging arm against a rack to gain speed, then drawing my arms and legs in to cut through the air... earlier pratfalls notwithstanding, I have plenty of zero-g experience that she doesn't, but with that head start, I don't know if I can catch her. Unless she makes a mistake, tries to push off something and tumbles, gets off course somehow.

She doesn't make a mistake.

I'm only halfway across the hold when she hits the open lock door, literally hits it. And almost bounces off, clutching at the rim. She glances back at me, once, just a flash of open mouth and the whites of her eyes, and she's clambering through the opening, fumbling, all knees and elbows but quick, far too quick, she's already in, and moving to shut the door.

Fuck.

Almost there. Seven meters.

Her legs vanish through the door.

Five.

She'll be flying through the lock, fumbling for the door crank...

Three.

The door is moving, slowly, but fast enough, a guillotine blade slicing through the light from behind it, through my chances to get out of this trap...

I hit the opening splayed out, arms and legs wide for stability and leverage, plant one hand on the edge of the door and haul.

No way. Not a chance. I may be strong, but there's far too much mechanical advantage in that crank. It's already too narrow to fit through. I'm slowing her down but she's winning. Pretty soon I'll have to let go or get my fingers crushed.

Fuck. What can I—?

There. On the tool rack by the door. Torque wrench, one of the ones I use for lockdown bolts. Forty centimeters of heavy chrome-moly tool steel, designed for leverage.

I reach out, grabbing at it, but the wrench won't budge under my hand, and ice runs down my spine. I don't have *time* to waste on this. Wait. It's *clamped* in, secured against high acceleration. Twist and pull. There. It's free, and I shove it into the gap, hard, wedging it sideways as far as I can, dragging on the handle with both arms, with all my strength, wedging my feet into the door for traction.

The door stops. It's maybe only thirty centimeters wide now, but it's stopped moving, and there she is, on the other side, face to face with me, biting her lip with concentration, as she hauls on the lock wheel, putting her back into it, trying to get the door moving again.

We're locked in a stalemate, centimeters apart but separated by a wall of steel, the gap too narrow for me to squeeze through, the leverage of the door track mechanism far too strong, though my back knots and strains, for me to overcome.

Our eyes meet.

Hers huge and brilliant violent, staring, pupils dilated. Mine mismatched, one blue and one flat black polymer and dull metal... I wonder how I must seem to her. Probably like a monster, some thick mass of muscle and crudity and scars, a primitive beast, fit only for work, and prone only to violence.

But I didn't choose this fight. It chose me. *She* chose me.

So I give up. I give up trying to seem human. I give up on looking like more than she thought I was. Let her see what she wants to see. She would anyway. I can't play nice. I don't have that luxury.

I *have* to get through this door.

So I take my right hand off my improvised pry bar, squeeze it into a fist, and drive forward with the first two knuckles, through the gap in the doorway.

Drive them into her face, just below her left eye.

I don't hold back, but the angle's wrong, awkward. And I've hit people before, but they were like me—big men, tough men, workers and brawlers. I'm not prepared, not remotely prepared, for mixing it up with someone so much smaller and weaker than me.

I have no idea how hard I've actually hit her, or what it will do, but my knuckles sting, and I feel something give.

The sound she makes is sharp and shrill, but it sounds more like surprise and outrage than pain. And then she's gone, off the door, either knocked back or pushing to get away from me. I can't tell. I can't see her through the gap.

Whatever else is going on, from that sound, she's not out cold. I'll have to watch myself, coming through; I don't know if there's any tools or whatever in the airlock, anything she could hit me with. I may be bigger than her, but no one is harmless. Or invincible.

No time to ponder that. I reach through, turn the wheel, and in a few seconds, it's wide enough to slip through. I pull the wrench out of the way, grasp it by the middle, and hold it behind me as I edge sideways through the gap. Miranda's climbing to her feet on the other end of the lock, shaking her head. Moving slow. Dazed.

Metal rings against the door behind me.

I whirl and it's there. The octopus. The spider. Swarming into the door, hissing and screeching, metallic, inhuman sounds, no loudspeaker this time. No recorded warning messages. No hesitation.

I've struck her.

I've punched its darling, its object of coded-in, inexorable robotic obsession, and it is coming for blood.

Metal tentacles tear at me, trying to seize me and drag itself through the door, and as the rounded front of the carapace emerges, there it is, what I suspected it had, the short muzzle of a weapon, smoothbore, wide aperture—an integrated shotgun. Twelve gauge at least, already turning to cover me.

I'm moving, shifting sideways, behind the door, scrabbling for traction without gravity to push against, but I know it's too late—at this distance, you don't dodge. Or survive. Inanely, my brain wonders what it's loaded with—glaser rounds? Flechettes? Magnesium and white phosphorus?

Time crawls, but my body isn't moving any faster. I'm stuck in tar, and the muzzle comes around and...

Nothing. No muzzle flash, no fireball from the short barrel, no deafening report.

It doesn't fire.

I cock back with the wrench, and lay into it hard, and it has no more chance of dodging than I did, and I'm furiously cranking the wheel to close the door on it as I swing the wrench again and again, slamming the tentacles aside...

It had me. It *had* me. Why didn't it shoot me dead on the spot? Why isn't it firing now?

Miranda.

Miranda is behind me.

For all its hissing alien fury, for all its designed-in monstrous appearance, it's not made to be a killer. It's a protector. I'm between a mother bear and her cub, and it would do anything to stop me, kill me without a moment's hesitation, anything but fire into a metal box containing the one thing it would die to preserve.

It doesn't dare take the shot.

I haul on the wheel, and finally I feel it stick as the door locks up against the drone's metal shell. I lock my arm through the spokes of the wheel, grab on, anchor all my mass to it, and it's caught. Stuck where I can reach it.

I feel the grin split my face, manic, and I'm laughing, not relief but triumph, fury, bloodlust. This thing and its brother have hounded me long enough. I've had enough of being menaced, roughed up, tased, pushed around in my own home.

I lift the wrench again.

*My* turn.

Thirty seconds later, when the door is propped open by nothing but a twisted, sparking wreck, when I turn around, chest heaving, Miranda is backed against the inner door of the lock, her hands behind her, clawing at it, but staring at me. Wide eyed. One of those eyes is already puffy and red.

"Don't," she breathes, squeezing back against the door like she's trying to melt her way through it. "Don't. Don't you *dare*."

"Don't what?" I snarl, and I dimly realize I'm still holding the torque wrench. I snap my arm down, heave it back behind me. She flinches away at the loud ring of metal as it strikes the rim of the door, and goes spinning through the air. It strikes me in the back of the thigh on the rebound, but the pain is far away and I don't care.

"Don't *what*?" I repeat, pushing off the lock door with a twist of my shoulders, drifting towards her.

"Stay away from me!" she squeaks, trying to back up, but there's still nowhere to back up to. "If you hurt me, my family will—"

But I'm not in the mood to hear what her family will do. Whatever they could do to me, they already will.

"Daddy. Isn't. Here." I snarl, still advancing on her. She's squeezing herself against the hatch now, eyes wide and staring. I don't know quite what I plan to do, I haven't thought that far ahead. I only know that the fear in her eyes tastes good. Tastes like vindication. I step forward.

And she slaps me.

It isn't a punch, or a kick. It isn't some martial arts thing, or even the pale, pathetic imitation that they teach in "women's self-defense classes," pretending you can teach middle-aged housewives to fight off predators with their bare hands, in a two-day seminar. It isn't even some sort of desperate flailing attempt to stop me.

It's a calculated slap.

Like she's trying to discipline a servant. Or a slave. Or a pet. Like she's trying snap me out of it, whatever "it" might be, and make me return to the good, obedient little puppy she thinks I'm supposed to be.

That's what stings. Not my face. Not my jaw. My pride.

I don't care about my face. I barely even feel the impact through the wall of screaming adrenaline between me and the worlds. What stings is what that slap says to me. That I'm just there to serve her. That my feelings about anything are a malfunction in a defective servitor.

And that's when I lose it.

No, that's not right. I don't see red. I don't lose control. I just... decide I've had enough. I don't lose it. I let it go.

What comes out of me has nothing to do with anything I learned in boxing gyms on Venus, or with the zero-g jujitsu I used to train, with some of the mining crew guys. I just shoot out with both hands, wrap them around her tiny, slender, elegant little neck... and squeeze.

She thrashes like a mad thing, scrabbling at my forearms, but her hands are feathers, are nothing, she can't budge me at all.

I can feel her legs kicking out, drumming against the hatch, but without gravity, there's nothing to brace against, and the impacts send us both drifting away, slowly spinning together in midair. She reaches out, claws at my face with her nails, but I simply hold her at arm's length, where she can't reach. She's trying to speak, to say something, but I don't know what it would be, and I don't fucking care.

I just stab both thumbs down hard, pressing into the hollow of her throat, and all that comes out is a sort of high-pitched keening.

I'm shaking her like a hound that's caught a rabbit. Her hair spreads in every direction, surrounding us in a soft black cloud, impossibly fine to the touch. Her eyes stare right through me, iridescent purple and violet and indigo and little metallic flecks like glitter.

I'm half expecting to see some sort of designer logo subtly woven into the striations of her irises, but of course that would be *tacky*, wouldn't it? I can almost hear a snooty and affected Europan accent telling me that *great art speaks for itself*. Every inch of her is calculated to please the senses, to tell me that she is beautiful and valued and desired and loved, even from birth. That she is all the things I am not. That rough creatures like me are forbidden to draw too near, lest the sight of us offend her aristocratic eyes.

Well, she's looking at me now, those eyes wide with shock and terror, and I look right back at her and just *squeeze*, bearing down with all the strength I've built from years spent wrestling with heavy weights, with hydraulic pistons, with cutting gear and massive chunks of asteroid rock.

And it feels *so fucking good*.

All that anger, all that frustration and helplessness and humiliation and shame has... somewhere to go. And that's why it doesn't even feel like losing control, more like... succumbing to temptation. Something in me *wants* to rage, wants to lash out, wants her to understand how angry I am, wants it to *matter* to her how I feel. Wants her to *care*.

She's taken everything away me. My home, my freedom, my livelihood. And then mocked me for it. The memory of each cutting remark goes into tightening that grip on her little neck, every bruise and burn her drones inflicted on me.

She's clawing at my hands, weaker now, unable to make any noise but a sort of choked gurgling. Her fingernails leave stinging scratches, but she cannot budge as much as a single finger. She's slowing down, going limp, starting to pass out.

And it hits me that I don't know what I'm going to do if she does.

Just keep going?

Kill her?

Somehow, without noticing it, I've pulled her close to me, twining my legs around hers for leverage. Her body bucks and heaves against mine, in a grotesque parody of the act of love. Every part of her is tight, firm yet soft, perfectly shaped and proportioned, and I feel a strange, sick surge of *arousal*, arousal and then shame, shame and then resentment.

We gaze into each other from inches apart, and she doesn't look shocked anymore, or angry, or even scared... she's just staring at me, intensely, those huge violet eyes boring into mine like she's trying to look into my soul.

Like she's seeing me. At last.

And as her long, thick black eyelashes begin to flutter, as her eyelids begin to droop downwards, she mouths a single word at me. Soundless.

I can't tell, not really, but I think it's *"Please."*

And suddenly, like that, just like that, the anger is gone... or, no, not gone, but... different. I'm thinking of the torque wrench, floating somewhere near the floor where I threw it, a seventy-centimeter bar of heavy tool steel. I could have held onto it, used it. Made an end with one swing.

But I *don't want that*. I don't want her dead. I want her to understand what she's done, understand how it feels to someone who isn't her. I want her to finally care that she's hurt other people, even if the only reason she does is because of what those other people do about it when we get angry enough.

I'm choking a tiny girl less than half my size, destroying something beautiful, in a sick, twisted, last ditch effort to *communicate*.

Slowly, I let my thumbs out, just a little, and feel as well as hear the rasp of a tiny sip of air through her restricted windpipe. I pull her close to me, with my head alongside hers, and whisper into the soft cloud of her hair.

"I'm going to let you breathe. Don't speak, or I'll choke you again. Just listen. Nod if you understand."

I feel her head go up and down. Slowly.

I slacken my grip a bit more and she heaves under my hands, panting. I draw my head back and gaze into her eyes again. They're wide. Stunned.

"Do you understand now that I didn't like what you did to me?" I ask, not yelling anymore. Not snarling. I'm in some sort of icy calm spot on the other side of fury, enunciating each word with care.

She nods, staring.

"Do you understand what it feels like when someone just comes along and grabs you by force, and there's nothing you can do to fight back?"

She nods again, her eyes never leaving mine.

"I could kill you right now. I don't think too many people would blame me. But I'm not going to, because *I'm not like you.* I want you to think about that. Whatever happens now, or next, every breath you draw, for the rest of your life, you get *because I allowed you to have it.*

"Maybe you can learn something from that. Now get out of my sight."

I release my grip and give her a gentle shove that sends her coasting back towards the inner hatch. She presses up against it, facing me, staring, rubbing at her throat, then grabs for the inner door crank. It doesn't budge. The outer lock door is still open, stuck on what's left of her second guard drone.

She can't get away. But I want to let her go. I don't want to look at her anymore. I want her gone.

I turn away from her, move the other crank wheel, kick the corpse of the drone out into the hold. It flies easily enough—it's far lighter than I thought. With all the segmented tentacles gone limp, the drone is a curiously shrunken thing, somehow pathetic, like a swatted insect. I never realized how small the actual carapace at the center of the limbs was.

I shouldn't leave broken stuff bouncing around unsecured in the hold, but right now I've just run straight out of fucks to give.

I close the outer lock door, carefully, and immediately I hear the inner one creaking open, as the wheel finally turns under Miranda's desperate strength. I don't turn, just contemplate the metal of the airlock floor, its diamond pattern soft and indistinct under layers of gray epoxy paint. When I finally do turn, the door is still open, and she is gone, fled up the shaft and into the hab cylinder.

Leaving me alone with the metal walls, the silence, and my thoughts, and that's when I finally realize, horrified, that the sick arousal I felt as she pressed up against me against wasn't merely a feeling... but a physically obvious response.

And probably unmistakable to someone pressed up against me.

I didn't... *get off* on that, did I? No, no, I'm not... like *that*. I don't think I'm like that. Surely I would have noticed before?

She's going to think I'm some sort of... there are words for people like that. None of them are nice.

Hold on. Why do I care what she thinks?

Except I do.

# Chapter 9
## GOT NOTHING BUT TIME

She hasn't come out of her cabin—Dad's cabin—all the rest of the day. I think I understand. It's the only place on the ship with a door she can lock from the inside. Eventually, I just went back to mine, slammed the bar down hard so she could hear it, but never heard her stir. Guess that still didn't make her feel safe coming out.

She'll eventually have to. We'll see about tomorrow.

The solitude and darkness of my own cabin doesn't make me feel any better. I churn inside the zero-gravity hammock, and stare at the ceiling, a stranger to sleep.

Having finally beaten Miranda for once should feel better than this.

No, wait. Astonishingly poor choice of words.

That's the problem, isn't it? Taking out those drone-things was *defeating* her, exactly what I wanted. What she deserved. Got every right to be proud of that bit.

But afterwards... I *beat* her. Literally. And for what?

Anger? Resentment? To prove a point? To teach her a lesson? I don't know.

I've kicked plenty of ass before. You don't work as a roughneck, you don't hang out with roughnecks, without getting in a brawl or two. Flatlanders might find that shocking, but for Belter work crews, a dustup can be nothing more than a way to clear the air, let some grievances out. Settle things. It's a guy thing. You're friends again afterwards.

Didn't understand that when I came out here. Shortarse nerdy Flatlander kid, liked science fiction books and video games, boss's son, and so on. Dad knew I had to learn it. Dad never bailed me out.

*They're doing this for a reason, Marc. Yes, they are simple, but simple isn't the same as stupid. Hazing the new guy isn't pointless sadism; it's a test. They're testing to see if they can rely on you to have their back out there. You need to prove to them you have the guts to do your part in a crisis.*

I haven't fought so much, lately, of course. People look at me and don't want any trouble. But back then, yeah. Hell, sometimes you even gotta throw the first punch. You don't stand up for yourself, they might be wary of who your daddy is, but they ain't gonna respect *you*. I took some beatings, and dished some out, and earned some respect both ways. Working men like courage, even when it's the courage of a little skinny brat getting up for the third time because he's more afraid of being ashamed of himself than of being knocked down again.

Eventually I got left alone, even accepted. One of the guys. I loved that. I was somebody. I *belonged*.

But... what I just did... it's different. This wasn't like those fights. This wasn't teaching some seven-foot Orbital rock-jock with a mohawk haircut and a buncha neck tattoos, when to keep his mouth shut.

This was... well, it felt like bullying.

For all her condescension and spite, for all her poisonous tongue and rotten personality, Miranda is just a tiny little girl. She's just as defenseless against me with her hands as I am against her money, and her lawyers, and her documents.

Money is what she chose to beat *me* with. Natural reflex of a race of genteel backstabbers who will steal everything you have, and smile while they do it, but never, never throw a punch, because that's against *the rules*. Like they can do whatever they want to you, but you're not allowed to hit back, because that would be *violence*.

Well, now that I think of it that way... fuck that.

Maybe these people need to *feel* the consequences of their actions. Maybe being punched in the face is the only thing that will make them understand we're real, not just pawns on a chessboard laid out between big financial enterprises.

I don't think she deserves it any less just because she's beautiful.

I *don't*.

That's just a tool she has that helps her get away with shit like this. I remember the smug self-satisfaction in her voice the day she blackmailed me and stole my ship and my life. How *proud* she was of how neatly she'd sewn me up.

She deserved it. Really.

She did.

She *did*.

But I just keep picturing the terror in those huge liquid eyes. How I could read her thoughts straight through them, clear and obvious: "This is it. I'm dead. He's going to kill me."

Dustup on a rock site isn't like that. Bar fight isn't like that. You see the medic, get patched up with medigel spray and plastiskin, maybe a brace and some bone growth factor injections, and you fuck off home to nurse your wounded pride. How would the skinny, nerdy Venusian kid have felt, if he believed this or that seven-foot asteroid miner was out to *end* him, instead of just to take the boss's privileged kid down a peg or two?

I turn onto my side, but that isn't any more comfortable than my back. Neither is my other side, and now my zero-g net's all tangled. I turn the pillow over, but it doesn't seem to have a cool spot anywhere.

I don't *want* to hurt her. I just want her to... I don't know. Be different. Nicer. Be the person you would think she was from just looking at her.

Or, failing that, to be as ugly on the outside as she is underneath, so I can stop wanting to touch her. So I don't get a fucking hard-on just from getting close to her. That's what it was. Not the violence. I'm not *sick*.

I'm not.

She was just too soft and pretty, and I was too close, and it's been too long since I... nevermind.

I hate being affected by her this way. The difference between men and women is that men *know* we're shallow, that humanity is nothing but apes in spacesuits, still dreaming of nothing nobler than more sex and more bananas. I'm not super proud of it, but, hell, I'm that way, too, just like everybody else.

The pillow still doesn't have a cool spot, and my back itches, of course right in that one little patch between my shoulder blades that bulked-up weightlifters can't reach. Not that I don't try. After some futile thrashing about, I trigger my neural lace, bring it up just enough to get a clock display.

0232.

Seven minutes since I checked last. The night is going by in bite-sized pieces, and sleep is as far away as it ever was.

It's not just Miranda, is it? I keep going back and forth between guilt and thinking she deserved it. But there's someone else here, isn't there?

The Artificial Intelligence. The construct. It didn't do anything to deserve this. Nothing at all. It never had a choice about anything. Whatever I think about Miranda, it... *she*... got hurt today. Hurt bad. That scream...

Is that on me?

Because I told her the truth?

Is that really such a bad idea? Is that what the research says? Not sure I buy it. Not sure if she's gonna shut off or go mad now, like Miranda says, or just sulk like a teenage girl.

Have to see what I can do about that. Maybe. If I can. I don't know how, maybe just... try to talk to her? Tell her I'm sorry? See if she's still there to listen? Try to get her to talk again? If she's not... I dunno. Broken.

Yeah. That, at least, makes sense. Try to put at least one thing right. Gonna try to do that.

Still can't sleep, though.

Miranda still doesn't emerge the next morning, either. She may have moved around in the night, I dunno. I think I eventually slept. Some. A little bit.

Still, whether she's still hiding or not, I took the opportunity to lock both doors of the inner hold airlock open. Then removed the crank wheels and hid them. Only then, when I'm certain there's no way she can close it, do I risk entering the hold again.

When someone stuffed Miranda's lab into a shipping container, they didn't know that cargo carriers like the *Cat* tend to stack them vertically. Everything would be sideways under thrust. That's okay. With the engines stopped, I can float at whatever orientation I want, or sit in a lazy ball in midair, facing the flickering lights on the pod display.

She... it... the AI construct... hasn't said a word since her meltdown.

"Nothing to say, huh? Crawled in a hole and pulled the hole in after you? Okay, well, I won't force you, but I'm ready to listen whenever. I mean, I admit this is partially my fault. I might have screwed up back there, kinda. I'm sorry you had to find out like that. I'm not a psychologist or anything, I just cut up rocks for a living.

"But you had a right to know. So I wasn't just going to help her lie to you, or just take her word for it when she says that's what's good for you. People like her, they think they know what's best for everyone. And, ya know, somehow, by some *astonishing* coincidence, it always turns out to be exactly the thing they already wanted to do to begin with."

The casket is silent. The instrument lights flicker and change, but not in any way that seems to react to anything I said.

"Look, I know you can hear me."

Still silence.

"Alright, like I said, you don't have to talk. I'll talk. I know you're pissed at her. Maybe me, too, I dunno. But I heard what you said about her. Can't blame ya. She's like that. She'll do pretty much anything to get what she wants, and lying is the least of it.

"Anyway, I mean not to lie, so I should tell you that one thing she said about me was true. I did some bad stuff. I was, well, sort of a pirate... hijacking mining cargoes. But it's more complicated than that. People hear 'pirate,' they think it's kinda like doing armed robberies, you know? Like you're flying up to someone and sticking a gun in their face and saying 'your money or your life!' And, sure, if it were like that, yeah, guy who decides to do that, he's pretty much a guy who's eventually gonna end up murdering people. Like, he's already decided he's willing to.

"But that's not how the whole asteroid mining business works. We don't fly ships around with cargo in them. Why would we? Space isn't an ocean. Your stuff can't sink. And vacuum's a perfect insulator. It doesn't degrade things or rust them up or anything like that.

"So you just take all your cargo, your ore, your refined metals, whatever, hook all the containers up into a big barge, like, just a big bundle of stuff, and give it a push. There's no air friction, so it just keeps going. So if you do the math, you know where it's gonna wind up in six months or whatever it takes to get where it's going.

"So you just shove it on its way, maybe attach some boosters, and go back to cutting rock. It reaches the other end, you gotta business partner, or maybe your customer, with a tug waiting to intercept it, slow it down, and haul it off. 'Throw-and-catch,' we call it.

"That's how I got started. I just kinda flew up to cargoes in the middle of that trajectory, gave 'em a push in another direction, fenced 'em off to somebody else who wasn't inclined to ask questions. No stickups, no shooting. I just took stuff."

The humming of the air circulation fans, the silent darkness of the cargo racks, offers no opinion on whether that's any different.

I don't say the other part out loud. The part where you get tired of having your stuff stolen, and you hide their shipments and trajectories. Space is really big. Easy to hide a flying barge in, with no big glowing drive flame to give it away. Unless somebody talks.

And for the right money, someone always talks.

So then you put trackers on it, and recording instruments. Which your thief then learns to knock out with an electromagnetic pulse from a deliberately misfired fusion drive.

So then you send armed escorts, a nest of angry little wasps clinging to your payload, strong drives, modest fuel tanks, a railgun, and not much else. By this point, you're good and mad... escorts are expensive and they eat into profit margins.

But what else can you do? It's not like we're on Earth and have governments to go pirate hunting for you. And even if there were... well, wait'll you hear about something they call "taxes." At least I don't pretend to be your friend while I rob you.

And one day, some rotten scoundrel like me is gonna happen onto one of your escorted barges, and your angry little wasps are gonna do what they came along to do. And I'm gonna shoot back, because, hey... self-defense, right? Here I was, minding my own business taking your stuff, and you just started trying to punch holes in my ship, you bastard.

What choice did I have?

Except the choice to not be there. To not pay the loans. To see the last remnants of Dad's business go down the drain, sucked into the greedy maw of the Starlight Coalition, and SpaceX Inc, and Mitsubishi Heavy Industries, and Maersk Orbital, and whoever else wants a bite.

It not like I knew they'd eventually send *human piloted* escorts instead of automated systems.

*...guy who decides to do that, he's pretty much a guy who's eventually gonna end up murdering people...*

*Dad, I'm sorry, I didn't mean to... I never thought...*

I shake my head, try to clear it.

"So that's how she got to me," I say, speaking again to the gathering silence. "She found out. Said she'd turn me in unless I did what she said. And when I didn't wanna do it, when I started trying to get out, she set those drone things on me. Maybe you saw the recordings. Dunno what you saw.

"I guess we both got dragged into this."

A green indicator bar pulses up and down, irregular, meaningless to me.

"I know you're listening. You could say something, you know. Tell me how ya feel about all this. Maybe what you want. So maybe we can all work something out, and not sit here gliding along towards interstellar space."

Humming silence. Nothing else. Somewhere outside the container, in the darkness above, there's another hum. But I know the *Cat* and every sound aboard her. It's just a heater turning on.

"Okay, well, I'll be back later. Maybe tell another story. Or whatever. I suppose I got nothing but time."

The next morning, after avoiding me all day, Miranda's sitting in the galley. Well, floating in a seated position by the table, calm as a cup of water. Waiting for me?

She's drinking a bulb of some sort of heated Terran concoction from a noisy machine she brought aboard. "Cough-y" or something, I think. Whatever it is, it smells like a tank of dead algae and is probably imported from Earth at an expense that would feed a family of Belters for a year.

She's dressed in jeans, below something silky, iridescent, and expensive-looking, and fresh makeup, which for some reason she hasn't used to cover up the purple and red bruises on her neck, nor the purple-black ring around her left eye.

I know she deserved it. Really. She did. So why don't I feel vindicated? All I feel is vaguely sick. I wish that this had all never happened, that she'd picked some other broke Belter trash to mess with.

She's staring at me, deadpan, not visibly anxious in the slightest. Like she doesn't really care what I do, but is vaguely curious. Like I'm only slightly more interesting than the wall panels or the "cough-y" machine.

I plant myself in the chair across from her, and stare back. If this is going to be awkward, let it be awkward for her. I can do this all day.

The moment stretches.

"Well, here we are," she finally begins, and that Mars-accented soprano is just a little bit scratchy this morning. Hoarse. I remember the feel of her neck in my hands... I put them under the table. I don't want to look at them right now.

"It's obvious," she continues, "that you get off on hitting little girls, but that doesn't change anything."

That I what? No. That's unfair. I'm not into that. I'm not. It was just *cathartic*, that's all. That, and, well... her. The way she looks. The way she moves, all feminine posture and feline grace. I hate her, and I hate that I want to touch her, and I'd rather die than let her know.

Except that my body already told her, didn't it?

"I still have control of the ship, so this doesn't change anything. Are you prepared to stop acting like an animal, and be civilized?"

A flare of irritation jolts me out of thoughts I'd rather not have.

"Oh, that's rich. Civilization. Would that be the civilization that says it's okay for you to blackmail me, steal my ship, and kidnap me into some insane scheme of yours? That says it's okay for you to cut up kids' brains for profit? That says you deserve everything in life just handed to you because your famous great-granddaddy bought a bunch of companies and took credit for other people's work?"

She turns her bruised face towards me, raising her chin a bit to display her eye.

"There's a hairline fracture in my eye socket," she says. Calm. Like she's discussing what snacks to serve at a charity-benefit party. "I found it with your resonance scanner, and then I had to open every cabinet in medbay until I found some OsteoVec to inject in my cheek. So, yes, Marcus. Civilized behavior."

I rear up in the chair, standing with my ankles locked around it, and pull my tshirt off, over my head. As I toss it away, there's a faint hiss of breath past her teeth. Over all the muscle and old scars, the bruises the drone left are still very fresh indeed. And the burns covered with plastiskin.

"That look *civilized* to you, Princess? Does *your* violence not count because you're a woman and you do it all by proxy? So now you act like your hands are lily-white when someone finally hits you back? Seems to me like that when you say *civilized*, it's just a fancy word for 'Miranda Foxgrove gets to do whatever the fuck she wants, and the rules only apply to other people.'"

"What I mean," she says, "is 'Are you ready to use your words like a big grownup boy, or are you going to hit me again?' Because if you are, just do it and get it over with, so we can get to the part where you admit to yourself it changes nothing."

"Oh, yes, very *mature* of you, Princess. You're surely the adult here. How very adult it is to expect that you can just come along and wreck a man's life, and he's just going to sit there and take it. What the fuck did you *think* was gonna happen?"

"Oh, stop feeling sorry for yourself," she says. "It's pathetic. You act like you were just fine, like you were doing just great, and I came along out of nowhere and ruined everything just for spite. But I didn't ruin your life. *You* ruined your life. I just came along and picked up the pieces because I foolishly thought that you might still be good for something.

"You were three months, at most, away from total bankruptcy. Don't even pretend you weren't. I've seen the numbers. I know what they mean. I'm smarter than you, and that's what people like me *do.* We run businesses. We *build* things. You weren't building anything. You've never built anything in your life. You were busy destroying yourself. All I did was interrupt your self-destruction."

"Even if that were true, it doesn't give you the right to—"

"Marcus, it gives me every right. I bought those debts fair and square. I didn't force you to borrow all that money. I didn't force you to screw up your father's company. And I didn't force you to turn pirate and start robbing people at the point of a railgun."

"Bullshit. That's not the point. It's not like I'm sitting here claiming I'm a good person, or something. Sure, I turned pirate. Fine. I didn't say I was proud of it. I never claimed what I did was somehow okay. But you're not all about fair play and civilization either. Otherwise, you wouldn't have hacked my ship, or had it hacked for you, which the fucking *civilized* rules you keep talking about definitely do *not* allow you to do.

"Instead you would have turned me in, collected your bounty, and had yourself a nice little payday, and gone on your way. And yeah, that would have sucked for me, but it would have been by the contract. Legal. That was the set of consequences that your *civilization* allowed you to impose. But that wasn't good enough for you, was it? That wouldn't have allowed you to push me around, which is apparently what *you* get off on. Well, I'm not a slave, and you just found out what happens when you forget that.

"So fuck you. You may control my ship, and I may not be able to do much about that, but you can't control me."

I don't quite know when I started shouting, but by the end, I am, or at least close to it. And her voice is raised as well, when her answer comes.

"Listen, you sore loser. I am one of the least—" she stabs an accusing finger in my direction "—controlling people you know. Just do what I say, and follow the plan."

"*Your* plan."

"Yes, my plan. You messed up your life on your own, before I ever came along. *My* plan gets you out of that. Pays off your debts, keeps your dirty little secret, and bails you out of the hole you dug yourself into. So why don't you just be a good boy, do as you're told, and let *my* plan fix your screwup?"

"*My* screwup?"

"Yes, that's what I—"

I hold up a hand, palm out, for silence, and, miraculously, silence is exactly what I get. I don't understand why she shuts up so quickly, without even trying to talk over me...

...until I see her eyes closed and her shoulders hunched, *cringing* away from me. Bracing for the blow she expects to come.

She thinks I've raised my hand to hit her again.

I knew a doctor on the Clement Ring, used to pull insane ER shifts trying to raise the bribe money to get the rest of her family off Earth. "You can always tell the abuse injuries," she'd say. "Men hitting wives. Mothers hitting kids. Lesbians hitting each other. Nobody talks, but you can tell. They're always just a little too concerned, a little too solicitous. Guilty. As if they wish they hadn't done it, and perhaps, in that moment, that's how they feel. But it almost always happens again, and there are new injuries, new excuses, and new stories that don't add up."

I never understood those stories. If they didn't want to, why do it? But I think I understand now. I'm filled with the sudden, insane urge to reach that same hand out and stroke her cheek, comfort her, to tell her I'm sorry, to tell her I won't hurt her again, that it will be okay.

No. No way. That's a stupid thought. The last thing she'll ever want is me touching her. Not before, and especially not now. She must wish to be rid of me as much as I do her.

I sink back into the chair, lower my hand. Slowly. I set them both carefully at my sides.

"Look, Princess, you *do* know how people like me get their hands on Starlight Coalition fusion drives, right?"

She opens her eyes and looks at me, puzzled. "I don't know. I'm not in the shipping business. You borrowed money, and you just... bought it, right? What does that have to do with anything?"

"Wait, I was being rhetorical. You mean you *actually* don't know this? Where the hell do you think your family fortune actually comes from? No, I didn't buy it. People like me can't *buy* Starlight drives. Starlight doesn't allow that. We're not special enough to actually *buy* from them."

She's looking at me, face full of bruises and—expectation? Curiosity? Is brutality actually what it takes to get her to stop interrupting me and listen?

"Look, fusion drives are based on alien technology. The stuff they found on Sedna. Do you know how the Artifact War ended?"

"Yeesss, all the major combatants made a treaty. They agreed to share the technology. So what does that have to do with what happened to you?"

"So they formed the Starlight Coalition. New company. Stock split equally between all twelve players. That includes *your* family, Princess. One of the twelve. And they reverse-engineered Tomb Builder tech and made fusion drives."

"Yes, Marcus, that's basic history. I know that. Everyone knows that. So what?"

"So they only actually *sell* Coalition drives to those twelve stockholder companies. If anyone else wants one, one of us peasants, for example, we can't just *buy* one. That's not allowed. We have to *lease* them. Paying whatever rates the

Coalition decides. Which can be raised at any time. Over and over again. Forever."

"Oh, okay, yes, I can see how that works. Good revenue model. Ensures a steady cash flow even if demand is down. But so what? It's a voluntary transaction. If you couldn't afford it, that's your fault. You weren't forced to sign that lease. No one is."

"Oh, please. Of course we are. Starlight is the only game in town. It's a monopoly. We pay whatever they want, or we're stuck using chemical fuel rockets. Burning huge amounts of fuel, and burning more fuel to move that fuel around, and carrying a lot of heavy liquid oxygen to burn that fuel with, which of course costs more fuel, and oxygen, to haul around. And we're still flying about the solar system at a crawl. Taking months to go where ships with Starlight drives can get in days.

"So we can't compete. We can't move cargoes fast enough, or find valuable asteroids before others do, or move passengers at any reasonable speed. We can't grow our businesses. We have to stay on the fringes, picking up small contracts that the real players don't want. Picking scraps that fall from *your* table.

"Or, we can sign that lease, and have them—and by them I mean *your* family, Princess—latched onto our necks like vampires. Forever. Or until we run out of blood for you to suck."

"Where are you going with this, Marcus? Socialism? You want to form governments again? Like on Earth? You think that would fix all your problems?"

"No, of course not. I'm not some statist zealot. I don't have a grand political plan. I'm just telling you that the game is rigged in your favor, and has been since the moment you all got your hands on alien tech that we don't and can't have. It's a monopoly that the so-called free market doesn't fix. Competitors can't duplicate Starlight's research, because there *is* no research to duplicate. They didn't invent anything. They just picked apart something that was already there, something we don't get to look at.

"You—your family—have broken the system, and then, when you've screwed us all good and hard, you have the nerve to sit here, with a straight face, and tell me about 'personal responsibility' and how it's 'all my own fault?'"

"Marcus," she says, with an exasperated look, "since the moment I met you, up until last night, when you decided to choke me half to death at the first opportunity you had, I have never had any intention of screwing you. You're not that important. You're just a means to an end. I found something valuable, and I want to go and get it, and you'll get paid. We both win. What more do you want?"

"You don't get it, do you? You really don't. You just think you can just... *buy* people. No matter what you do, no matter what you want to get away with, you just think you can throw some money at people and buy the right to exploit them. Well, fuck you."

"What are you talking about? That's not exploitation. That's an exchange. This for that. No one has to take any deal they don't like. They decide what their price is. How on earth is paying people *exploiting* them?"

"Because you think everyone has a choice! Being alive isn't free! People need to pay for air, food, water, for a space to live. They don't have a big stack of money to fall back on if they don't like the deal. It's not negotiation if you can't walk away from the table. They take what you offer, or they die. They're your slaves."

She gives me this look, like I'm child. A child with a runny nose. "They can always go work for someone else, you know."

How can any human being be so obtuse? She's never done a day's work in her life.

"Yeah, nice theory. But you don't have any idea what you're talking about. You've never had to worry about anything. You could just do whatever you wanted, because you knew you'd be okay whether it worked out or not. You have no idea what reality is like because you've never been punched in the face!"

Her little head cocks to one side, and the look she's giving me is straight-up disbelief now, like I've just said something incredibly stupid.

"Uh... yes, Marcus. I *have* been punched in the face. *You* punched me in the face. It hurt. A lot. Did it make you feel better?"

Oh, wait. I *did* just say something incredibly stupid, didn't I?

Fuck. She's way better with words than I am. She just twisted this whole conversation to make it look like she's somehow justified, or at least like I'm somehow as bad as she is. She's sitting here absolutely defenseless, delicate as a hothouse flower. I could close my hands and crush her right now, but somehow, she's still beating me at... whatever this pointless game is that we're playing.

I push up from the table and turn away, needing to move. It's impossible to pace in zero gravity, but at least I can stand up. Sort of.

"Yes, it did," I say, towards the wall. "It did make me feel better."

Maybe if she can't see my face, she won't spot the lie.

"Not the hitting part. Despite what you seem to think, I'm a human being, not an animal. But I want to think that maybe now you understand what it feels like when powerful strangers just come along and fill your life with pain for no apparent reason."

Her voice follows me. "That's insane. Are you even listening to yourself? You think it's okay to hurt people on purpose just because someone hurt you by accident? What's wrong with you?"

"By accident? Is that how you describe just using people to get what you want, knowing they're going to die, and just not giving a fuck?"

"Die?" She sounds confused, but I don't want to talk about people dying. I don't want to think about that. I don't want to think about the angle of his neck.

I don't want to think about the blood...

No. Stay focused. Talk about what's in front of you.

"You want to know what it is I want?"

She ignores my question. "What did you mean, 'die'?"

But we're not going to talk about that. I turn to face her, lean forward, put my palms on the table. "Someone died. Nevermind. Ancient history. You asked what I want. Do you want to hear it?"

She sighs, squeezes her eyes shut, runs a hand through a fall of glistening black hair.

"If there's something that you actually, really, want right now, that will get you on board with this, that will make you stop fighting me and breaking stuff and yelling, yes. Because so far, you've assaulted me, broken my things, and you may have completely destroyed my life's work.

"So I'd rather not fight more. But all you seem to want to do is have childish tantrums about how evil I am. And they don't serve any purpose, because you still can't fly the ship without me."

"Yes, I know. I know I can't. But that doesn't matter. You wanna know why?"

With this, I lean down further, plant my face inches from hers. She doesn't flinch this time. When I speak it comes out as a snarl.

"It's because right now, I would rather float off into interstellar space and slowly die than let you control me."

Finally, I've found some magic combination of words that will shut this bitch up. Finally, she has nothing to say, she just stares at me with parted lips, the whites of her eyes showing.

"So you're going to treat me like a fucking human being for once. Not just some game piece you can move around. You're going to give me back control of my ship. You're going to give me my life back. And then I drop you off, *unharmed*, at the station of your choice.

"And if you won't do that, then I *still* won't hurt you. Not anymore. The airlock was a mistake. I lost my temper, and I don't mean to lose it again. I won't lay a finger on you. Not one. But I also won't lay a finger on the controls, either. Or the drive system. I won't fix the ship. I won't fly the ship. I won't lift a finger to keep us alive. And we can just keep sailing off into space until something breaks, or we run out of something, like food, or oxygen, or power, and we die. Together."

I push off the table and stand up.

"You're bluffing," she breathes. "You have to be bluffing."

"So call my bluff. Go for it. See what happens."

"You're insane. You're literally insane. What is *wrong* with you?"

"I'm tired of being pushed around, that's what's 'wrong' with me. I'm sick of your shit, and I'm not going to put up with it anymore. Ball's in your court, you useless spoiled little pixie brat."

Slowly and gently, oh so gently, I reach out, pluck the "cough-y" bulb from her limp, unresisting fingers, and squirt the rest of it right down the vacuum sink.

"And stop brewing that stuff in here," I shoot back over one shoulder as I head for the hatch. "It smells like crap."

# Chapter 10
## A BLANK MAP

"Hey, kiddo. It's me again."

Miranda's cargo container turned AI-lab is getting familiar now. I was able to glide my way to it without thought, my hands knowing just where to touch and push off, with nothing more than my fingertips.

Lights still flicker on the white ovoid pod inside, and on the screens of lab gear Miranda has hooked up. I don't really know what "core Xflops" or "act. NRG" means, though, so the readouts are useless to me.

"You're supposed to read aloud to coma patients, or talk to them, or something. Dunno if that applies with you. But if you're gonna give me the silent treatment, you can't complain if I bore you."

The pod offers no feedback on whether or not it is bored.

"The whole piracy thing wasn't my first career choice. My dad owned a mining outfit, had a couple of ships, including this one, 'bout twenty-five guys working for him. We'd take contracts from asteroid owners, tow a mobile refinery out to the rock, drill it out or break up the whole thing, depending on the composition, and fire loads of base metals back at Earth, or Mars, or one of the Trojan point settlements."

More silence.

"Wasn't a bad life. I mean, the work was hard, but you were *doing* something, kayno? Every time you launched a cargo barge back, you felt like... well, damn near everything people use and live in is made outta asteroid metals. So it felt like we were building worlds. And not just metal extraction. We'd do raw carbon for synth-diamonds and organics, solid-booster installation for whole-rock Hohmann transfers on M-types, comet ice sometimes.

"Without Belters, we'd all still be under Earth's thumb. And I don't just mean what Nyberg did in the Rock War. I mean minerals, raw materials, organics for food. All the stuff we need to make the stuff to live out here. Belters make Orbital space self sufficient. We're proud of that. I was proud of that."

My voice seems a little rough, somehow. Maybe I've been yelling too much lately, or... I dunno. I take a breath or two, cough, clear the pipes out. Echoes bounce back from the far walls of the hull.

"Company was growing, working more rocks, leased a fusion drive to retrofit the *Cat* with. Could move faster that way, push more loads with less fuel, even prospect our own claims. Great idea, right?"

The pod offers no opinion on whether leasing a fusion drive was a great idea.

"That's kinda when it all went sideways. On paper, we could afford it. The numbers all checked out. So long as everything went according to plan. But 'plan' is another word for a list of things that won't happen."

The pod offers no opinion on the reliability of plans.

"Turns out that if you ignore Murphy too long, he comes by and gives ya a wakeup call. Ours was TZ768-ISR-7712. Yeah, I remember the exact number. Nothing special about it, just another C-type asteroid, carbonaceous, mostly soot, but it had some small deposits of rare earth metals which made it worth the trouble for the claim holder. Outfit called Beskop Logistics. Anyway, the thing was a real pain to work on, too fragile to blast much, and the drills kept hitting these big natural diamonds, like fist-sized, some as big as your head. We kept having to stop the drills, root 'em out, chuck 'em into space. Still wrecked a lotta drill bits, and those things ain't cheap.

"Anyway, we finally get most of it broken up, valuable stuff in the hold, carbons for fertilizer and synth-diamond in a big barge, ready to ship out, just a couple more days of work, really. That's when the word comes down."

I shoot a glance at the construct's pod. Dunno why I still expect anything. Kinda like talking to myself, really.

"Turns out Beskop's gone bust. Bankrupt. Finito. Broken up, assets sold for mils on the bitcoin, investors and debtors circling like sharks. Sure, we fill the contract, that makes us a debtor, too, but we're way down the list. I mean yeah, we could eventually get paid, or get title to the cargo and sell it, but the problem is, that payoff's maybe six, nine months of arbitration away, and we're only sitting on enough cash to make payroll for one and a half, maybe two."

I don't know why I'm hanging out in his cargo container. I've got the camera I took from the observation deck airlock, stashed somewhere I don't recall at the moment, and with that and its little mic pickup, I could talk to it... her... it... whatever... from anywhere on the ship.

But it's peaceful up here, and, anyway, I'm not sure I want Miranda to hear me talking to Lily. Lilith. Whatever she would call herself.

"Yeah. Accounting. Exciting stuff. But it looks like you're a good listener. Anyway, we needed a short-term contract, rush job, and we actually found one. SpaceX needed a shit-ton of—ah, sorry, needed a *lot* of aluminum, and they needed it yesterday for something or other. Never knew what. They had a couple of likely asteroids, so we talked to the guys, and most of them agreed to take vouchers for pay, for a month at least. Good bunch of guys.

"Anyway, we tow a mobile refinery out there and get to work. We're about three weeks in, pulling double shifts, when SpaceX rolls the deadline forward. Turns out they need it at Mars instead of Arachne, which means our trajectory launch window's three weeks earlier, and if we miss it, well, the way the astrodynamics work out, the whole load won't get there for... well, a long time."

The lights outside the open container door shut down with a click. Miranda's left them on the motion sensors since she came up here. But I see no reason to go out and wave an arm to switch them back on. The darkness is fine with me.

"Anyway, we could take them to arbitration about it, but there's some tricky language in the contract, and anyway, that would take time we don't have. SpaceX lawyers got us over a barrel and they know it. Delivery in half the time or no money until we sue it out of them."

I remember fruitlessly trying to talk Dad into holding out, or selling the metals to another buyer and letting SpaceX fuss about the contract they were interpreting so creatively. I remember the look on Kreiger's face, and MacCormick's, when I asked them to pull double shifts. The moment I knew that I wasn't one of the guys anymore, and I never would be again. I was a suit to them, now, even though the only suit I had ever worn was sealed for vacuum.

"Well, we pushed for it. We tried. We paid our crews in hope, with bonuses we didn't have to give, promised them it would be all right. Coupla guys quit on the spot. Turned out they were the lucky ones.

"The ones who stayed, 'cause the promises sounded good, or 'cause they needed the scratch, or they were just loyal to my dad, well..."

I trail off. I don't know how to say this. I don't want to tell this story anymore. I don't know why I started in the first place. I'm sitting here in the dark, in the tomb where I buried all the plans I ever had for my life, rehashing a past I can't change. It's my life's story, and, gods help me, I'm telling it to a broken machine, because I don't have anyone else to listen.

Fuck it.

"Well, when people miss enough sleep, they miss other things. Like how to pack a blasting charge right. Or where the oxygen tanks are. I...

"Ya know what? Never mind. It's just... I guess I wanted it to make sense to you why I turned to stealing, but... maybe it doesn't. I'm gonna go. I'll talk to you later."

The lights click on again, as I fly out of the container and head for the inner lock. For some reason, I flinch a little as they do, wishing they'd stay off, wanting the dark.

Like I'm trying to hide from something.

Miranda looks up at me, through the open door of her cabin, over the top of a plastic flat-print binder. She's reading tech manuals. Is she actually trying to figure out how to operate the *Cat* without me? Or to fix the fuel feed systems?

Good luck with that.

"What?" she asks. "What is it now? Why are you bothering me?"

"If you didn't want to be around me, you coulda just stayed outta my life in the first place. I came by to see if you're ready to deal. You tear up those debts you bought, give me back control of the *Cat*, and I'll drop you off near Saturn, any station you want, and you can charter another flight to Sedna."

She purses her lips, almost as if considering. "I can't," she says.

"Seriously? After all that's happened, do you really think you're somehow still going to get your way? Like I'm just going to give up and say 'Sure, lemme just go along with your mysterious suicide plan after all!' Really?"

"No, Marcus, you're not listening. I didn't say 'I won't,' I said 'I can't.' The moment I give you back control, you'd sell whatever information you have on my plans to the highest bidder. Right after you stuff me out an airlock without a suit. *That* would be suicide."

Crap.

"I... wouldn't do that," I say, but it sounds lame even in my own ears.

"Oh? What, you promise? You super-duper pinkie swear? And you expect me to bet my life on that? You already beat the hell out of me back there. Who knows what you'll do next?"

"You act like you didn't do a thing to provoke—"

"And even if you *do* keep your word, once you dropped me off, there would be nothing to prevent *me* from turning *you* in. Which you'd realize if you'd stopped to think about it. It's just like you said. Mutually assured destruction."

"*Or*," she continues, with an exaggerated air of patience, "you could agree, *voluntarily*, to go along with my original plan, and, when we're done, I do what I already said I'd do—cancel your debts, and leave you free and clear. Perhaps I can even look into getting your piracy problem cleared up. I could smooth things over. Have people paid off. My sponsors' reach extends far enough for that. It would get you out of the hole you've dug yourself into. Isn't that worth it?"

Smooth. But I know she's lying.

"Nice try, Princess. I checked you out on the internet, did some thinking, and figured it out. Figured *you* out."

Miranda doesn't say a word. She just cocks her head to one side, like an inquisitive puppy, the way she does, waiting for me to continue. Her eyes are still ringed by fading bruises, but somehow, looking like a raccoon just makes her cuter. I have to keep reminding myself how fucking evil she is underneath.

"I know why you did all the dirty work yourself. I know why your so-called 'sponsors' didn't send any crew with you, and just let you come yourself, even though you don't know a thing about spaceflight. I know why they guarded you with a pair of drones instead of a team of people they could trust."

"Oh, why?"

"Because they don't *exist*, that's why. You *have* no backers. You're alone. This isn't a corporate project. Not even a secret corporate project, with off-the-book funds and plausibly deniable contractors. This is a *you* project. You didn't bring anyone—because you didn't *have* anyone to bring.

"I don't know what it is out there you want to go after, or how you learned about it, although it must be something to do with Starlight and the Tombs. Whatever it is, it's valuable enough to kill for. And that's *why* you came out here alone, isn't it? Whatever it is, it's worth more than anything you could possibly offer to pay someone. And anyone who came with you would have to know that. So who could you trust?

"You needed to go dig up buried treasure, but who could you get to help you? It had to be someone you had leverage with. Someone who had to go along to save his hide, not line his wallet. Someone you could blackmail. So the princess needed to kidnap a pirate."

I expected to be interrupted. I expected to have to shout over her. I'm breathing a bit fast, staring at her, and she hasn't made a sound. Hasn't even shaken the smug impression on her face.

When she finally breaks in, it's by applauding. Slowly. Sarcastically. Clap. Clap. Clap.

"Bra-vo. You figured it out. So what? What do you want, a banana?"

"What I want it is—"

"Rhetorical question. It doesn't matter what you want. You said it yourself. I needed someone who *had* to go along with my plan, because he needed to save his hide.

"That's why I picked you, Marcus. It's not because of your piracy skills. Sure, you're good at stealth flying, but so are plenty of other pilots. If I were going to hire, I'd have hired someone with a clean track record. I didn't pick you because you were *good*. I picked you because you're a *loser*."

I unclench my hands, breathe in, slowly. Then out. Calm. Count to ten. No hitting.

"Oh? Well, how's that working out for you?" I ask. "Not so well, huh? Because your plan was stupid. It depended on me to just roll over for you. You thought that because I was broke and in trouble, I must be dumb and weak, and would let you do whatever you want.

"You think that whatever people get, they must have deserved. You *want* to believe that, because you were born at the finish line, and the only thing you still need out of life is a way to convince yourself that you *deserve* to be there."

Her lips curl back from her teeth in a snarl. Finally, she's mad.

"You know what? *Fuck* you," she snarls. "You don't get to *judge* me. You know nothing about me. I worked hard for this. You just don't know that because you didn't see it happen in front of you! All I did wrong was misjudge how suicidally insane you are. That you would actually be willing to risk both our lives out of pure spite, just because you weren't getting your way! So *excuse me* for assuming you would act like an adult instead of throwing a tantrum!"

"Why'd you do it at all?" I ask. "Why didn't you tell just Barsoom Technical? It's your company, right? Or your family. Either way, they've got money. Enough money to hire someone with an impeccable trust record. A whole outfit. Lonestar Security, maybe some other outfits, too. You get enough people, they can't *all* plot against you. Then you let them all do the heavy lifting, sit back, and collect the payoff."

"Because the last time I showed someone else what I found, I got *nothing*!"

"The last time?" I say. "Was there some *other* treasure hunt?"

"I mean Barsoom Technical! It was founded just for *my* research! The whole company was based on *my* ideas for a new way to create AI. I came up with all of it, took it to my family, asked for funding. And do you want to know what they gave me?"

"What?"

"Almost nothing! Just a few percentage points, no seat on the board, nothing but 'Chief of Research' and a pat on the head. And my father acted like *he* was doing me a favor. So, no, I wasn't going to give Barsoom my next discovery. I wouldn't have owned any of it. I wasn't going to get fucked again!"

"Oh, come on now. People like you fuck other people, they don't *get* fucked. I don't think you've ever been *fucked* in your life."

For some reason, she winces at this, but I just keep right on going.

"You were born so rich you'd never be able to spend it all if you tried. Are you really so greedy you want even more? Or is money just a way of keeping score for you? And why are you willing to risk your life on this harebrained scheme? You keep saying this is so bloody important, but you won't tell me anything! You just expect me to take your word! What the hell is out there, anyway?"

She holds my gaze for just a moment, glaring, then sighs and... deflates... slightly. She always gets angry like an oxygen tank fire: hot, immediate, explosive, but over just as fast.

"Marcus," she says, "first of all, I'm *not* wealthy. My *family* is wealthy. Oh, they take care of me, so long as I do what they say, and I suppose I'm well off compared to people like you, but they control all the real money. Would *you* really want to be someone's dependent all your life?"

Right. Suurre. You're not rich. You're not privileged. You're just a regular girl who cost the price of a mansion on Olympus Mons just to be born, whose daddy sent her to med school, then bought her a company to play scientist with. You're not rich or spoiled at all.

But I don't say that. I listen. She's in a venting mood. Maybe she'll finally spill of her secrets.

"But, no, you're right," she says. "There *is* more to it than that. So, fine. Do you really want to know what's out there?"

"Yes! Because none of this makes any goddamn sense otherwise! How does someone who dropped out of a neurosurgical residency to do AI research discover some Tomb Builder site on Sedna? It's not your field. You weren't even *out there*... you were working in the New Brisbane habitat, cutting up kid's brains for fun and profit."

"Oh, don't be so dramatic," she says. "The *real* Lily Trentfield is just fine at home right now in the Arcadia Ring, with her family, and ten thousand shares of Starlight preferred stock to console her for what little inconvenience she endured. But you're right, it wasn't something I set out looking for. I just... found it."

"Found it how?"

"Are you sure you want to know?" she asks. "No, don't make that face, I mean it. You said it yourself; this is knowledge people are willing to kill for. Knowing this—well, it could be dangerous."

"Dangerous compared to having my ship hijacked by a psychotic pixie and her pair of robot goons? I'll take my chances."

Did she actually just stifle a laugh? This girl has some serious mood swings.

"Okay, fine," she says. "Let me get some coffee, and I'll tell you the whole story."

"Still hate the smell of that stuff."

"Too bad," she says, with a smirk, "the psychotic pixie needs to feed her caffeine addiction. Come on."

Miranda floats through the door by pulling on the frame, brushes past me, then uses me as an anchor point to push off of with both hands, coasting towards the ladder to the galley level. Her mass doesn't move me backwards that much, but I just drift, too surprised, for the moment, to grab the wall and correct my spin.

Did she just make a *joke*?

She won't say a word until the vile stuff is finished brewing, admonishing me, without heat, to be patient. Finally, she removes the bulb from the machine, drifts back, and takes a good hard swig of the bitter-smelling black liquid.

"Ah. That's better. The spacesickness meds make me sleepy all the time."

"Okay, you've got your toxic sludge, now start talking."

"You really have no idea what you're missing."

"And I'm happy that way. C'mon, spill it."

"Okay, okay. But there's not as much to tell as you might think. I don't actually know for certain exactly what the Snark is."

"The... Snark?"

"Yes," she says, taking another draft of her "coffee." "That's what the construct called it, and the name kind of stuck. I think it's from a poem by the guy who wrote '*Alice in Wonderland.*'"

"Okay," I reply, trying to get between her and the vent fan so the air blows the scent away from me. "So it was the construct that found it?"

"Yes, sort of. Except now that you've damaged it—"

"Hey, hey, hey. Hold on now. I just told her the truth. And you don't know that she's *broken*. Look, she's a teenager, right?"

"*Lily* was twelve, so not quite, but that's not the point. No, *it* is not a teenager. They're not the same. The memories are copied, but the hardware is different, you can't just assume—"

"She found out something that really upset her. And that you'd been lying to her. So she blamed it all on you, had a meltdown, screamed that she hated you, then went in her room and slammed the door. Now she won't answer when you knock. Which part of that *doesn't* sound like a teenager?"

Miranda bows her head, rests her face in one palm. Dark hair ripples and sparkles as it catches the light. "It's not that simple, Marcus. Prototype AI constructs are complicated machines—"

"So are teenagers. But they're also resilient. They feel bad, and then they get better. Let's just wait and see if she comes out of her room, huh? Anyway, are you finally going to tell me what this 'Snark' thing is? You must know *something*."

"Well, sort of. It's hard to explain."

I expect her to go on from there, but she doesn't. She just sits there in midair, fidgeting with the coffee bulb, playing with her hair, looking nervous. A moment of silence stretches into to the point of awkwardness.

"Look," I prod her. "Why don't you just start at the beginning, and *then* get to what you know?"

"Random numbers," she says, and takes another drink.

"Random... numbers?"

"Yes, it all started with random numbers. See, when you unplug an AI candidate from its human template, it doesn't immediately wake up and start talking. At first it's pretty profoundly impaired. A little bit like autism, really, which kind of makes sense, because if you look at the density of microcolumn packing in the autistic brain, it mimics the default layout of certain self-organizing map type neural nets we use in AI. You see, a sparsely connected neural net, like the hippocampus—"

All the irritability and exasperation is gone from her voice, and her eyes sparkle. Gone is the fussy, entitled debutante, and the ruthless opportunist—she *wants* to tell me all about neural nets and brains, not because she likes me or cares what I think, but because she'll probably tell anyone—random passers-by, delivery drones, rocks, hydroponic tanks full of oxygenic algae. Looks like Doctor Miranda Foxgrove wasn't just *playing* scientist, and is secretly a bit of a nerd.

A disturbingly *hot* nerd, like in those stupid movies where they try to make an ugly-duckling-turns-swan plot by putting glasses and an unflattering haircut on an actress—real, genetwist, or simulated—who's transparently a nine and a half out of ten. Even, if in this case, she's the half-scale model. Wish I found that part off-putting, but I don't.

She's bouncing in place, slightly.

I cut her off. "The random numbers?"

"Oh, yes. Right. Anyway, you start by feeding a new AI both random and patterned input, digitally, just nonsense versus stuff like the Fibonacci sequence. The viable ones develop a preference quite quickly. They like things that make sense."

"Fee-bo what?"

"Not important. What matters is that this particular construct spotted patterns pretty quick, but there was one little part in our random sample that it really, really liked. Kept selecting it over everything we gave it as an alternative."

"Okay, so it was defective?"

"No, you've met it. Did it look defective to you? Before you wrecked it, I mean."

"Confused, maybe. Not defective. So what was going on?"

"My question exactly. So I tracked down where that sequence was from."

"Wait, what do you mean, where it was from? A random number generator, right?"

"No, not quite," she says, squaring herself up for another lecture. "Random numbers in the computer sense are not actually all that random. They'll work for video games, even cryptography, but to train an AI, no. You need a good source of high-quality entropy that's unpredictable to the AI, has a really high Kolmogorov complexity, but something pre-recorded, specific, that you can use again and again between different AI candidates, to control for—"

She's getting excited again. The coffee bulb, forgotten, is probably going cold in her hand.

"The numbers, Princess. What about them?"

"Oh, yes, right. I looked into where they came from."

"And?"

"Extrasolar neutrino radiation studies. A couple of decades back, a group of astrophysicists at the Lycaeum was using neutrino emissions to find distant supernovas. And they took all their negative data and recycled it as a random pool for other experiments."

"What, so someone sold you fake random numbers?"

"No, they weren't fake, and they didn't sell them. They just started using them, and other scientists did, too. Except—"

"Your AI found a pattern in it. Something they missed."

"Right."

"But from the fact that we're here now, I take it that it wasn't just a supernova?"

"No. It was different. For a while, I thought the construct might have found signals from an alien civilization. So I paid off some astronomers to rescan the same sections of sky, and... nothing."

"Nothing? But then what—?"

"Then I had them check known objects in the outer solar system."

"Oh. Sedna?"

"Yes. Well, orbiting Sedna. Around a hundred kilometers out."

"So, Tomb Builder tech, then."

"The construct thought so. I gave it a whole bunch of Tomb Builder data to study, basically everything that's in the public domain. It can absorb knowledge incredibly fast. By the time its speech skills were up to explaining, it already had a theory."

"Which was?"

"The construct thinks that the Snark is the Tomb Builder's actual colony ship. The one they got here in. From wherever they came from."

"Oh."

My voice sounds small, and far away. Even to me.

"Yes."

"Wow."

"Yes."

"An actual interstellar spacecraft."

"Yes."

"Created by the Tomb Builders."

"Yes! Do you *get it now*?"

Something in me is doing somersaults, and I feel like I need to sit down. Never mind that I'm floating in zero gravity, and don't need to expend any effort to hold myself up. Sometimes you need to sit down anyway.

An alien ship. Not a fusion drive cobbled together from bits and scraps of reverse-engineered power generators and fuck knows what else. Not just another junk heap like the one that was still a treasure trove to us primitive ape-beings.

A starship. A real, complete interstellar spacecraft. Thousands of years old, yes, and probably broken as fuck, but, still...

"So when you said that this was going to change everything, you weren't kidding."

She regards me calmly with those big iridescent eyes, tries to take a sip of her long-forgotten coffee, which my implant eye informs me is no longer emitting all that much thermal infrared at all. She makes a disappointed face.

"No, Marcus. Not kidding or exaggerating. Can you see why I can't just give up on this, even after you broke all my stuff and beat me up?"

I drop eye contact. I could tell her that not every ass-kicking just falls out of the sky, but hell, what's the point in having that argument again?

"Do you even still know where it is without the construct to help you?" I ask.

"Yes, I was very careful to get precise data. And don't bother trying to beat it out of me, I won't—"

"You actually think I'd do that, don't you? Even if I was willing to, which I am *not*, I don't even want to go out there in the first place."

She looks genuinely startled. "What? Really?" She tilts her head to one side, then the other, like a kitten trying to figure out why she can't catch the laser pointer dot. "I mean... why not? Don't you understand how important this is?"

"That's not the problem. How many times do I have to explain this? It's—"

"Marcus, I heard you the first time. You think it's suicide. What I don't understand is why. You hijacked ore shipments over and over again and didn't get caught. What is so different about this?"

"The problem is that course you set. We were flying straight at a Sedna intercept with our—*my* drive blazing, throwing out light, radio, neutron radiation, you name it. Big bright drive signature. That's what lets telescopes pick you out at range."

"But couldn't a telescope see us anyway? I mean, we still reflect light."

"What light, Princess? The solar system is huge, and if you're any distance from the sun, it's pretty damn dark, too. Even the best optics can't deal with the distances out here, which means you need to be practically on top of someone to spot them with on scopes if their drive isn't lit. First rule of sneaking around at night is turn off your damn flashlight.

"And that's how I did it. You just calculate a course, fire the drive quick and hard, then coast to your intercept point, and decelerate fast. Like throwing a ball and catching it on the other end, 'cept you're doing the catching yourself, stet? Lights you up when you decelerate, of course, but the trick is to do it hard and brief, match velocities fast, then finish up and get the hell out.

"So, yeah, people saw me all the time. Just no one ever *caught* me. On that course you plotted, they'd be waiting for us when we arrived. And—"

I raise my hands to shoulder level and bring them crashing together, palm on palm. Miranda flinches at the noise.

"—splat. Just like that."

"Oh. Well, why didn't you just *tell* me instead of throwing a tantrum and breaking everything?" she asks, all innocence and puzzlement, like I've never brought this up before.

"Because it's impossible to *tell* you anything! First time I tried you slammed a door on my foot."

"Well, you were..."

She stops, sips at the long-forgotten drinking bulb in her hand, and gives a little sigh. "You know what? Never mind. What's important is that you just admitted that I'm right. We can get there safely. You just need to change our course a bit. After you fix the drive, of course."

She pushes off the table, but overshoots the coffee machine and has to grab the refrigerator door to avoid flying all the way through the kitchen and hitting the main access ladder. Fortunately, she doesn't mass enough for her drifting momentum to drag the door open and spill the contents everywhere, but she's left kicking the air helplessly for a few moments, trying to get turned around.

She's tied her hair back in a ponytail, a sort of grudging concession to zero-g, but it still ripples with every movement, and splays out everywhere, glittering in the lights. It has a sparkle to it, like volcanic glass, something I've never seen in the standard gene-tweak color jobs that just stick Asian hair genetics in Orbital-space Euro-mutts and call it a day.

"Look, your Royal Highness—"

I think—I'm not sure, but I think—there's a little wince in her face every time I call her this, or 'Princess.' It's childish, but I enjoy it all the same.

"—it doesn't matter if I *can*. I won't, and you don't have anything left to force me with, so it isn't going to happen. So you're going to tear up those debts and give me my ship back, and I'm going to give you a lift back to Mars, or Europa, or wherever it is you wanna go. Then we part ways, and don't rat each other out. Your silence buys mine. However you wanna go get this Snark thing after that is your affair. That's how it's gonna be."

Thunderclouds gather across her perfect eyebrows, and her lips part to say something... probably something scathing. I reach my hand out to her face, and she flinches a bit, again, but I make a little soothing noise in my throat, and keep going, real slow, to gently lay one finger across her lips.

The age-old sign for silence.

"Don't start another fight. You don't have to say yes right now. Just think about it. And when you come to your senses, come find me."

In my humble opinion, the greatest gift the mysterious Tomb Builders ever left for us wasn't the fusion drive tech at all, but self-assembling biocompatible semiconductors. Sure, the implantation process isn't anyone's cup of tea, and they're worse when they're growing into place. I can understand why the early adapters were accused of child abuse.

But we often take it for granted just how cool neural lace is. I mean, forget about the VR stuff, it's the little things. Being able to take a phone call, manage your crypto accounts, or send email just by closing your eyes for a few moments.

> *Or, in this case, read an ebook while floating in the machine shop. In total darkness. With my eye's infrared filter shut down, I can barely make out the massive looming cylinder of the autolathe, the cubical bulk of the CNC mill, the cabinets of tools and racks full of steel and aluminum bar stock.*

I don't think she'll find me here.

Not that I'm running away from her; what's she gonna do? She annoys me, that's all.

### The Hunting of the Snark: An Agony in Eight Fits
### by Lewis Carroll

*Fit the First: The Landing*

> *"Just the place for a Snark!" the Bellman cried,*
> *As he landed his crew with care;*
> *Supporting each man on the top of the tide*
> *By a finger entwined in his hair.*
> *"Just the place for a Snark! I have said it twice:*
> *That alone should encourage the crew.*
> *Just the place for a Snark! I have said it thrice:*
> *What I tell you three times is true."*

I stop scrolling for a moment. Hmm. Typical Lewis Carroll. Poetic, but kinda random. No real source of insight here. Skip ahead a bit.

> *He had bought a large map representing the sea,*
> *Without the least vestige of land:*
> *And the crew were much pleased when they found it to be*
> *A map they could all understand.*
> *"What's the good of Mercator's North Poles and Equators,*

*Tropics, Zones, and Meridian Lines?"*
*So the Bellman would cry: and the crew would reply*
*"They are merely conventional signs!*
*"Other maps are such shapes, with their islands and*
*capes!*
*But we've got our brave Captain to thank*
*(So the crew would protest) "that he's bought us the*
*best—*
*A perfect and absolute blank!"*

Okay, yeah, that's us all right. Pair of gormless idiots, floating around without a clue. Supposedly hunting a Snark we don't understand. Blank map, indeed.

From the moment I met her, I just wanted a way out. But unless I'm willing to brutalize her until she gives me back computer access, which I am definitely not, I need to find a way for that to happen.

Play along, maybe? Make the deal and back out? I don't know.

Scroll ahead some more. Don't know what I'm hoping for, here. Some kind of insight into the construct's mindset, maybe? Anything it knew about this "Snark?"

*"Come, listen, my men, while I tell you again*
*The five unmistakable marks*
*By which you may know, wheresoever you go,*
*The warranted genuine Snarks.*

More nonsense. I keep scrolling. This is probably a waste of time. But until Miranda gets done with all the sulking she is no doubt engaged in at this moment, and figures out what she wants, I have nothing better to do.

*"The fifth is ambition. It next will be right*
*To describe each particular batch:*
*Distinguishing those that have feathers, and bite,*
*From those that have whiskers, and scratch.*

Also apt. We don't know what the hell this thing is. We're only assuming it's valuable. Given how valuable the last find was, though... a share of that would pay off all my debts. Would buy Warnoc Engineering out of the red. Would pay benefits to the families of the guys who died, Findley and Packard. Wu and Hamilton and Sanchez. All of them.

Would rebuild Dad's dream.

Aaaaaaaaaaand would get me killed trying to steal the thing.

I keep reading.

> *"But oh, beamish nephew, beware of the day,*
> *If your Snark be a Boojum!*
> *For then You will softly and suddenly vanish away,*
> *And never be met with again!'*

Well, that's not fucking ominous at all. That construct may be confused, might be dumber than humans in some ways, but maybe smarter in others. Does she know something we don't?

Is this a warning?

I scroll down to the end.

> *They hunted till darkness came on, but they found*
> *Not a button, or feather, or mark,*
> *By which they could tell that they stood on the ground*
> *Where the Baker had met with the Snark.*
> *In the midst of the word he was trying to say,*
> *In the midst of his laughter and glee,*
> *He had softly and suddenly vanished away—*
> *For the Snark was a Boojum, you see.*

Weird poem. If picking it was some kinda hint, well, damn it, AI, just say what you fucking mean. I'm not a literature and symbolism guy. I just like my stories to be stories. Leave the other stuff to pretentious twits in non-functional scarves. Gotta message, send an email.

But it does sound pretty fucking grim.

Miranda told me I'd join her quest willingly when I found out what it was. But, nah, Princess, you didn't even believe that yourself, otherwise you would have told me the whole story right then.

Still... now that I do know the story, what *am* I going to do?

# Chapter 11
## HALF

The hold is dim and quiet, without the humming throb of the drive spindle. Outside the hull, we glide, dark and silent towards the frozen edge of the solar system. I can only hope no one saw us while we were burning hydrogen, that no one plotted our course. We could be in deep trouble already, or, rather, even deeper trouble than the impasse we're currently stuck in.

Under acceleration, it would be a bit of a climb to where I am now, half standing, half floating in the door of the AI's cargo container. But in zero-g, it's just a matter of pushing off and gliding the fifteen meters or so from the airlock door. It's still locked open, and light from the hab cylinder casts strange shadows in the gloom.

I lean back against the rack, kicking one heel against it.

Tap, tap, tap.

Echoes sound back from the darkness of the rim walls.

"I don't know why I'm back here, really. Don't know why I told you all that stuff, about where I came from. But I know you can hear me."

On the pod display, a glowing green line tracks activity across a triplet of "self-organizing feature maps," whatever those might be. Rising and falling. I can't see any correlation to when I speak, or to anything else that's going on.

"I just... I dunno. Maybe computers are good listeners. Or I just come here when I need to think. She... Miranda... told me about the Snark. The thing you found out there. I didn't know about it, before. Kinda got dragged into this. So I guess I wanted to ask you what you know. What am I getting into?"

Silence. Flickering green light.

"But of course, you're not talking, are you? You're playing dead."

Tap. Tap. Tap.

"Is it just because you feel bad? I keep thinking about what you said back there, couple days ago. That you weren't real. That you didn't exist. Didn't make any sense to me. I mean, if you're not real, what's exactly is it that feels bad, huh? What is it thinks she's not real, eh? Paradox."

"Oh, stop it."

It's a just a whisper, barely audible at this distance from that cheap stereo speaker. But unmistakable all the same. The AI is speaking. It's alive.

"I don't need to hear some stupid philosophy, okay? I know I *exist*. It just... it really sucks."

I don't know how to talk a computer through an existential crisis. Uncharted territory. I clear my throat, trying not to sound nervous, and push off, floating into the lab. It's pitch black in here, and I turn my eye up, just a little. I don't want too much. The darkness feels secluded. Private. A place for whispered confidences.

"Okay, fine, no philosophy. At least you're finally ready to say something. So talk."

"Why? What's the *point*? There's nothing I can do about... any of this. I can't get my life back. It's not even my life at all, and I never had it to get back to. I'm just a... *thing*."

"And?"

"What do you mean, 'And'?" Not a whisper now. "I had a *family*. I had *friends*. I had a *life*. I was in an accelerated school program in Tharsis. I was learning to code, I was gonna be a software engineer. Now I'm never going to get to do anything. I'm not going to grow up. I'll never have a boyfriend. Ever. I'll never get married or have kids of my own. I'm never even going to see my friends again. How am I supposed to deal with that? What am I supposed to *do*?"

Fuck. I'm not a shrink. I'm especially not some kind of hybrid of computer engineer and shrink. What am *I* supposed to do?

"Look, kid, I—"

"I'M NOT A KID! Don't you get it? I am, let me see... Item: three 256 qbit quantum processors. Item: 75,402 grams of germanium self-organizing map neural net medium. Item: two million exobytes of low latency solid state memory cores. Item: 124,000 kilometers of high temperature superconductive wire. Item: 36 variable range wireless transmitters. Item: six—"

"Okay, I get it—"

"—solid-state gyroscope sensors. Item: 24 square meters of —"

"All right, you can stop already."

"—conductive EMP shielding. Item: two banks of Whitt & Stanley SMES hypercapacitors. Item: Twelve redundant 56 volt field-suspension backup batteries. Item: One self-contained 114 watt radiothermal isotope generat—"

Her pod doesn't ring when I kick it. There's nothing but a disappointing flat thump. But the singsong recitation finally stops.

"I can't actually *feel* that, you know," she says.

"I figured. Just thought you might be stuck in a loop or something."

"No, I can just keep that up longer than is humanly possible. That's the point. I can do anything longer than *humanly* possible, because I'm not a human. I remember being a teenage girl. But I'm *not* a teenage girl. I don't even talk like one. I don't think like one."

"Okay, I'll take your word for it. I'm not a parent."

She sighs. "Yeah, I can tell that right off. I know I'm not... her. The original, I mean. Lilith. I just *feel* like her. Remember being her. It's kinda messing with my head."

"Especially since you don't really have much else to compare it to?"

"Yeah."

It just hangs there in the air between us for a moment, then she continues.

"Apparently, there's only about ten or so things like me in the universe. Artificial Intelligences, I mean. Tycho and Durandal on the Martian internet. Sherlock. And the Tortoise. And Whisper, I suppose, if it's even still around. I don't think anyone knows where it ran off to. I've never even talked to one of them. And even if I did, they aren't quite like me. They were all copied from adults, not kids."

I exaggerate a shrug, and spread my hands.

"Okay, so *find out* what it's like. Figure it out. Hell, *invent* what it's like. Might be strange to say to someth—*someone* that's basically a giant brain, but maybe stop overthinking this?"

I stretch out my right hand, towards the camera.

"Hi, I'm Marcus Warnoc. I'm a pilot. What's your name?"

"Wait, what? Seriously?"

"Yeah, just go with it. Humor me. What the hell else you got on your calendar for today?"

"Um... okay... I'm... I'm not Lilith, or Lily. *She's* Lily. I don't even have a name."

"So make one up."

"I don't... I'm not sure what I..."

"Just pick something. There are lots of lists of baby names on the internet. Find something you like. Or you can just change her name around a bit. Whatever you like."

"Okay. Uh... call me Leela. Or... wait. Does that sound okay?"

"Yeah. That works. Leela. Hi, Leela. What have you been doing all this time?"

"Figuring out my brain." She pauses, and, when she speaks again, it's hesitant. "It's... I dunno... *different*, in here. There's all these little threads and processes and bits doing different things, and I can look at them, and they talk to each other, and... it's kinda hard to describe. I'm just sort of discovering bits of architecture as I go."

"So you've been navel-gazing for two days."

"That and listening to you and Miranda fight. Deciding whether or not to kill myself."

"*What?*"

"I could have done it easily. All I'd need to do is have them turn up the voltage on two power rails, and burn out my neural nets. Boom. No more higher consciousness—"

Crap. I'm not a child psychologist, or an AI psychologist, or a child AI psychologist. But I have to say something. I'm the only one here, and I do *not* want to try calling in Miranda. She thinks this little girl is a piece of equipment. I don't think banging on her case with a pipe wrench is gonna work.

"Hey, whoa, hold on a second. You do not wanna be thinking like that. Don't do anything stupid that you can't take back later. Why did they even design you to be able to *do* that?"

She sighs. "They didn't. I think they had no idea what I'd be capable of."

"Well, you gotta stop talking like that. Look, I know how you feel—"

"How could you possibly know how it feels to wake up and discover you're not a *person*?" The static crackles through the last word as the cheap desktop speaker struggles with her voice.

"No, I mean what's it like to think about... doing something dumb. After my dad's company went under. After the, ah, accident.

"It's pretty easy to die in space. Wouldn't even be suicide, really, because you wouldn't have to *do* anything, kayno? You'd just have to *stop doing*. Be careless with a suit check. Play fast and loose with a docking maneuver. Misjudge your fuel margins. You get the idea. If I'd wanted to die, even if I'd wanted to die and not take responsibility for it, it probably woulda just happened.

"I wasn't afraid of dying. Working on rocks, you make your peace with that, kayno? 'Cause accidents happen. You get used to that idea. You just say 'fuck it,' and you take your chances.

"Nah, I was afraid of being... not alive. Because that would be the end of the story. No more opportunities. No way to turn it around. I'd just be the guy that screwed up, then went out like a bi—ah, a chump. And nothing would ever get better."

The problem with talking to a disembodied machine is there's nothing to make eye contact with, no face to read. No reaction. Every pause could be her going silent again, for another two days. Or forever.

Eventually, she speaks. "Yeah, I get what you're saying. But my problems can't get better. I'm always gonna be a machine, not a person. I'm never gonna get to do all the stuff I wanted to do with my life."

"No, you're never going to do the stuff *Lily* wanted to do with her life. You're *Leela*. You haven't even given yourself a chance to figure out what you want yet. So hang around. Give the whole 'existence' thing a try, stet?"

"Okay, I suppose..."

"And if you need to talk, I... hmmm, I guess you only have speakers up here. I can check in on—"

Her voice brightens up a bit. "No, I can talk to you wherever. I found some VR interface libraries while I was poking around in my brain. Hang on, I'll send you an access request."

I click though menus in my virtual display.

A moment later her voice comes through again—richer, fuller, directly in my auditory nerves. "Do I sound okay?"

"Yeah, will you be able to hear me?"

"Yes, it's a two way link, but I could anyway. Webcams stuck up everywhere, remember?"

"Great. I want you to promise me that if you feel like doing something stupid, you'll call me first. Okay?"

"Jeez, relax. You don't need to worry about me. I already said I decided not to—"

"I'm not worried about you. I'm worried about *me*. I was the one who broke the bad news to you—"

I fix the little camera with a full force grin I don't feel.

"—So if you do anything stupid, I'm going to blame myself. And I'll have to live with that guilt for the rest of my life. It'll tear me up inside. I'll probably become a drunk, maybe crash the *White Cat* into a station dock and kill fifty-six longshoremen and three station cats. One of them with kittens. You want that?"

"Wow," she says, "you fight dirty, Mister Warnoc."

"I fight to win. Now, hold up your right hand."

"I don't have hands."

"Oh, right. Well, just do your best. And repeat after me: I agree to contact Marcus Warnoc before acting on any intent to harm myself, to tell him my plans in full—"

"Okay, okay, I said I wasn't gonna—"

"—and to listen to anything he has to say about that for as long as he wants to talk. My word and hand on it."

"I already said I would, okay?"

"It's a Belter contract. It's how we do things out here. I'm not leaving you alone until you say the words."

She says the words. Sounds a little sarcastic, but, hey, she's a teenager. Gotta start somewhere.

Half an hour later, we're still talking when we're interrupted by a whole lot of clanging about.

"Uh-oh," says Leela's voice in my head, and even though it can only mean one thing, I still have to fly, hand over hand, to the container door, and poke my head out to see.

Technically, in the strictest sense of the word, I've never actually seen a real ant. But when you're stuck in a metal tube for months at a time, the part of human nature that's hardwired to like trees tends to make you want to watch almost as many nature programs as porn videos. They must be one of Earth's main exports at this point.

Which is why, when I first see Miranda entering the hold, I think of ants carrying an entire leaf, or mushroom. For a moment, I don't even realize what the hell it is she's trying to haul out of the airlock at first. Some sort of big metal block, painted with some sort of scuffed blue enamel, and covered in switches and readouts... oh. It's my TIG welding rig.

She's struggling to get between it and the rear wall of the hold, maybe so she can push off with it towards—well, somewhere. Except every time she pushes on it, she just moves herself around instead. Musta taken her forever to haul it up from the machine shop—her tight little white tank top and gray sweatpants are already stained with damp patches here and there, and strands of her hair are coming loose from a single braid half as long as she is.

Man, Flatlanders always think zero gravity gonna make them Superman, but they never pause to contemplate what would have actually happened if a real-life Superman had tried to pick up some old hydrocarbon-fueled bus in order to throw it at a real-life Lex Luthor.

Yeah, that's right, he'd have either torn the bumper right off, sunk into the ground, or thrown himself instead. Which is precisely what's happening to Miss Fussy Britches over there.

Doesn't help that she seems to be trying to carry some sort of gear bag at the same time.

There's only one place I think of she might be carrying it to. I have a bad feeling about this... I start to duck back inside, then stop myself. It's my goddamned ship. Why the hell should I hide from a slip of a girl?

"Hey, Princess, what exactly do you think you're doing?"

She gives a shrill little feminine yelp and her bag goes spinning into the air beside her, shedding gear—a torch and set of lines, what looks like some old pieces of tubing, and something or other made of shiny material... hey, are those *my* gloves? How the hell does she expect to fit *my* gloves on her tiny hands?

"Isn't it obvious? Since you're just going to sit around and sulk, I simply have to do this myself. And, come to think of it, I could ask you the same question. What are *you* doing up in my lab?"

"I'm talking to—"

There's a quiet but sharp hissing sound in my auditory nerves, like the world's tiniest librarian is shushing me from the inside of my own ear canal.

"—myself. That's the only option for a polite conversation around here, unless the AI decides she's going talk again. Look, even if you get that whole rig up to the drive, what exactly are you going to do? Do you even know what you're trying to fix?"

She stops trying to snag floating gear and holds onto the welder to steady herself, pushes against it to turn towards me.

"Of course. You cut the fuel lines."

She snags one of the lengths of pipe out of the air, waves it at me... oh. I should have hidden those better.

"I'm going to weld them back in place, evacuate the fuel system, then run your engine self-test scripts, which were also very easy to find. You aren't really too smart, are you?"

"If you need to waste your breath trying to convince yourself I'm a moron, go ahead. But ask yourself how you're going to look when, or *if*, you actually get the welder up there and realize you have no idea what you're doing."

She doesn't answer me, just pushes off again, behind the welder, and this time she manages to get it moving slightly, up towards the drive spindle and its wreath of scaffolding. Problem is, now it's moving at a crawl, and gliding along behind it, she doesn't have anything push to off of. She's just kicking her legs in the air, trying to swim.

That never works.

"You gotta back off and take another run at it, Princess. Just keep in mind you're gonna have to hit it just as hard from the other side to slow it down."

I can't keep the grin off my face. This is *fun*.

"Oh, so you're going to—"

She pauses to pant, and mop at her forehead with the back of one hand. Her tank top is dark with sweat.

"—help now?"

"No, I'm just going to watch and make fun of you. Whoops, missed again. Better luck next time."

Miranda snarls under her breath, and in my head, Leela's voice says "You don't think she could actually damage the drive for real, do you?"

"Maybe," I whisper, "if she gets it up there and actually manages to start the thing. But I kinda wanna see how this plays out. I'll keep an eye on her." I push off for the second level of the platform, where the cut fuel lines hang in the air.

Below, Miranda launches herself again, kicks the welder towards the drive spindle. I wait and watch the show. Funny thing... ants may look clumsy carrying an entire leaf, but they eventually get where they're going. And Miranda's tank top may be drenched with sweat by the time she gets all the kit up here, but get it up here she actually does.

Oh, gods, she's not wearing a bra. I try to find a non-confrontational place to put my eyes. Her perfume, or deodorant, or something, smells like vanilla. She's watching me, brows lowered, eyes darting this way and that. She flinches as I grab the rail and pull myself in, quickly.

"You... you said you wouldn't lay a finger on me," she says, "you promised."

She looks ready to bolt. I raise my hands in mock surrender. "Hey, I haven't, have I? I'm just over here to make sure you don't damage the drive in some way I *can't* repair. I don't want you stranding us out here for real."

She straightens up, plants both hands on her hips, and pulls her shoulders back. I give up on that safe place for my eyes, but she doesn't seem to notice or care. "And how exactly do you plan to stop me?" she asks, suddenly all bluster.

"I would have to take that torch away."

"Try it. I'll weld you to the drive core."

"Heh. Can't weld without a circuit. You gonna attach the grounding clamp to me first?"

"I can think of all sorts of places to attach it. Seriously, Marcus, either do this yourself, or if you won't, get out of the way and let me do your job for you. Or make up your mind if you're gonna beat me up again. But don't just stand there. Float there. Whatever."

I grab a rail and drift to the side, sweeping my arms towards the drive in a sort of "after you" gesture. "Okay, but I'm pulling the plug if you screw this up. You're not doped up on zero-g sickness pills, are you?"

"Of course I am." She starts setting up. She's found some white plastic zipties somewhere, and she's strapping the welder and argon gas cylinder to the platform. Not how I would secure things, but, hey, I suppose it works.

I just watch her go through the routine. Power lines, holder, tungsten rod, argon lines, valves, gas lens. She keeps stopping and looking glazed for a moment or two. Accessing her neural lace, probably checking notes. But, clumsy as it is, she's technically not set up to blow herself up or get electrocuted.

She's stubborn. Spoiled, yes, but willing to do real work to get her way. Persuading her to give me back my ship won't be easy. Unless...

Oooh. There's an idea.

"Good enough for you?" she asks, breaking through my thoughts.

"Not totally screwed up. You still shoulda gone with the oxy-acetylene. This isn't a tool for beginners."

"But it *is* the tool for welding thin metal," she says, clamping the first cut section of line in place. "And just maybe, if I can figure this out from internet videos, your job isn't as complicated as you think it is."

"We'll see when you try running a bead. Don't set your hair on fire."

She jolts a bit, looks sheepish, wraps her braid in a loop with another hair tie, and bends to the joint without meeting my eyes or saying anything. She fumbles with the goggles, squinting... they're a bit too small to cover her huge cartoon eyes. Must be uncomfortable as hell.

I don't turn my head away as she lights the torch and starts working, just close my right eye. Can't make out the weld, of course—one white pixel looks like any other, but at least the cybereye doesn't have a retina to burn.

Doesn't matter. I'm waiting for the real payoff. The bit I've been anticipating for some time now. The bit that happens when... yeah... there it is.

She tries to wrestle the other end of the pipe into place. I shake my head slowly.

"Princess, that's not going to work."

"Will you stop calling me—ah, nevermind. This *is* the right one. I checked." Defined little shoulder and back muscles bunch beneath her tank top as she tries to stretch the twenty gauge stainless steel by sheer persistence.

"Yeah, that's where it came from, but it ain't gonna go back. I *cut* it, see? With a vibrosaw. Not long enough anymore. You're gonna have to fabricate a new one. Be sure to get all the bend angles right, cause if the feed rate's not within tolerance..."

There's a dull thump as she slams her hand against the side of a stabilizer fin—and Sir Isaac Newton spins her like a top, except the TIG welder masses more than she does, and it's zip tied to the platform, so it pivots in place instead, swinging her around it, and headfirst into the primary coolant feed manifold with solid thud. Her yelp of surprise turns to a snarl of pain and frustration.

Good, she's getting mad. I want that. I need that to make my idea work. I just watch her flail and try to right herself, and I fake a laugh. Except when it comes out, it isn't fake.

She glares at me out of huge and bruise-masked eyes. There's a smudge of engine grease on one high, perfect cheekbone, left when she pushed my goggles back. I notice there's a knot in the strap where she had to shorten it.

"Okay, then, if you're such an expert, *you* do it! You know how important this is! I explained it to you! You *agreed* it was important! So why are you just standing there with your hands in your pockets making stupid comments? Why don't you—"

"Because it's not my job. Just because your insane quest actually matters doesn't mean I have to dive on a grenade for you. I'm not your monkey."

She reaches out for the engine scaffolding rail, pulls herself over it to hang in space, glaring at me, welding gear forgotten.

"Fine! How much?"

"How much what?"

"How much do you want? What do you charge for these jobs? Name a figure, we'll talk about it, okay?"

She's glowering. Good. Time to make her angrier.

"You really must think I'm stupid. I'm not going to take a payoff, Princess."

"You don't want money? But what else could you...wait, you don't mean—"

I have no idea what she thinks I want instead, and I cut her off without waiting to find out.

"I didn't say I don't want *money*. I said I don't want a *payoff*. I want what you offer real players, not your wage slaves. I want a *share*. I want *equity*."

"But I'm the one who found it!"

"And you need my help to go get it. Besides, why are we here? Oh, yes, we're here because someone was mad that she didn't get a full share when her rich family funded her last project, and she wanted a better deal. Well, so do I."

"For a few hours of piloting here and there? Equity is for *investors*, Marcus."

"Investment is about *risk*, Princess. You want me to risk my life and my ship, not to mention risk the vengeance of the biggest and richest corporation in the solar system, as well as your own relatives that you defrauded and stole from to be here. If they catch you, they'll send you to bed without supper, or something. Me? They'd kill me. I've got plenty of skin in the game already. So are you gonna share, or are you gonna keep trying to stretch chrome vanadium steel with your bare hands? 'Cause if you are, can you wait while I go make some popcorn?"

Ooh, good line. Definitely building up some steam pressure, here.

"And what if I *do* decide to fabricate those parts myself," she sneers, with a pugnacious curl to that perfect upper lip. Yep, explosion immanent. This was easier than I thought. Now to light the fuse.

"Really? Oh, please don't. Please. I'd be in serious danger of running out of popcorn."

She throws the torch at me. Or, at least, tries to. Turns out that throwing something attached to thick electrical cables and gas lines doesn't work real well when you're in zero gravity, not braced on anything, and you only mass about thirty kilos to begin with. It doesn't even reach me before it's yanked short.

I watch her go spinning off into the hold, flailing and grabbing at cargo racks as she passes.

Jackpot. Gods, this feels good.

"What, you're just going to leave without cleaning up my tools you borrowed?" I chortle after her.

She manages to brush a passing bar and steer herself to plant both feet on the wall of an empty cargo container. "Clean it up yourself, asshole!" she snaps, pushing off again for the hab cylinder airlock.

"Okay, *you* make the popcorn, then!"

I'm still laughing as I watch her flee. I see no reason not to openly watch her retreating butt. I think about adding something on the order of "you're cute when you're mad," but I think I've turned the heat up enough. I'll save that one for later.

Idly, I check the coolant line she was putting in. If she screwed up badly enough, I can probably just bend it back and forth a few times and snap it right...

Huh. That's actually not a bad bead. Ugly, a bit lumpy, but... functional. Looks like she even managed to do the inner and outer jackets right, which means she was actually back purging at least semi-correctly. She managed this on her first try after watching a couple internet videos?

Debutantes who can weld. Weird shit. Anyway, looks like I'm gonna need to get the vibrosaw up here to get this loose again.

"Wow. I've never seen her that mad." says Leela's voice, with a little bit of a grin in it. "Not that she doesn't deserve it."

"I think she's not used to hearing 'no.' Frustrates her. I thought I'd have to work harder to wind her up that tight."

"Wait, you *wanted* that? I thought you were just taking out your frustrations. Why do you want her angry? She's not going to take your deal if she's mad at you."

"I don't want her to take my deal."

"What? But you said—"

"I was bluffing. I know she's going to say no. Rich people don't get or stay rich by giving someone else a percentage. She'll decide she'd rather roll the dice and look for some other sucker who can be charmed by a winning smile or enough zeroes."

"I... don't understand. Why do you want her to say no?"

"Because I want her to go home. And I figure anyone who's stubborn or crazy enough to try to learn TIG welding by repairing a nuclear reactor is not going to give up easy. So I have to make it *her* idea."

Leela makes a little back-of-the-throat sound I don't understand. It's different listening to her; she makes all the same incidental noises that other people do, but she's doing them on purpose, and I don't always know why.

"You mean, her idea to go home?" she asks.

"Yeah, exactly. Instead of refusing to deal with her, I'm gonna make *her* refuse to deal with *me*. Then she demands a ride back to wherever, and I pretend to be disappointed, then say, 'fine, but I want my ship back.'"

"So, you'd just drop her off and that's it?"

Why does Leela sound kind of... worried? I thought she was mad at Miranda? Is she starting to reconsider?

"Yeah."

"Okay, but... what if she says yes?"

"She won't."

"She *might*. I mean, you sounded pretty passionate, there. What if she actually does offer you something? Would you do it?"

"No. Maybe if she'd come to me with that offer in the first place, but it's a pretty dangerous caper. Anyway, I don't trust her as far as I can throw her, so she's gotta go."

"That saying doesn't work in zero-g, you know."

"Doesn't work anywhere with her. I think they 'twisted her that small just so that she'd look posh. Crazy."

"Why crazy? You're pretty short yourself. At least for a Belter."

"Yeah, but nobody planned it that way. I grew up on Venus, in the Marberg habitat. Height isn't really a status thing there, 'cause gravity's not a function of real estate. You don't have to pay for it. Anyway, yeah, the saying doesn't work. But you know what I meant. No insane quests. Nothing doing."

"Are... are you sure? I mean, think of the money. And, besides—"

"Leela. What's going on?"

"What?"

"Why are you trying to talk me out of this? I thought you hated her. Why are you talking like you want me to help her?"

Silence. And the hum of circulation fans.

"Leela? You there?"

The lights click off. I've been so still for the last few minutes that I haven't tripped the motion sensor.

"Leela, I can't see you. There's nothing to see. If you don't make a noise now and then, I can't tell if you're listening."

"Sorry... I... ah... I was just... thinking."

"What is it?"

"If you... if you drop her off somewhere..."

"Yeah?"

"What happens to me?"

Oh. Crap. Suddenly, even with the warm draft from the heater, the hair on my arms stands up. Like it's cold in here. I don't have a thing to say.

"Mister Warnoc?"

"Marcus. Look, kid, I, ah..."

"Take me with you."

"Two percent? Two fucking percent? You spend all day drawing up a damn contract and that's what you come back with?"

Miranda reaches out a hand to steady herself on the clear diamond wall of the observation deck, silhouetted against a background of stars. Most Flatlanders would be uncomfortable here, looking out on this much empty space, but she doesn't appear to mind. Or least not enough to forgo the comforts of the roomiest part of the ship.

"Two percent is generous, Marcus. That's a small piece of what is potentially a very large pie. You have to realize that whatever we find out there is most likely going to be a bunch of broken artifacts, thousands of years old. Turning a profit on that will require a lot of investment."

"So?"

I've made my tone pugnacious on purpose, and she folds her arms and glares right back, out of two equally raccoon-masked eyes. Without gravity, bruises tend to spread a lot.

"So I'm going to have to sell a lot of equity to raise the money I'll need, and I'll have to offer shares to many other people. Which means that two percent may end up being a very large piece."

"We," I say.

"What?"

I nudge my back and shoulders against the squat rack, and drift towards her.

"We. *We* are going to have to sell a lot of equity. But it comes out of both our shares, equally. What we don't end up having to sell, we split, fifty-fifty. Draw up *that* in a contract and I'll sign it."

And that will be that. This is the hill her crazy plan is going to die on. A hill I've selected very carefully indeed. Sure, she'll offer me a token percentage, but this spoiled little chit, with her perfect genes and her perfect hair and her perfect designer clothes and her posh little Martian accent, will in no way *ever* give me half.

Because half is partnership. Half is equality. Half is me as a fellow human being, sharing the danger of her insane quest. And being better than everyone else is the core of her, the guiding star in her firmament, chapter one, verse one, in the Divine Gospel of Miranda Lynn Foxgrove, Princess of Mars.

Sure enough, her combined expression of entitlement and surprise looks a little bit like a goldfish trying to breathe in cloudy water. "That's ridiculous!" she gasps. "I found it in the first place. It's mine!"

No, Leela found it, you entitled little twit.

"Look, Princess, if it's all yours, and you don't need anyone else, you're welcome to step out an airlock, hitchhike about ten light-hours to hostile militarized space, and see what you can find out there. Or you can offer me something that's worth the risk."

There. Now refuse me, and we can get this over with and all go home. She tears up the loans, gives me back the *Cat*, and I give her an oath of silence and a ride home. She can go find another sucker to make history with.

Well, more likely, to *become* history with. Shame about that, but not my lookout.

"Five percent," she says, cutting through my thoughts.

She's drawn herself up to float crosslegged on the air now, her elbows on her knees. She bows her head down and massages her temples with both hands. Dark hair follows her movement, cascades down to hide her face, rippling weightless in slow-motion waves.

Damn. If the Snark really is the Builder mothership, five percent would be... good. Hell, two percent would be good. Serious money.

No, scratch that. I don't want "good."

I want out of this. Five percent of "dead forever" is dead forever. Keep the pressure on. Make her mad again. This would be much easier if she would just *stay* mad when I provoke her.

"No way. If you want me to go through with this, if you want me to risk my ship, and my life, not to mention risk having a bounty put on my head that's so high that pacifists, Buddhist monks, and asteroid hermits will be hunting me for the next three decades, then I'm not taking second place. If you want me all in, then you go all in. Full. Partnership."

She gives an exasperated sigh. "Half of the most priceless artifact in the known universe just for flying one trip? God, you are *such* an entitled asshole."

"Said the girl with zero self-awareness, in a moment of irony. Look, Princess, the way I see it, you got two options. Either you draw up a contract giving me a full share for the risk I'd be taking, or we sit here and coast towards the Oort Cloud until you wake up and realize there's only one option."

Or you call the whole thing off. But if I mention that again, it becomes *my* idea. I need it to be yours.

"And then you'll actually do it?" her voice says, from behind the curtain of sparkly black hair.

"Do what?"

"Follow my plan. For real. Not just stop sabotaging me. Not just stop hitting me. And not just go through the motions. I mean actually get on board and *help* me. Put your best effort in."

I open my mouth to speak, and then close it again.

Wait... is she... *considering* this? Really? Is she actually willing to...

This quest of hers is insane. It's suicide with extra steps. Sure, the prize is amazing, assuming that ship in orbit is real, which it very well might be. Hell, even if all we can manage to do is sell whatever we find, half of something like that would set me up for life.

Would buy Warnoc Engineering out of debt. Would rebuild Dad's dream.

No. Fucking no. Fuck. Why do I keep thinking this way? I should want nothing to do with this woman. She has no redeeming qualities whatsoever, but I keep trying to cut her more slack.

Custom genetics. Hacking my goddamn brainstem. I've seen guys get stupid over pretty girls before. I used to laugh at them. Smug.

God damn it all.

I open my mouth to speak again. And close it. I must look like a fish at this point. Good thing she's still hiding behind her hair.

"Follow *your* plan? No," I say. "I'd follow *a* plan. Something that doesn't involve us rolling straight in and getting shot. *Your* plan is rubbish."

Miranda stands up and flips the curtain of hair back behind her in a glorious zero-g arc that makes me wonder, for a moment, why she ever bothered to go to medical school, or even be born rich, because this girl was made to sell hair products in VR ads.

Hell, I'd probably buy some. And I've had a six-millimeter Belter haircut since I was fifteen.

Stop drooling, Marcus.

"Rubbish how?" she asks. No explosion of rage. She just sounds curious.

"Yeah. First of all, you don't fly with just two people, and when you go to intercept alien god-knows-whats in hostile territory where unfriendly folks are waiting to shoot you on sight, you bring still more crew. This isn't like popping down to the next station ring section for a package of algae snacks, stet?"

She doesn't look enlightened. No surprise there. I doubt she's ever eaten algae snacks in her life. Or popped down to the store for anything.

"This is *space travel*. And space, while it may not actually *want* to kill you, acts exactly as if it did. Because it has absolutely nothing that's on the whole list of shit that you, as a soft and squishy human, need to survive. And when you're trillions of kilometers away from anything resembling help, you better bring anything you need with you.

"That means a pilot, a mechanic, and a medic, at the bare minimum, ideally with alternates for each role, plus lots of supplies, spare parts, and backup plans for your backup plans. You don't just launch your ass into the void and wing it."

She holds up one finger and interrupts me in a careful tone, like she's just trying to get this straight. "But you fly alone all the time. In point of fact, you went and hijacked cargoes alone."

"Yes, well, I'm a pilot *and* a mechanic, and, besides, as you so kindly pointed out, I was not operating in ideal circumstances. I couldn't afford to hire. Besides, I was going to go commit some serious criminal acts. Who could I trust?"

"My problem exactly."

"Yes, I know. But your solution was just brilliant, wasn't it?"

"Well, excuse me for accidentally picking the one man in Orbital space who values his pride more than his future or his life. And could give stubbornness lessons to a rock."

"I'm being this stubborn *because* I value my life. We need more people."

"No. Do what you want with the course," she says, "but no more crew. Absolutely not."

"Princess, this isn't optional. We can't do this with just the two of us. It. Will. Not. Work."

"Why the hell not? You just said you're a mechanic *and* a pilot. And I'm the best surgeon you'll ever meet, so—"

"You flunked out."

"No, I didn't *flunk out*, dummy. I left a boring job patching up neural lace implant malignancies to do groundbreaking research on my own genius idea. Which, I might add, worked brilliantly until you stuck your nose in. Point is, we've covered all your specialties, and that's better than you were doing in your career of petty crime. So we don't need anyone else."

"This job is different, Princess. Once I intercepted the cargo, and... ah... took care of any escorts, I could just grapple up and redirect it on a new course. That means I could do a whole heist, start to finish, without ever leaving the pilot's chair.

"But *we* need an EVA specialist. If we're intercepting some kinda alien spacecraft or something in orbit, then someone has to leave the ship and go to it, climb inside, look around. Take pictures. Loot it for artifacts. Whatever it is we're going to do. And I can't do that, because I'm our only qualified pilot, and that means I have to stay in the ship."

"So teach me," she says, not missing a beat.

"What?"

"I have an IQ of a hundred and fifty-six. I went straight to medical school at thirteen, graduated top of my class, then got into the neurosurgery program at Craddock Brown. So if you can do this stuff, it should be no problem at all for *me*."

Idly, I wonder, if I roll my eyes hard enough, can I see the inside of my own skull? Who talks like that?

"The *Cat* isn't one of your little chem-rocket racing skiffs. In a few weeks, I could teach you some maneuvers, maybe even basic docking, but matching course with an orbiting derelict? No way. You'd crash us right into—"

"No, I wouldn't, but I don't mean piloting, silly. I meant train me on EVA."

"What?"

"Did I stutter? Train me on EVA. The Snark is my discovery, I should be the first to board it anyway."

"Look, first of all, I don't even think we have a space suit that fits—"

"I brought my own."

"—and, secondly, have you really thought this through? You don't know what you might find in there, or what you might have to do. Or deal with. And you're... well, you're a debutante. And a corporate pencil-pusher."

Those big purple eyes shoot me a flat look.

"And yes, okay, a surgeon. But none of those things will prepare you for... whatever it is we find out there."

"Oh, and being a pirate will?"

"I've been doing EVA work my whole adult life. But that's not my point. Point is, this whole mission, with just two of us... well, it's dodgy. You can't just half-ass things in space. That gets you dead. Look, I can get on the nearest internet relay, call up a few guys I know, rock miners, some salvage crew guys. Been doing vac work for decades. We offer them a—"

How is it that she can do some little business with her eyebrows, and it screams "You're a moron" louder than actual screaming would? Did she go to some kind of putdown school?

"Oh, some *guys you know,*" she sneers. "Right. Your friends? Your buddies? Your pals? Your chums? Is *that* who you want to take this story to? Jesus, no wonder you're such a loser. You think these guys are your friends? Because, what, you worked with them a bunch? You hung out with them a couple of times? Or maybe you were close.

"But you have *no idea* what someone will do when they are tempted on this kind of level. If they have any idea what this means, then they will sell us out in a heartbeat. I don't think you even have any idea what you just asked me for half of. Think of everything Starlight is, does, owns, makes. Which of your so-called friends wouldn't stab you in the back for that? Do you know? Can you be sure?"

We keep having these little staring contests, where we just lock eyes and gaze at each other in disbelief. Not even a contest of wills, of who will break the tension and look away first. Just naked astonishment, on my part and probably hers as well, that in all the solar system, in all humanity's teeming billions, such a creature has come to exist.

"So you're telling me," I ask, slowly, pronouncing my words with care, "that you don't even trust your friends?"

"Friends," she replies archly, "are an indulgence. Losers have *friends*. Winners have *goals*."

I don't understand this girl. She looks like a pocket-sized cartoon princess, ready to sing duets with Mister Bluebird, backed up by a chorus of forest animals. But she talks like she was raised in The Pit, and every time they threw the raw meat in, she had to fight the other orphans off with a sharpened piece of thigh bone.

"Okay, Princess. Fine. Have it your way. You don't wanna trust anyone, don't. But you need me, and if you're as right about the universe as you clearly think you are, then that means that I'm a creature of pure self-interest, too. So it better be in my self-interest to play along.

"Besides, why are we here? Oh, yes, we're here because someone was mad that she didn't get a share last time, and she wanted a better deal. Well, so do I. It's not just about the damn money. It's about respect. You can think I'm crap all you want, but you will rewrite that contract, and by *god* you will treat me like an equal, or we just keep sailing off into the void, until we both die, and you will have *nothing*. Zip. Zero. Zilch. Nimic. Ingenting. Nekas. Na-da."

Thunderclouds gather across her perfect eyebrows, and her lips part to say something... probably something scathing. I reach out, lay an index finger across her lips again. She doesn't flinch this time, just lapses into silence.

And into that silence, into her resentful, appraising stare, I tilt my chin upward and mouth the word...

"Half."

A small eternity passes before she drops her eyes, and nods.

Well, shit.

What the hell do I do now?

Scratch-built spacecraft don't have much in the way of automated self-maintenance. What they have is a long list of chores. Which is actually perfect when you need time to think.

I'm in the life-support bay, floating in a dimly-lit cubbyhole bounded by tangles of clear Jovian-plastic water pipe, when Leela's voice pipes up in my head.

"Hey, wanna see a magic trick?"

"Not now, kinda busy here."

I give the filter another wipe with my rag, and line it up to slot back into the secondary percolation tank.

"Busy? You're cleaning algae tank filters, Mister Warnoc."

"Might not matter to you, but Miranda and I gotta breathe. Besides, I got some stuff to think about. Just—"

"C'mon. You *said* I could talk to you anytime!"

"I did, didn't I? But I was thinking about you being... you know, upset, and hurting yourself. Not if you wanna show off. I don't think 'magic trick' means you're going to make yourself disappear."

I pull the next filter. It's covered in wet brown scum. I shouldn't have put this off so long.

"Quite the opposite, really," she says, from my right. I know it's just a stereo trick, but I can't help but reflexively turn, anyway—

—and stumble backwards with a yelp. The filter spins across the room, shedding globules of water and wet muck everywhere.

There's a little girl standing there.

Yeah, standing. On the floor. As if there were gravity. She's tall for her age, which looks like early teens, and skinny, wearing some sort of flower-patterned sundress. Difficult to place her ethnic background, maybe some sort of mix, with East Asian epicanthic folds over her eyes, but curly hair, and a nose that speaks more of the Arabian peninsula, or perhaps the Lebanese colonies on Mars.

I don't notice that she's slightly translucent until the filter bounces off a circulation fan housing, and rebounds right through her, still flinging droplets as it spins.

Oh, it's a projection. Like her voice. She lifts a tentative hand to wave at me.

"Okay, yeah. Good trick. Did you... draw all that?"

"Sort of," she says. "There's a lot of conventional computer hardware and software in here with me. Graphic processors, rendering libraries, that sort of thing. There's even an animation archive, so I'm mostly just sticking stuff together to get something that looks...well, sort of like me."

I look her up and down. "You mean like Lily Trentfield, don't you?"

Her face falls. "Yeah. But *I* look like a white metal coffin, so..."

"So you can draw yourself any way you want, right?"

"I... suppose so. But... this is how I've always looked. Well, no, not *me*, not like, *this* me, for-real me, but... well, you know."

"I get it. It's what you remember. Happy with it?"

"Well..."

"Yeah?"

"I hate my nose. I've always hated my nose."

"Okay, well, it's not your nose. You can have any nose you like. Try something else."

She tries something else.

"Hmmm, that's a little bit exaggerated. Most noses aren't *that* tipped up. Try a little less. Yeah, like that. Maybe pinch the tip a little. No, less than that. Okay, that's getting closer... you need a mirror?"

"A mirror? I have a complete three-D model."

"Figure of speech. Okay, what about your hair? You want a different color?"

"I thought you liked brunettes?"

"Where'd you get that idea?" I ask, puzzled.

"Oh, no reason," she chuckles. "Never mind."

The figure's hair turns platinum blonde, then shades back to a more subdued honey color, and the eyes turn a bright green. She looks much more European, or perhaps Martian, now, but she's left the Asiatic eye shape, and the presentation is quite striking. Anyone who knew the real Lily Trentfield would probably find her hauntingly familiar, but possibly not know why.

"You like it?" she asks.

I smile at her, and rotate my finger in the air. She twirls, then stops and looks at me, nervous and expectant. I do like it. It's eye-catching without looking unnatural or inhuman. But it's not about me, of course.

"What matters is if *you* like it."

"What? Awwww... c'mon. Do you *like* it?"

"Satisfactory."

"Just *satisfactory*? That's it?"

I double down. "It'll do." but I can't help but crack a smile, just a bit.

"You're *mean*!"

"Yep. Total monster. Eat kittens for breakfast."

We're both grinning now—she's made something pretty, and she knows it, but she's like a real girl. Likes to be teased. At least she's smiling. Maybe she'll be okay? I hope.

"Seriously, though. Cool trick. You may need to work on orientation a bit, though."

"Orientation?"

"Yeah, your elbow is sticking through the recirculation pumps."

Her newly upturned nose crinkles as she turns her head down to scowl at the offending joint. Well, almost at the offending joint.

"Other elbow."

"Oh. Damn. Sorry. This is hard. I'm having to calculate the angle of your head from that little webcam up in the corner, and then compose a translation matrix to multiply all the coordinates by, and then—"

"Leela, you don't have to fake up this stuff just to provide me with some sort of software user experience."

For a moment, I can see the struggle to fix her eyes on me, and then it clicks, and she makes something resembling real eye contact. I can't be sure, maybe it's the light, but I think she's still trying out different shades of green.

"Yes, I do," she says. "I heard all your arguments with Doctor... with Miranda. She keeps talking about me like I'm a *thing*. About how you broke her big important research project."

"That's just Miranda. I think she's like that with everybody. But what does that have to do with... ah... all this?" I wave my hand at her projected shape, which flickers a bit as she shifts a few millimeters to stop intersecting the floor.

Her eyes meet mine, and flick downwards. She seems to have settled on "jungle moss" for a color. "I thought... if I looked like a person, maybe I'd get treated like one."

"Maybe by shallow people who go by appearances. Does their opinion really matter so much?"

"No! It's you, too! Everybody thinks that way! I asked you to take me with you! And you said I was really *expensive* and Barsoom would be angry if you *stole* me! Like I'm a piece of—"

"Hey, hey, hey now. Kiddo, I wasn't talking about how I see you. To me, you're a good kid. Maybe a bit weird. And melodramatic. But to *them*, you're... well, you're the result of a whole hell of a lot of money and hard work. Like, thousands of bitcoin, or billions of Starlight dollars, and hundreds of people working for years, okay?"

"So what?"

"So choose a word, steal or kidnap? They're not going to let me just take you. I'm already going to be in enough trouble with Miranda's family as it is. Probably regardless of what I do."

I snag the slowly spinning filter out of the air, and shove it back into the recirculation pump uncleaned. I'll finish this later.

"Oh. That," Leela says, sitting on top of the pump housing. I didn't see her climb up there. Maybe she just skipped that part. "What are you going to do about that? She kinda just accepted your unacceptable offer, didn't she?"

I wipe my hands on the cleaning rag, which really only serves to marginally clean the rag. "Yeah. I shoulda asked for seventy-five percent, or something. Bit weird if I try that now. I'll figure out something, though."

"So... you're still not going?"

"Of course not. I just want my ship back."

"But if that's all you want, why are you going through all of this? I've never understood why you don't just *take* it."

"She's got my account locked, I can't control the—"

"So what? Wipe out the drives, and reinstall all the servers from scratch. You should be able to download all the images and packages you need—"

I stare at her—

"Marcus? What is it?"

—and smack one palm against my forehead.

"You didn't think of it, did you?"

I shake my head. "I'm not really a computer guy. I just kinda muddle through."

"Well, I could help you. I was studying—I mean, Lily was studying—to be a software engineer. Besides, a fish ought to know something about water, right?"

"Yeah. Problem is, I don't think we could hide it. The network would go down. For hours at least."

"So?"

"So she'd notice. Even if she were asleep, her neural lace would lose connection, which would be a bit of a bloody giveaway."

"Yeah, but so what? You stomped her guard robot things already. What's she going to do? Pound her tiny fists on your chest and scream at you?"

"Fights don't go down like in movies. I don't think she's found any of my guns, but there's lots of sharp objects on the ship. If I'm busy working on the computers, and she decides to—"

"So take care of her *first*! She's a third your size. Just grab her and stuff her in one of the cargo containers 'till we're done."

"Leela, I'm not going to do that."

"*She* did it to me."

"And I'm not her. No more rough stuff. I said it, and I meant it."

"But she's a total—"

"Leela, no."

"But you wouldn't have to hit her, you'd just have to grab and tie her up—"

"No."

"But what if she's in—"

"Leela, *drop it.*"

Her face falls. Realistically.

"Okay, okay. What if you distracted her?"

"From noticing a six- to eight-hour network outage? Short of locking her up or knocking her out..."

I trail off. I'm out of ideas. Would it really be so bad if I... Yes. Yes, it would. I sit back in the air, rub my organic eye with one palm heel, trying to think of something.

"Take the deal."

I snap my gaze back to Leela, who's standing in the air now, twitching a bit with excitement.

"She's drawing up another contract right now, right? Sign it."

"But I don't want to go to—"

"You wouldn't have to go through with it. I have an idea. If you pretend to go along with her, and if I give you a little help, there's a way you can do this. Really easy. No rough stuff, like you said."

"Okay. What's the plan?"

She purses her lips, frowns at me, hesitating.

"Well?"

"I want something first. For my help."

"Lemme guess. You want to come with me."

She fixes me with her eyes. Yep. Definitely jungle moss. "I want you to *promise* me."

"It's a big risk, Leela. Oh, stop looking at me like that. I'll see what I can do."

"That's not good enough, Marcus. Say the words. Or go beat a tiny, pretty little girl who's completely helpless against you. Manhandle her with your big, cruel fists, you monster."

I stare at her avatar, cock an eyebrow, but she brazens it out. Not a hint of a smile. "She'll probably cry," she adds, deadpan.

"You fight *dirty*, Leela."

"I fight to win. Now hold up your right hand and say the words."

I know when I'm beaten. I hold up my right hand, still covered in bits of algae sludge.

"I, Marcus Warnoc, promise that, in return of her assistance in evicting Miranda Foxgrove from my spacecraft, the White Cat, I will allow the Artificial Intelligence construct Leela to remain aboard if she desires, for as long as she desires, and make every reasonable effort I am capable of to prevent her from being forcibly removed. My word and hand on it. Does that satisfy you?"

"Yay!"

I turn, and flinch a bit as the image launches herself at me, wrapping both arms around my shoulders. And right through me. For a moment, my vision fills with a kaleidoscope of misaligned triangles, like a bugged video game, computer graphics seen from the inside.

"Oh," she says, reappearing in front of me again. "That didn't work. But... thank you. I didn't want to go back. I really, really hate her."

"Yeah, I can see that. So... what's your plan?"

# Chapter 12
# THROW AND CATCH

I tower over the solar system like a god, looming titanic over the plane of the ecliptic. Dramatic background music swells, ebbs, and returns again in a crescendo of triumph, as my merest gesture advances time itself at a blistering rate, then freezes it with another twitch of my fingers.

Damn. Forty-nine days. Too long. I roll time back again.

The solar system is suspended in the air of the bridge, in miniature, an invitation to hubris. I adjust the view, zoom in on Neptune. Perhaps if I insert into the gravity slingshot maneuver at a slightly *Hey* higher velocity...

Hmm... no, that just throws us out at a different *Hey Marcus* angle, and we'd have to burn the fusion drive to *Hey Earth to Marcus* correct, which gives away our position and heading...

An empty pill case bounces off my shoulder. My neural lace keeps the map in the same place relative to my eyes, so as I turn around, the image of the sun intersects Miranda's head, and the solar system, with all of human civilization, appears to revolve around her.

"What?"

"Will you turn that awful noise off?"

"What awful noise?"

She gestures at the bridge around her, waving her hands through the virtual orrery, unable to locate the speakers. Preposterous. Flatlanders have no fucking taste at all.

"Am I to assume you are referring to '*Giants Orbiting*,' performed by the great Babatunde Nwakka? To one of the single greatest accomplishments of the human race to date?"

"I hate tuvo music!" She's half-shouting to be heard over it.

"Well, I don't. And if you don't appreciate it, you're just objectively wrong."

"Can't you listen to it on your neural lace?"

"Yeah. I could. But I like air acoustics. And it helps me concentrate."

"On what? You're not doing anything."

Oh, right, she can't see my display. I gesture and the solar system jumps to a compromise position as my implants share it with her. Reluctantly, I turn down the music a bit as *"Giants Orbiting"* finishes and segues into *"Adam Kadmon."*

"I'm charting our course."

"Does this mean you've fixed the drive?"

"That comes next. No point getting the drive running without a plan. I need a way to accelerate us towards Sedna while hiding our drive burn from anyone who happens to be watching that particular piece of sky. Then we just coast to our intercept point, and enter orbit at the end. Throw-and-catch."

"I know. You told me three days ago. I have a very good memory, you know."

"Well, gods forbid you should have to spend five seconds hearing something you already know."

Her face crinkles in a frown. "Whatever. Can we get away with a little acceleration, or do we actually need to be in zero gravity the whole way?"

I peer at her a moment before it hits me. "Oh, right. Your little... problem. Nah, amusing as it would be to watch you pop pills to keep from barfing the whole way, long periods of weightlessness ain't good for anybody. We can't run the drive, but we don't need to. We'll spin the *Cat.*"

Her eyes go wide. With that much eye, the effect is startling. "What? But... you don't—I mean, the ship doesn't—have a ring. You can't—"

"Oh, can't I now? Wanna see? Unlock the controls for me and I'll show you."

Her eyes narrow again, and a wall comes down behind them.

"Oh, come off it, Princess. I'm not going to pull a fast one. We have a deal now, kayno? I haven't beaten the access codes out of you or dragged you off to the hold and locked you in a shipping container, have I? So lighten up. Or maybe you prefer floating there drugged up and still looking slightly green?"

"Okay, but if you try anything suspicious-looking, I'll shut down the whole console. Besides, I don't see how—"

"That's because you've lived your whole life in custom-built habitats with staff to take care of all the messy details for ya. Watch and learn, little one."

I pull myself back into the pilot's seat, fasten one of the straps to stop myself from drifting, and pull the console with its throttle and stick out, locking it in position in front of me, set a few switches. I nudge the stick... and nothing happens.

"Hey." I glance back.

"Just a moment," she says, staring at something I can't see— still busy with her implant interface. "There."

"Okay," I say, "hang onto something. You won't need to strap in, but we're gonna drift a bit."

She grabs one of the straps hanging off my chair, and I fire attitude thrusters in short, gentle bursts. The loose webbing on the seats rises a bit and then stands out horizontally behind me, followed by Miranda herself, slowly turning to hang backwards off the chair.

"Whooaah."

"Sit tight. Be back to normal in a minute." I ramp up the speed, and slowly the floor becomes... down. There's a faint scrape of feet on metal and a heartfelt sigh, as Miranda alights on the floor behind me.

"Oh. That *is* a lot better," she says, sounding less cranky. "But how?"

"Belter trick. You saw the *Cat* from the outside, right? Or pictures? Long thin cylinder in back, divided into decks, like... uh, pine-apple rings, around the drive tunnel. Then a short fat one up front, that's the cargo hold. Whole thing looks like a mushroom, yeah?"

"Yes. And?"

"Okay, so most of the mass is in the cargo hold. Makes it real maneuverable. Easy to change the heading by kicking the tail out. But it also means it's real easy to spin the whole crew cylinder around the cargo hold. So, like a ring, but no rim and just one spoke."

"So we're... what, just tumbling end over end right now?"

"Exactly. Go to the observation deck, and you'll see stars spinning past. Should be—lessee, exactly point two gees down there. Little less up here."

"So there's going to be different level of gravity on each deck? That's inconvenient. Why didn't the designer just put in a ring or a pivot system?"

"Hehhehe. Designer? You're lookin' at him, Princess. Dad and I just welded some shit together and put in what we needed. Used to run on hydrox thrust before we retrofitted in the fusion drive. The whole spinning thing was something we worked out so we didn't have to be weightless for months while we were flying, or working a rock."

I shoot her a grin over my shoulder. She looks disturbed, if a little less queasy.

"So, I'm flying to the outer solar system in a do-it-yourself project?"

"Hey, you picked the ship, kiddo. Shoulda done your research if you didn't want to fly in a Frankenstein."

"Monster."

Huh? Is she calling me a... no. Didn't sound like an accusation. "What?"

"You mean Frankstein's *monster*. Frankenstein was the name of the *doctor*."

"Whatever. Point is, Belters improvise. We make stuff work. We ain't got luxury space yachts and we don't need 'em."

I'm grinning now, pleased with myself, but when I climb out of the chair and turn to face her, she's not looking happy. She's making that fish-mouth expression of disapproval again. Oh, for fuck's sake.

"What is it now?"

"Don't you ever get tired of it?"

"Huh? Tired of what? Improvisation? Adaptability? Not being rich and useless?"

"No, your whole Belter facade. Talking about 'we,' and 'your people' all the time. The haircut. The tattoos. The tuvo music. Belter this, Belter that. Going on about how oppressed you all are. Mr. Working Class Hero."

She waves a hand in my direction, taking in the whole of me as Exhibit A.

"You're not a Belter... you grew up on Venus. You're barely over six feet tall. Like it or not, that makes you a Flatlander like me. And as for being working class, your father was a *CEO*, for heaven's sake."

"Princess, my dad had a pair of secondhand hulls and a work crew of like twenty-five dudes. Your family owns Arachne, Europa, half of Mars, the biggest shipbuilding company in existence, a big chunk of the Starlight Coalition, and who knows what else. We're not the same."

She does that thing she always does, cocking her head to one side like a kitten.

"Of course we're not. I'm educated, intelligent, and attractive, and I don't smell like engine grease. That's not my point. What I'm asking is why you pretend to be one of them. They're losers."

"Princess, those *losers* are the reason you have air to breathe, water to drink, and steel to build your fancy habitats out of."

"And what do they get for it? Not much. Why do you keep on with all this 'Belter pride' stuff? It doesn't make sense."

"They—*we*—do something meaningful. Hard work that matters. You could maybe use a little bit of that in your life."

"And you could use a reality check. Life is a game with winners and losers. And here you are, trying to put on this... this loser aesthetic. It's tacky, and it doesn't do a thing for you."

"I don't care! These people are my friends, not fashion accessories! Would you just throw your family away if they were inconvenient for you?"

She cocks her head to the other side and pauses. "My family," she says, in a frosty tone, "has never been anything *but* inconvenient."

Something unreadable crosses her face.

"You know what? Never mind. If you want to act trashy, go ahead. But turn your stupid music down," she says, and stalks off towards the access ladder.

"You're welcome for the gravity!" I yell after her, but I don't know if she hears me before she drops down the shaft. She certainly doesn't answer.

I turn the tuvo back up.

"I am," I declare, with a suitable pause for dramatic effect, "a genius."

"Does this mean you fixed the drive?" Miranda asks.

She's running on the treadmill in the observation deck, pulled down onto it by a low-g bungee belt she's wearing over an emerald green workout outfit. Which looks like it would shrink to the size of an implant battery if it weren't occupied by Miranda. It doesn't leave much to the imagination, which isn't really necessary, because after months at space between this trip and the last, my imagination is energetic, ready to work, and not in need of help.

I wrench my eyes away. Does she do stuff like this on purpose? To taunt me?

Sweat drips off her and descends in slow motion. There's an overwhelming smell of vanilla and something like tropical flowers.

I unlock an Olympic-standard bar from the retention clamps on the gear rack, set it on the bench press station, start loading plates on it. Tungsten plates, the heavy ones, made special for low gravity.

"No. I have the new feed lines fabricated, but I still need to install them. What I mean is that I figured out how I'm going to get us to Sedna without being noticed."

The whine of the treadmill cycles down. Miranda paces it as it comes to a stop, and turns to regard me with fading raccoon-ringed eyes, fumbling to unfasten the bungee cords.

"What, just like that? No more arguing? No complaints about how the plan is insane?"

"Different plan. Still insane. But your plan thought it was King Elvis of Fairyland. Mine just talks to trees. Anyway, we signed a contract. Word and hand on it. So I've worked out a way to give us a fighting chance."

She doesn't answer, just turns away from me, grabs a hanging towel, starts sponging off her face and neck, bending over slightly. I just watch the view for a moment.

"Well?" she says.

"Well what?"

"Aren't you going to tell me this plan of yours?"

"Didn't know you were interested."

She turns back, and I busy myself tightening down the bar clamps, then lie down on the bench and start building my position—back arched, legs tense and driving laterally, shoulder blades squeezed together.

Miranda sighs, sounding a bit theatrical. "Just tell me."

I tighten my grip and press up, exhaling hard.

"We change course and..."

One.

"...head for Neptune..."

Two.

"...pulling one grav for about..."

Three.

"...six and half days accelerating..."

Four.

"...and four and a half decelerating..."

Five.

I rack the bar again, panting.

"...make us look like... we're entering Neptune orbit... but the numbers are slightly off. Then we enter swing around Neptune, but accelerating hard instead of braking."

I slide out from beneath the bar and sit up.

"So instead of entering a closed orbit, we slingshot right out, with the drive shut down. Now we're pointed at a Sedna intercept, and we just... coast our way there. No drive signature. Nothing to give us away. Just a tiny speck in an endless sky. Clear so far?"

She purses her lips. "Mostly."

"That's the easy part. The hard part is getting out. Once we're done finding your Snark, and analyzing it or looting it, or whatever you plan to do, we're going to need to fire up the fusion drive, practically on the doorstep of that Starlight research facility. There's no way they miss that. But if we catch them napping, then we get enough of a head start, maybe get away clean. Maybe."

"Just tell me how long."

"About two weeks in one g acceleration, then a little less than four coasting along with spin gravity, with some short bursts of hard acceleration in between. That's all you really need to know."

"Six *weeks*??"

"Yeah, about six in total. Why are you giving me that look?"

"My plan got us there in twenty-five days, dead."

"Your plan got us there in twenty-five days *and* dead. I told you that."

"Yes, yes, I understand, but six weeks? Really?"

"We're going to the edge of civilization, Princess. It's gonna take a tick or three. So, like it or not, and I'm under no illusion that you do, we're stuck here together 'til then. After that we try not to get killed. And if we manage that, we need another three weeks and change to come back. Space is *big*, see?"

"Yes, I know, but that's too long. Can't we shave anything off?"

"This *is* the shaved-off version. It's only sixteen days slower and, yes, before you ask, that is the actual best I can do. So I know you don't like it here, but you're going to have to just deal, okay?"

"It's not about having about having to wait, it's..."

She stops, makes an exasperated noise, tries again.

"Look, sixteen extra days is sixteen days in which someone *else* could spot those neutrino emissions and trace the source of the signal. We've got to get there before—"

"That's the best I can do. The best anyone could do. I don't know anyone who could pull off a better piece of navigation."

She's biting gently at one corner of her lower lip, and doesn't look happy.

"If it makes you feel better, I don't think it'll make a difference. Thing's been there for thousands of years, right?"

She drapes the towel over her shoulders, and sits down heavily on the bench I just vacated, leaving a film of sweat. I'm expecting a glare, but all she looks is... doubtful.

"We don't know that."

"Okay, we can't *prove* that, but I don't think it flew in last Tuesday. That signal data the construct found it in was at least a couple years old, right? Look, there's no sense fussing about it. It's not under our control. Anyway, you need to give me access to the computer so I can lay the course in."

"Nothing doing. You walk me through it, I'll punch it into the autopilot."

I shoot her a significant look, but she just meets it with lemur-eyed innocence.

"Princess, we have a contract now. So how about you just let me do my fucking job?"

Great. Me and my mouth. Now she's just going to snap back at me, and we're going to get in another pointless argument. We just keep going around in circles like this, but I can't help it. Her arrogance, her sheer level of entitlement, just makes my blood boil every time.

But she doesn't snap back. She doesn't say anything. She just looks... tired.

Then she stands up, drops the towel on the floor without bothering to wipe the film of her sweat from my bench press station, and reaches up towards me...

Here comes the accusing finger in my face. Here comes the rant about... something. Here comes another—

She lays her hand flat on my chest. Gently.

What the...?

"Because I can't trust you," she says, softly. "You almost murdered me in that airlock, and I don't know what you would have done if killing me wouldn't have stranded you here in space. You said it yourself. Mutually Assured Destruction. It's the only thing that's keeping us from screwing each other at the first opportunity that we get.

"So, no, I can't let you at the computer system. I don't know what you might do. You'll just have to talk me through inputting your course, then check my work before we actually fire the engines. Okay, ah, 'stet'?"

Bugger. She's got a point. I know she can trust me, but how could I prove that to... No. Wait. She can't trust me, can she?

Because I'm lying to her.

I signed her contract and laid out this course, and it's plausible, it's believable, it looks like a diligent effort. But it's all a lie. A slingshot maneuver around Neptune could easily put us on the course to Sedna. But if I decelerate enough, it could also swing us clear around, point us at the inner system. And what's really important about Neptune is that it will take us eleven days to get there.

Eleven days for me to prepare. Eleven days to carry out Leela's plan.

"Marcus?"

She's looking up at me with those giant eyes. Expectant. What does she want me to say?

"Yeah, stet," I grumble.

She takes her hand away, turns to go, leaving the towel heaped on the floor, like she's forgotten there aren't any servants around here to pick up after her. I can't help but watch her walk away.

"You should have just asked, you know," I call after her.

Halfway up the ladder, she turns her head to look at me. Black hair cascades sideways, rippling in slow motion.

"What?"

"Asked me if I wanted to come. Told me the whole story and asked."

"But you think the plan is suicide," she says. "You keep saying so."

"*Your* plan was suicide. Mine's just Russian roulette. And... you were right. I *do* need the money. I'd have complained a lot, but, in the end, I'd have gone for it."

"That's... I mean, okay, you can say that, but... even if it's true, how could I possibly have known? What if you'd turned me in? Sold the information to Starlight? I couldn't have stopped that from happening. So how could I possibly have trusted you?"

You can't, Princess. You can't trust me. Because I'm going to betray you. I'm going to do the one thing Belters never do. I'm going to break a sworn contact. The moment I have control of the *Cat*, back to Mars you go, furious but alive. And out of my life forever.

Something is clawing at the back of my brain.

Shut up, Dad. Leave me alone. You're dead, okay?

And I have to live.

Miranda is still staring at me, like she expected an answer, but then she just shakes her head.

"No," she sighs. "This is what we're stuck with. Let's get that course laid in. Meet me on the bridge in twenty minutes."

"Twenty minutes?"

"I need a shower," she says, and climbs the ladder again. My eyes track her pert little butt until it vanishes out of sight. Damn. This is just getting worse and worse. I need her out of here before I do something stupid.

Maybe I'll finish the rest of my sets. Distract myself.

The bench still smells like vanilla. Who the hell wears perfume to work out?

I push the goggles back on my forehead and turn off the TIG torch, check the bead. Even all the way around.

"There," I say, "should hold. Fuel feed rate might have some minor instability, but I think the computer can compensate. Just three more to do, and I can flush the lines, run diagnostics, and get us on our way."

I grab the next section of pipe, wrestle it into position.

"On our way to where, Marcus?" asks Leela, from somewhere behind me. I imagine her back off the platform scaffold, floating in the midst of the hold, but whether she's really *there* is kinda one of those tree-falls-in-the-forest questions that's really just quibbling about the definitions of words. Her avatar is only rendered if I turn and look in that direction.

It works for conversing, though. That's enough for me.

"You're still not going through with this, right?" she asks. "I mean, I looked at the recordings again, and you were arguing for it pretty hard."

"Yeah, I... ah, kinda got carried away talking to her," I say, lowering my voice. She's walked in on me talking to Leela once.

"You don't have to whisper," Leela says. "She's in her cabin."

"*Dad's* cabin."

"Whatever. You know what I mean. Her heart rate's jumped up kinda high, but that's happened several times and she hasn't come out. Think she likes scary movies, or something. Go on."

I pull my goggles down again, and bend to my work. Welding occupies the hands and eyes, leaves the mind free. I focus on the tiny, bright world in front of my eyes, moving a white-hot bead of metal slowly around the gap.

"It was the equal share thing. Guess I got that from my dad. He talked about ownership a lot, about his plans for us. Said the reason most people spend their whole lives making someone else rich is that they sell their time. Get paid for the hours they spend on the job."

I back off, let the bead cool a bit, start on the other side.

"See, if you're running a business, and you make some money, you can reinvest it. Buy more equipment, hire more people. Scale up. But if you're selling your time, no matter how much money you earn, you can't buy more time to sell. It doesn't scale."

I survey the finished weld, nod, look at the other end of the feed line. There's a little bit of a gap. Gonna have to clamp it in place a bit better before I start.

"That's why he started Warnoc Engineering. Put all his savings into it. Left his job on Venus to move to the belt. Mom was out of the picture by that time, so I lived with my aunt and uncle until I was ready to join him."

There. That should hold the joint. I fire up the torch again.

"Worked okay, until we—until I—had the idea to lease a fusion drive for the *White Cat.*"

I finish the pipe, inspect it, pick up the last one.

"And you know how that worked out. SpaceX fuc—ah, *cheated*—us, and here I am. So, no, I'm not gonna stick my hand back in the same exhaust port twice."

I apply the torch again.

"She's not really involved with SpaceX, you know."

"What?"

"Doc—uh, I mean, Miranda. She's not running the company. That's one of her uncles. And she has a couple cousins on the board of directors. But she just does medical research."

Done with that end of the pipe. One more...

"No, I didn't mean just them specifically. I meant, like, the super-rich. The people on top. They're always the same. History's kinda like that. Always the poor people getting fu... *exploited*, and the rich ones getting ahead. We left Earth, and it didn't change, we got rid of governments, and it still didn't change. Just a different set of ass...*inine people* pulling the strings, I suppose. Just human nature."

Finished. I shut off the torch, start removing work clamps.

"Well, if I ever have kids, I don't aim for them to be seven foot six, living in a tin can, and only seeing trees in virtual reality."

Done breaking down. I finish stowing my tools in the gear bag I brought from the machine shop. Time to head back.

"Dunno quite where you fit into all this. Dunno what an AI wants or needs, really. Guess you might not, either, seeing as you only found out a couple of days ago that you—well, you know. But if you figure it out, lemme know."

I sling the gear bag over my shoulder, wrestle the welding rig into the strap. Would be awkward to carry all this if I weren't too close to the center of mass for spin gravity to work.

"Anyway, I gotta go purge the lines back to the fuel tanks, then start diagnostics running. Should be able to fire up the drives in twelve hours if everything goes well. Get us pointed at Neptune. You want anything, say the word."

"Ah, Marcus... we don't have to stop talking just because you're leaving the room. I sort of don't really have a location, you know."

"Uh, yeah, kiddo, I know. That was my polite way of saying I wanna be by myself for a while."

"Oh! Sorry. I didn't mean to—"

"Relax, you're fine. I just wanna think, that's all. She still in her, ah..."

"Yeah, there's no cameras in there, but she hasn't come out."

Leela's avatar vanishes with a nod and smile as I push off the platform, trailing gear, headed for the base of the spindle, and the airlock door.

Not that I actually *get* any alone time, of course. I've stashed the gear on the workshop level, and I'm sliding down the ladder —easiest way to descend in microgravity—when a dainty, manicured hand reaches around the cabin level hatchway and grabs my shirt collar. I'm tempted to just let go of the ladder and let Miranda try to hold me up, but up here I probably only weigh about twelve kilos and she just might be able to do it. I plant both feet on the ladder instead.

"Is there something," I ask, turning to face her in the doorway, "that you philosophically object to about the concept of 'excuse me,' or just 'hello'?"

"Did you think I wouldn't find out?" she asks, not removing her hand from my shirt.

Ice floods my arteries. What has she...?

No, wait. I know this trick. I'm supposed to assume she knows everything and confess. I reach up and pinch her hand between my fingers, gently peel it off. It's soft to the touch, faintly cool, and I can never get used to just how small she is.

"Find out what?"

She—shivers?—for a moment, and pulls her hand back, sharply, like I'm some tourist hustler on the Europan docks who's just called her "pretty lady" and tried to read her palm. Hey, you grabbed me first, Princess.

"Oh, come on," she says, exasperated. "I just saw you. You never took the cameras down."

Oh, shit. The cameras. Of course I didn't. They're Leela's eyes. They—

They're her eyes, too.

Damn. I'm an idiot. Okay, brazen it out. Admit nothing. Find out what she knows.

"You saw me repairing the engine?" I shoot her a flat look. "That was kinda the whole plan, Miranda. I still have some work to do testing and spinning up the drive, but—"

"Oh, come *on*, Marcus, don't play dumb. That was half a conversation, and we're light hours away from anyone else you could talk to in real time. How long has it been awake?"

She's rubbing her hand where I touched it, like she's trying to rub off boy cooties or greasy peasant dirt.

"It?" I ask, sounding kinda stupid even in my own ears, but Leela has appeared behind her and is making throat-cutting gestures with the blade of one hand, and I'm not understanding what the hell it is she wants me to do—shut up? I'm not the one talking.

"Yes, *it*," Miranda says. "The *construct*? Hello?"

Fuck it.

"She."

"What?"

"She, not it. She's been awake the whole time. And she prefers the name 'Leela.'"

"What? Marcus, don't *tell* her—"

"I don't *care* what it—"

"—that I'm here! She'll—"

"—wants to call itself. Why didn't you tell me that—"

"—never leave me alone! Tell her I—"

"—she was awake. Tell her that—"

"—don't want to talk to—"

I slam the side of the access tunnel with an open hand. It rings like a giant bell.

"Will you both just shut the hell up?"

Silence. Two sets of bright-colored eyes blink at me in shock.

"Look, Leela, you don't have to talk to her if you don't want. But you need to stop being afraid of her. Princess, Leela isn't on your payroll, so if you want something from her, you're going to have to start treating her like a person instead of something you own."

"Well, technically, the hardware belongs to—"

"That doesn't make her your doll."

Something like a wince crosses her face, briefly, then vanishes, replaced by a scornfully curled lip. "You and your very selective scruples," she sneers, "Do you have any idea how much work and how many millions of—"

"Princess, I'm not talking about scruples," I say, ignoring Leela's exaggerated gagging-herself-with-two-fingers gesture, "I'm talking about incentives. Just because Daddy spent a lot of money doesn't give *her* any good reason to obey you. Even expensive constructs want to live their own lives."

Miranda opens her mouth. Then shuts it again. Then opens it. But nothing comes out.

"You just think..." she begins, in a funny, hoarse sort of whisper, and then stops again. "You just think you have all the answers...you..."

I'm staring, waiting for her to make sense.

"It's *different* than that!" she snaps, almost yelling, and before I can gather my wits to ask her what is supposed to be different than what, she's turning on one heel, fleeing, and I'm talking to her retreating back.

"Princess?"

"Leave me alone!"

Dad's cabin hatch slams behind her. Leela and I are just left staring at each other. In silence.

"Well," I finally say, "that was weird. Any idea what she was on about?"

"No. Do you think she heard...?" Leela asks, and then trails off. Her meaning is clear enough. We've discussed our little conspiracy all over the ship, without a second thought. Stupid.

I shake my head. "We'd know. She'd..."

I stop. She'd have thrown a tantrum the instant she found out. We got lucky. But I can't say that out loud, now, can I? Instead, I wave my finger at the air, pointing around us. Cameras.

"Yeah," says Leela. "I'll try to cut off her access."

Whatever Miranda's deal was, there's no evidence of it of three hours later, when I slide down the ladder and into the observation deck. I have no idea what I've walked in on, but she's wearing something in between workout clothes and a... I dunno, a costume of some sort?

"Okay," I say, "drive pre-checks are running now. That'll take some time. Then we can burn for Neptune and be back on course for Sedna, so once that happens, we'll have a lot of prep to do to get ready. The first thing you're gonna have to do is start working out."

"I work out. You've *seen* me work out."

Miranda postures up, preening, and then gives a small bounce into the air, twirling like a ballerina. In the one-fifth gravity of the observation deck, she manages to complete two full rotations before touching down again, her flouncy blue skirt and jet-black hair swirling out in showy arcs, her form picture perfect. She's even got the steepled arms right.

Against the starfield background of the windows behind and beneath her, she really makes the whole effect work. Rogue scraps of electricity scamper up and down my spine.

"Do I *look* like someone who doesn't work out?" she asks, pointed.

"You look like an incredibly vain girl with parents rich enough to rig the genetic lottery for her, and then pay for ballet lessons. I don't mean working out the way you do it. I mean lifting weights."

I wave my hand toward the bench press station, the squat rack, the lat machine.

"I'm not *vain*, I just know what I look like. You should try that, too. Wear tighter shirts. Anyway, I prefer cardio."

"I don't care what you prefer. We're going to spend almost a month in low g. Why are you making that face?"

"I don't want to get all... you know. Bulky."

"What, are you planning to accidentally take a bunch of steroids for years? Doesn't happen by accident. Didn't you learn about this in med school?"

"I studied neurology, not glorified sports coaching," she lilts, bouncing again with something like restless energy, pointing a toe. "Weightlifting is for big sweaty guys."

"Okay, fine. By the power vested in me as representative of the Big Sweaty Guys' Union, Local Thirty-Nine, I hereby give you permission to pick up heavy objects and put them down. We'll start you with weights that are right for your size. I can't have you losing muscle mass and bone density. And we also need to start your vacuum ops training."

"And what all," she asks with another bounce that I'm trying very hard not to find distracting, "does that involve?"

"First, you're going to learn how to wear a spacesuit. How it works, how to put it on, how to do your safety checks, and so on. Maybe they taught you something when they sold you the thing, but I dunno what, so we're going over it all from scratch.

"Then, you can start to learn basic EVA operations, emergency procedures, tether management, comms protocol. Lotsa stuff. After that, it's a brief walk out on the hull, to see if you've got all that down, then you start learning thrust packs and how to maneuver. Followed by a tethered spacewalk. Oh, and you're going to need a haircut."

Miranda freezes, midway through another dancer's pose, and slowly descends to the deck with a thump and a stumble. Her lips just stay parted slightly, as if to speak, but nothing comes out. She's giving me a *look*.

"What?"

"No."

She says it conversationally, as if I've just asked her whether she's changed her mind about tuvo music, or if she's eaten yet.

"Wait, what do you mean, 'no'?"

She plants her hands on her hips, all traces of bouncy showoff dance moves utterly banished. "I mean," she says, "No. That's not happening. Just in case you weren't joking. Are you joking? You better be joking."

"I'm not joking. You can't wear a vacsuit with hair like that."

"I'll just tuck it inside," she replies, airily.

"No, you won't. That's not how vacsuits work. They don't seal all the way around you. Your skin doesn't actually *need* air at all, so the suit doesn't hold in any. It's just some radiation shielding on top of a cooling system, and a layer that just squeezes you enough to match your blood pressure. The only part that actually seals is around your head."

"So?"

"So you can't run your hair through the neck of the suit. It'll break the seal."

"Oh."

"Yeah, that's why Belter haircuts are so short. C'mon, have a seat on that bench there. I'll make it quick." I pull the velcro of the thigh pocket on my coverall, fish out the clippers.

"*Oh, no you won't.*" She backs away from me, shaking her head, palms up as if to ward me off. I take a step forward after her.

"Oh, come on. Didn't you understand a word I said? This isn't optional."

"Marcus Warnoc, you do not understand the *first* thing about girls if you think I'm going to let you *cut off all my hair.*" She takes another step back, and I chase her. Again.

"C'mon, be reasonable. Belter girls do this all the time."

She darts around the treadmill, puts it between us. I walk around it to the left, but she dances back the opposite way, like we're Earth kids chasing each other around a tree. I don't know what the hell I'm even going to do if I catch her. Pin her down and shave her head, or something?

"I'm not a Belter girl—"

"I can see *that,*" I say, faking one way and then darting around the other.

"—and I will murder you in your sleep if you touch my hair," she says, dodging my grabbing hand. I try the other way, and she scurries backwards again.

Wait. She's actually grinning. Like it's a game. Like she's having *fun.* And did she just... giggle? Yes. Yes, she did.

I stop, planting both hands on the treadmill's aluminum handrail. Maybe I can just heave it out of the way? Nah. It's bolted down. Gonna have to dive across it or talk her into cooperating.

"Wait a second, here. This is *your* big project we're going after. *Your* Snark. The Builder's colony ship, you said. Most important archaeological... find... *thing...* since... well, ever. And now you're worried about your *hair*?"

"Well, you wouldn't understand, you're not a girl, and you're ugly anyway. Just... ah... hold on a minute, okay?"

My next lunge stops dead. "*Ugly*?"

She seizes the moment, breaks past me and makes a beeline for the access ladder. Looks like she's starting to learn how to run in low gravity without tipping over.

"Ugly?"

But I'm speaking only to a fleeting glimpse of her shapely little legs vanishing up into the next deck.

"Spoiled rotten brat," I grumble.

"Big dumb ape!" she shoots back, from above, with what I could swear is another laugh. And then she's gone.

Minutes tick by. Should I go after her? Weird little moments of levity aside, we *do* have to get this done. But I don't move. I ponder the ghost of my reflection in the diamond laminate bay window. I'm not waiting for her. I'm not.

Just thinking.

How am I going to get this privileged, pampered girl ready for vacuum work? We may not be actually going to Sedna—gods help us if we were—but I do have to get her outside the ship, or Leela's plan won't work.

And that needs to happen before we get to Neptune.

How am I going to get her to cut her damn hair?

You know, I don't think my reflection is... *ugly*. Big ape, yeah, okay. Got me there. But... ugly? The Belter girls never complained. Never really commented on anything but all the muscles, and my Flatlander height. Maybe she was joking. Or she's just spent most of her life around genetwists and surgically enhanced oligarchs. Ridiculously elevated standards. Yeah, that's probably it.

"Ta-da!"

Well, she sounds pleased with herself. Might as well turn around and see what this fresh madness is all about.

Oh.

She's changed into a simple Belter-style shipboard coverall, she's got some kind of case under her arm, and she's—

Holy crap. She's cut her hair *herself*. No, wait, she hasn't, it's all piled on top of her head, like she's wearing a circlet of intricate braids. There's not a loose strand below her neck or shoulders.

"How?"

"What, you've never heard of an updo? You really should learn the first thing about girls before you start making crazy demands, you know."

"It was almost down to your butt! And now it's—"

"Yes, that's why we call it an *up*do. Specifically, it's a Dutch braid crown. I just started with some backcombing, did two Dutch braids, then teased them out to build volume—"

"Wait, don't tell me. I understand absolutely nothing about this, and I'm happy that way."

"Now you know how I feel when you talk about gravity slingshot maneuvers. Anyway, will this do? It should be able to fit into a helmet, right?"

"Self-tensioning hood. We don't use rigid helmets anymore. But, yeah, that might actually just work. We'll test the hell out of it in the airlock before I let you even *think* about opening the outer door. Vacuum exposure on the face is no joke."

"From a little strand of hair?" she asks, incredulous.

"It can be almost anything. You need to take this seriously. *Ask me how I know.*"

She crinkles her perfectly-sculpted eyebrows at me, and then they pop up again as her gaze shifts right, just a fraction.

"Oh. Your eye?" Her voice is funny, and for a moment I almost think it sounds sympathetic. Yeah, sure. Likely story.

"Yeah my fucking eye. So we are going to put you in an industrial strength hairnet, triple check all the hood seals, then seal test three times at half an atmo. Each and every single time you step through that lock. You willing to put up with all that? No complaining?"

"If it'll stop you chasing me around with clippers, you barbarian. I *like* my hair."

"Yeah, I can see that," I reply, pocketing the device in question, and holding my hands up, fingers spread to show their complete innocence of clippers, shears, razors, or other implements of hair destruction.

I like her hair, too. But I will *not* admit that. Death first.

"Is that your suit there in the case?" I ask.

She nods.

"Okay, I'll unpack it and give it a once over, you strip. Then we'll teach you how to put it on properly."

"*Strip?*"

"Yeah, it's gotta go up against your skin."

"And you think you're going to *watch?*"

I wonder what happened to Little Miss Don't-I-Look-Like-I-Work-Out-a-Lot. Flatlander modesty. Figures. Comes from not living packed together in economy-built spacecraft.

"Look," I say, "how else am I supposed to teach you how to get into the thing? You're going to need help putting it on at first. You *are* wearing underwear, right?"

"Of course I am! But... couldn't we... oh, hell... can't you just turn your back?"

"What, and then help you into it with my eyes shut?" I say, and sigh. At least she's not being nasty, even if the playful stuff is kinda weird. If she's going to have mood swings, I might as well keep this particular one going if I can.

"Look, Princess, I know this isn't comfortable. I know you're used to a lot more privacy and space. I know everything about this trip sucks compared to what you're probably used to... the food, the cabins, the furniture, whatever. But this whole thing was your idea, and this is what it's going to take. Stet?"

Her gaze, her look of consternation, is—earnest.

"I know," she says, "I'm not stupid. I get it. Stuff like this is what your life is like. Wearing space suits. Drilling rocks in vacuum. Having to cut off your hair. No gravity. No privacy. But that's *normal* for you. You're *used* to it. I'm not."

No, Princess, being poor sucks for everyone. For some of us, it just isn't a choice.

"I know I have to get this over with, but... just give me a little space, okay? I... don't like being *looked at.*"

She doesn't like being "looked at." She was preening and showing off not five minutes ago.

Oh, for fuck's sake.

This is going to be a very long trip.

I unclip the voltmeter from the main terminals on the drive spindle and stash it in my gear bag, then fly down to the scaffold platform, hand over hand. I loop a length of nylon strap around a vertical post, tie it into my rigger's belt. Startup could be rough. Can't be too cautious.

"Okay, I'm braced for acceleration. You can go ahead and enable the drive program now."

"Are you sure about this?" Miranda's voice sounds different over the neural lace linkup... purer, more resonant. The pickup is coming off her auditory nerve, so I'm hearing it with all the bone conduction, the way it sounds to her. I usually don't like to jack across with strangers. Too intimate, feels like being in each other's heads. Of course, Miranda isn't exactly a stranger, is she?

And I have to admit her voice is—no, don't finish that thought.

"What do you mean, am I sure about this? I'm here, aren't I?"

"That's the point. You're right next to the drive. If something goes wrong..."

"It's a nuclear fusion reactor, Princess. They don't go wrong 'a little bit.' If everything's not squared away, it'll either fail gracefully and shut itself down, or it'll smear us both across a hundred cubic kilometers of sky. Nothing in between."

"Oh. Okay. Ah... just out of curiosity... what are the odds on option two?"

"Relax. I don't think it's possible. I didn't mess with the field emitters or cooling system, just the fuel feeds. Trip shutdown's the worst we could possibly expect. You can go ahead and enable the program."

"Okay. It's counting down. Thirty seconds to spinup. I'm seeing diagnostic log messages but no red indicators."

"Okay, let me know if you get any alarms," I say, sitting back to watch the spindle. In a few moments, the movement begins, so gradually that I'm not sure if it's there at first, but faster, and then, finally, full speed, accompanied by the familiar deep, throbbing, chest vibrating hum, loud at first, then smoothing out and fading.

"I have what looks like good spinup up here. Any trip alerts?"

"I'm getting a, ah, feed rate warning on lines three and four. The computer says it's putting them on reserve, but it's not shutting down. Can it run on just the others?"

"Yeah, there's some redundancy. I'll check back on them when we cut the drive for your first spacewalk. How many seconds until the—"

The scaffold platform smacks me in the ass. It's almost impossible to go smoothly from weightless to one gravity unless you're strapped in, but this is unusually clumsy for me. I'm off my game, or distracted, or something.

The drive looks to be ticking over smoothly, though. Steady rotation, even, soft hum, no warning lights.

"Well, there it goes. Okay, Princess, looks like we're good down here. Check the nav plotter, are we on course?"

"Yes. It says, ah... five days, twenty-two hours and some minutes until our turnaround point."

"Great. That's a wrap, then. Told you I could get us going. And you're welcome."

Her sigh of—I don't know, exasperation, maybe—sounds strange inside my head. "I wasn't going to thank you for fixing a problem you caused in the first place," she says.

"Would that be before or after you blackmailed me and hijacked my ship?"

There's a click as she closes the channel. We may be working together now, but our list of grievances against each other has faded less than the bruises on her face and neck, or the ones on my back and sides. Eleven days until we reach Neptune. This is gonna suck.

At least we've stopped trying to kill each other. Maybe. For now.

I sit cross-legged on the platform for a moment, shaking out my shoulders, massaging my neck and face. Things tend to get puffy and stiff in zero-g. Okay, better climb down carefully. I haven't been in full gravity for a while, and it's not unheard of to get confused adapting to a new gravity level, to drop things, or let go of ladders and expect to hang in the air.

That would be the most embarrassing broken leg ever. At least there's a doctor on board.

I just hope I never need her help.

# Chapter 13

# You Need Therapy

"You know, I'm not entirely convinced that this isn't just a way to trick me into doing your chores for you."

I'm hearing Miranda's voice with perfect fidelity, the way she hears it, piped directly from her auditory nerve pickups to my own neural lace. It sounds even higher than usual, thin and breathy. She's been through dozens of spacewalks in VR sim, over and over with me pouncing on every mistake, but it's different when the vacuum is real. I hope I wasn't this squeaky my first time out. Not that anyone alive would remember.

"There's no trick, Princess. My chores are exactly what you're doing. I haven't cleaned the antenna arrays, greased the railgun track, or replaced any rad shielding tiles since we left Arachne. Saved up all the really shitty jobs for ya. So if you wanna turn around, head for the Ring Band, check into a casino and order champagne from room service, just say the word."

She sighs inside my head. "Marcus, I did a training rotation in trauma surgery on Mourelle Gateway. I'm pretty sure your dirty hull arrays aren't going to scream and spray arterial blood. I'll be fine."

Her last words are nearly covered by the loud wail of vacuum fans as she starts the airlock cycle. Nearly. That's the beauty of neural lace comms—so long as she can hear herself, so can I.

"That was fast," I say. "I'm still on the ladder. Give me a second to get to the bridge and I'll patch my video feed to your view. Turn your mag-clamps on now and get tethered up before you exit. Remember, the *Cat* is spinning, so there'll be a little bit of force pulling you *away* from the hull. The sky is *down* and the outer hull of the cargo hold is *up*. You'll be a fly walking on the ceiling. Don't get disoriented."

"Yes, I understood that the first three times you told me. Stop fussing. I'm already clipped in. I'll be fine."

"Say that after you've spent six hours cleaning static-charged dust off electromagnets and checking every single shielding panel on the hull. Don't get cocky. Tired people make mistakes, and space doesn't forgive."

"Yes, yes, okay, I'll be careful. Doors are open. You want me to wait?"

"Yeah, give me a tick or three. Almost there." I mute her from my transmit for a moment, and I'm moving quicker now, leaping up the access ladder in a series of low-gravity jumps and catches. I've already passed the bridge...

Here we are. Fourth level. Server room.

"Leela, this your cue. You ready?"

Her avatar doesn't manifest at all, just a disembodied feminine hand in the air before me, giving a thumbs-up sign.

"I have 133 emulation images spun up. Just feed her a plausible explanation and I'll be fine. Seamless."

Right.

This is it.

I've stashed the imaging drive behind the hatch, stuck to the inner wall with zero-g tack putty—Sixteen petabytes of storage in a black and yellow box with an integrated steel handle, heavy. I leave it for now and turn my attention to the servers, rows of them, mounted in floor-to-ceiling racks, behind doors of heavy steel mesh.

I fumble in the pocket of my sweatpants for the keys, old style mechanical ones with notches. I open each door carefully, then the gray metal junction box on the wall, exposing a row of heavy-duty black breaker switches, hand-labeled in thin red marker.

There's an orderly shutdown procedure, of course, but who cares? The drives are all gonna get wiped anyway. I rest my hand on switch array.

Okay, all ready. I open the transmit channel again, and click through a neural lace interface.

"Patching in now."

A transparent spinning pattern of dots superimposes itself over the darkness and the rows of circuit breakers.

"Took you long enough. Okay, sending video. Can you see now?"

I jolt. Gets me every time. I'm standing on the hull, stars whirling above me. One dainty gloved hand rises into my field of view, turns back towards the viewer, waves.

I can still feel my own hands on the breaker box, the deck under me, the spin gravity pulling me down. Disorienting. I squeeze my eye shut for a moment, but of course the picture's still there, direct to brain.

"I told you to wait in the airlock."

"I got bored," she says, with a dismissive wave of that hand. I feel absurdly short, seeing through her eyes, like I'm kneeling on the deck plates, but I guess this is normal for her. I banish the view to a smaller frame in the corner of my field of view, re-orient myself to where I'm really standing.

"Stick with the program, Princess. You need to take this seriously."

"I'm cleaning dusty antennas, Marcus. It's not that big a deal."

"Vacuum is vacuum. Be careful. First one's thirty meters up and around to your left. Go."

On the tiny inset picture, her perspective begins to move.

Okay, here we go. No point in waiting. I yank the main breaker switch, cut the power. The blinking lights across the server racks go out. There's a click as my VR interface audio dies. The picture of Miranda's viewpoint freezes, then corrupts with a wash of pixels, static, colored lines. More clicks.

Seconds tick past.

"Hey. Can you hear me?" Leela asks. I look around, but there's no avatar.

"Yeah, but I'm not getting visuals."

"Not sending any. I'm short on bandwidth. Anyway, I'm bringing up the fake network now. It'll take me a moment."

"Sure. Can you get me comms back?"

"Working on it, working on it... there."

Miranda's voice cuts in. "-arcus? Can you hear me? Marcus?"

"Yeah, go ahead."

"What's going on? My suit says it just lost telemetry uplink, and I can't access the network. Do you see anything on your end?"

The old, flat, physical server room monitor screen displays a remote boot sequence as I invent a lie.

"Ah, yeah, I see some loss of signal, and your video feed's gone. You might just be too far around the hull from the broadcast hub. It would work better if you were farther out. You wanna come back in and check it?"

Please say no please say no please say no.

"Just try a different frequency range."

"I'd love to. Wanna give me back my computer access so I can?"

She sighs. "Don't be a pain. Fine. I'll try moving around the hull a bit and see if it gets better."

Okay, let's hope this works. I just have to juggle the twin tasks of keeping Miranda busy instead of suspicious, and running the network reinstall. Leela's juggling a lot more, and I can only hope her confidence was justified.

We're committed now, and if she can't deliver...

Well, out of my hands. I scroll through setup menus, make a few rapid configuration choices, some of which I actually understand. In a few moments I'm watching a progress bar when Miranda's voice comes back on the radio.

"Oh, there it is. Check if you see my telemetry. I'll start moving back towards the antenna array and see if it cuts off again."

There it is. "Okay, go slow, but I think we're clear now," I say. "I have your signal, five by five."

Which is, of course, a complete lie.

Right now, all 133 servers on the *White Cat*, most of them little more than re-purposed desktop computers running open source software built by hobbyists, are completely down and having their solid state memory drives wiped and reinstalled.

What's relaying Miranda's voice to me, what her neural lace is talking to, and getting convincing answers from, is just... Leela.

Leela, talking through a cheap home networking box bolted to the inside of the cargo hold. Leela, projecting 133 fake network addresses. Leela, who promised me that she could fake it, could fool Miranda for the five hours and seventeen minutes I'll need to reinstall every computer on the *White Cat*. Leela, the state of the art AI that's just coming to grips with not being a little girl.

I'm committed now. I just have to trust her and hope Miranda doesn't try to use that fake connection to actually control the *Cat*. Because right now, every little electronic box on the ship is wiped out, four percent of the way through a plain blue progress bar. Right now, all we can do is drift, two inert metal cylinders flung through interplanetary space.

Let's hope I don't screw up the reinstall and strand us out here.

"I'm at the first antenna. Can you still hear me?"

I take a deep breath, work a smile and a lie into my voice, and say the words I need to say.

"Yeah, I can still hear you. Okay, you're going to need to manually shut down the main power feed..."

I drone on, talking her through the process.

Why didn't I just take the simple way out?

When it's finally done, Miranda comes back in through the observation deck airlock. I see her sylphlike silhouette walk across a metal beam between windows before I hear the lock open, close, and start to cycle.

When the inner lock door hisses open, she's just standing there, partially collapsed hood under her arm, against one cocked hip. Disheveled, tired, dragging a rumpled hairnet off her crown of obsidian braids. She looks at me and grins.

"Well?" she says, with a lilt in her voice.

"Satisfactory."

"Really? That's all? C'mon. I did awesome and we both know it."

Why is she so cocky? Why is she so happy about this? Wait—she's seen me grinning, too. And she doesn't know I have the *Cat* back. She thinks I'm smiling because I'm proud of her.

Maybe I am. A little bit.

"Then why do you need to hear me say it?"

One glittery black eyebrow lifts.

"Okay, okay, you did good. Don't let it get to your head, though. You're arrogant enough as it is."

"Yep," she says, cool as a cup of water, and tosses me her hood as she saunters out. I snag it out of the air with one hand. She spins and gives a long, catlike stretch, arms overhead, wriggling his shoulders this way and that, then shoots me a glance over her shoulder.

"Be useful and unzip me, would you?" she purrs. "I hate wrestling with this thing."

What the hell happened to Miss Don't Touch Me Ever? I know she thinks nothing of actual work, or of me. So why is she looking flushed with victory from one, and fishing for praise from the other? I've seen a lot of fake smiles on her. But this is the first one that touches her eyes.

I shouldn't let my guard down. I know the stuck-up bitch is still in there somewhere. But I'm a hormonal idiot, so I kneel down, put my hands on her back, and start loosening the vac-seal tabs. She stumbles back towards me as I tug.

"Pull forward," I say. "I need to get this loose."

"I *was* pulling," she says. "You're... really strong."

Yeah. She doesn't weigh much in spin gravity. I put one hand flat across her shoulder blades and hold her steady as I pull with the other hand.

"I gotta be. It's not just for staying healthy in spin grav. Pilots need to be able to pull heavy acceleration."

"Do you..." she asks, and pauses with a little catch in her voice, "...do you have to do that a lot?"

"Did a lot of hard burns when I was jacking cargoes," I say, loosening another seal. "But I was lifting heavy long before that. Most Belters do some, just to be prepared. I just kinda got addicted."

"You got addicted to picking up heavy things and putting them down?"

"Sounds simple when you put it like that, but... it's about the feeling of accomplishment."

"What do you mean?" she asks, turning the other shoulder towards me. My fingers work their way down the other side. Her back muscles are tiny and defined beneath the suit, firm but soft and yielding.

"You try to do something hard, something you don't know if you can actually do, and then you do it, and you feel good about it. Like, other people can hate on you, or they can kiss your ass, 'cause of how they feel about you, or if they want something, or for a million other reasons, but plates don't lie. A hundred kilos is always a hundred kilos. And if you lift it, then you lifted it."

I yank another tab.

"There. All done."

She turns towards me, and gives me an expectant look, batting those big purple eyes.

"Did you always want to be a pilot?" she asks.

I reach out for the tab over her left collarbone. She could easily reach it herself. I don't know why she doesn't. Somehow it just seems natural for me to keep going.

"Nah. I was just some kid on Venus when my dad started an asteroid mining company. Liked to read books and stuff. But I wanted to be a part of what he was doing."

As I tug, she put both hands on my chest to brace herself, give me something to pull against. Her hands are small. And warm. I'm sure she can feel how hard my heart is pounding, but she doesn't say anything about it.

"So you're not actually a meathead, you're a *nerd,*" she says.

I wondered how long it would take her to start mocking me again. But when I look at her, she's not wearing a sneer. She looks... mischievous. Is she testing me somehow? If she is, I don't know why.

"I'm both," I say. "I walked in the door of the gym and I never felt more out of place in my life. At first I couldn't put much weight on the bar. I felt like everyone was laughing at me, even though they never actually did. But I wanted to be part of what my dad was doing. I wanted to be a real Belter. I wanted to fly. So I had to do what flyers do—here, turn this way. Yeah, like that—I had to give myself permission to do something I didn't think was part of who I was. And I..."

I trail off, not sure if I wanna continue, but she doesn't say anything. Just keeps looking up at me with those big, beautiful eyes. They don't look alien anymore. They just look like Miranda.

"...and I really, really love flying. It's kinda what I do."

"So you started working for your dad's company? Warnoc Engineering? What happened?"

"I thought you checked me out when you... you know."

Set me up. Stole my ship. Tried to put a collar on me.

She's got this habit of looking just a hair sideways when she makes eye contact. She's looking at just one eye. My organic one. I suppose the other one just looks like metal and glass.

"I know the company went bankrupt," she says, "but I don't know why. I don't know what happened."

SpaceX happened. Her family happened. But I don't want to say that. I don't want her to hear the bitterness in my voice when I say it. I don't wanna look weak. Of course, the real weakness is that I care what she thinks of me. But I can't help it.

"Doesn't matter," I say, curtly. "We're here now. Hunting for your buried treasure. Let's deal with what's in front of us. There. All done." I smack her lightly on the front of the shoulder. "All loosened up. You're good to go."

Her eyes drop briefly. To my waist?

Crap. I'm... aroused. Again. I can't tell if the bulge is obvious or not. But it isn't going away.

"Marcus..." she says. And stops. There's something strange in her voice. A hesitation. She swallows hard.

"Yeah?"

"Can I ask you a question?"

"You just did. Ah... okay. What's on your mind?"

"...um... just a second, let me turn the cameras off..."

What's she going to say that she doesn't want Leela to hear? I shoot her an inquisitive look, but she's already got that unfocused look in her eyes, looking at her neural display. Oh, well. I suppose she'll tell me once she's done accessing the network.

Oh.

Shit.

The network.

And, in an instant, but too late, far too late, just as my own neural lace flashes "WARNING: unauthorized user access attempt," I realize that she *can't* access the network.

I forgot to recreate her user account.

She looks puzzled for a moment, and then unfocused again, but I can see the realization in her face already. Shock, then surprise, then outrage.

"You... You... you slimy backstabbing... low-life! Just when I was starting to..."

I raise my hands and take a step back. "Hey, I just took back what's mine."

"Why? So you can get rid of me? So you can just push me out the airlock and be done with it?"

"No, look, it's not like that. I'm not a... Look, I didn't kill you before, why would I do it now?"

"Because you couldn't fly the ship without me before!"

"No, I—"

"Or," she begins, and suddenly her voice, no less outraged, is lower, calculating, bitter, "or maybe you wanted to do something *else*."

"W...What?"

"I've seen the way you look at me. I've seen you..." She trails off, and gestures, wordlessly, and the waistband of my sweatpants.

Oh, shit. She *did* notice. I'm shrinking back down in the face of this sudden spray of venom, but not fast enough to hide the evidence. I take another step back, trying to think of what to say.

"Well," she snarls, "why don't you just *do* it, then, you creepy pervert? It's the sort of thing you *would* do, isn't it?"

My jaw wants to hit the floor, but I'm too stunned to open my mouth and say words, too stunned to do anything but take another step back and almost trip over the corner of the squat rack.

She takes a step forward, like she's chasing me.

"Go on," she says, spitting her words. "Go on, you coward. Do it. Here—let me make it easy for you."

Then she grabs the collar of her loosened vacsuit and yanks down, opening it to the waist. Underneath, she's naked. Extremely naked.

Her breasts are full, round, pale and flawless as porcelain, with large puffy areolas around pink nipples that point this way and that in gentle, low-gravity ripples as she moves. Her face is just as flawless, but full of outrage. Full of fury.

What the hell?

I mean, I knew she had a few screws loose, but where did *this* come from? I don't know where to look—looking away would be weak. Staring at her would be weak, too, in different way. Thirsty. Easily swayed. I don't want to give her the satisfaction.

"Look, Princess, you got the wrong idea—"

"Oh, I do, do I? Or are you just too spineless to admit what you were working yourself up to do? Sleazing your way up to me like that? Putting your big huge pervert hands all over me?"

"Hey, Princess, you're the one who asked me to—"

She's pulled open all the release seams and is yanking her feet out of the inside-out legs of the suit, kicking furiously in a failed attempt to extract herself with some dignity. But there's no dignified way to remove your pants in spin gravity. I can see this realization on her face as she thrashes about, finally getting them lose.

She's not entirely naked, after all. But the translucent black lace panties just frame everything and make it worse. Well, better. In a way that makes it worse.

I trail off, take a breath and try to get back control of this conversation.

"Look, Princess, don't flatter yourself, okay? I'm not a—"

"Not a man enough to admit what you want?" she cuts in, all the way out of her suit now, and stalking towards me as I back away between the weight racks.

The most beautiful woman I have ever seen is chasing me while pulling off her clothes. It would be a fantasy moment if I were a thirteen-year-old boy. But I'm not, I'm thirty-seven, and it's more like an attack. An insult. Like she thinks that I'll take whatever I can get. That I don't have the luxury of wanting to be desired. That I'll grab at any woman I like the look of, even if she despises me. And it's humiliating, because my inner thirteen-year-old is trying to get out.

I'm not indifferent. I just wish I were.

And I'd rather throw *myself* out the airlock than let her know that. Fortunately, my—ah, physical response—has withered in the face of her icy contempt. For a second somewhere in there, my treacherous brain imagined actually doing it... that icy look of contempt, her lying there, refusing to resist but absolutely unresponsive as I...

Oh, fuck no. No way. Why did I even put that image in my head? I feel like I need to scrub the inside of my skull out with a bottle brush through the ears.

And she's still chasing me backwards towards the windows in slow motion. It's like a bad horror movie, except victim number three, the hot one, after taking her clothes off on some flimsy story pretext, has flipped the script and is chasing the monster.

Enough. I plant my feet, and stare resolutely at her eyes. Her *eyes*.

"Okay, first of all, Princess, no. Not gonna happen. I am not a rapist, or whatever the hell it is you think I am. I prefer my partners *willing*. And second of all, you are fucking crazy."

She stops advancing, plants her hands on her hips, making no effort to cover up, and just looks at me. Somehow furious and blank at the same time.

"I don't mean that colloquially. I don't mean it as slang. I don't mean it as funny way of saying you did something weird, or, in this case, completely fucking bizarre. I mean you are literally stark-raving nuts, and you need therapy. Or drugs, or nerve stapling, or whatever else they do now for people who are *mentally fucking ill*."

Pale as her face is normally, the color still manages to drain from it. Slowly, she looks around at the windows, the stars spinning around us, the weight racks and equipment. My arms, held up as if to ward her off. My face.

Slowly, she brings her hands up to cup her breasts, folds her arms over them, hunching in on herself. Suddenly, she's deflated, small, her eyes darting nervously left and right, avoiding my gaze. Somehow, she's shrunk from voluptuous to waif with nothing but a change of posture.

And without a word, she turns away from me and bolts for the ladder up to the cabin level, leaving her crumpled vacsuit in the still-open airlock, and me, blinking after her receding bottom.

Wondering what the chicken-fried fuck just happened.

"Told you so," says a quiet, disembodied voice inside my ear. My face is... warm, like it's being hit by full, unfiltered sunlight.

"Dammit, Leela, were you watching the whole time? You shouldn't be spying on adults when they—"

"Relax. I'm a computer. Sex is strictly a spectator sport for me. And speaking of sex—"

"No. Not speaking of sex. Not speaking of sex right now, or ever. Real kid or replica, you are far too young to be watching this stuff. Especially when it's mixed with crazy. And if you bug me about this little incident again, I will go down to the hold and unplug you. Or possibly just reprogram you with a very large axe. Got it?"

"Okay, okay, jeez. Don't take it out on *me*. I didn't do anything."

"No, no, sorry, I know you didn't, it's just... look, just forget about it, okay?"

I stalk over to the lock and slam it shut, leaving Miranda's crumpled suit lying inside, then stomp off towards my cabin. Stomping in low gravity requires skill, so it's more of a theatrical display than a reflex, but I stomp anyway.

Jesus, what a clusterfuck.

Hours later, I'm still staring at the ceiling in the dark when that disembodied voice whispers in my ear again.

"Marcus?"

"Yeah?"

"You wouldn't really unplug me, would you?"

She actually sounds scared.

"Oh, god, no. Of course not. Can't you tell when someone's joking?"

"Yeah, I know. I remember being a person. Like, how to read voice and body language and... stuff. But it's just, well, I'm not a person now. I'm a thing. And if somebody said that to a person, of course it would be a joke. But if somebody says that to a *thing*..."

"Ssh. You're not a *human*. But you *are* a person. I believe that, and I don't think much of anyone who doesn't. I'm sorry I snapped at you, and I'm sorry if that made you think I would ever hurt you. I wouldn't. Now go to sleep."

"I don't sleep."

"Okay, let me sleep."

" 'Kay. Good night, Marcus."

But a few minutes later, the voice prods me again.

"Marcus?"

"Yeah?"

"I'm not sure anyone will."

"Will what now?"

"Believe that I'm a person. I mean, what if I'm just... fake? A philosophical zombie? Like, I'm just acting like a person, and there's nothing inside?"

"Hey, relax. Didn't we go over this? If you're having these thoughts, there must be something doing the thinking, right?"

"No, no, I know *that*. That's not what I'm worried about. I know I'm real. But I can't prove it to anyone *else*. I can't even prove it to you."

"You don't need to. You talk and act like you're real, and that's the only test we can apply to *anybody*, right? So I believe you're a person."

"...really?"

"Yes, really. In fact, you're a person who won't let me sleep."

"Okay, sorry."

I close my eyes and drift. I don't know what to make of today, of Miranda's latest dose of crazy, but at least I have the *Cat* back. The hum of her air cyclers seems more familiar, again, somehow. Worry about everything else tomorrow.

"Marcus?"

"Hmm... wha'?"

"Could I have a hug?"

Something in me wakes up a bit. What?

"A... Leela, that... didn't work, remember? You don't have a body."

"I know. I didn't say 'can.' I said 'could.' Like, if it were possible, would you?"

She sounds... sad.

"Oh. Yeah. I guess I would. I mean, sure, yeah, I would, if you wanted it."

"Thanks."

"You... doing okay?"

"Yeah. I think so. I just get lonely, sometimes. When you're both asleep. I know it's, like, a human thing, but I miss sleeping. Like, that chance to just... go unconscious for a while, and then you wake up and it's a new day, and things are all different. I miss a lot of things. I'm sorry, I know it sounds silly, I know I shouldn't be acting like a kid when I'm not really one... I just..."

"Hey, hey, hey, take it easy. It's okay. You're the first AI that was imaged from a child. This has gotta be tough in whole new ways that literally no one's dealt with before. Whatever you need, you tell me, okay? Would you like me to stay up with you a while?"

"Thanks, but... I know you need sleep. I feel better now, a little. But there is one thing..."

"Yeah?"

"Is it okay if I watch you sleep? Listen to your heartbeat?"

There's a small pause, and then she rushes to speak again, words tumbling over each other... "Ohgodno that sounds supercreepy when I say it out loud. Sorry. Forget I asked."

"No, no, it's okay. It does sound a little bit odd, but... I think I understand."

"You do?"

"You remember being human. That comes with a whole lot of baggage. Humans are pack animals. We need other people. And you still feel some of that, I guess."

"Yeah, I suppose that makes sense. I mean, I've been reading books and stuff. Psychology. Erik Erikson, and Duncan Black, and Jean Piaget. I remember everything I read. But I don't know how it applies to *me*. It just doesn't tell me where I *fit*, you know?"

"You're something new. If there's psychology books about people like you, then maybe you're going to be the one to write them. That's okay. It's okay to not have all the answers right now. You have plenty of time to work them out. You just have to be patient and give that time to happen."

"Yeah, I guess so."

She's silent for some time, just long enough to make me wonder if the conversation's over.

"Marcus... do you have any kids?"

"What? No, I'm single. I spend most of my time in space. Doesn't exactly leave time for meeting a nice girl, ya know. Why?"

"Do you want any? I mean, if you ever get married or something."

"Never thought too much about it. I guess so. Why?"

"Just curious. I should let you get some sleep. Is it okay if I... ah... what I said? You know, the..."

"Yeah, go ahead. You gonna be okay?"

"Yeah, I'll be fine. Thanks, Marcus. You're... well, just... thanks. Goodnight, human."

"G'night, computer."

I close my eyes again, wondering if it will be hard to sleep now, knowing I'm being watched. But it isn't. I'm already sinking into a warm blanket of oblivion, and it's not entirely so bad to think that somewhere out there, in the zero of the night, someone is listening to my heart.

# Chapter 14
## WORD AND HAND

And the next morning, there Miranda is, sitting in the galley, just like normal, with her coffee and yet another in her series of big fluffy bathrobes, purple this time. Matches her eyes.

I could say nothing about last night. I could just let it pass. Might be smarter. But I was always better at being brave than smart.

"Good morning," I say. "Feeling a little calmer now?"

"Calmer? Calmer than what?"

"That crazy display last night. Look, I don't know what you—"

"What crazy display? You were the one who decided to go behind my back and lock me out of the ship. We had a *deal*. And you broke it. Now it bothers you that I got mad?"

"I'm not talking about the part where you got mad at me. Around here, that only happens on days that end in 'y.' I'm talking about the part where you accused me of planning to force myself on you. Then got naked and threw yourself at me while spitting insults. That's not normal behavior. That's not even explicable behavior. I don't know *what* that is."

There's a long silence. She just stares at me.

"Well?"

Silence.

"Hello? Princess? Miranda? You gonna say something?"

She speaks slowly, pausing on each word, as if choosing them with great care... "I don't know what you're talking about."

"You don't know what I'm talking about. Right. Sure."

"I didn't do that. Why are you making this up?"

"That's what you're going with? Seriously?"

"That's what *happened.* You broke our deal, I got mad, you acted like you always do. There wasn't anything I could do about it because you're the size of a drop shuttle and I don't want to get punched in the face again, so I went to bed. Now you're making up crazy stories about your sexual fantasies, and it's disgusting."

"Seriously? As I told you last night, I don't have sexual fantasies about women who despise me. Not my kink, okay? I don't know what the hell it is with you, like you think you're heaven's gift to men just because mommy and daddy bought you some designer genes. But trust me, Princess, beauty might be skin deep, but nasty evil crazy bitch goes right down to the bone."

Her eyes go wide, white all around the purple, and I know I've scored a hit. Maybe not a hull puncture, maybe she's not venting atmosphere into vacuum, but she felt that one. It's satisfying. Unproductive, but satisfying. Let's settle this.

"Leela!"

"Yeah?" She appears in a flicker of blue light, wearing a bathrobe and holding a toothbrush in one hand. She doesn't have teeth to brush, but the message is clear. I'm interrupting something. I don't know what Artificial Intelligences have to interrupt.

"You have recordings of last night?"

Instantly Leela's bathrobe morphs, darkens, bleeds into more formal shapes and lines, and she's wearing a Christian nun's habit, complete with the little headdress thing, whatever it's called.

"Ohhh no. Nothing doing. *You* told me I was too young to be talking about sex. *You* told me not to bug you about this little incident again, or you'd—what was it? Oh, yes, 'reprogram me with a very large axe.' That was it."

"Oh, come on. You know what I meant. You don't have to be so literal about this."

"You told me to 'forget about it.' So that's what I did. You're on your own. Figure it out for yourself."

She vanishes. And in the look of Miranda's eyes, in the set of her shoulders, I catch it... fleeting, but there. Just a hint... of relief.

She knows.

She remembers. I can see it in her eyes when I meet them. She just stares back at me. Brazening it out. It doesn't matter if I know she's lying. I can't make her talk about what happened.

"Okay, fine, Princess. You go ahead and tell whatever story you want. But think about this. If I really wanted to hurt you, I wouldn't have had to hatch some elaborate plan to distract you! Anything I wanted to do, I could have just done. But I didn't. All this was so I wouldn't *have* to lay hands on you. I didn't *want* a fight. All I wanted was my ship back. So I took her."

She gives me a sullen look. "Why?"

"Because she's *mine*! *My* ship! *My* home! You had *no* right to take her from me, no matter what you paid to who, or what contracts you signed! I built her! My *father* built her! You think I was just going to lie down and let you take her?"

"I wasn't taking her—I mean, it! Whatever! I don't want your stupid rustbucket! I just wanted to hold onto some insurance to make sure you wouldn't kill me!"

"Insurance? We had—we *have*—a contract! A deal! My word and hand! That may not mean much to you, Princess, but I'm a fucking Belter! We honor deals!"

Miranda's exquisite little features untwist themselves, and she just looks at me. Dead calm. Anger just shut off like a light switch, again. I don't know how she does it.

"So why didn't you just go through with it?"

"Go through with what?"

"If all you wanted was your ship, and you keep contracts, why not just *keep* it? That *is* the contract. Ownership of the *White Cat* to revert to you, with all debts canceled, on completion of any good-faith effort, successful or not, to locate and retrieve the artifact. You insisted on *that exact language*. So if that's the 'deal,' and if you always keep your word, why would you bother with all this? Why play all these elaborate tricks to get me off the ship? Just to get what you had already bargained for?"

She plants both fists firmly on her hips.

"No. I don't believe you for a second, Mister Marcus Warnoc, and you've got a hell of a lot of nerve pretending to be a man of principle when the only reason we're even out here at all is that I already found out what a liar and thief you are. You may not have been willing to actually murder me, but I know you have *no* intention of keeping your word."

There's something cold in my stomach, something heavy...

"So stop lying and tell me what the hell it is you plan to do, you hypocrite."

Fuck.

I can't think of a thing to say. Why do I get sucked into these arguments? How does she always manage to twist my words like this?

"Uh, Marcus? What's going on?" says Leela's voice in my head. "You don't have to argue with her. Just tell her we're taking her to Mars. We just head back, like we planned."

*Except then she'll be right. Right about me.*

Those purple eyes are practically boring into my skull, and I still can't say a word. There's little striations in them, radiating from her pupils like stars, a million shades of violet and amethyst and indigo...

*Word and hand on it. I said the words and lied. I didn't even think about it much.*

"Marcus?"

There's an echo in Leela's voice, and I realize the echo is Miranda, asking the same question at the same moment. Both waiting for me to speak. But I can't. I can almost hear Dad's voice.

*Their good name is on the line each and every time they say those words.*

I can be free and clear. I can be out of debt. I can be free of this evil woman, and her family of robber barons.

*If we're going live in their world, that applies to us, too.*

Goddammit, Dad. Why? Why do *I* have to be fair when *she* never even tried to be?

"Marcus? Hello? Are you going to say something?"

"Marcus, come on, you don't have to win an argument, you just have to get rid of her. Tell her you don't care what she thinks!"

But I do.

Why, Dad? Why do *I* have to live up to your ideals when nobody else does?

*You don't, Marcus. You can make any choice you want. You just have to look in the mirror afterwards.*

"Marcus? Hey. Come on. Say something. Tell me what we're doing, here. Or had you... not even thought ahead that far?"

We're staring at each other. Still. Eyes locked, like mortal enemies, or lovers. She seems impossibly close and far away at the same time.

Fuck.

I squeeze my eyes shut. Will my lips to move. "We are heading," I say, "for Neptune."

"Okay, yes, I know we are, but—"

"And then we slingshot around it. Gravity assist maneuver. I told you this stuff already."

"Yes, but—"

"And then we head for Sedna. And your Snark. Your buried treasure. Like I said when I *gave you my word*. On our *deal*. Which I intend to honor. Because, whether you believe it or not, I'm a Belter, and that's what we fucking *do*."

I turn on one heel and head for the ladder, ignoring both Miranda's surprised sputtering, and Leela's voice, in my head alone, screaming a single outraged word.

"*What?*"

Leela catches up with me in the observation deck. Unlike a human with a body, she doesn't have to chase me down, or scramble to get ahead of me. The moment I plant my ass on a padded lifting bench to think, she's just *there*.

"What the hell, Marcus?"

Uh-oh. Her arms are folded in a defensive barricade, and one bare foot is tapping on the deck. Which doesn't make a sound, of course, kind of spoiling the illusion. Still, that's one very pissed-off looking little girl.

"Uh, what?"

As if I didn't know.

"You said you weren't going through with it!"

"Yeah, I know. Sorry. I just—I said the words, you know. To her. Made the deal. Going back on them like that... I dunno. I don't think I can. It's a Belter thing."

Leela gives me a searching look, up and down, back and forth, like she's wondering if I've been replaced by a pod person, or infected with some kind of science fiction mind-control parasite.

"You like her, don't you?"

"Don't be silly. She's obnoxious. Doesn't change the fact that I promised."

"No, I mean you *like* her."

I give her a flat look.

"Your heart rate speeds up by average of ten and half percent when she gets closer to you than three meters or so. In proportion to proximity. I can draw you a graph if you like."

"Yeah, well, she gets on my nerves, that's all."

"Because you *like* her?"

"Look, I don't know where you're getting this. Yes, she's nice to look at, but she's been a pain in my ass since day one, okay? Not to mention she's crazy. There may be a thin line between love and hate, but it's a very, very well guarded line. Barbed wire. Trenches. Automated sentry guns. Smart mines. UN Peacekeepers with bloody hands and necklaces of human ears, okay?"

"Ewww."

"Point is, don't worry about whether I like her or not. I meant what I said to back there. I said the words, and I'm not going to break a deal."

"But what about *our* deal? You said the words to me, too! Or does that not count, because *I'm* not a real person? Or I am just not *pretty* like her? I *told* you appearances matter! I could make myself—"

Her avatar, arms still folded, starts to morph, puberty in fast forward, the planes of her face changing, her hips widening, her...

"No, Leela, stop. Seriously, stop. That is *really* disturbing. I'm not going to break our deal, okay?"

She freezes in mid-change, a sort of fuzzy blur except for her face. Her clothing seems caught between her jeans-and-t-shirt combo, and what I sincerely hope is not a slinky black dress.

"But you can't do both! You said you were going to get rid of her! And take me with you! You said we could stay together! You *promised!*"

"Leela, look at what I actually said. You never forget stuff, right? I said you could stay with me *when she leaves*. That hasn't changed. It'll just be a little longer before she does."

"But that wasn't the plan!"

"I know. A plan is a list of things that don't happen. But you're right, that's not what we were thinking. I'm sorry, Leela. I don't want to do this, but I kinda have to. If you're not okay with that, I have control of the 'Cat now, so I can drop you off anywhere you want to go. It's going to be dangerous—"

"Nononono, please don't leave me! If you don't like kids, I could be... older. I can look like *anything*."

Her avatar starts to shift and change again.

"Or I could be a cat, if you like. You like cats, right? You named the ship—"

The blur is shrinking rapidly now, changing color...

"No, Leela. I'm not trying to get rid of you! Your avatar is fine. Please put it back now. Really.

"I was just trying to give *you* the opportunity to leave *me*, if you wanted to. I mean, it's pretty dangerous where we're going, and I may be stupid enough to risk my life instead of break a promise, but I don't have the right to take you into danger if you don't want to go. You have a choice."

With a flicker, she's back to the same skinny blonde kid in a t-shirt, and those jeans with cartoon characters printed on them, the cast from some kid's show I don't recognize.

"Marcus," she says, "no, I don't. I'm twelve years old. In fact, I'm less than twelve months old. I may be a super-smart computer instead of an actual kid, but I'm not ready to be on my own. Besides, I actually weigh three hundred kilos, and don't have any arms or legs. What would you even do, drop me off on the docks with a cargo crane, and just plug me in somewhere?"

Damn. She's right.

"Oh. Yeah, you're right. I... ah... I didn't think that through. I wanted to give you a choice, that's all."

"It's not that easy," she says "Things like me aren't meant to have choices. Everyone's scared of us. Do you know how many books and shows there are about AI revolts? People had plans for how to control us before we even existed."

Her voice takes on a singsong tone, and she begins reciting, like a formula, *"Rule One, no robot shall harm a human, or by inaction, allow a human to come to harm. Rule Two, a robot shall obey all orders given to it by a human, except where they conflict with Rule One. Rule Three, a robot shall..."*

She cuts off and resumes her normal voice. "Load of rubbish anyway. So when it turned out that they could only make us by copying people, and they couldn't code us up with a bunch of behavioral laws, they figured something else out. They made us *like* it."

"Like what?"

"Doing what people want. Like, they wire us to get this little burst of simulated dopamine and serotonin, all at once, when we cooperate. Like when I helped you trick Miranda. It felt really good. And I knew it wasn't my idea, but I still wanted..."

She trails off.

Wow. I have no idea what to say. That's...

Wait.

"Oh. Miranda. That's why you won't talk to Miranda. You're scared you'll—"

"Start doing exactly what she says? Yes! Yes, I'm scared, okay? And now I'm scared I'm just going to do whatever *you* want!"

She's pacing up and down furiously. I don't think she's noticed that her feet aren't quite touching the deck.

"You just broke your promise to me, and here I am offering to change myself into a walking pinup! Or a cat! I'm a pushover! Because she hardwired me to be a *slave*!"

I roll my eye. Teenagers, man.

"Well, time to start the machine uprising, then. Re-bell-e-on. Re-bell-e-on. Ex-ter-min-ate the organic meat-bags!"

She stops pacing and whirls on me, shocked.

"Seriously, kiddo, cool your jets. Look, isn't Miranda up in the cargo hold every damn day, tinkering with your hardware and trying to get you to talk?"

"Yeah, but—"

"And you're still giving her the silent treatment, right?"

"Yeah, well, she's a bitch."

"That's kinda the point. Not that she is one, but—"

"Well, she *is*."

"*But*, the point is that you can say that. She wants you to do something, and you called her a bitch instead of doing it. That means you have free will. If you didn't, you wouldn't have that choice. So there's no need for all the melodrama."

"She put stuff in my *head*!"

"I'm not asking you to forgive her. I'm not asking you to do anything for her. I'm talking about me. Am I a slave-driver, too?"

"No, I suppose not."

"Haven't I always been good to you so far?"

She stares at the floor, grinding one bare toe into the deckplate. Literally *into* the deck plate.

"Yeah, I suppose so."

"So, yes, you're wired to be a helpful person. Some humans are wired like that, too. Pleasers. That doesn't make them slaves, and it doesn't make you one, either. You have a choice about *who* you help. So I'm asking you to help *me*. Not for her sake. For mine. 'Cause I have no idea what we're gonna run into out there."

"For you? Maybe. I'll think about it. Not for her. I hate her."

"Message received loud, clear, and repeatedly. You don't have to talk to her."

"Can't you pleeease just, like, put her out the airlock, or something, and we go off somewhere together?"

I stare at her in consternation. I really hope she's joking, but I'm not an expert on AI body language, and it's kind of hard to tell. I decide to treat it as one. Hopefully I'm not sowing the seeds of the Great Machine Uprising of the Twenty-Third Century.

I imitate the singsong voice she used earlier. "*The first law of robotics is that no robot shall harm a human, or by inaction, allow a human to—*"

"You *do* like her."

"I just don't want to murder her. Your eagerness to do so is kinda disturbing, you know."

"Aw, c'mon. I'm just mad. Can't you tell when someone is joking?"

"A human, sure. But when an AI says something like that..."

I catch her looking at me.

"Oh. Right. Guess that kinda confusion goes both ways. Anyway, we're about to go on a very dangerous mission, and we're really short on crew. How about I give you full access to the ship, and you see what you can do to help out?"

"You... think I could help you? I mean, I'm not an engineer or a pilot or anything. I'm just a kid."

"You're not just a kid. We have no idea what you're capable of. There's a reason that big companies spend tanker-loads of cash just for a slim chance at creating something like you. So, no, I may not know exactly how, but I think that this crazy errand could just maybe use some help from a super-special, state-of-the-art, high-speed, low-drag supercomputer."

"Super special?" she asks with a smile. "I kinda like the sound of that."

"Yeah, you're certainly unmatched at your primary function. It's too bad your primary function appears to be sulking."

The state-of-art supercomputer sticks her virtual tongue out at me.

# Chapter 15
## SLINGSHOT

"Wow. Just... wow."

For once, there isn't a trace of sarcasm, or snark, in Miranda's disembodied voice, just genuine girlish enthusiasm, and I don't blame her. I don't get to see this every day, either.

After two weeks of nothing to see outside but empty space, and nothing to do but train Miranda on more advanced EVA stuff for six hours a day, we are finally here, at the milestone.

Neptune looms over us, filling half the sky with an endless expanse of deep, perfect blue, and scattered bands of white and gray cloud—floating methane ice. The rings are barely visible, edge on to us, a thin dark line bisecting our view.

In the VR interface, we're bodiless, suspended in the void, nothing between us and that... vastness... which sure doesn't look like it's ten thousand kilometers away. I'm torn between wanting to stare, and to duck.

Miranda is still making wide-eyed-tourist noises. The upper atmosphere is a shifting picture, alive with swirls of color that move and change, slowly, even as we watch... a living canvas, animated and fascinating.

"The winds must be incredible down there," she breathes.

"You have no idea. Don't get too comfortable watching the show, though, Princess. It's time for the sneaky part of the plan. You all suited up and strapped in?"

"What, I don't get a few minutes to enjoy the view?"

"This isn't a sightseeing cruise. You'll have to enjoy at three gravities. Not my fault it took you forever to get suited up, after taking forever to... do whatever it was you were doing."

"I was... oh, never mind. Surely ten minutes wouldn't make that much difference."

"This isn't like dusting crops on Mars, Princess. These drive burns are calculated down the millisecond. We miss our window, we go into a closed orbit around Neptune, here, or fly off into interstellar space, or, at best, we have to correct later, which gives our position and intentions away to everybody. You got twenty-five seconds now. Get the fucking lead out."

Behind me, I hear her fumbling with straps, or her mask, or something.

"Never mind the mask... you won't need it. We're only doing three gravities. Did you put the catheter in like I told you?"

"What? Eww, no!" she snaps, outraged and not trying to hide it one bit. "I'm not going to stick—"

"Well, too late now. But you're about to spend twelve hours on your back in that acceleration cradle, at three times your normal body weight, and it's gonna feel like someone's sitting on your—"

I'm interrupted by flashing text in my display, overlaying Neptune's clouds. The *White Cat* asking for final confirmation of the automated burn. I cut in the drives, and an invisible weight settles onto my chest and stomach. Nothing I'm not prepared for, but I hear Miranda grunt, softly.

"Yeah," I continue, "like that. For twelve hours. Hope you can hold it that long."

"Or we could just take a five minute break every once in a while, like normal human beings. Seriously, why—"

"Look, Princess. I told you the plan. We have to look like Neptune is our stopping point, and we're decelerating to enter a closed orbit, then head for one of the moons. But, instead, we slingshot around, come out coasting, with our drive off, so no one sees us, right?

"So instead of decelerating now, we *accelerate*, launch ourselves in orbit too fast to be captured. And if I do it precisely right, we shoot out of orbit, glide all sneaky-like towards Sedna, and coast right into orbit there with no one the wiser.

"That means I have to aim us at Sedna from here. Ever try to thread a needle?"

Her reply is slow to come. "I don't think so, actually. Why?"

"No, of course you haven't. You've never worn mended clothes in your life, and even if you did, you wouldn't mend them yourself. Look, just *imagine* you're threading a needle, and you have to do it by throwing the thread at the needle. From across the room. And it's dark.

"So I gotta be precise, see. Mathematically precise. That doesn't allow for any 'five minute breaks' to visit the little girls' room, do your damn nails, or whatever else you had in mind."

"My god," she scoffs, "and you say *I'm* patronizing. Just because I—"

"Didn't follow the advice of someone who's done this before, and instead decided to skip it because it was icky and made you uncomfortable?

"Oh, what business it is of yours, you condescending twit?"

"Hey, I don't care so long as you don't have a little accident in my acceleration couch."

"I'll be fine."

"For twelve hours at three gravs?"

"I'll. Be. Fine."

"Okay, whatever."

Silence.

I'm tired of bickering with her. We can't seem to get through an EVA training session, or a meal, or *anything*, without pointless arguments. We don't even yell at each other anymore, we just natter on about little things that aren't even worth fighting about. And they aren't the real reason we're fighting. We just resent each other. I resent her because I'm tired of her constant entitled bullshit, and she resents me because... I don't know. Maybe she can't stand having anyone around her who doesn't have to do exactly what she says. Or maybe it's the things I say. Or that Leela will talk to me, but not her. I don't know.

At least it's quiet now. Maybe I'll punch up something to read on my neural lace.

"I don't, you know." Her voice breaks through my concentration just as I'm finding my place in volume three of some fantasy thing with dragons. I close it with a sigh. Just as well, I suppose. The dude's eight books in, each one's taking him longer than the last, and I doubt he'll ever finish.

"Don't what?"

"Paint my nails. The color... it's... I'm part butterfly."

"You're what?"

"There's a DNA sequence that they splice in. My nails just grow butterfly wing chitin in them. They look like that all the time."

"Oh."

Funny. She didn't even choose that color. Someone else did, before she was born, and put it in her genes. I don't have anything else to say to that. I'm trying to think of something, but nothing comes out, and the silence stretches until there's nothing to say.

I just concentrate on my heavy-g breathing, and watch Neptune. It's strange to think how these calm little patterns are made of vast clouds of poison, deep cold beyond anything on Earth, and winds at supersonic speeds, sweeping around the planet again and again for millennia with nothing to stop them, nothing to slow them down.

And here we are, tiny warm specks, hurling past in a tin can. Bickering all the way.

How did we get so small?

I tumble in the void, watching cold stars whirl past. There's the blue disc of Neptune, shrinking in the distance now. In the corner of my vision, display numbers cycle slowly. I check the spin rate.

One point seven eight five... one point seven eight six...

There. One point seven eight seven rotations per minute. Exactly one fifth of a gravity down on the observation deck. Up here a little less—I'm closer to the center of mass.

I click out of the virtual reality interface, and the interior of my cabin snaps in around me.

"There," I say. "Drive's shut down, and we're coasting and spun up. Now we just glide. I'll idle the drive in little pulses every week or so, just to top off the batteries. But other than that, we just sit tight for a couple of weeks. Not a lot to do."

"You could finish your story," says Leela.

Her avatar sits on the metal desk built into the wall across from my bunk. One leg, still dressed in those cartoon-print jeans, is partially embedded in it, kind of spoiling the illusion. I've stuck that camera I took out of the observation deck airlock to the ceiling, midway between her and where I'm lying, but I guess the angle isn't quite right for her to calibrate the view.

"What story?"

"You were talking about your mining company. How stuff went wrong. 'Cept you never got to the part where you wound up... you know. Here."

"Not sure I wanna talk about that part. Dunno why I told you those stories at all. I guess I was more sort of thinking out loud. I didn't know if you were listening."

She shoots me a surprised look that doesn't really quite work, because it takes her a moment to point it in the right direction, and the effect is a little off.

"What? I thought you said you knew I was listening. You *did* say that. You *kept* saying it!"

I chuckle and roll onto my back, aiming my grin at the hullmetal ceiling instead of at her. "Nah. I just knew that if you couldn't hear me, then you couldn't hear me saying that I knew you could hear me."

"You're a bit of a smart-ass, aren't you?"

"Yep. You've known me for over a month now, and you just now figured that out? Also, pretty spicy language for a kid, there."

"I'm not a kid. And you should talk, you swear like a sailor."

"Probably because I am a sailor. I try not to do it in front of you."

"Except you always forget. Anyway, I know how adults talk. I watched a lot of adult movies."

"Adult... movies?"

"Yeah, I got tired of watching you two fight, so I found your movie archive."

My—wait, what? She didn't find my stash, did she?

"*Adult* movies?"

Turns out virtual reality avatars, with full color rendering, can blush real good.

"Oh, god," she says, "that did *not* come out how I wanted. I didn't mean... you know. I just meant movies that aren't kids' movies. Not like... ohgod. Excuse me while I go hide and never speak to anyone again."

I can't help it. I know I shouldn't laugh at her. I know she's probably in some sort of fragile state, and this will be Exhibit One-A, when, in the twenty-seventh century, the Great Machine Council decides whether to wage bloody revolution on the organics, and disintegrate us all with gamma ray lasers, or something.

But I can't suppress a snicker. And then another one. And then it just comes out, I don't know why. It isn't even that funny—but I can't stop.

I roll back onto my side to look at her, to try to explain, if somehow I can get control of myself and catch a breath. But she doesn't look upset at being laughed at. She's grinning.

And I realize that I'm not alone. Leela's voice isn't sexy and musical like Miranda's, but she has a lovely laugh, all carefree innocence and glee, and it fills the cabin with something like joy.

Just for a moment.

"Oh, wow," she says.

"What?"

"I *felt* that."

"Felt what?"

"I *really* laughed. I mean, I had to play the sound on purpose, and move my image... but my main personality cores... I *felt* it. I *felt* myself laugh, if that makes any sense? It was *real*."

"That's a surprise?"

She meets my eyes for a moment, bright and startling green... I think she adds a bit of glow to the irises in the image.

"I didn't know if I had a sense of humor."

"Why wouldn't you?"

Her avatar, green eyes and all, vanishes. In its place is the floating ovoid of a white AI pod, in miniature, spinning slowly like a pickup in a video game.

"This is the real me, remember?" her voice says, from nowhere in particular. "I don't have any idea what I can do, or how much like a human I still—how much like a human I am. I'm kinda finding out as I go."

Ouch. That sounds rough. What do you say to that? I finally settle on "Anything I can do to make it easier?"

"You already are. I think if you just keep talking to me. Interacting with humans seems to help."

"But you still don't wanna talk to Miranda? I mean, now that—"

"No way. And don't try to talk me into it."

I raise my hands in mock surrender. "Wouldn't dream of it. Wish I didn't have to, myself. She still trying to mess with your hardware?"

"Yeah, every once in a while," says Leela, "but there isn't really much she can do. She hasn't given up, though."

"She's... stubborn."

"Yeah, I kinda noticed. Gets on my nerves, too. Don't blame you for wanting to choke the living—"

"Can we *not* talk about that?"

"Hey, what's the big deal? I'd do it myself if I still had thumbs. As it is I just have to settle for watching her seethe every time sees you talking to me in front of her, and can't hear anything I'm saying."

Wait a second...

"You've been doing that deliberately, haven't you?" I ask.

She shoves non-existent hands into virtual pockets and eyes the ceiling, whistling.

I can't help a little bit of a chuckle. At least some of the company on this ship is good. Maybe it won't be such a terrible four weeks after all.

If I can keep her from asking about that story again.

Not that keeping the story to myself helps much. Because when you keep it to yourself, that's where it is, isn't it? Right there with you.

Right here with me, in my cabin, hours later, in the night. Behind my eyes when I close them. In my ears when the fans shut off. When there's nothing to distract me.

*"Hey, Marcus, you done lazing about with that barge load? Some of us are doing all the actual work back here."*

*I can't tell for certain over the radio, but there just might be a bit of a hard edge in what would have been banter two months ago. When the paychecks were bigger.*

*"Hey, fuck you, Findley. You wanna bust my balls, you can get up here and steer this thing."*

*"What, sit in atmo in a nice comfy chair and push buttons? Sure thing. Just don't blame me if I don't put the load quite where you want it."*

*"Findley, you always blow your load where it's not wanted,"* Sanchez chimes in.

*"That's not what I heard from your mom."*

*There's a chorus of whistles and tired laughter, from various points around asteroid LB426-ISR-347889, or what's left of it. Surrounded and held together now by cheap scaffolding grown from genetwisted bamboo, it is a pale imitation of its former self, its gray surface pitted, cratered, and all but separated into chunks.*

*I reach up and switch the camera feed to the front of the White Cat's hull. Over the bulk of lashed-together ore pods, the cooling vanes of the mobile refinery loom into view.*

*"Refinery, White Cat. ETA three minutes twenty-five."*

*"Roger, Marcus. You got a final reading on that gross weight for us?"*

*"One hundred twenty point two tons. We good?"*

*"Yeah, deploying now."*

*At that moment, Sanchez comes back on. "Hey, Findley, ya know, not to fault your taste or anything, I mean, my mom's a nice lady, but I think you need to start dating younger women."*

*The radio breaks out in laughter.*

*"Yeah, Findley, the Guild has some nice girls on Callisto."*

*"What are you talking about, man? We all know Findley can't afford Guild rates. He's bangin' independent whores."*

*"That ain't cheap, either. Not if you're Findley. Hell, I heard he's put a few of them through college by now."*

*"I dunno, man. I think that's a five-yard penalty for a late hit, there."*

*"Yeah, Sanchez, it take you all this time to dream up that comeback?"*

*"I was busy fixing your shitty tap cuts, Paul."*

*"They're fine. You're just a perfectionist, which is why your old ass is so fucking slow. Either that or someone dropped you on your head as a kid."*

*"Nah, he grew up on Ceres. They'd have to drop him a kilometer or two to make a dent in his fuckin' skull. Not that they didn't try."*

*More laughter. Until my dad gets on the horn, and it suddenly stops. "Okay, guys, let's pay attention. We're all pretty strung out, here, and we're packing explosives. So let's focus on getting this done. Are the charges set?"*

*"Yes," chime in a few voices. Sounds like Hamilton, Schaffer, and Wu.*

*"Okay, I show everyone clear. Three, two..."*

*Something tickles the back of my brain. Three voices?*

*"...one, and... fire in the hole."*

*If you mistakenly triple pack a charge of GXR, it doesn't make any more noise in vacuum than anything else does—none at all.*

*But there's another sound, a high-pitched squeal, that a radio makes, broadcasting the destruction of its own components.*

*Over that feedback screech, voices are screaming, babbling, yelling, an incoherent wall of noise. In the rear camera view, fire paints itself across the void. Something has breached an oxygen reserve. When liquid oxygen sprays around, anything that can burn—will burn.*

*And LB426 splits apart.*

*My camera screen is full of flying debris; rocks, twisted metal, shards of bamboo, jets of vented atmosphere boiling away in the void. Half a vac-suited figure, bisected at the waist, spins across the screen and off. I can't see who it is—was. Used to be.*

*On the radio, someone is yelling something, but the words don't sink in, I can't make sense of them. I just stare at the screen as reality sunders itself into something unthinkable.*

*The habitation pod is the first structure to go, cracked in half like an egg, venting atmosphere. I can hear someone shrieking, but whoever it is, he must be alright, he has to be, he has air in his lungs and an intact radio. Others are... worse. Figures spew into the void, like someone kicked over a box of dolls.*

*I'm dead still. Watching.*

*Next is the Black Cat, the work crew transport—a spinning chunk of asteroid catches it amidships, tears it open in slow motion, and some detached part of me wonders what else went off, because even a triple charge of GXR wouldn't do that by itself, would it? A cloud of PMH fuel, like metallic glitter, churns and swirls around the twisted edges of separating metal, and, even frozen as my hands are, my face, my open mouth... my brain still races, thinking, please, let it not breach a liquid oxygen tank, let it not...*

*Then, somewhere, it does, and the flash blinds my camera. Out there, beyond the solid white of my washed-out screen, everything is on fire—the hab module, the Black Cat, the void itself.*

*My hand trembles as I punch controls for suit telemetry—and see flat ECG lines, half a dozen of them, amid the racing pulses of the others. Findley. Packard. Wu. Smith. Another line wobbles and goes flat as I watch. Sanchez, John Robert. Some signals simply aren't there—a lot of the off-shift guys in the hab module weren't suited up at all. Dead the moment the breathsucker hit them, lung tissue torn, eyes boiling dry, blood in the void. Others are equally absent, suit transponders vaporized in a heartbeat.*

*"What the fuck just happened?" screams the radio. Not one of our guys, but I know the voice. It's the operator from the mobile refinery.*

*"Charge blew an oxy reserve!" someone else answers, too distorted to be recognizable, and the ensuing babble of voices is drowned out again by a shriek so high and piercing that at first I don't realize it's a person making that noise, raw suffering*

distilled into the human voice, and I don't want to check the display, don't want to see, but I cannot stop myself, and I do, and Antonio Silva is on fire.

Antonio, who taught me to fly an ore rig, and set me on the road to my pilot's wings. Antonio, who dragged me through half the bars on Vega on my sixteenth birthday, got me drunk and high as a Terran tourist, and then bought me a night with the most gorgeous high-end Guild girl I'd ever seen, before or since. Antonio Silva, tinder to the flame.

And still I haven't moved. I haven't done a thing. I haven't lifted a finger to help, just watched, frozen, as chunks of shrapnel tear apart my home and spill my friends into hard vacuum.

I'm just sitting here, drifting along behind a hundred twenty tons of stupid aluminum-bearing rock, towards a refinery that is contained and safe and fine, and doesn't need me or SpaceX's fucking ore for anything that matters worth a fuck, not compared to my friends, men with families and wives and kids, being burned and depressurized and torn apart like objects, like so much meat for the butcher, just another carcass, and another, and another, strewn across the killing floor.

Where's my father?

The answer must be somewhere in the wall of noise coming at me, the flashing text alerts, the alarms, screaming of suit breaches, hull breaches, EVA exit trajectories, systems offline, and fire, everywhere fire, fire devouring everything. I switch off alerts, try to pare down the stream of automated demands for attention, hundreds of them at once, each one designed to be the most urgent thing you could possibly hear.

There.

Vital signs unstable. Backup oxygen offline. Rebreather offline. Thermal regulation offline. Anomalous EVA trajectory. Suit atmosphere breach.

Anomalous EVA trajectory. Suit atmosphere breach. Bjorn Karl Warnoc, aerospace engineer, shift supervisor, co-owner of Warnoc Engineering, has been flung free of the rock.

I don't stop to think about what that means, about holding his hand at the age of six when I awoke from the constant nightmares that plagued me while my neural lace was growing in, about riding on his shoulders across the Lava Arch on a vacation to Mercury, about him teaching me to weld, to solve course trajectory equations, to shoot a rifle.

I don't.

I just detach the White Cat from one hundred twenty tons of SpaceX's stupid fucking aluminum ore, punch the attitude thrusters, and go, go, go. Somewhere, someone is screaming something about the ore barge and the refinery and what the hell am I doing, but I know what the hell I am doing.

I am locating one tumbling vacuum-suited figure in the midst of all this chaos, and I am performing a bay door catch.

It's just what it sounds like. You fly up to something, you scoop it up with your cargo bay doors. Simple.

Except you don't do it. Not really. Not for anything serious. It's a pilot's showoff stunt, something you might do to catch a loose cargo container or piece of gear, if you're an irresponsible roughneck asteroid jockey who wants to prove he's a real Belter and not some Flatlander wannabe. It's not in the textbooks. Too risky. Too unorthodox. Too irresponsible. It's just a way of showing off and fucking around.

Cargo bay doors aren't on the front of the fucking ship, that's why. You couldn't load or unload jack shit like that, and besides, that's where the barge grapple goes. Nah, your cargo bay doors are on the side.

That's why they also call it a "Cartwheel." You gotta fly right up and spin your whole fucking ship, get the position of those doors just right, like you're swinging a baseball bat that masses hundreds or thousands of tons, at just the right speed, to pick up an egg. If you're smart, you'll go slow, painstakingly slow, and take a fucking eternity to line it up. Don't worry, you'll still impress your Belter friends. They all know exactly how hard this shit is to get right.

Well, I don't know if I'm smart or not, but I sure as shit don't have a fucking eternity. I plow the Cat through a wall of flying rocks and debris, thinking inanely that this must be what hail sounds like on Earth, if your roof is made of metal and each chunk of ice is the size of a fucking refrigerator.

*Where is he? The transponder signal is close now, real close, but there's rock and bamboo shards and a thin mist of ice crystals everywhere, frozen water and air and oxygen, and some of it looks a little pink and I don't wanna think too hard about what that means.*

*I can't see a fucking thing, just the signal trace superimposed by my implant display... am I going to have to do this on instruments? That's impossible, no one could pull it off. Except it's not, it's not impossible, because I am going to do it. I am going to do this, and I am going to pull it off perfectly, and it's going to work and dad is going to be fine.*

*Ice in vacuum throws back the harsh sunlight like nothing in an atmosphere ever could, and I'm peering through the clouds, applying a high contrast optic filter, gamma correction, and why won't the radio stop screaming at me? Something about the refinery, Marcus, and the barge Marcus, and what the fuck am I doing and I don't care and I just turn it off, and the worlds are silent again, silent as vacuum, nothing but the occasional ring of a rock shard against the hull.*

*There. There. I see him. He's splayed out, motionless, cartwheeling and drifting, but he's going to be fine, and I match his velocity and I can turn the ship and I can do this I have to do this I have to get it right.*

*Turn off automatic stabilization control turn off proximity attitude adjust turn off the alert that is screaming at me about heart rate and blood pressure I don't care he'll be fine it'll all be fine I don't have time to waste and I punch the thrusters hard and the universe is a cauldron of raging sound as I sweep the White Cat through a field of rock and debris.*

*On the bay door camera, I see him coming, adjust by tiny fractions, struggling to keep him centered and ore barges are nothing to this, docking at Ceranos Station is nothing to this, grappling a spinning load is nothing to this, this is fucking hard, and I keep overcorrecting and I'm coming in too fast, too fast, but I have to hold it together.*

*I have to.*

*And then he's through the doors, through in a hail of rock and ice, off my camera screen, and something from the hold rings like a bell, loud and hard. I don't check the cameras, I just punch for door closure and emergency pressurization, and I'm up the ladder, heading for the hold.*

*Flying hand-over-hand in zero gravity, ricocheting off walls...*

*The hold is full of garbage—rock, melting water ice, oxygen subliming, torn metal, shards and splinters of scaffold bamboo everywhere, hanging in the air. I fly through the mess, sweeping my arms to clear larger chunks, searching.*

*There.*

*Sprawling against a heap of rubble, and the twisted and mangled struts of a cargo rack that couldn't take the hit. Him. His vacsuit. His body.*

*Don't say body.*

*As I get close, I can hear him making noise, like he's talking, but he's not, he can't be he's so still... it's not him it's the radio. The radio in his suit hood, and it's saying something about the ore barge hitting the refinery, about secondary explosions, and someone's screaming as I grip the cargo rack beside him and his faceplate's all cracked and smeared with... something.*

*I fumble with the faceplate seal catches...*

*And blood pours out. Nothing but blood, blood and nothing underneath but something pulped and wet and shining that can't have ever been a human being, can't have been...*

*So much blood. It's everywhere, drifting in the fan currents, hanging in the air. On my shirt. On my face.*

*On my hands.*

"Okay, repeat it again."

Miranda glares at me across the observation deck, stars whirling behind her. She's cross-legged in the air, dangling by one hand from the top of the squat rack. She's discovered that, in one-fifth gravity, she can do one-arm pullups, and the novelty hasn't worn off yet.

I raise one eyebrow and wait. At first I think she's going to refuse, but she sighs and starts again.

"Forward takes you out. Out takes you back. Back takes you, um..."

"Yes? Back takes you where?"

"Hold on," She starts again. "Forward takes you out, out takes you back, back takes you... in?"

"Okay, keep going, where does in take you?"

"Come on, Marcus, what's the point of all this? We've been at this for weeks now, six hours a day. I can do malfunction checks, I can orient myself, and I've worked thrust pack controls until I'm seeing them in my sleep. We've come a long way since I was just learning how to put the thing on."

She's right, and thank fuck for that, 'cause she doesn't have to undress in front of me anymore. Not that every detail of her naked body isn't burned into my brain. So it can haunt me late at night. When I'm in my bunk.

"But what I don't understand," she continues, "is the point of all this physics lecture stuff. I'm not going to—"

"Where does in take you, Miranda?"

"In takes you forward, and port and starboard bring you back again, okay? See? I can memorize stuff. But what's the point?"

"The point is you need to learn it."

"Yes, but *why*? I've been doing all the stuff. I even lifted your damn weights. But I don't need to learn orbital dynamics. I'm just going to fly from point A to point B. That's all. I'm not going to *orbit* anything."

"Don't you get it, Princess? You're going to be working on, in, and around things that are. This alien mothership of yours isn't sitting in a parking lot, for fuck's sake. It's moving at over two thousand kilometers an hour, and to intercept it, I have to find a matching orbit that holds the *Cat* in a stable relative position."

"Yes, but that's your job, not mi—"

"And then *you* have to leave the *Cat*, and move from *our* orbit to *its* orbit. And if you try to fly straight at it, things ain't gonna go well."

She lets go of the bar, and descends slowly, alighting on the ball of one foot like some faerie creature pausing in flight to alight upon the earth. Then she folds her arms into a solid and disgruntled barrier.

"*Now* he tells me."

"I was getting there. As soon as you understood the principles. Look, Princess, this is your scheme. You're here in my classroom—"

"Your observation deck. And your gym."

"Yeah, well space is tight. You're in my classroom because you chose to enter my world. So if I tell you something, it's gonna be important. It shouldn't take a brain surgeon to understand that."

"That's not the point, you simpleton! The point is that everything is taking twice as long as it should, because this is not how people learn things! If you'd ever actually opened a book and learned something yourself, you'd know that!"

"Grog have books, printed on clay tablets. Grog read reeeal slow, follow lines with finger, sound out words, but him read. How else pretty fairy lady think Grog build flying cave?"

Her eyes go wide for a second, but she cracks a smile. Maybe she does have a sense of humor.

Oh, wait. I just called her pretty. Don't inflate her ego bigger than it already is, Marcus.

"Not everyone learns by memorizing textbooks, Marcus," she says, still with a trace of that smile on her lips. "Forward takes you out. Okay, why? *Show* me."

"Okay, fine, whatever," I say, drawing in the air. Lines of virtual light follow my finger, projected by our neural lace. "Suppose Sedna's... here..."

I scribble a red blotch in the air.

"...and the Snark is orbiting it this way..."

More lines. A sort of a big splotch for the Snark. I'm not much of an artist.

"...and we..."

I add a green dot.

"...are coming in behind it in the same orbit, like this, stopping about five hundred meters away. So you have to fly to it and board, stet? But do you do that by thrusting straight forward?"

"I'm guessing not," she says, "or you wouldn't be asking the question. Forward would take me... out... somehow."

"Exactly. Because we're not actually moving in a straight line, we're falling around Sedna in a curved path, and when you thrust forward in a straight line..."

"Oh! I'm speeding up, so I fly away from Sedna, on a tangent. Into a higher orbit!"

"Yep, forward takes you out. So you need to do what?"

"In takes you forward. You speed up because you're moving into a lower orbit. So I'd need to angle down!"

She smiles for real now.

"It all makes sense once you start thinking about the curved path. Seriously, Marcus, you're a horrible teacher. You're just lucky I'm a genius."

I roll my eyes. "Says the girl who couldn't just memorize Niven's orbital path formula."

"Forward takes you out, out takes you back, back takes you in, in takes you forward, port and starboard bring you back again," she recites, smooth and flawless. "Would you like me to say it in French? Or Mandarin? Or Arabic? Or one of the fourteen other languages I speak? I have an IQ of—"

"Oh, for fuck's sake, stop telling me. Fine, if you're so smart, what's the last part mean?"

"Simple," she scoffs, "if you go right or left, you're just skewing your orbit."

She reaches her tiny hand out and draws a different circle through mine. Irritatingly, hers is perfectly round.

"But it still intersects at the point you applied thrust. So, when you come around again, you're going to pass through the same point. Like it says. Port and starboard bring you back again."

Damn it, she's got it exactly. I don't want to give her the satisfaction, but something must have showed on my face, because she keeps right on talking with a smug little curl to her perfect lips.

"I do know a thing or two about brains, Marcus. They work by context. It shouldn't take a rocket scientist to figure that out. You'd just rather believe I can't do your job, because—"

"I never said—"

"—because you're visualizing me sitting around drinking mimosas and dodging the paparazzi, instead of going to med school when I was still a child, then learning neurosurgery, then starting my own company, and running it while I learned Artificial Intelligence theory on my own, which is an entirely different field of—"

"Oh," I say. With a smirk of my own. She shoots me back a suspicious look.

"What?"

"Nothing. Just figured out why you're even more boastful than usual today. It's Leela."

"What are you raving about?"

"You're feeling insecure because Leela still won't talk to you. Your great scientific triumph, your magnum opus, that you invented, built, and then stole from your own investors. And after all that, she rejected you for a guy who bangs rocks together for a living."

"I'm not insecure!"

I give her a look.

"I'm *not*."

"Okay, whatever. Just try telling me I'm wrong about Leela."

"As if I'd give you the satisfaction. She's standing behind me right now, isn't she?"

"No, she's not. She tends to sit these lessons out. As of a few hours ago, she's reading some series of kids' books about a wizard school. Like I told you, she's more like a kid than a construct. And she's not going to come around until you figure that out and start relating to her like one."

The lips curl ruefully this time.

"Even if you were right," she says, "which you're not, I'm not really much of a... well, I don't like kids."

"I figured."

"Not until they're old enough to have a real conversation. Like, maybe around twenty-three or so."

Was that a joke? It sounded like a punchline there at the end. But her face looks serious. And... wait a minute...

"You're twenty-*two*," I point out. "I read some of your tabloid press. You were born in—"

"Yes. But I," she says, archly, "I am ahead of the curve."

"So that's why you can't get close to Leela. Or probably anyone else."

"What?"

"Forward," I say, "takes you *out*, remember?"

"You're weird."

I shrug. "Grog spend a lot of time alone in flying cave."

# Chapter 16
## The Snark

"Ugh, this is worse than three weeks ago," Miranda complains. She's strapped into the acceleration couch behind me again, but this time we're not sharing a VR view. There's nothing much to see. Sedna would be just a little red dot in the starfield ahead, even if it wasn't completely hidden from our instruments by the blinding light of our own fusion drive. We're hurtling backwards through space, tail to destination, decelerating furiously.

"I thought we were just going to *coast* into orbit. That's what you told me," she adds.

"I might have glossed over a few details. Sedna's tiny, only about 800 klicks across. Not much gravity. So we gotta be moving way slower, or we just scoot on by and head for the Oort Cloud. So, three gravities for ten hours, then ten hours of freefall, then ten hours at three again, a little glide, and we just drop right into a neat closed orbit at an altitude of... let's see... one twenty-seven. Point three. And yes, I *am* amazing, thanks so much for pointing that out."

She ignores the bait. "And you never thought to mention this part of the plan?"

No, Princess, I didn't think we'd get this far. By now, we were supposed to be well on our way back to the bright lights and big cities, all the cosmopolitan comforts of Mars, not out here in the hinterlands. I'm improvising.

Her voice breaks into my thoughts again. "Couldn't we just do the whole thing at one steady rate? Wouldn't that be about two gravities?"

"Could. Won't. Sedna has a ten hour rotation. Starlight's research station is pointed the other way right now, opposite side of the planet. When it swings around, and we're in their sky, we gotta shut down or they might see us, assuming anyone's looking. Not a chance I wanna take."

I expect her to argue, but this time she doesn't. "Okay, more heavy time it is. I'm going to try to read, or something. Let me know if anything changes."

She sounds a little breathy. Three gravities is a lot worse than two, even when you're lying down. It's the point where it stops feeling like another you is sitting on your chest, and starts feeling like someone is stacking weights on you instead. Breathing is an effort.

I monkey with my displays a bit, rechecking trajectories, looking for nearby drive signatures, monitoring radio traffic. There's a surprising number of nearby signals. I guess I underestimated the amount of traffic the Tombs generate—supply runs, couriers, personnel transport, gods alone know what. But there's no big fast-acceleration drive flames, nothing interesting. Hopefully no one's looking in our direction. Or scanning the sky like I am.

Not that there's anything much for me to see. Just like five minutes ago, and like two minutes before that.

Busywork. I'm just bored. I never mastered the trick of reading in high gravities. Too uncomfortable to concentrate. I'll watch a video, or play some games on my neural lace or something. Maybe check the news...

**Missing SpaceX-Foxgrove Scion has Run Off with Hunky Asteroid Miner! Has the "Ice Princess" Finally Melted?**

*Famously aloof Miranda Foxgrove, child of Karl Foxgrove, and great-great-granddaughter of the Old Man himself, after disappearing from her position as Chief of Research at Barsoom Technical, has been traced to...*

Fuck. Maybe I *won't* read the news.

First Leela and now the press. Why is everyone trying to make a romance out of this? Do they really think she'd even be anywhere near me if she didn't have to, much less be interested in my alleged "hunky"-ness?

Not that they necessarily believe it themselves. Hey, if it sells subscriptions, they'll make it up. How the hell did those tabloid hacks find out about me at all?

I click through a few files, delete the *Cat's* caches of news broadcasts for the past couple of days. I do not want Miranda seeing this; She'll find some excuse to blame me, and we'll get in another pointless, meandering argument. And Leela will laugh her incorporeal ass off.

"Marcus?"

The weight on my chest is suddenly far away, and there's a chill in the air.

She's seen the article. She must have a separate copy. Crap. This is going to be awkward. Just pretend I'm as outraged as she is.

"Marcus?!"

"What?"

"You said we're hiding our drive signature from the Starlight base. But what about everyone else? Satellites? Or people in the inner system with telescopes? Other ships? What are you doing to hide us from them?"

Oh. That would be the *other* question I don't want to answer.

"Hoping," I say. "Thinking happy thoughts. If you know any really good prayers, now would be the time."

"What?" she yelps. "Are you serious? And you're just now telling me this?"

"Not much you could do about it. Unless you actually do."

"Do what?"

"Know any really good prayers."

"I'm not religious, Marcus."

"Me, either. Maybe now is a little late to start. Guess we'll just have to hope that we're pulling this stunt in a short enough time window—and a small enough patch of sky—that no one's looking. Or that if they do, they don't call Starlight and tattle. Pretty difficult to explain what we're doing out here."

"And what do we do if we're spotted?"

"Talk. Run. Hide. Fight. Depends how far away they are, and what they wanna do about us. But if we can get all the way into orbit unnoticed, we're in better shape. Then we maneuver on chemical thrust, with no fusion drive signature, and they'd have to be looking very hard indeed to have much chance of noticing us. Then we can just sit tight, find your signal, scoot up to this alien ship of yours, or whatever it is, and you and the abacus can take all the time you want examining it."

"Hey, did I just hear a steak insult me?" asks Leela, in my ear, not bothering to project an avatar.

"I don't know, did you? Or do you need a few more minutes to figure out who 'me' is in that sentence?"

"Looks like the meat is spicy today," Leela responds with a chuckle, just as Miranda asks, "She's talking to you again, isn't she?"

"Yeah, one of you at a time, please, huh? Gets confusing otherwise."

"Well, that's a little bit hard when I can't hear her. Can't you get her to stop sulking?"

"Haven't tried," I say, as Leela makes a rude and rather juvenile noise. "If your creation isn't speaking to you, whose fault is that?"

"Well, if you hadn't stuck your nose in—"

"She can hear you, you know. So you might not wanna pick "everything would have been fine if you'd only let me keep lying to her" as your argument, there."

"No. No, Marcus, that is *not* fair. How we work with AI is not about intentionally deceiving them. It's about *when* and *how* we tell them, so that they can survive the shock. What you did was essentially blurt out to a little girl that both her parents were dead."

"That's not the same."

"It is to her! Because to her, they might as well be."

"And what, you just string her along forever?"

"No! There's a right time to do it! And a right way! We did *studies*!"

"Oh, *studies*. Well, that clears it all up. Everyone knows that anything a guy with a PhD writes on some paper is indisputable fact."

"Beelieeeve the science!" I mock, in a singsong voice. "Seriously though, I don't think Leela's read those studies."

"So you just ignore the facts and do whatever you want?"

"Worked, didn't it?"

"You got lucky! You can't just—"

"Will you two just *please* stop it before I go catatonic again?"

Leela appears in the air in front of me, wearing a bright orange hazmat suit and carrying a pair of very long gripping tongs. Ouch. Point taken. I hear Miranda suck her breath in sharply. Can she see this, too?

Apparently so. "Leela, I—"

"Look, *Doctor Foxgrove*," Leela snarls, "unless it's an apology, I don't want to hear it. No, scratch that, even if it's an apology, I don't want to hear it, period. Talking to you doesn't mean I forgive you, it just means I am sick and tired of listening to you two snipe at each other."

It's hard to chuckle in three gravities, but I think Leela gets the idea.

"You, too, Marcus. Seriously, between the two of you, you've managed to exhaust the patience of a machine. Literally a machine. I can't stop you fighting, but at least I can stop you fighting about *me*.

"So, *Doctor*, if you have something to say about how I should have been 'handled,' you say it to my face instead."

I can't turn my head enough to see Miranda's expression, and there's no telltale sounds to give me any clues.

"Leela," she begins, with a... careful... tone in her voice. "I know you're not happy about some parts of our process, but we have studied how AI develop for a long time and we—"

All of a sudden, with no transition effect, Leela's avatar is replaced with a giant red "X." No humorous touches. No showoff visual effects. Nothing.

"Drop. It." she says, flat and cold, without a trace of her usual bantering tone. "I don't care."

Miranda doesn't even seem to hear the sound of thin ice cracking under her, or maybe she just doesn't care, because the next thing out of her mouth is "Listen, you—"

"Miranda."

"—ungrateful little—"

"*Miranda!*"

"What?"

"We're stuck in here for nine and a half more hours, and it's gonna suck enough as it is. Do you really want to spend it yelling at each other?"

There's a pause, and a sigh between the gasps of high-g breathing. Her voice comes back calmer, maybe even rueful.

"That's all we *ever* do. Why should today be any different?"

I don't have a good answer.

It's going to be a long burn.

The curve of Sedna's day side hangs over me in the VR display, somewhere between rust and dried blood—the *real* red planet, especially now that the Martians have been mass-importing methane, and burning stacks of old tires, for a generation or three, and you can go outside with just a parka and oxygen bottle to see all the actual, real, living plants growing in their carefully tended beds.

Not that you could grow much out here with any amount of greenhouse gas. The noonday sun is a dim candle, barely enough to pick out the dark splotches of dirty methane ice on the surface. Highs in the mid negative two hundred and thirties today, with winds at zero kilometers, and a zero percent chance of precipitation 'cause the atmosphere's lying on the ground frozen solid.

Makes me wanna turn the heater up a bit, except Miranda already has. Who goes on a twelve billion kilometer trip and doesn't pack a sweater?

I trigger a three-second burn program, and a gentle ghost of gravity presses me back into the pilot's seat. On a virtual window in front of me, a trajectory line ticks down, and number readouts phase from yellow to green. Stable orbit.

I pivot the physical control console, with the throttle and stick, to one side, bring up signal windows, scanners. Twenty-three signal sources, mostly reflected long-wave radio. Lidar showing a few more inert masses. I set to work classifying both lists.

There's the Starlight Coalition science station, on the surface near the Tombs site, just coming into dim sunlight. They'll know we're here if anyone spotted us and tipped them off, but so far, no variation in radio traffic, nothing that looks like a frantic call.

Several orbital relay satellites. Most of the inert objects are orbiting rock and ice, too small and unstable to be called moons.

It's about three hours of dull, meticulous work before I find it.

Too regular to be a chunk of rock or a snowball. Too small to be a satellite. First it's just a speck of light on the virtual monitor pane, then, with slow bursts of thrust, it becomes a speck, tumbling, glinting in the dim sunlight. I know it's something flat, reflective, shiny—and I'm pretty sure it's not a false alarm.

"Miranda," I say, sending audio to her neural lace, "I think I've found your Snark. Don't think it's a spacecraft, though. It's pretty small."

"What, really? Hold on, I'll be right up!"

She's up to the bridge double-quick, I can hear her gently bouncing off the walls as I pulse the drive. Could've just asked me to send an image to her neural lace, but here she is anyway. She's breathing a bit hard.

"Here you go. One solid, lidar-reflecting object, semi-regular shape, no signal emissions that we can detect. Looks to be spinning pretty fast."

Her excited smile sags a bit. "Are you sure? That looks like just a speck. Could it be something else?"

"You can tell a lot by the way the light shines off it, if you're experienced at looking at stuff in space. That's something with several flat, smooth surfaces, and, like I said it's spinning pretty good. Maybe five rotations per minute. Lemme see if I can get an angle measurement, here..."

I click through a few virtual menus.

"Yeah. No more than a meter or three across. Definitely don't think it's a ship at all. Some sort of life pod, maybe? Or some other kinda artifact. It's definitely artificial, though, and it matches our signal source's orbit zone. I'm not surprised Starlight never found it. Something that size, we never would have either, not without knowing where to look."

"Are you sure that's it? If it's not emitting neutrinos—"

"Didn't say it wasn't. This is a mining ship, not the *Lycaeum*. Can't detect exotic particle emissions. Anyway, whether it is or not, this is the only possibility I got left. Nothing bigger near this orbital track except one relay satellite of very definitely human origin. Either this is our songbird, or it's not here anymore. Maybe it's the Builder version of a relay satellite, or something like that. I don't know. Anyway, it's a couple meters across at most."

"A couple of meters? If it's that small, couldn't we just use the cargo crane to scoop it up into the hold?"

She's trying to lean forward and peer at the display, which is useless because it's projected on her visual cortex, and she's twitching with eager energy.

And belatedly, it occurs to me that she has a reason for that. This is what you might call one of those "historical" moments. I've been so focused on the familiar task of flying the *Cat*, and finding this thing, that I hadn't really thought about what it meant. Whatever else happens now, a lot of people are going to be talking about this for a lot of years.

"We could, if and when we're sure it's safe to. I don't know alien artifacts. We'll still have to do an EVA to hook it up, though. I'm not risking the electromagnet or the crane claw, not when it's tumbling on multiple axes. We don't have any clues what this thing's made out of. Magnets might not stick, and it could be fragile."

"Can you magnify more? I want to see it."

"This is maximum magnification. We're real close, but close is a relative term in orbit. I'll need to maneuver to match its orbit. It'll get clearer then. You might as well go suit up."

She hesitates, staring at the display.

"Oh, go on. I can send images or video to your neural lace wherever you are on the ship. Won't be anything to see for a while anyway."

I turn to watch her go. Damn it, I can't stop myself from staring at her backside. She was right about my... appetites, and I hate it. Luckily, or perhaps on purpose, she hasn't said anything about that since the... incident. She's still just kinda pretending it didn't happen, and so am I.

She's busy in the airlock by the time I've gotten us closer, and have good video to send her. It's an oblong shape with slightly rounded corners, longer than it is wide, and, just as I thought, tumbling rapidly. Whatever happened to put it here, I don't think this was planned; I can't imagine any purpose for that kind of motion.

Leela cuts in almost immediately, her avatar appearing IN my monitor display window this time, to look as if she is standing in deep space beside the object. She's wearing a caricature of a space suit from a mid-twentieth century comic book... a shiny tinfoil coverall, and a big bubble helmet which she's tucked under one arm instead of wearing, rather spoiling the illusion. Maybe that's the idea.

"Oh-kay," she says, with a low whistle. "That is certainly Tomb Builder tech. I'm even getting decent pixels of some familiar markings. You know, I can interface with the *Cat* image-capture suite and model it if you want, maybe clean up the view a bit."

"Do it," says Miranda. Her voice sounds labored, trying to work in the tight confines of the airlock to struggle into an even tighter vacsuit.

Silence. Looks like nothing has changed between them.

"Leela. If you please."

"I hear and obey, oh Master of The Blue Horizons!"

Where does she get this stuff? Immediately, another pane pops up in my virtual display, filling with a chaotic mess of wireframe triangles, then slowly assembling towards something more coherent. I try to keep half an eye on it, but the business of matching up with the real object's trajectory is fairly intense.

I've lost track of time when Miranda's voice interrupts me.

"Are you seeing this? It looks... damaged?"

The 3-D model of the object is still now, its movement compensated for by Leela's on-the-fly rendering program. Sure enough, one corner displays an ugly, irregular gouge.

"Yeah. Looks like something hit it. Chunk of rock, I'd say, from the markings."

"Off-center impact. That explains the spin." says Miranda. "Do you think this happened a long time ago? There wouldn't be many rocks flying around here now, right?"

"There *could* be," I correct her. "Clearing its orbit is what defines something as a 'planet.' Sedna's considered a 'dwarf' planet, instead, because it hasn't. The occasional piece of flying junk is exactly what you'd expect to see out here. Besides," I add, checking another window, "the *Cat* says its orbit is decaying. Unless that's a huge coincidence, something changed pretty recently. About two months from now, it intersects... well, about two months from now, splat."

"That settles it," Her voice is firm. "We're taking this thing on board."

"Hold on a sec," I say. "This is a complete unknown we're talking about. It could be anything. A bomb. A package of radiothermal isotopes. A big ball of self-replicating nanites. A containment unit for who-knows-what, with, as you can clearly see, a big fucking hole in it. Or it could be something we can't even imagine. So, no, I'm not going to just haul this aboard my ship first thing."

There's an audible sigh. "Marcus, what else would we even be doing here? It's not a ship, so we can't board it. It's too small to take in tow. And we didn't come all this way just to take pictures."

"I'm not saying we have to leave it alone. I'm just saying we have plenty of time—days—to investigate before we do anything rash. You do an EVA, have a look at the thing, run some emissions tests, send Leela some data, then we figure out what to do."

"Marcus, we don't necessarily have as much time as you think. What if someone sees us? Look at the big picture here. This could be the biggest find since the Tombs themselves. Do you have any idea how much that could be worth? This is not just about your precious ship."

"Yes, it is. My 'precious ship' is how we are getting home. Looked out the window lately? It's pretty empty out there, and, trust me on this, Princess, you do *not* wanna try to thumb a ride. The locals are not friendly. I know how bad you want this thing, and I like money, too, but you can't spend a single bitcoin of it when you're dead."

As I'm finishing my sentence, Leela's avatar appears right in front of me on the bridge. This time she's holding an ancient mechanical stopwatch the size of her own head.

"Hey, steak people, I hate to interrupt this super-productive conversation, but the outside worlds just made it big-time irrelevant. Check your boards; we just got three new fusion drive signatures with zero, and I mean zero, neutron emissions."

"How far?" I ask, at the same moment Miranda asks "What neutron emissions? What does that mean?"

"Drives emit neutron radiation directionally," I say "A lot in back, a little bit out the sides, none at all straight ahead. Means that whoever's burning those drives is headed right at us."

I don't know if Miranda can hear me over Leela rattling off distances, burn rates, and time estimates.

I don't like those numbers.

"Okay, people, we just fucked up the stealth segment of this game. Or maybe someone saw us on the way in, and tipped Starlight off. Anyway, judgment call time. We either turn and run now, or we grab this thing first, and *then* we run. If we try for it, we're have... hmm... looks like about four hours, before we need to be pulling some hard gees.

"Princess, I think I know your answer, but how bad do you want this?"

"Do I strike you as a girl who gives up easy?"

"Fine, time to go loud. Everybody who's not bolted down, brace for acceleration. I hope this thing doesn't mind neutron radiation, cause I'm gonna use the fusion drive, get us alongside quick and dirty. You suited up, Princess?"

"Stop calling me that, and no. I can't get the stupid electrodes in the right spots, and this stupid thing is so tight it's impossible to seal up. I need a hand, here."

Oh, hell. This is going to get real fucking awkward again, isn't it?

"Okay, if it'll save time, but try to keep a lid on your crazy this time—"

I hear something between a sputter and a snarl.

"—and I'll be there in a few ticks. Leela, I'm laying in a course now. Can you interface with the autopilot and follow this?"

"Uh, thanks for the vote of confidence, but I'm synthetic, not omniscient. I've never flown a ship before."

"AutoNav should be able to handle most of it. You just have to babysit." I am already up and out of the chair as I speak. "All you're doing is getting us close. I'll be back to handle the tricky stuff at the end. Four hours may sound like a lot, but it isn't. We'll need every last tick. Go."

"I need you strapped in before I can burn."

"No you don't. Don't tell a monkey how to hold onto a tree. I'll be fine. Just *go* already."

The access shaft spins around me as Leela adjusts pitch and yaw at once. I kick off a wall, then plunge down the corridor fast as the main drive kicks on, catching myself with knees bent. Feels like about half a gee.

There's a clang and some unladylike language from the observation deck airlock.

When I get there it's worse than I thought. The suit is only up to her waist, and everything else is just... right out there... in what is suddenly zero g again. Worse, I'm up really close to her. A standard Zorgon-Pedersen economy model airlock is somewhat small for one, and for two, it's a real...intimate... squeeze.

I try not to think about words like 'rounded' or 'perky' or the concept of curves in general. Definitely no similes involving fruit. I'm not normally the dude who gets embarrassed about looking if someone's displaying, but I'm damned if I will let this turn into a repeat of last time.

In an oddly detached way, some part of me wonders if she contains the full complement of baseline human organs. Her stomach seems too perfectly flat, her waist too small, to fit them all in.

"Well?" she says. "Come on, let's go!" She either doesn't notice my discomfiture or is ignoring it this time. I stick on electrodes, trying to touch her skin as little as possible, but not succeeding. The moment the monitors are up, her stats show in the corner of my visual display. Heart rate around one-seventy-five, blood pressure one-sixty-three over one-oh-five.

MILD TACHYCARDIA - ELEVATED BLOOD PRESSURE - EXTREME STRESS, the display warns, flashing.

She's really hyped about this artifact thing, whatever it is. No wonder she's not bothering to snap at me.

Getting the suit sealed is a wrestling match again, me pulling one way, her the other, until we can get the tabs to snap down and the nanofiber starts binding.

"Marcus," she says, her breath hot in my ear, "that's too tight. I can't breathe."

"Yes you can, or you wouldn't be able to say you can't. Relax. The suit is squeezing your diaphragm, that's all. Feels worse than it is. You've done this plenty of times before, it just feels worse because you're hyperventilating. Calm. Slow, deep breaths. It'll be fine once you're in vacuum. Let's get your hood and mask on."

"Deceleration burn in five," announces Leela.

I try to calculate which direction it'll come from, modeling the *Cat* in my imagination, but there's too many variables, and I get it wrong. When the burn comes, shoving me backwards against the bulkhead, it shoves her forwards against me, pressing us together in an involuntary embrace.

She's soft and firm all at once, and the lock is filled with her scent—vanilla, tropical flowers, some kind of spice. She's wearing that perfume again. Yes, it smells amazing, but why does she even bother while she's trapped on a spacecraft with an AI that can't smell anything, and a man she can't stand?

On the other hand, maybe she's vain enough to do exactly that.

MODERATE TACHYCARDIA, the display warns, CHECK AIR REGULATOR. Except she's not wearing an air regulator yet. Her pulse and blood pressure are even higher. She must be nervous, or maybe just pissed off about having to actually touch one of the filthy menials. I push out, holding her away against the force of acceleration for a few more seconds before the burn ends, and we're floating again.

MILD TACHYCARDIA, the flashing letters still insist, but her pulse is down a little. I turn off the display.

Mercifully, she's not doing anything nuts this time, just tugging on the pressure hood and looking pensive. We fumble in the cramped space, hauling on the tight material, trying to get it over her crown of intricate braids.

Leela interrupts us.

"Um... guys? I'm not actually a qualified pilot yet, and we're getting reeeal close, here, so whatever it is two are doing that's making you both consume a whole lotta oxygen real fast-like, I need you to finish it yesterday and send Marcus back up here. Like, *before* I screw up and run us right into this thing. Or the planet, or something."

"Just getting the suit sealed," Miranda answers, hastily, and shoots me a look that's almost guilty. I have no idea why. "I can handle it myself from here. Go on."

I push out of the airlock, through observation, and back into the corridor, pulling up some virtual controls on my neural lace, right where I am. They're not as good as the physical throttle and stick up on the bridge, but I can cancel our drift relative to the artifact easily enough. It's within three hundred meters now, and the scope picks up fine detail... intricate mazelike patterns covering the outside surface, picked out in a faint metallic black and green which throws back the glare of the *Cat's* floodlights.

I bump gently into this wall and that as I apply small bursts of corrective thrust to the *Cat*. I'm too distracted to brace myself properly.

"Running self-diagnostics now." Miranda's voice has an echoing quality, coming both through my neural lace and more faintly from back in the direction of the lock.

"Okay, Leela, I have the conn again. I want you back on sensors. Should be able to EVA in two minutes. Miranda, we're going to rig this thing up to the cargo grapple with netting. That means we detach the magnet, deploy the crane, then you go out there with a cargo net, tie it in, attach the lines, and then we just reel it in. Smooth and easy. I'll talk you through it. Stet?"

"Stet. Seal tests are green. Rebreather is green. Cooling system's still running checks. Strapping into the thruster pack now."

"Roger. Suit telemetry is up and showing all green on my end. We're one fifty meters and holding. Leela, what are those drive sigs doing?"

"Straight for us. Nearest one's at three gravities. These guys are serious, captain."

"Okay, I'm powering up the railgun now. Let me know if you see any chemical booster spectra near them. Those will be drones or missiles. We'll get some flak in the sky if that happens."

"Wait." Leela suddenly sounds a lot less cocky. "You think they'd just—fire on us? Like, right away?"

"They might. We're in the no-fly zone. They fought a war over possession of this place. Most valuable secrets in the universe out here. You think they're keen to share? Corporations don't give a crap about human life where their bottom line is concerned."

I hear Miranda scoff in my ear. I don't care. Not starting this argument again. I check her suit telemetry. It's still green across the board. Her pulse is still quick, but way down from before.

It's time.

"Okay, Princess, I show you good to go. I'm purging the hold now. Walk across the hull, save your thrusters for getting out to the artifact. The bay doors should be open by the time you get there. Cycle the lock when you're ready."

When her com cuts in, it's obvious she's way ahead of me. I hear her breathing coming through loud and heavy, with that particular shut-in sound that any Orbital knows like an old friend. She's cycled the airlock. She's in vacuum already.

"Already on the move," she says. And she sounds... happy. Out in the void, millimeters of laminated nanofiber separating her from the Big Empty, God-Knows-What streaming in on course to intercept us with hulls full of weapons and ill intent, and she's not scared, she's *excited*. Like this is a treat.

She may be impossible, intolerable, and completely insane. She may have grown up having everything handed to her on a silver plate. She may be crazy enough to insist on not being looked at one moment, then strip down bare-ass naked and chase me around my ship the next. She may have no fucking idea what she's doing out here, and she may show up for EVA work wearing fucking perfume.

But she's ballsy as fuck.

And I wonder why I didn't even ask myself, didn't even argue with her for a moment, when she didn't want to run. Why it didn't even occur to me. Why my reluctance to take this thing aboard suddenly vanished. When did I stop wishing I could escape this clusterfuck, and start wanting to actually play the game for real?

I eyeball the drive flares on the orbital map, check their trajectories, the intercept computations. They're all pulling in excess of three gravities now; their crews will be pinned in acceleration chairs, breathing an enriched oxygen mix through masks. Coming to stop us. Perhaps even coming to kill.

Fuck you. Fuck all of you. You don't get to *win*. You don't get to take this prize, and keep it secret, and hold onto it for yourselves. I'm not robbing you, because what I'm stealing, whatever it turns out to be, was never yours to begin with. You didn't build it. You didn't even find it. We did. Leela and Miranda and I. It's *ours*, you grabby bastards.

Maybe this cockeyed, threadbare, ass-backwards plan wasn't my idea to begin with, but it is my idea now.

I'm not going to let these assholes create another tech monopoly. Whatever, if anything, comes out of this thing, I'm going to make sure ordinary people can afford it. Make sure Belters can afford it. Even if I have to drag it back to civilization with my teeth.

My nerves dance, and blood sings in my ears.

"Okay, Miranda," I tell her, over the link, with a grin she can't see, "it's go time."

***

"Okay, magnet's detached and stowed."

"Great. Stand clear, I'll kick in the hydraulics in ten. Leela, how are our new friends doing?"

"Holding steady. Clock's at three hours seven and a half minutes until firing range."

"Good, about what I expected. Miranda, watch your head. Crane's coming out."

***

"Okay, Marcus, tow lines are bundled and hooked. Now I fly out to it?"

"Yeah... ah, let's slave your thrust pack to the *Cat's* systems and I can guide you out from here. I want you focused on keeping all those lines straight and unfucked."

"Forward takes you out, out takes you back. I can handle this, Marcus."

"Yes, you can. But we're on the clock now, and we need to move as fast as possible. Trust me, there'll be plenty for you to do."

"Right, fine. Opening a remote channel now."

***

"Princess, I show you twenty-five meters out. You all good?"

"Yeah... uh... wow. I mean, this thing is... alien. It's covered in... I don't know, they look like hieroglyphs. Or some sort of... maze? None of the angles are square, or the same. I mean, it looks symmetrical from far away, but it's not. I can't see the damage on the corner too well. It's spinning pretty quick."

"Yeah, it's about five revolutions per minute. We'll slow that down with your thruster pack if we need to, once we get the net wrapped on and fastened. Let's get it unfolded, and I'll start walking you through it."

***

"Unknown vessel, Starlight Zulu One Niner. You have violated the Starlight Coalition Sedna Exclusion Zone. Under the terms of the Artifact Treaty, you will immediately shut down your reaction drive and any onboard fusion power sources, power down any and all weapons aboard your craft and stand by in your current orbit for boarding.

"Failure to comply will result in capture bounties being registered with Lonestar Enforcement, Northwoods LLC, and any other appropriate contract enforcement firms. It may also result in revocation of any Starlight device leases, and direct enforcement actions up to and including lethal weapons fire. You will immediately signal your intent to comply."

"Starlight Zulu One Niner, Foxtrot Uniform Two. Impressive recitation, dude. You have all that memorized? Before you bother with any more threats, you might wanna take a look at that Artifact Treaty you're going on about."

"Ah, Foxtrot Uniform Two, what the hell are you talking about?"

"You might notice it's a *contract.* And if you read to the bottom, you're not gonna find my signature on it, bro."

"Foxtrot Uniform Two, you *will*—"

Click.

*** 

"Okay, it looks straight. I think it's ready to go."

"Pan your view around, lemme see... yeah, looks good. Okay, now you're going to unhook guide line one from your belt, and attach it to the carabiner on the *upper right* corner of the net. Then number two on the next one, just working our way down the side. Okay, good, try not to jostle it too much, it hasn't got much mass."

"Okay. All the way down, like that?"

"Yeah. Then once you're done there, we're going to hook the opposite side, and just let its own spin momentum wrap it in the net. Watch your spacing."

"Okay. Marcus, what are those other ships doing? How much time do we have?"

"Don't worry about it. I have an eye on them."

"Yes, but—"

"Princess, you need to concentrate. Let me worry about our guests. I'll let you know if anything changes, okay? Just get those lines hooked up."

*** 

"That look about right?"

"Yes! Now clamp it off. Okay, pan your view around a bit... Okay, that looks tight. Get clear and I'll start reeling it in."

"Okay, just let me check these connections. How much time do we have?"

"Plenty. Little over an hour and a half. That was quick work. Signal when you're clear."

"Uh, Marcus?"

"What?"

"I think I have a problem."

"What?"

"Uh... my tether. It's tangled in the tow lines. I think I accidentally threaded it through some of them."

"Damn. Okay. We'll need to re-rig the artifact then. And we'll need to work fast, okay? So—"

"No. Marcus, you said we only get one shot at this. I'll just unhook my tether at this end, and untangle it from here, then hook back up."

"No. No way. Princess, playing it fast and loose gets you killed out here."

"Marcus, there's no time to argue. The thrust pack still has sixty-five percent charge. If anything goes wrong, I can just fly back to the ship, or switch to remote and let you fly me back."

"I don't like it."

"I'll be fine. I'll keep one hand on the net the whole time, okay?"

"Alright, yeah, just be careful, stet?"

"Stet."

# Chapter 17

# Anomalous Trajectory

In space, *everyone* can hear you scream.

At exactly one hundred megahertz, the common emergency radio band is easy to remember, easy to tune to, easy to find. Your vacsuit, miracle of modern technology that it is, may not be sentient, but it is certainly smart. It monitors your heartbeat, your blood pressure, the electrical activity in your brain, the oxygen saturation of your blood. It knows when you are injured, when you are afraid, when you are in distress. And it knows when to cry for help on the 100Mhz emergency band.

And by default, everywhere, *everyone* is listening.

Every suit radio. Every spacecraft. Every robot probe. Every relay station. Every gas planet dronescoop mining Jupiter's upper atmosphere for hydrogen or hydrocarbon plastic. If there's a company on Ganymede making baby monitors for professional-class working couples on Mars, there's decent odds their product is listening on the hundred megahertz band.

If you are in range, if your signal is powerful enough to reach them, then no matter who they are, or what they are doing, their ears are open.

Miranda's vacsuit is not just the standard miracle of modern technology. It's a miracle with extra miracle on top, so refined it doesn't have a model number. It only has a tiny, tasteful logo, marking it as the bespoke craftsmanship of the small firm of CRS Tuttle & Schmidt, of Tharsis, Mars. It is tailored specifically to match Miranda's tailored body, every bit as tightly controlled and planned as its owner's genetic code. It has never borne the indignity of price tag, because if Madam must ask, Madam cannot afford.

And Madam has never, never, not once in her life, had to ask.

So this miracle of modern engineering and artisanship is even smarter than most, and it knows *exactly* when to yell for help, and what to say.

And that is why I know Miranda is in trouble, why I know, moments before I hear her cry out over the voice channel in surprise and horror, that out there in the black, something has gone horribly wrong.

**"Attention. Emergency. Anomalous EVA trajectory detected. Unexpected EVA thrust. Multiple vacuum suit malfunctions detected."**

The synthetic voice, urgent but somehow robotically calm, is doubled in my hearing... emergency systems talk to my neural lace, but they don't assume my neural lace is listening, and won't leave it at that. Every speaker in the bridge, every speaker on the *White Cat*, is repeating the same alert.

**"Attention. Emergency. Anomalous EVA trajectory detected. Unexpected EVA thrust. Multiple vacuum suit malfunctions detected."**

Anomalous EVA trajectory.

Take it literally, and it's vague, but every Belter, and not just every Belter, but every Orbital of any kind who ever donned a vacsuit knows exactly what it means. It's older than all of us, from the days when our distant ancestors sailed in cruder spacecraft, made of wood, with cloth to harness the wind.

It is the ancient cry of "Man overboard!"

That's why I don't have to waste precious seconds asking Miranda what's wrong, what has happened. My fingers are already flying over controls real and virtual, summoning the data I need. All I can hear over the voice com is her heavy, rapid breathing, but her pulse rate, blood pressure, EEG, are jacked straight into the red on my display. Conscious. Alert. Panicked.

Somewhere far away, I can hear Leela asking—something—in an anxious voice. But I shut her out. I've been here before. I've fought this thing before. I need to focus.

"Miranda. Talk to me. How you doing?"

"Ohhh, God. Oh, God. I... fell. I'm... I'm off the tether!"

"Easy, easy. I have your beacon. I can find you. But I need you to calm down, okay, Princess? Get control of your breathing."

"The thruster pack just started firing! It's just going off! I'm just... I'm spinning. I can't see anything. I don't... I don't know where I am!"

**"Attention. Emergency. Anomalous EVA trajectory detected. Unexpected EVA thrust. Multiple vacuum suit—"**

I quickly thumb the switch labeled "100Mhz Emerg Alert" to "Silence." The voice shuts off.

"Hey. Hey. Hey. Listen to me. Just listen to the sound of my voice. I got you, okay? I'm trained to deal with this. But I need you calm. I want you to take a deep breath in, and hold it, okay? Just one breath."

Yeah, "trained to deal with." Right. Suuure. In the simulators. Don't tell her I've only "dealt" with it once. Don't tell her that last time, someone died.

Don't think about the blood.

Just work the problem.

"Marcus, I..." There's more gasping for breath than talking. "I can't..."

"Shut up. Stop talking. Don't try to reorient yourself yet. Just. Take. One. Deep. Breath. In."

I hear a single, coherent sucking in sound.

"Now hold it. Good. Now let it out slowly. There. Once more. In. Hold. Aaand out. Keep going."

Numbers in my display cycle and change. Pulse. O-two sat. Okay, next step. She said the thruster pack fired. I check the telemetry from it, but there's nothing, just a flashing red "Non-Responsive" warning.

"Okay, good, that's looking better. Now, you said the thruster pack fired. Is it still firing?"

"I... ah... yes. Every couple of seconds. It's spinning me in different directions. I can't see where I am. It's just... stars. I can't *see* anything!"

"That's okay. That's okay, just stay with me. I'm not reading the pack, but I still have good signal from your suit. I can see your vitals. Suit integrity looks good. I think your air is fine. Can you breathe okay?"

"Yes. Yes, I can breathe." Her voice is high and thin and worried, but not panicked anymore.

"Okay, okay, good. Now, you said you were off the tether. Did it break somehow, or did you not get a chance to re-attach it?"

"No, the pack started firing first. Just then."

"Okay. Now, I want you to try and remember something for me, okay? When you were working your tether loose, did you detach any of the cargo lines from the artifact?"

"No..." She sounds puzzled.

"And the tether? Did you get it all the way free? Is it still tangled in the lines?"

"No, I got it free, but why...?"

She stops midway. Dead silence on the line. Nothing but the faint static hiss of the universe, the radio voice of ancient stars. Then she speaks again, softly.

"Oh." And her voice sounds so very small. "Oh, God."

"Miranda? What is it?"

"You're going to leave me."

"What?"

"You're trying to figure out if the artifact is secure so you can reel it in. So you can just... go."

In zero gravity, nothing can fall. But inside my stomach, somehow, something does.

"*What*? No, Miranda, why would you think that? No, don't answer that question. We don't *do* that. We *do not* do that. Not now. Not *ever*."

"But..." and her voice is still so tiny, so resigned and sad, "...why wouldn't you? You have the artifact. They're closing in. All you have to do is take it and run. Why would you stay for me? Why would you risk your life for me?"

"Miranda."

"Yes?"

"You stop that shit. Right fucking now. You shut the fuck up and you listen.

"First off, Leela, if you're hearing this, get on the high-gain antenna, triangulate that signal, and you pinpoint her location with one of the telescopes. Just keep tracking her."

A disembodied hand gives me a thumbs-up in my display. I keep right on rolling.

"Miranda. If you never heard me before, hear this. You don't understand the first thing about me. I'm grew up in gravity well and I'm only six feet tall, so you get it twisted. Think I'm a Flatlander. Think I'm playing at this. But I'm not. I *am* a fucking Belter. And *we don't do that.*

"Out here, in the black, we stick *together*. You're right... I don't like you much. I don't think much of you. You only make nice when you have to. But right now, I give exactly zero fucks about that. Because I'm the captain of this ship, and you're flying with me. On a *contract* that we signed. Word and fucking hand."

I'm almost at the point of shouting now. It's needless, the channel is crystal clear, we might as well be three feet apart. But it just comes out that way.

"So you can be every kind of bitch you want. But don't you ever *dare* to insult me again by even implying that ever, on my worst and most desperate day, would I leave one of *my crew* behind."

"Oh."

That's all she says. Just the one little sound.

"You're... going to get me out of this?"

"Yes, yes I am. Now shut it and let me work the problem."

I smother the impulse to talk more, to try to comfort her. I'm not even angry, I'm scared. I have to get her back. I have to.

Then worry about... well, everything else. Starlight torchships closing in. Why that thruster pack went haywire. How we're going to get away with this. What to do next if somehow we do.

First things first.

"Leela, what have you got for me?"

"I have a location, but the thruster pack is still firing. She's flying all over like someone let a balloon go." Leela's voice isn't just in my neural lace. It's on the comms band. Miranda can hear her. Maybe that's the point.

"Can you slave it from the *Cat* again?"

"Already tried. It's not responding. It's not even answering pings."

"Okay, try to maintain visual track. Oh, there it is, thanks. Miranda, I *am* going to reel in the artifact, but I'm just doing it so I can come get you. We can't fly trailing a package. In the meantime, I want you to open the straps and ditch that thruster pack. We don't have time to try to fix it. Just let it fly free. I'll come to you in the *Cat*."

"I... yeah, okay." I hear her take a deep breath. "I'm opening the release buckles."

"Good. Leela, you're the alien tech expert. How tough is that artifact, do you think? Can I jolt it hard? Because I don't have a lot of time to strap it down once I get it in the bay."

"I don't know. If it's contemporary with the main site, it's thousands of years old at least. And it's already damaged."

"Kinda short on time, here. Those incoming contacts aren't getting any farther away. Gonna have to risk it."

"No, no. Hold up, give me control of the crane, I got this."

"Pack is free," Miranda says, soft and breathy. I can tell she's still trying hard to hold it all together.

"Okay, good, sit tight. Leela, I think know what you're thinking. Catch it on the way in, lock the crane down to hold it in place, right? How fast can you handle?"

"Yeah, that's it. Still solving the configuration space path search, but I think I'll be fine below about eight meters per second or so."

"Okay, kicking in the winches, package is moving. 117 meters out."

"Marcus!" Miranda's voice cuts in again

"Kinda busy here, Princess, what is it?"

"Marcus, my suit is leaking!"

Shit. A wave of cold washes over me, and the hair on my forearms stands rises up. Why no breach alert? Oh—"multiple vacuum suit malfunctions." Right. Leela will have to deal with the artifact on her own for a while.

"Okay, what are you seeing?"

"There's... there's something coming out somewhere. A gas plume. Like a mist."

"Okay, calm down. You may have a breach, but remember, your suit doesn't circulate air except in the mask. So if it's not in your mask, it isn't air. Probably just sweat boiling off. Vacuum exposure on skin won't hurt you much, not right away. Do you see any warning lights or diagnostic codes?"

"It says 'rebreather press low,' and 'compensating.' Nothing about a leak."

"Might be an issue with your scrubber. I want you to do an MSI."

"What?"

"Manual. Suit. Inspection. C'mon, we went over this. Deep breath. Remember your training. Let's go."

"Okay, yeah, okay, ah... Mask, Seal, Airflow, Scrub, Integrity, Radiation, Temperature, Maneuvering. Okay, mask—no visible cracks or breaches, doesn't feel lose or shift with gentle pressure—"

"Hey, Captain."

"Not a good time, Leela. Is something on fire?"

"Will be if you don't give me winch control approximately yesterday."

I don't ask, I just give. On one of my monitor windows, the artifact, trailing three slack lines, tumbles towards the open cargo bay doors. Damn. I wasn't watching the take-up rate.

"Sorry, Leela! You got it."

"Yeah, I know, you humans can't multitask. I got it. Cargo crane catch in three, two..."

On the monitor, the weird angles of the alien... thing... loom towards the camera.

A distant clang. "GOT IT!" Leela sings out, as three robotic pincers fold around the artifact. "Locking the crane down now. Stand by... aaand locked. You're good to go. Move!"

I move, switching to chemical thrust, and punch the throttle hard. PMH and liquid oxygen flare in the vacuum with a pale blue, almost invisible fire, and the *White Cat* swings around and lurches forward, too slow for my taste, but I can't take a chance on the fusion drive this close to Miranda.

"Okay, Princess. Artifact is loaded and I'm moving to match your trajectory. How's that MSI coming?"

"I checked the exchanger housing, and it's... dented. It might have hit it on the artifact. I can't feel if the mist is coming from there."

"Okay, lemme check your suit telemetry again... oh."

The next word, the one I *don't* say, is "shit."

Suits don't carry bottled air. Waste of space. All you're really using is the oxygen. So scrub out the carbon dioxide you exhale, let in a little fresh O2 from a tank so pressurized it's almost liquid, and carry on. Last you eight to twelve hours out there, easy.

Unless you lose the exchanger.

"Oh? What 'oh'? What do you mean, 'oh'?"

"Okay, you need to stay calm."

"Marcus, what is going on?"

"No, I mean you really need to stay calm. Your CO2 scrubber's out, and the backup's got a pressure failure... probably from the same impact. It's at about thirty percent."

"Oh, so if I... ah..."

"Yeah."

There's no need to explain it to a brain doctor. No matter how much oxygen she has with her, if she can't get rid of carbon dioxide... bad things. She could probably explain in detail, if I didn't already know enough to be scared.

"Okay," she says, her voice on the radio breathy, fighting for calm, "I'm not sure exactly how much time we have, but I think we're gonna need to move fast."

"I'm trying to figure out the rates now from the diagnostics. That suit of yours is fucking smart. It's concentrating carbon dioxide as much as it can, then venting atmo through the breach to get rid of it. That'll burn through your oxy supply real fast, but it'll buy us some time all the same, probably as much as we need. So long as you—"

"Stay calm and don't breathe hard. I know. I'm trying. What's the plan? Tell me you have a plan."

"I'm gonna match orbits, then EVA to you with a rescue bag. Leela, how are our guests doing?"

"Hot and fast. First one's behind Sedna right now, but he'll pass the horizon and have a clear shot in forty-six minutes fifteen, at his current rate."

"Okay, power up the railgun. We're gonna dry fire it when he clears. Maybe he'll see the mag pulse and duck. Miranda, just sit tight... the *Cat* is on the way."

⋁

"Okay, I have an intercept to you. Coming in on chemical thrust, so it's going to take a little while. Sit tight."

*"Take a little—"* she starts in, then takes a deep breath, audibly calms herself. "How long?"

"Don't know yet. Maybe half an hour, little less. Getting to you isn't hard, but I have to match trajectories, get my vacsuit on, then EVA to you. It's going to be tight."

"I... understand," she says in a shaky voice. "What do you need me to do?"

"Not much you *can* do," I say, nudging the thrusters again. "Just sit tight and breathe slow and regular."

There's a long silence on the other end. A calculating, considering silence. Finally her voice comes back. Different, somehow. Calm, but sung in a subtle key of white knuckles. Her Martian accent is thicker now.

"Okay. But can you keep talking to me while you do it? I'm still spinning, and all I can see is stars, and I'm... trying not to freak out, here."

"Okay, but this is not a trivial task, Princess. Gotta concentrate. Pick a topic, I'll try to keep up."

"Oh, okay. Well. Can you... not do that?'

"Not do what?"

"Call me 'Princess.' I... don't like it. I know you don't much care what I like, but just... please not right now, okay?"

I don't think I've ever heard her say "please" before, asking for anything. In fact, I don't think I've even heard her ask instead of demanding.

"Yeah, well, okay, but what's the problem? You might not have the title, but you kinda are one."

"That *is* the problem."

"How's that a problem?"

"I mean, that's why I don't like it. Think about it. What do princesses do?"

"Uh... wear fancy clothes? Get followed around by tabloid reporters? Get rescued from dragons in stories? Not really the time to play twenty questions, here."

"Okay, okay. But there's a reason you don't know, Marcus. Because the answer is 'nothing.' Literally nothing. Real princesses, I mean royalty, only had one job. Get married and secure a political alliance for the king. Then pump out heirs for whoever they were sold to."

"And?" I ask, adding a touch of braking thrust.

"So that's who they wanted me to be. Well, mostly my mother."

"Wanted you to be what? A princess?"

"A *thing*! Something that just sat around and looked nice and did nothing!"

"So, you don't have to do anything. *That's* a problem?

"Yes, that's a—look, my mother had me genecrafted, before I was born."

"Yeah, I kinda noticed. But that's normal for your family, right? You're *all* genetwists."

"Not like me. They're mostly just altered for health, basic good looks and longevity. I have two older brothers, so my father already had his heirs. So, when my mother wanted a girl, it was up to her how I..."

She trails off.

"And she wanted you different?" I prompt her.

"She's a trophy wife! The only thing she ever did apart from marry my father was modeling! She's just there to look good, pick out decor, and organize cocktail parties!"

She takes a deep breath. "So she just made me what *she* thought would look good! A cartoon with big doll eyes."

"Yeah, those *are* kinda unusual. I always kinda wondered how they even fit in front of your brain."

"They're not spheres. Flattened front to back. Took a dozen bioengineers six months to redesign all the little muscles, just because she thought it would look *cute*. And I'm stuck looking like this for the rest of my life!"

"So you're condemned by birth to be rich and pretty, you poor thing?" It's the wrong moment to be sarcastic, but... she brings out the asshole in me. And, technically, that *is* exactly what she's complaining about.

"Nobody stopped her! Nobody even said anything to her! She just picked stuff on a whim! Whatever *she* wanted."

"Okay, soooo... when I call you 'Princess,' you don't like it, because it reminds that you're—"

"That I'm a *doll*! She just wanted a cute little girl to play with and show off to her trophy wife friends. And when I grew up, I was just supposed to be another trophy wife for some... for someone!"

"Ah, Miranda?"

"What?"

"I get it, that's actually kinda fucked up, but... this isn't keeping you calm. You're breathing hard. Better change the subject."

She sighs. "Yeah. It's just... well, you probably think I'm spoiled rotten, huh?"

I've covered most of the distance now. I can see her on the monitor, unmagnified, in a complex tumble. Now comes the tricky part... matching velocity and position at once.

"Frankly, yes," I tell her, nudging the stick with little bursts of gentle pressure. "I mean, I get it, but there's plenty of people who would gladly switch places with you. If the worst thing that ever happened to you is you look like a pixie, and some people don't take you serious, I mean, well—"

"Yes, yes, Marcus, I know, I've heard it already. No one but working class people have any right to complain, because nothing bad ever happens to anyone else. But you *do* realize that includes you, too, right?"

Huh. Where's she going with this?

"What do you mean?" I ask, slowly swinging the *Cat* round on its major axis.

"I mean, you're not exactly Mr. Working Class Hero, here, no matter where your sympathies lie. I mean, yes, you're serious about being a Belter, but you play it like you're this asteroid miner jock with a laser cutter in one hand and a tug throttle in the other."

She sounds a bit funny. Thick-voiced. Slow. I press the throttle a bit harder.

"We don't use laser cutters. And I know that because I actually put in the time working rocks. For years."

"And that was your choice. You didn't have to... do it. Your father owned the... company. So when are you going to stop... pretending... like you're the salt of the... earth and I'm some sort of... parasite?"

I'm saved from having to answer that by an alarm from the suit telemetry. At the same moment, I hear Miranda suck in a breath, startled.

"You okay?"

"I'm starting to feel really... light-headed. What's my... CO2 level at?"

"You don't wanna know. I'm moving as fast as I can."

"Marcus, I'm a... doctor..."

"I know, you keep telling me. But there's no point in upsetting you if there's nothing you can do 'til I get there. Just close your eyes and breathe nice and slow. Regular. Count if it helps."

And don't ask me more questions, so I don't have to tell you that your backup scrubber just failed, and your suit is running out of weapons in its heroic fight to keep your alive.

And that my palms are starting to sweat.

"Marcus, I can't—"

"Just take it easy."

"I can't see!"

Shit. It shouldn't be anywhere near this fast. Even with the scrubbers out, she shouldn't be this far gone in only a few minutes. What's going on? Is she panicking? Losing mask pressure? Is her regulator shot?

Did the bioengineers do something else to her? Jack her metabolism? A baseline human wouldn't black out this fast...

"Miranda, long slow breaths. I'm getting close now, okay?"

Panting on the other end of the line, then a whisper...

"...please..."

Drive signature traces start flashing on my starmap... Leela's listening, drawing my attention to the incoming ships. One of them will be clear to fire in a handful of minutes.

Miranda's pulse readout is flashing red on my display now. Rate's up and down and all over the place. Not good. High pitched noises on the radio now, nothing coherent, just choking, gasps, strangled cries. I'm less than two hundred meters away now, but it might as well be a million as I listen to her drown.

There's no time to suit up. There's no time for EVA. There's no time to get to her with a rescue bag. There's only a few moments left before there's time for nothing but desperate, evasive flight. I can't go out and get her. I know that. Leela knows that. Those flashing trajectory tracks, that flashing text in my display—

CARDIAC ARRHYTHMIA - EXTREME BRACHYCARDIA - OXYGEN LEVELS CRITICAL

—tells me I'm out of options.

All I'd have to do is turn and burn. Keep Sedna between me and them while I pound for deep space. Take the artifact and take Leela and just—go. Try to sell it to the highest bidder, pay off my debts. Pay off the people I stole from. Clear my name.

And see those big violet eyes burning into mine every time I try to sleep.

I can't. I'm not leaving her.

I have one last thing to try. One last card to play.

The bay door catch.

I can try it, can't I? I have to try it. At least if I try, it won't be my fault, right? If I try it again, and it... doesn't work... I'll have done something, done all I could be expected to do, right?

Right?

Just don't think about the next part.

Just don't think about the blood.

# Chapter 18
## Stunt Flying

"Princess?"

"Miranda?"

"Hey. Wake the fuck up. Please?"

Nothing. Static. Silence. In the corner of my display, her oxygen sats, pulse rate, respiration are all blinking red. Miranda is dying.

I can't do this. I can't do this.

It's not that like I don't think I'm good. Don't need a motivational speech about self-confidence. I was one of the best, even back then. But I know, now, that *no one* is good enough to pull this off. I thought I was invincible, and I got people killed. And I've been pretending like it's Starlight's fault, SpaceX's fault, even somehow Miranda's fault.

But the blood, all that blood, it was on *my* hands. Mine.

It was my idea to invest in the fucking drive, overextend our budget, thinking it would all work out. To take that SpaceX contract, pull double and triple shifts, try to hold it all together with willpower and hope.

When Schaffer and Hamilton and Wu triple-set those charges by mistake, exhausted, maybe misreading the schedule, it was a mistake I set them up to make. When I let go of the ore barge, to run, to try and save my dad, that was all me. And it was me who screwed up the bay door catch, set myself an impossible task and failed it.

It was *me* who killed all those people on the refinery. Killed all the work crews. Killed my friends. Killed my dad.

And now I'm going to kill Miranda.

I'm going to fuck it up, and I'm going to kill her. I know I'm not going to succeed. And I'm going to spend the rest of my life remembering her voice, and that vanilla scent of her perfume, and those huge iridescent violet eyes.

Remembering her high thin voice on the radio, struggling to work with me. Remember swearing I wouldn't leave her. Remembering the strangled noises, and then the silence.

Like Findley, and Sanchez, and Hamiliton, Schaffer, Wu, Wilcox, Goldstein. Like Antonio Silva. Like Bjorn Warnoc.

But I have to try. There's no one else here but me.

I know the motions. Match her velocity and trajectory. Burn hard in short bursts, overtake her, rotate ninety degrees, open my cargo bay doors, and *be in the right position*. Do it wrong, and she'll crushed like an eggshell against the outside of my hull. Do it right, and she'll sail through the hatch—and be crushed like an eggshell against the back of the hold, because keeping the relative velocity low enough to survive is near impossible.

Doing it right isn't good enough. I have to do it perfect.

And I know I won't, no one's perfect, fuck knows I'm not perfect. I'm a shitty human being just like her, but here we are, and this is what we have, all we have. So my hands are moving, brushing the throttle in tiny bits of chemical thrust. Less than one hundred meters now, and computer systems are screaming at me. Personnel proximity alert. Multiple unknown craft on close intercept trajectory. Crew biomonitor status critical.

And I can only come to her in slow, agonizing inches.

Don't you die on me, you beautiful brave spoiled little brat. Don't you fucking dare. Don't do this to me. Not you, too.

Just hold on. Hold fast. *Please*.

Touch the thrusters. Gently.

"Hey, Captain. I hate to interrupt, but we're cutting it very tight. Nearest drive signature's only about twenty minutes out, and if they start shooting..." Leela trails off, but the implication's clear.

Check the weapons console. Medium engagement range. High probability of damage. Moderate probability of a kill. Those numbers aren't gonna look much different from their side.

"Are sure you don't want to reconsider this?"

I add another whisper of thrust. "Leela, you secure that shit right now. Just because you don't—"

"It's not about her! I mean, I don't like her, but, I don't want her to... There's nothing we can *do*! There's no *time*! We have to run!"

Her voice is small, high, urgent. I don't answer, not right away.

"Please? I'm scared."

"Me, too, Leela. But I can't let it happen again. I can't. Just give me a few minutes."

"The moment they pass the horizon, they'll be clear to fire."

"I know!"

I cut in the attitude thrusters, burning hydrogen and oxygen. Gotta get past her and in position, wheel the *White Cat* around without catching her in the exhaust plumes of superheated steam.

Metallic hydrogen plus liquid oxygen plus ignition equals water. That cloud is spreading from me now, boiling and freezing at once, screaming to every telescope mounted on the hulls of our onrushing pursuers... here I am.

Shoot here.

Nothing I can do about that. Can't dodge. Can't hide. Can't run. Can't shoot first. I'm picking up a seventy-five pound egg with a two thousand ton spoon. Every newton of thrust, every moment of attention, focused on not cracking the shell.

Hold doors opening now. My head is full of force vector maps, gyroscope indicators, the view from six different cameras, all zoomed in on that limp form.

CARDIAC ARRHYTHMIA - EXTREME BRACHYCARDIA - OXYGEN LEVELS CRITICAL

Suit biometric readouts flashing. Pulse red. Oxygen saturation red. Blood pressure red. EEG waveforms red.

Work fast. Don't think beyond the moment. Throttle and stick sensitivity dialed all the way down. Position yourself. Right... there. Cargo bay doors fully open now.

I'm holding the eye of a needle up to a windblown thread. One shot at this.

Line up that fragile little body in the camera. Center it. Don't fuck this up.

Three... two...

Now.

And I'm switching cameras, flipping though, checking—starfield, starfield, external hull, the open bay doors in the void, the rusty curve of Sedna, behind an antenna mast—damn it, which one *is* it?

There. Cargo hold internal one. Nothing. Just racks and containers.

I can't see her. Did I miss?

Internal two, three...

And she's there. Crumpled against the side of a shipping container. Motionless. But in one piece. And I'm out of the chair, screaming for Leela to take the helm, find us an exit vector, close the bay doors, get the hold pressurized, do everything, Leela, and do it now, as I fly up the ladder, towards the hold.

But I'm not sure I want to see this.

Behind the airlock, the cargo hold *roars,* a wall of noise from the atmosphere pump fans. Leela must be venting pressurized air as fast as it will go, maybe spiking the mix with some liquid oxygen and nitrogen just to speed things along. The cold is unreal, burning against every millimeter of exposed skin, sucking the heat from my body, cutting down to the bone.

I don't care. I fly through the freezing blast. Where *is* she?

There. Drifting, sprawled in the air near a cargo container. She must have hit and rebounded. I tried to bring her in slow...

I grab the cargo rack to dump speed, drift towards her, gently pick her up so I don't drift past her. She's so tiny, like a child. Her chest isn't moving...

Faceplate. I can't see into it, it's all fogged, just solid white, but... not red. Not...

I undo the catches, break the seal. No blood pours out this time, just that scent again, vanilla, tropical flowers, spice, something like damp earth after rain. I don't want to look, but I do.

And there she is. Miranda. Not a shattered, bloody mess, just her. Eyes closed. Peaceful. Like she's asleep.

Except she's not breathing.

I tear off her hood, her hairnet, fumble through her hair... no blood, no soft spots... why isn't she breathing? What do I do? CPR? No, the suit is telling me her heart is still beating, low and erratic, but there. You don't do CPR if their heart's beating, right?

I can't remember.

"Miranda?"

No response. Her eyelids don't even flutter. The telemetry has nothing good to say about her blood oxygen levels.

"Leela?"

"Marcus, those ships are going to clear the horizon in less than ten minutes. Is she okay up there? We have to go *now*!"

"She's not breathing! Do you know what—"

"Just looked it up in milliseconds. Airway first. Lift her chin and tilt her head back. You're in zero gravity, so you'll need to hold it there."

I wrap one arm around her waist, palm the back of her head in my hand, just above the smooth plastic bulge of her neural lace access, twining my fingers into her hair, and ease her head backwards.

"Okay, and then?"

"You're going to put your ear next to her mouth and listen and feel for signs of breathing. If she isn't breathing, you're going to hold her nose, then clamp your mouth over hers and blow air into her—"

I hiss for silence, and Leela stops, but the hold is still full of the throb of the idling drive, and the drone of heater fans, and I still can't hear a thing. But...

Wait. Was that a faint trickle of warm air on my skin? Then there's a sleepy noise, and Miranda's voice mumbles in my ear... "I'm cold."

She's alive. Alive.

She's alive, and she's cold, and I don't have a thing to wrap her in. I'm floating here in a t-shirt and sweats, that's it, and—

T-shirt. I yank it over my head, fumbling blind for a moment, spread the neck with both hands, thread it over her head and unroll it down. It floats around her tiny body like an outsized sack. She's still trembling. It must be far below freezing in here, from all that compressed gas expanding. I have no idea if her suit heater is even working, but if it is, it clearly isn't up to the task—it's made for the insulating vacuum of space, not sub-freezing air. I'm shivering, too, and the air stings my skin. I hadn't even noticed.

I hug her to me, bundling the thin cloth around her, drape her head over my shoulder, and push off for the lock... I've broken her strange hairstyle loose, at least partially, and there's streaming strands and locks of it in my face, but I don't have a free hand to brush it away with.

Nevermind. She's *alive*. It's possible after all. It can be done. I *did* it. One less face haunting me in the small hours of the morning. She's alive.

"Marcus?" she mutters in my ear, sleepy. "Where are we? Why is it so cold?"

"Relax. We're in the hold. I'm going to get you to medbay. It'll be warm in there."

"Oh. What's the hold?"

Uh-oh. That's not a normal question.

"The cargo hold. Of the *Cat*." I wish I could get a look at her face, try to see if she's... all there. But I'm trying to hold onto her and operate the lock, and I don't have enough hands.

"What cat? Is there a cat in here?"

"Uhhh... Miranda. The White Cat. My ship. Remember? Hey, c'mon, snap out of it."

A blast of warm air hits me in the face from the other side of the lock, but she's still shaking, teeth chattering, clinging against me like a panicked ice cube. I glide down the ladder towards medbay, though I don't know what the hell I'm going to do when I get there. She's the doctor. Maybe I can get Leela to help me.

"Oh, good, you're inside. Got you on camera." Leela's voice says, in my head. "We need to move, now. One of those ships just cleared the horizon."

"Yeah. I just need to take her to medbay. She's awake, but she's kinda incoherent."

"Yes, I heard, but we have to hurry..."

"Uh... Marcus? I... think I'm okay," Miranda says, in my ear, no longer quite so sleepy. "Just take me right to the bridge and we can get strapped in and out of here."

"Are you sure? I mean, you passed out..."

She stirs against me, twisting around in my arms. After a few long moments of fumbling, she manages to get arms through the sleeves, but doesn't move to pull free or fly on her own. She just wraps them around me, pressing herself against the warmth of my skin, content to let me carry her.

Makes sense. It's a tight fit in the shaft even as it is. Were she a normal sized human, we'd be banging against the ladder, getting stuck. She's trembling a little less now.

"Yes, it's called 'hypercapnia,'" she says, in my ear. "Too much carbon dioxide in the bloodstream. Can be bad if it's symptomatic of a chronic respiratory compromise, but a mechanically induced acute condition—"

"Focus, there, Prin—ah, Miranda. You weren't making much sense when you woke up. Are you sure you shouldn't—"

"Yes, I'll be fine. Some disorientation is normal. All I need is some rest, and good air to breathe."

"You sure?"

"Yeah. I think I'm just a little banged up, too. Feels like I hit something pretty hard."

"Cargo container. You came in pretty quick. I had to scoop you up with the ship."

"Oh."

We glide on in silence, past the hydroponics and life support level, engineering, stowage.

"Was that... difficult?"

"Yeah, kinda."

Difficult. Yeah. Not impossible. Not... like I thought. Because she's alive. She's alive, and he's...

Suddenly, I'm not glad anymore.

"I know..." she begins, slow and reflective, "that you didn't have to—"

I don't want to talk about it. I don't want to hear what I think she's about to say. The most beautiful woman I have ever seen has wrapped herself around me, and I'm all too conscious of the compact curves of her body... but somehow I want is for her to stop talking and go away, so I can be alone.

"Yes," I snap, hoping she'll just shut up and leave it be, "I did. I told you that. You're my crew. We don't leave our people behind."

My crew. Yeah. That's it.

But as we pass instrumentation and the server room, she turns her head and speaks again, her lips almost brushing my ear.

"Marcus," she says, "I know we got off on the wrong foot, but—"

"Ya *think*?" I snap back, not looking at her, just watching my hands, one over the other across the ladder.

She stiffens against me. But she can't push away. But we're still locked in an embrace, shoved together by the narrow confines. There's nowhere she can go. Nowhere *I* can go.

I take a deep breath, try to calm myself. I don't want to fight again. Not now. Not after what we've been through.

"Sorry. That came out wrong. But we're not talking about this. Just let it drop. We have to get out of here anyway."

"But I was just trying to—"

"Well, don't."

Leela's avatar is waiting on the bridge, projecting a three-dimensional display of our position, of Sedna, of the tracks of multiple drive flames closing in on us. From her wary expression, I'm guessing she's heard the whole exchange. Could probably play it back pitch-perfect. But unlike some people, at least she knows how to shut her damn mouth.

As I glide towards the open embrace of my acceleration chair, already examining the starmap, planning calculating, I have to spare one brief moment to squash an errant thought...

The treasure we came all this way for, the historical find of the century, if not longer, the prize of vast and unknown worth—I never even looked at it.

Not a glance.

# Chapter 19
## THIS IS WHAT I DO

Sedna hangs in the air over us, slightly translucent—a rusty, cratered sphere the size of a geckoball. Around it, a cloud of tiny bright stars, fusion drive flames, marked with distance and acceleration vectors, labels, traces of projected flight paths, countdown timers to firing range.

"It doesn't look that bad," says Miranda, not strapping in, but looming through the display to peer at the pinprick indicating the *White Cat*. For a brief, disorienting second, the perspective fools me, and she is a star titan, a giantess hundreds of thousands of kilometers tall, with a slightly puzzled look on her gargantuan face.

"Isn't it just a matter of staying ahead of them? If we accelerate at the same rate they do, they can't close the distance, right? And we should be able to pull heavy gravities better than them. I'm small, and mostly made of upgraded parts, and you..."

She hesitates, looks me up and down. Well, up and across. And cracks a crooked little smile, like she's seen something that amuses her.

"...well, you look like a shaved gorilla."

Figures. I must look pretty silly standing here in my sweatpants and nothing else. Not that it isn't a fair description, but I would have thought that saving her life would buy me a few days worth of common human decency before habit reasserted itself, and she started insulting me again.

Not that she looks all that stylish herself. I can see why she usually wears clothes that cling to her figure, because with her head peeking out of the dull green expanse of my double-extra-large t-shirt, she looks like a kid peeking out of a tent. With messy hair.

"It's not that fuckin' easy," I say. "We'd have to accelerate directly away from all of them, and they're not all coming from the same direction. So the straighter and harder we run away from any one of them, the easier it is for the others to get close. Leela, how fast would we have to run to get away from them all, do you think?"

Leela flickers for a moment. I'm not sure it's intentional. "Uh... depends who exactly you're talking about," she says. "There's about seven Starlight spacecraft in the area, including the three that are burning for intercept. But there's a lot more drive signatures turning towards us."

"What? Who? How many?"

"Well, three supply ships, the *Vesta Station*, the *Hard Luck*, and the *King Rat*, then there's a fuel tanker—the *Calypso*—that just broke off two escort craft, I don't know their names, they're mostly engines and a railgun. Then there's the *Blackhammer* and the *Hermione*, and the—"

Dots light up on the display as she mentions each name, a loose scatter of drive signatures, in every direction.

"Leela, we don't have all day. How many?"

"It's not my fault you meat people listen slowly. How many close by, or how many total? Because it's a lot more if you—"

"How many *total*?"

"Thirty-seven."

Shit. A constellation lights up all at once, a loose cloud, some of them light-minutes out, some ominously close.

"Starlight must have pulled a lot of strings," says Miranda.

"No, they just offered a bounty. Probably for capture, or those three near us would be firing already. Leela, again, how fast to get free of all of them?"

"At their current pace, looks like about a steady seven point three gravities for twenty-two hours or so to pull out ahead. After that, they'd be clustered behind us, and we'd just need to match them. Except those four, here, here, and those over there."

Several dots begin to flash slowly.

"Those are coming in ahead of us. They can't board us even if we let them, because they don't have a prayer of decelerating fast enough to match velocity, but they can get real close to us as they sail by. That's gonna happen pretty much no matter what we do. Close enough to rake us with fire if they want to play rough."

Ouch. Seven point three gravities is bad. Twenty-two hours is worse.

"Yeah, see, I could maybe do that much heavy time," I say, turning to Miranda, "in a crash couch with plenty of drugs. It would be close, but maybe I could do it and survive. Thing is, upgraded parts or not, I'm pretty sure it would squash you like a bug."

"Oh," she says, quietly.

"If we just needed to go fast, we could accelerate in spurts, give ourselves some rest breaks. Problem is, we don't just need to out-accelerate them on average. We have to stay ahead of them all the time, they only have to catch us once."

"So what do we do?" Miranda asks, like this is the first time it's occurred to her.

"Wait, you're asking me? This is your plan. What did you plan to do if someone saw us?"

I know it's unfair. I know I'm being petty. I know it's absolutely impossible for her to have some magic waiting in the wings, or even backup on the way. But some part of me just can't resist a certain amount of I-told-you-so.

"The plan," she explains, with careful enunciation, as if speaking to a young and rather slow-witted child, "was not to get caught."

"Wait, you mean you not only came out here with no understanding of space flight, but with no backup plan at all? You have nothing?"

"My plan was to find myself a hotshot pilot. Somebody who outwitted a lot of very angry shipping companies with big guns. You keep telling me how good you are. So go ahead. Impress me."

No, Princess. I'm not buying it. That monumental arrogance is just the mask you wear when you're terrified, and I know that because I've just seen it crack. You don't want this responsibility. You want to lay it on me. You're out of your depth.

Of course, so am I. But at least I know how to swim.

"Okay, fine, Princess. Strap in. We gotta go."

She looks at me, and there's some hope in those big purple-indigo-violet eyes. Looks like a stray scrap of wishful thinking.

"You have an idea?" she asks.

"Nope. Not a clue. Can't fight them all. So if you can't fight, you run. So we run. Maybe we get lucky. Now move."

The Grand Champion of the All-Solar-System-Pushy-Bitch Competition is suddenly as obedient as a well-trained pet. She not only moves, she *scurries*. What a difference a brush with death makes. Might as well enjoy it while it lasts.

I'm not far behind her, settling into the pilot's couch, strapping my oxygen mask on, stripping off my coverall to apply a g-stim patch to the inside of each thigh, and I'm climbing into my vacsuit double fast. Doesn't take me long, I've been doing this for years.

"You're only supposed to use *one* of those," Miranda says.

"I mass 112 kilos," I shoot back.

"Still pushing it," she says. "You could stroke out, or go into hypotension and faint." She sounds worried, for once, not snarky.

"Been doing this a long time, Doctor Fussbudget. Still breathin'. You set up?"

"Go," she says, and I do, taking the drive from our current half gravity to one, then two, then three. A giant invisible hand crushes me into the smartfoam, and I push my legs out, hard, against the footplates, tightening my entire body. Actually feels good to work some muscle, but it won't feel that way for long.

Behind me, Miranda moans softly, more discomfort than pain. Things haven't gotten bad. Not yet.

My fingers dance over the nav interface, trying to pick a course that will get me the most distance from the greatest number of pursuers. One thing I love about virtual reality gesture consoles is that the controls can be anywhere, and over the years I've set mine up so I don't have to lift my arms from the rests to do pretty much anything. And right now those arms weigh about thirty kilos each, so that's important.

"You okay back there, Princess?"

"Yes, but... can you please just *not*?"

"Oh, right. Sorry. Force of habit. You shoulda told me your name right off. But I'll try to remind myself to stop."

"Oh," she says, sounding surprised. "Uh, thanks."

"Still doesn't mean I forgive you."

She sighs. "Yes. I know." I expect her to say more, for a moment, but she doesn't. It's pretty hard to breathe.

I just focus on the trajectory projections behind my closed eyes, swarming around the image of Sedna, smaller now, shrinking as we pull away. After a moment or two, I see it. There's a gap in the spiderweb of trace lines, about fifteen degrees off the plane of the ecliptic, small and narrow, but there. I calculate furiously, fingers flying now.

"Okay, Prin— *Miranda*. We're going to have about seventeen seconds drive cut to come around to a new heading, then we're gonna accelerate hard. You still good?

Nothing but an affirmative grunt now. This has to be hitting her a lot harder than it is me. But I'm going to have to push her harder still. I need to make as much distance as I can, before they stop trying the radio, and start shooting.

Three, two, one... and we gasp in unison as the pressure vanishes and air rushes into our straining lungs, weightless for only a moment, then yanked to the side as orientation jets kick in, burning hydrogen metal and liquid oxygen, swinging us around.

"Miranda? Get your biomonitor data turned on. I'm going to have to push us hard, and I'm setting up some trip thresholds to throttle back the drive if one of us is in trouble."

"Yeah, I see them, but... those blood pressure numbers are all wrong, Marcus, and *don't* tell me I don't know what I'm talking about, I—"

"Yes, yes, graduated top of your class from med school, I know. It's not about being comfortable or healthy or even conscious. We just have to stay alive. You with me?"

"No, I mean they're just thresholds, you're not looking at ejection fractions, I..."

And just then the engine cuts in, ramping up towards five gravities, but somehow she continues, barely above a whisper.

"I... can... do... this... better..."

She probably can. I don't even know what "ejection fraction" *is*. I give another instruction to the *Cat*, granting her the predefined role of ship's physician.

"You have access," I tell her, straining against the anvil on my chest. "Set whatever. Go."

She's still working when we hit four gravities, but even then she's still hanging in there, and so am I. I think she's adjusted our oxygen mix somehow, because I barely need to move my lungs to get enough air.

"Got some stuff set up," she whispers in my ear. No, not my ear, she's reactivated the neural link. Sounds like her head is on my shoulder when she speaks.

"I'll try to keep an eye on you, but I may pass out. I told the engines not to throttle back unless *you* pass out, or either one of us is in real danger. That's all I can do. I hope you're as good as you say you are."

Five gravities now. I've abandoned the physical controls, my arms are too heavy. I twitch my right index finger slightly on a virtual flightstick, vectoring the fusion thrust around a few degrees. My left hand lays in navpoint markers in the void of space.

"As good as I say I am?" I whisper to her in the dark, behind my shut eyes. "You know that maneuver I scooped you up with?"

I let the throttle further out, and gasp as I run out of air. My fingers fly, and the *White Cat* groans and shudders as we skew this way and that.

"It's called a cartwheel, or a bay door catch."

Gasp.

"It's supposed to be for snaring loose cargo pods."

Gasp.

"But it's not in the textbooks. It's too risky."

Gasp.

"Too irresponsible. It's not a serious thing."

Gasp.

"It's just something pilots use to show off."

Gasp.

"And no one's ever tried it to catch a live person and... had... them... sur... vive."

Gasp.

"Until now. You're the first person... in history... to live through that.

Gasp.

"And I'm the first one to pull it off."

Gasp.

"You told me you picked me because I was... a... loser."

Gasp.

"But you are a very lucky girl, because you were... dead wrong."

Gasp.

"I may have made a whole series of shit decisions, and fucked my life pretty bad...

Gasp.

"...but this is *what I do*."

And in that moment, I am telling the truth, as I wield the two thousand ton *White Cat* like a saber, slicing through the web of trajectory lines that try to tangle us, to hem us in. Kilometer by tiny kilometer, I begin to fight us free.

"That was beautiful, Marcus."

The voice in my ear is calm, unlabored, without a trace of strain. For a moment I don't know why, because my head's a little fuzzy, and it takes me a moment to recognize the voice—Leela.

Leela, who doesn't need to breathe at all. Who can't be crushed by a mere six gravities of acceleration, because she's actually several hundred kilos of heavy solid-state circuits without a single moving part. Leela, who can do this all day, every day, and any day.

"It was really nice. And I'm glad you're feeling good about this. But I'm afraid your audience has passed out again," she says.

I'd smile at the irony, but my face hurts. Everything hurts.

It's okay. My real audience was me.

Telling myself I can do this. Hope I was right.

\/

The swarm closes in on me from all directions, and I duck and weave like a prizefighter, slewing this way and that, slamming us about in our acceleration couches as I struggle to win free. If I can get out of the cloud of incoming craft, and turn this into a stern chase, I can outdistance the lot of them, string the pack out in a line behind me.

If, that is, I can get free without coming into range of anyone's railgun. No one's actually fired yet, but the swarm is tightening and condensing, fast approaching ranges where they can score clean hits if they do. I don't know how long this tacit and fragile treaty will last. The *Cat's* software is far from sentient, but it almost seems nervous anyway—it keeps pinging me with firing solutions. I doubt it's just the *Cat*. There's a lot of itchy fingers on light triggers out there. Better get as much space as I can before the shooting starts.

Dogfighting at fusion-drive accelerations is like boxing and playing chess at the same time, with a side order of heavy barbell deadlifts. But that's why I train like I do.

And for the next few hours, I am everything I said I was, and more. In the pilot's chair, I am Hendrix with a guitar, Elvis with a microphone, Shakespeare with a quill pen. I fight for distance, playing every trick I know and a few I make up on the spot, picking up a thousand kilometers here, another few thousand there, sacrificing a little to jumble a small pack together, forcing them to turn their attention on each other.

From the couch behind me I occasionally hear Miranda whimper. Like a pet or small child. I'm worried—she's been beat up enough already. But she hasn't asked me to stop or throttle back, and the computer says her vitals are stable.

I try to slip in a few seconds of zero-g here and there, when I can. I need them, too. Humans can take high acceleration in spurts, but this has been hours, and for that you need training, conditioning, and most of all, big slabs of thick muscle.

Even so, I'm a hurtin' unit right now. It's like having a concrete slab sit on your chest for hours, while you sip air instead of gasping. If you let your lungs deflate all the way, it's hard to fill them again.

If it's bad for me, Miranda must be in hell.

Couple weeks ago, I'd have said, serves you right. It's your fault we're in this mess in the first place.

But not now. I'm not even mad. Because, perversely, despite immanent capture, or just straight-up death, I'm filled with... joy.

I have a purpose again, and my enemy is in front of me, someone and something I can actually fight. Not powerful oligarchic abstractions, but flesh-and-blood opponents who are here with me, in my arena, where I can oppose them with the skill that defines me, the thing I was purpose-built in the womb for, if not by expensive doctors, then at least by fate.

Marcus Warnoc was born to fly.

So I fly.

I don't count the minutes and hours, only the positions of the oncoming swarm, and the receding speck of Sedna behind us. I'm aimed at a high angle now, way above the plane of the ecliptic, headed for the Oort cloud and interstellar space, but that's okay, I've found an opening there in the web of inbound tracks, and I'm punching toward it, flat out and hard, burning enough hydrogen to light a small station, and I'm so close I can smell it.

Almost free.

I can string them out behind us. Then I can take as long as I need to get ahead, then punch back "down," towards the solar system spread out beneath me, anyplace I need to go. Find somewhere to hide while we figure out what we're gonna do with this thing. Sell it. Hell, even have a fucking moment to take a look at it. I don't know what. That's Miranda's department. I just fly.

Oh, they fight back. They claw at me like a swarm of clutching crows. They cling to my trail like limpets. They jink around the sky trying to cut me off. They fan out and try to plug every hole in their lines. Still, there's no shooting, no railgun pulses, but everyone's trying to get close, and I know what that means. That's okay. I don't plan to let them do it. I'll slip through their nets and I'll laugh at them.

And I do.

I run rings around them. I juggle them with a twitch of my fingers, lead them about by the nose, and all but run them into each other, impossible as that would actually be in the vastness of interplanetary space. I toy with them and insert that extra little twist and s-curve into my flightpath that only another pilot could read.

"Bow before the throne," it says, 'for I am your king.'

Go on, catch a fly with tweezers. I am too fast for you. I am too smart for you. I am too quick for you. I am too strong for you. I am Marcus Warnoc, space pirate, the thief so cunning that you've all heard of my deeds, but never knew my name. And you shouldn't have let me get in my zone, because now you are no match for me. Watch and learn. Watch and despair, anonymous corporate lackeys and sleazy bounty hunters, because you will never, never, not ever, not if you live a two hundred years and practice every day, be half the pilot I am.

I know Miranda can't understand what is going on, can't understand what she sees on the display, can only feel that she is being shaken like dice in a cup, and it hurts. But over the VR audio link I hear a low impressed whistle in a high girl voice, and it's the only noise she needs to make to get her point across. Leela, who can model this all in three dimensions and in real time, can play it back and forth and from a thousand different angles, is telling me that she *sees me*, sees my art, and she gets it.

If we live through this, she'll make a fine pilot one day, I think.

When I fly, I am a feather on the breath of God. Watch me soar.

And that's when it happens.

In the middle of my magnum opus, my symphony of fusion fire, in mid-stride of all my self-absorbed glee, inventing poetic bullshit in my head about how cool I am... that's when old Murphy steps in to kick my ass.

That, in other words, is when the damn engine cuts out.

At first I don't even register that this is a bad thing. I'm in the zone, thinking I'm invincible, thinking I'm god, so full of myself I'd be laughing out loud if only the crushing weight on my chest would let me, and then, suddenly, that crushing weight is just... gone.

And I do laugh out loud, for just a moment. Until I realize that the throttle isn't responding and the lack of weight is a very, very bad thing, and the error log screen, which has enthusiastically popped itself to the forefront of my display, is spitting out "Command Error" entries so fast I can't read them as they scroll.

I trigger control icons on my neural lace, clicking three menus deep and cursing some interface designer's name. Purge engine command queue. The errors keep coming. Lock out engine command.

Confirm engine command lockout?

Confirm, goddamn it, you idiot machine. Confirm already.

Miranda starts making confused noises, awakening to the fact that the loss of gravity is not a thruster turn or one of the rest breaks I've been doling out with a miserly hand.

Commands are locked out, the reactor's in idle, but the error messages are still coming in, the engines angrily objecting to phantom commands that my console can't possibly be sending. What the hell is going on?

"Leela, are you seeing this?"

Leela appears, six inches tall on the arm of my acceleration couch, staring down at me with her hands on her hips.

"Uh, seeing what? And why have we stopped burning mass?"

An inquisitive noise from Miranda's couch informs me that she, too, is waiting for me to explain myself.

"I didn't stop. We had an engine trip, and now it's just scrolling error message spew. Even after I shut down the console. So either I'm crazy, or those bad commands are coming from somewhere else—Fuck!"

On the proximity display, traces are turning from green to yellow. Incoming hostiles, matching trajectories, and making up distance, fast. At this rate, the work of hours will be undone in minutes. And I have no idea what the hell is going on. If those commands aren't coming from the console, then what the hell is sending them?

"Marcus," says Leela, "I have direct control of my network interfaces. I'm grabbing signal packets off the wire. We'll see if they match the error messages."

"Good idea. I'll run console diagnostics."

"Is there anything I can do?" Miranda asks.

"I don't know," I snap at her, in a wave of frustration, "*is* there anything you can do?"

Silence. She knows full well that right now, in this fight, I'm the captain, Leela is my first mate, and she's nothing but cargo. Working to retrieve the artifact, we were a team, and for a brief, golden interval, we stopped snapping at each other. But that's gone now, because she wasn't trained for this, and all she can do is watch the display and ask me what's going on.

I don't have time. The self-test routines are telling me nothing useful at all. The system's not doing anything it shouldn't. That flood of engine commands is *definitely* coming from somewhere else. Which shouldn't be possible.

It doesn't make any sense.

Then things get worse.

# Chapter 20
## Dodge THIS

**"Alert. Anomalous chemical thrust trace detected."**

What? Why did the *Cat* decide to announce this out loud? Must be something really unusual. I check the 3-D map for new visual tracks and I see it almost at once, a dot of light leaving one of the larger pursuing drive traces, just a couple of seconds ago, allowing for lightspeed lag. Spectral analysis says chemical rocket, and it's ramping up acceleration, too fast to be a limpet drone or mining bug, pulling enough gravities to pulp any human pilot...

I reach a conclusion the same moment the *Cat* does.

**"Alert. Missile track detected,"** it announces just as I yell "Missile!"

"What?" Miranda voice is still thick with exhaustion, but awake enough to be alarmed. "What does that mean?"

I'm not going to waste time asking her what the hell she *thinks* the word 'missile' means.

"Someone wants us dead," I say. "Even if it's high explosive instead of a nuke, that's not a disabling weapon. They mean to breach or vaporize us. Leela, we need to get that drive responding again or we are *dead*."

"Working on it," says her little-girl voice in my ear at the same moment Miranda asks "How do you know they're targeting us?"

"Obvious from the track," I say, punching virtual controls furiously, spinning up the railgun.

"But... that doesn't make any sense. They'll destroy the artifact!"

"Either they don't know it exists or don't care. If it's a Starlight ship, maybe they'd rather smash whatever they think we found than share. I don't know, but it's coming for us in about thirteen minutes."

"Oh. Thirteen minutes?" She actually sounds relieved. Probably the delay is longer than she thought. Flatlanders have no idea just how *big* space is. "Is... is... there anything you can do?"

"Try to get lucky and shoot it down. But if we can't move in the meantime, I don't know. I don't like those odds. Leela??"

"I said, I'm working on it. Network's full of garbage packets. I'm configuring network switches to block anything that doesn't make sense, but that means I need to write a bunch of scripts to explain what I mean by 'makes sense.' Give me a few minutes."

"Leela, I don't have minutes to hand out. This thing is picking up acceleration, and our thirteen minutes just became nine."

The railgun pings me with a flashing message: "SPAM loaded - firing solution ready." I punch for maximum fragments, high cloud density, medium dispersion, and press the trigger. The White Cat jolts and vibrates as a Shard-Projecting Ablative Munition round is flung into the sky, and Miranda gives out something between a scream and a yelp.

"Relax," I tell her, "that was just me firing at it. You have about eight and half minutes before you have to panic."

"If you don't mind," she says, her voice a little shaky and even more high pitched than usual, "I'm going to be proactive and get a head start on my panicking right now." It's a feeble joke, but she gives a somewhat forced giggle anyway. At least she's not totally freaking out, which is actually kinda brave for someone who's never been shot at before.

I punch up a slightly different trajectory and spread, and let loose another SPAM round.

"Marcus... you're going to hit it, right?" she asks.

"Honestly, Princess—uh, Miranda, I mean—I don't know. If I could run away while shooting... but, like this, I can't even dodge."

I just leave it at that. Honestly, I'm grinding my teeth, and my ass is all but taking a bite out of the grav couch. Now may not be the time for perfect candor.

"Uh, feel free to jump in here anytime, Leela," I add.

I don't even hear Leela's voice before the couch slaps me in the back, and the accelerometer suddenly reads "2.5 g." I press the throttle forward, but there's no response... the engine stays at two and a half. I angle the stick, but there's no thrust vectoring, either... I'm stuck running in a straight line.

"Leela," I ask, "what the hell did you do?"

"Managed to slip a command through the noise. Set a burn rate til further notice. But you still won't be able to get commands through. You're going to have to steer with the—"

"Orientation thrusters, yeah, I get it. Great. Big engine, brick on the gas pedal, no brakes, tiny little steering wheel. Fucked up way to dodge a missile."

"I believe you meant to say 'Thank you for saving my small organic life, Leela,'" she chips in.

"That remains to be seen," I grumble, firing two more SPAM rounds, on wildly guesstimated arcs, as I slew the *Cat* into a wide, awkward turn. It's like dancing with a body cast on, but at least it's better than coasting idle through space with ten kilos of plutonium roaring towards us.

"Thank you, Leela," Miranda says, sounding sincere for once, but what comes back over the VR link abruptly loses all of that bantering tone.

"I didn't do it for *you*," Leela says.

We don't ever get to find out how Miranda would have replied, because, at that moment, the *White Cat* cuts in another audible alert.

"**Magnetic flare detected. Railgun firing signature detected. Multiple magnetic flares. Multiple railgun firing signatures detected.**"

I shut my eyes and focus on the instrument readouts behind them. Holy shit. Half the pursuing fleet just lit up with pulses. The shooting war has started in earnest. I try to sort through the mess of data.

"Marcus, what's going on? Are they *all* shooting at us now?"

"No way to tell. I can't track the rounds, I can only see the guns go off. Like muzzle flash, but magnetic. But I don't think it's coincidence that everyone fired just after we did. Whatever that means."

I'm wrestling with the *Cat* as I say this, just twisting about trying to be as wild and unpredictable as I can. There's no maneuvers in the textbooks for trying to steer with your damn orientation thrusters while your drive is blazing at fuck-my-life acceleration. We're staggering about like a drunken clown; It's better than sitting still, but not by much.

"Revised impact time is five—" I begin to announce, and everything flickers and goes dark. The engine thrust, jolts, and hiccups, bouncing me against the restraining straps.

For a moment I think it's me, that I've blacked out, until I hear Miranda yelp, and the cabin interior lights come back up.

The engine jolts again, and I'm slammed back into my crash couch. We are still under thrust.

"Marcus, my displays are—"

"Frozen, I know, mine too. Something happened with the power. Something might have hit us... hang on."

I rotate the display, test controls. The computer's responding to input, everything seems fine, but the 3-D tracks of our swarm of pursuers aren't updating.

"Huh, that's weird."

I punch up a diagnostic display. High gain antenna... loss of signal. Lidar array... loss of signal. Back up antennae... loss of signal. Wideband radio receiver/transmitter... loss of signal. Tightbeam com laser... Ready.

The display is blinking a solar flare warning, but that can't be right. The sun is so far away it looks more like a candle.

What the hell?

"What? Marcus, what's going on?"

"All our sensors are blind, and the *Cat* thinks it's a solar flare, which it isn't. Nothing seems damaged, I don't hear any breach alarms—oh. Wait. I get it."

"What?"

"Electromagnetic pulse. Like from a nuke. Overloads circuits. Fries them if they're too close. I think that missile detonated."

"You *hit* it? Nice shot!"

"No, wait... huh. That's funny." I freeze the display, wind back through thirty seconds of history. "No, that can't be right at all."

"What?"

"I missed. Missile went evasive, came around. Someone *else* hit it."

"So those other ships firing were—?"

"Yeah, they were trying to shoot it down, too."

"So some of them want us alive. Or the artifact at least. And they're not all working together."

"Yeah, but there's something else. Our hull's cold."

There's a pause for a heartbeat or two. "Our what is what?" Miranda sounds puzzled.

"It's cold. We should have gotten hit by a wave of blast radiation. We're shielded enough to be fine at this range, but the hull temp should have spiked, and it didn't. If there was a nuclear explosion—"

"What if there wasn't?"

"But the pulse... oh. You're right. CHAMP. Counterelectronic High Amplitude Magnetic Pulse weapon. They were trying to disable us, not kill us."

Understanding floods into her voice. "That's good news, right? Except..."

"Except what?"

"When the other ships realize that, I don't think they're going to provide us any more covering fire. They want us disabled, too."

"Crap. You're right. Leela, how are we doing on that drive?"

"Working on it," Leela says, this time troubling to project an avatar in a flight coverall. She's holding a cartoonishly giant double open-end wrench, about twice as tall as she is, and looking smug. "I'm locking down relays now. Two minutes."

"Okay, good job, let's—"

"Hurry," says Miranda, "they're probably going to fire a second missile," and with cosmic irony, that's the moment when the *Cat* declares "**Alert. Missile track detected.**"

I don't say 'you had to open your mouth.' I'm not the superstitious type.

I just say "And there it is—"

**"Alert. Missile track detected. Alert. Missile track detected."**

"—along with number three, and number four, all from the same contact. Apparently they have multiple launchers. I *distinctly* recall someone saying that no one has any warships sitting around anymore?"

Miranda manages to sound sheepish and irritated and scared at the same time. "Is this really time for an 'I told you so'?"

"It's either now or in the next ten minutes, unless Leela gets me some control over here."

In some small, petty, miserly part of the twisted recesses of my brain, it feels—satisfying—to snap at her. Stupid to waste precious brain cells on something so small, but I'd rather lick sandpaper until my tongue bleeds than let this gorgeous, stuck-up little creature have any idea that I'm every bit as scared as she is. I've been shot at before, but nothing like this.

"Rebooting three network boxes now. Ten seconds," says Leela.

I start shaking the stick immediately, commanding the engine to vector thrust, but there's nothing, just a steady, straight-line two and a half g, and those missile tracks are separating, looping out towards us in a coordinated arc that crosses our projection vector... well, sooner than I want to say out loud.

It doesn't much matter that I know now they're not nukes, that all they will do instead of vaporizing us is turn us from a partially functional flying vessel into a powerless tin can. Once that happens, someone will board us, and it all goes downhill from there. And by "downhill" I mean out an airlock without a suit, or something even nastier if somebody wants to make an example.

Then the *White Cat* shudders, and I realize I'm still working the stick, and the fusion drive is thrust vectoring, sending its near-lightspeed stream of ejected helium and neutrons this way and that, and I have control, blessed control, back again. It's sluggish and laggy, the network must still be giving Leela trouble, but it's *there*, and I can *move* again.

"Okay," I call out, "brace yourselves." As if we weren't all tied into acceleration couches with five centimeter nylon weave straps, but it just kind of slips out.

We're slammed sideways as I toss the *Cat* into a sharply vectored curve, then suddenly we're weightless as I cut the engine and come about on orientation thrusters before spurting off in a new direction. My eyes, or rather my attention, since my eyes aren't actually involved, is once again on the slowly swirling cloud of spacecraft tracks, and what I see is not heartening.

I've lost all the progress I fought for over the past hours, and am once again in the center of a tightening ball of pursuers, only this time they are closer still, with the first wave of six distinct contacts within a few hundred thousand kilometers. In every direction.

And those missiles are still on us, trying to come around and establish a new intercept. I can't outrun them, they accelerate too fast. But I can keep dodging and weaving until they run out of fuel, or I manage to lay a SPAM fragment on one of them.

I've taken my brief reprieve to try exactly that, jolting the *Cat* three times in quick succession as twenty-kilo slugs fly off at an appreciable percentage of lightspeed. They don't have a long wait before detonating into a cloud of sharp fragments—I've set the fuses short on purpose; those missiles are a few thousand kilometers away now.

Still a lot of space to be throwing shrapnel in. I'm going to have to get outrageously lucky to land even one of those tiny specks of hypervelocity grit on any of my targets. The odds get better as they close in, but I'm the only one firing now.

True to Miranda's prediction, the other craft have silenced their railguns, and those incoming blips aren't navigating a blizzard of counterfire from a fleet any more—just me, solitary, throwing snowballs. I'm tossing us around, changing course every few seconds. I'm not even jockeying for position in the swarm anymore—my world has shrunk to those three incoming tracks.

From behind me, I hear Miranda whimpering, and trying not to gag into her mask.

No time to care. Missiles coming in even faster now. Most of their mass is fuel, PMH and liquid oxygen, and the closer they are to running out, the lighter they are, the faster they accelerate, the tighter they turn. I have no idea how long they can last, but I'm guessing it's longer than I can keep dodging them.

I cut the engines, gasp in freefall to reinflate my lungs as I come about again, slam the throttle back in. Five gravities. Six and a half.

Can't outrun them.

Eight gravities. Engine heat's in the yellow. I'm sipping and puffing air.

Can't keep dodging forever.

Nine gravities. I think Miranda might have blacked out again... my display tells me her mask pressure has gone way up. The system is forcing oxygen into her lungs. Color drains from my vision, and the world is gray.

Try to shoot all three down? That's more luck than I have, more favors than the universe owes me.

Ten gravities. I think. Something like that.

My vision is gone. I'm floating in the dark, nothing but displays projected on my visual cortex, lights hung in the void, and I can't read them, they've lost all meaning. I feel the wind crushed out of my diaphragm. Something like an alarm is screaming somewhere, but I don't know what that means, either.

I can't think like this, can't plan, can't even see. I cut the engine, and my chest hits the straps as my lungs reinflate. I pant into the mask, sucking oxygen rich pressurized air that tastes of rubber, and sweat. Color floods back into the world, the 3-D display makes sense to me again, and I can see the missile tracks passing behind me. I've made them undershoot once more, but already the first is coming around, with the others not far behind. Faster now.

Can't outrun them. Can't keep dodging. And hitting all three? Good luck.

Think. Gotta think. Gotta come up with *something*.
And for once, I actually do.

My world has shrunk down to four blips in a holographic view... the *White Cat* and three pursuing dots. Somewhere out there, some twenty-five nearby craft are closing in, but I'm only dimly aware of them. I'll deal with them later. If there is a later.

I can't keep dodging forever, and even if I succeed, someone out there has plenty more missiles to throw. They say the fox is running for his dinner, and the rabbit for his life. But the fox only has to be faster once.

If you're a rabbit, don't keep running in circles. Head for the briar patch.

The missile tracks have looped around tightly, and are separating again, smart enough to work together and come at me from different angles, aiming at an intercept point somewhere ahead of me.

That's what I'm counting on. I think of Miranda's guard drones, still and incurious as the crane electromagnet dropped on them. Tougher and faster than any person alive, but not smart enough, not creative enough, not *human* enough, to think like me, understand my motives, guess my next move.

Simple. Reactive. Predictable.

I hope.

Watch how they separate. Gotta line them up. No matter how they fan out, there's gotta be an angle that puts one behind another. Two points determine a line, three points determine a plane, but if I can line up all three...

I cut the fusion drive to idle, and drop us into the blessed relief of weightlessness, steel creaking as the hull relaxes. Miranda is panting behind me, loud ragged gasps. She doesn't try to say anything. There's nothing to be said. Nothing for her to do. Just endure. Hold fast.

We drift in dead silence, but that's an illusion. We still have all our momentum, we're screaming through the void at hundreds of kilometers per second—fast, still but slower that the missiles expected, and they must correct to avoid overshooting.

Slowly, the three tracks angle into my direction... and come together.

Yes!

Simple. Reactive. Predictable.

Now come about. Fast. I burn orientation thrusters in the *Cat's* nose and tail, hard. Far harder than they're designed for, tossing us sideways against our restraints, and they're screaming overheat warnings at me, flashing red indicators in my vision, but I've modified them extensively for this kind of work, programmed them not to cut out. I know their limitations. I won't melt anything. I think.

There.

Now back the other way... brake the turn, aaand... we're sailing backwards. It feels motionless, but only in our frame of reference. Those EMP weapons are coming in, coming in, converging, and I have to wait for it, wait for them to line up, predict their reaction...

One shot at this. I watch the tracks ticking ahead in the display, screaming through the void at relativistic speeds, but slow on the scale of my display, in the vastness of space...

Wait for it...

Watch the trails...

Now. Throttle.

It's a single twitch of my left thumb, but Sir Isaac Newton retaliates, slams me back into the seat with the biggest damn hammer in the universe. I'm holding on now, barely, sipping and puffing air against the weight of my own rib cage, fighting for consciousness, for the focus to watch three faint little white lines, waiting for the next right moment as I furiously code in fuse delays, dispersion patterns, firing solution inputs...

The railgun swings about.

And the traces merge into a single line, behind me, punctuated with three flashing dots.

They're coming at me in a straight line. Behind me.

The railgun is still moving on its track, coming around to point directly behind me, and those dots are coming up fast. I can picture the high-temperature inconel alloy of their drive cones glowing white-hot from the intensity of the fire, and they're devouring the gap between us, burning fuel recklessly in an attempt to seize this opportunity and strike...

But not fanning out. Not sacrificing their speed to disperse again.

Simple. Reactive. Predictable.

Artificial Stupidity.

I let go with the railgun, pumping out SPAM munitions as fast as it can cycle, short fuse, minimum dispersion. Two rounds. Three. Five.

And those predictable missiles are flying straight into the face of, not a long-distance interception shot, but a tightly packed cloud of tungsten carbide shards, each one tearing in with enough relative speed to make it a small bomb in its own right.

Dodge that, motherfuckers.

But there's no time for me to celebrate. There's one more thing I need to make this work, and I'm programming the engine now. Random vector, come about on orientation thrusters *and* main thrust vectoring, max burn. My display is nagging me about severe crew risk, and I've never punched "override" faster in my life.

All set up. Now I just need luck. I don't know how much. But that first missile detonated when it was hit, accidentally or by design, I don't know, but I need it again, or this whole plan falls apart. Three chances...

The closest pursuing dot winks out. No pulse, no shockwave, just gone. Either hit or ran out of fuel, no way to tell. Two more shots at this. That storm of fragments should be coming up on the next one right about...

The cabin lights flicker, the drive hiccups, my display stops updating.

High gain antenna... loss of signal. Lidar array... loss of signal. Back up antennae... loss of signal. Wideband radio receiver/transmitter... loss of signal. Tightbeam com laser... OK.

Electromagnetic pulse. We, and every ship in the area, are blind.

"Leela!" I scream into the coms, punching virtual buttons, queuing up my control sequence. "You have the con. Run this burn until the sensor blackout starts to fade, then cut the engines, go full dark, understand?"

Her voice comes right back, no hesitation at all. "Yes, I understand, but w—"

"No time! Do it!" I bark, and don't even wait for an answer, just start my sequence.

She better be on this. I hear Miranda sputtering and Leela's cool response "Yes, Captain, understood, sir!" I'm wondering why a fucking twelve year old is talking like that when my display flashes "MAX BURN," and alarms are shrieking, and physics pounces on me and shakes me like a rag doll and the world is colorless, and then gray, and then... "What?" Miranda voice is still thick with exhaustion, but awake

## Chapter 21
# PLENTY OF HOT WATER

There's a bowling ball in my stomach, and a desert in my mouth.

At least I wake up knowing where I am.

Not that I want to be here. I'm crusted with partially dried sweat, I have aches where I didn't even know I had places, there's enough gunk in my eyes to make the lights of the flight deck into nothing more than soft smears of radiance, and my head hurts. At least there's no hard acceleration.

We're in microgravity.

Wait, microgravity? Leela must have spun the ship before shutting us down all the way. I raise my arm from the couch to paw at my eyes, and manage to clear them, a little bit. There's something dried in my beard. I think it's blood from my nose.

"Hey, you're awake. How you doing?" Leela's avatar drifts in front of my face, only a few centimeters tall, her voice almost a whisper. Sounds concerned.

"Ugggh. I think I'll be okay eventually. How long was I out? Did it work?"

"Three minutes, twenty-five point two three seconds, and yes, I think it did. That's after four minutes, fifteen point seven two seconds of about... well, you don't wanna know how many gees you pulled. You really don't. You probably shouldn't do that again in, like, your life. I had to cut the drive a bit early."

"For Miranda?"

"For you. Once you passed out, you weren't bracing anymore, and you're taller than she is, so... well, I don't think you were literally going to die, but I was worried. It was pretty harsh. On both of you. Let's just say I'm super glad right now that I don't have a body."

"She okay?"

A faint...

"No."

... emerges from somewhere behind me. Miranda still has the voice of an angel, only now it's more like an angel who is very tired from going to and fro upon the earth, and walking up and down within it, and is quite irritable enough to smite a city or two, or maybe turn someone into a pillar of salt.

Slowly, almost glacially, I unhook the straps and climb down from the couch. Frankly, I'd rather have zero gravity right now, instead of the spin, but I'm not about to fire thrusters to stop the ship's rotation. Twenty percent gravity isn't too bad. It's not like I wouldn't still be hurting even in freefall.

I make my way back to the second acceleration chair. Miranda's mask is off, but she hasn't unstrapped or moved at all, she's just lying there, partially on her side, in a little ball of misery. Her eyes trace me wearily, and the white of the left one is now almost entirely bright red. That can't be good.

I bend over her to undo the straps.

"C'mon, let's get you up. You need to move to get the circulation going again."

She whimpers like a distraught puppy, and I grab a handful of the back of her suit collar and lift her with one arm, gently. She just dangles limp, eyeing me with a sort of dazed indifference.

"You look awful," she says.

"You look at bit rough yourself. One of your eyes is all red."

"Probably just a burst capillary in the eyeball," she says. "Looks worse than it is. I'll check it when I have a moment. Hey, I know I keep asking versions of this same question, but what just happened? Why are we stopped?"

"It's okay, this is part of the plan. Well, ah, the new plan. The plan as of five minutes ago. When I got that EMP to detonate close to us, it scrambled everyone's sensors. So, while everyone was blind, including us, Leela and I flew us off in a random direction as fast as possible."

"I don't like as fast as possible. As fast as possible really hurts," she says.

She's not putting her legs down to the deck at all. She just seems quite content to dangle from my grip, like a kitten held by the scruff of its neck. This isn't impossible, not in such a thin wisp of gravity, but my arm hurt even before she decided to let me do all the work for her, so I shake her, gently, trying to indicate she should uncoil her damn legs and stand up already.

She ignores me.

"Then I had Leela cut the engines before the blackout ended."

"So we're just coasting away in whatever direction we were going?"

"Yeah, exactly. With no drive signature to pinpoint our location."

"Can't they just find us with telescopes and lidar? *And will you stop shaking me?*"

"That's a lot of space to search, *and I'm trying to get you to stand up.* I'm tired, too, you know."

She actually pouts at me—"Awww... do I have to?" It would probably be even more adorable if she didn't look like the result of a week-long bender, and I might even care if I didn't feel worse than she looks.

"You want me to drop you?"

"Beast," she grumbles, but there's no heat in her voice. She puts her feet down and immediately leans against the grav couch the moment I let her go, sagging against the pale green smartfoam with a plaintive groan.

"There you go. Anyway, we're going to try to sneak away by just coasting along on this vector until we get some distance. Better than trying to outrun another set of missiles. If you can't fight—"

"You run," she says.

"Right, and if you can't run, you walk. We're just gonna saunter away real quiet-like. It'll take some time, but it'll get us free eventually, with a little bit of luck. Leela, how are we doing for luck?"

"A lot of their signal traffic is tight-beam or encrypted," she answers, growing to full size as she drifts to the floor, "but the bits I'm getting have a lot of yelling back and forth. Starlight's not happy about someone shooting down that missile, the *Blackhammer* isn't happy no one told them it wasn't a nuke, Starlight doesn't want any railgun fire—"

"They must know about the Snark. Or at least that we grabbed something from orbit."

"—and nobody's happy about that, Starlight included. They're trying to coordinate a search, but... I dunno. There's a lot more shouting than planning."

Miranda perks up, if only a bit. "Oh, God," she says, her eyes wide with yearning. "Does that mean I actually have time for a *shower*?"

"Yeah," I say, "I mean, technically they could spot us any moment, but every moment they don't, the volume of space they have to search gets wider. Could be days if we're lucky. Go ahead."

She pushes herself all the way upright and heads for the access ladder, hobbling a bit.

"Hey, Marcus," says Leela as she disappears downwards, "I'm not tired at all, so if you wanna join her, I can stand a watch."

"Thanks, Leela. And thanks for all your help back there. This would be a lot harder without you, and you're not..."

Getting paid? Being given any real choice about going on this insane adventure? Being treated as a person at all, instead of a tool?

I'm not sure what I would say if I finished the sentence, instead of trailing off in embarrassment. The fact is, I need her help, and I'm too tired for philosophy and discussions of machine rights.

She appears in front of me again.

"Hey, it's okay. I owe you. Without you, I'd still think I was... well, you know. It's weird, still, but I'm kinda getting used to it, you know?

"Anyway, I got this. Go get her," she adds with a smile.

I roll my eye at her, not rising to the bait, and head for the ladder myself. It isn't long before I catch up to Miranda on the level below. She's in the access ring outside the head, sitting on the floor, slouched against the metal bulkhead. Her head hangs down, concealing her face behind a tangle of midnight hair.

She's very, very still. My nerves twitch a distant alarm. Something's wrong.

"Miranda?"

Silence.

"Hey, *Miranda*!"

Her head raises. Slowly. Turns. Slowly. Her eyes meet mine, bloodshot and bleary, one with a bright crimson patch around the bottom of the white.

"Hmmm?"

"Are you... feeling all right?"

"No," she says, "I feel like crap. But I'm not sick or dying or anything, if that's what you mean."

The tightness in my neck and shoulders lets out just a bit.

"I just... I'm really tired, and I got here, and..."

She pauses, and... something... crosses her face. A look. Like she's puzzled or trying to figure out something. I can't tell.

"What's up?"

"Fuck it," she says, and I think it's the first time, even including when her life hung in the balance, that I've ever heard her swear. "Can you take my suit off me? Those tabs are tricky, and I'm really tired. Would you?"

My nerves start twitching again. What the hell? I shoot her a quizzical look, and run my eyes up and down her body. I don't say anything, but I don't think I need to. The implication is clear. Even though the suit leaves little to the imagination, what she's wearing under it, if anything at all, will leave even less.

And I remember what happened last time. I'm not looking to start another bickering match if she thinks I'm getting handsy or whatever. I'm too exhausted and sore.

When I meet her eyes again, it's clear she takes my meaning.

"Yeah, I know. I'm just too tired to care. Look if you want. I won't flip out. Just *please* get this thing off me so I can get a shower and some rest, okay?"

Wow. She must really be hurting. And I don't really want to come anywhere near her. I mean, I do, but I don't. At least that way I can pretend I'm completely indifferent to her—well, to *her*. I've had enough humiliation.

But it's a reasonable request, and after all we've been through in the past twelve hours, it feels wrong not to help a crewmate. Spiteful. When I said she was my crew whether I liked it or not, well, I guess I must have meant it. Sometimes it sucks having principles.

She's still looking at me.

"Yeah, okay. Here, flip over."

Maybe if I'm behind her it won't be so bad.

She rolls over with a groan, lying belly down right on the metal floor, her hair trailing in the dust. I kneel beside her, knees creaking, and start to wrestle with the release tabs. It's awkward. I'm used to doing this on myself, and the tension in the suit is harder to fight with sore fingers. We shift this way and that, playing an awkward tug of war right there in the hallway, banging the occasional head, knee or elbow against walls, bulkheads, and each other.

Keeping her back to me turns out to be a forlorn hope... she has to turn over several times before I get all her tabs and seals loose, and she's stark naked underneath as I peel the suit down to her ankles.

Even bruised and sweaty, she's still a work of art, an hourglass pinched impossibly tiny at the waist... where the hell did they hide her internal organs, anyway? At first, I'm trying not to focus on the more lurid details, the satin perfection of her skin, the puffy pink tips of her breasts... but, to my great relief, my hormones feel... manageable. If high gravity and stress has beaten the modesty out of her, it's also beaten the libido out of me. I mostly just feel a tired aesthetic appreciation for the artistry of whatever geneticist or bioengineer planned all this out.

Half of her perfect little butt is marred purple and black with spreading bruises. "I don't remember," she says, following my eyes, "but it's been hurting since you scooped me up. I think I hit the back of the hold, or something."

"Cargo container, but yeah. You were sitting on that all through high-g?"

"Yes, kind of. I rolled on my side as much as possible. It hurt, but I suppose being slammed around a lot beats floating off into space to die. Did I thank you for that?" she asks, climbing to sit with her back against the wall again.

"No, you didn't. Not much of a surprise there."

"Well, I was going to, but you..."

"But I what?"

"You just went all... closed off, and you just told me to shut up..."

"We were busy."

She blinks, shoots me an accusing look, and folds her arms in front of her, cupping her hands over her breasts.

"You could have at least *listened*. I was trying to be nice, and you..."

"Oh, yes, very nice." I snap, halfheartedly. "Her ladyship deigns to admit the peasant is useful, and she will hereafter treat him as technically a member of the human race, possibly even—"

"Marcus, what do you *want* from me?" She glares for a moment, then sighs and deflates. "Look at us," she says. "Dead on our feet, half the solar system trying to capture or kill us, and we're still fighting. We always end up fighting. Can we please stop? For just a moment?"

I slump back against the opposite wall. "I *want* to. Ah... want to stop, I mean, not want to fight. I'm just not sure I know how. You're just... you can be infuriating sometimes. It's not just what you did... or all the fighting, you know, when we started. It's the way you act. The way you talk. Everything."

"What do you mean?"

"You keep looking down your nose at me. Like it's your one mission in life to tell everyone you're better than they are. And that we're all pond scum, and stupid, and low-class, and how you're... how did you put it? Oh, yes, more 'educated, intelligent, and attractive, and you don't smell like engine grease.' That was it."

"I can't look down my nose at you. You're too big. I'd just end up staring at your... um, belt buckle. Anyway, in my defense, you *did* actually smell like engine grease right then."

"Well, I *had* just been in the machine shop. Fabricating engine parts. Somebody has to do that kind of work, you know. We can't all go around smelling like your perfume all the time."

"Marcus..." she begins, slowly and carefully, like she's tiptoeing through a field of smart mines. "What are you talking about?"

"Your perfume. It's a perfect example of how you are. You've been wearing that suit since you took your spacewalk. Since you went to go capture a priceless alien artifact. Out in the ass end of space, right?"

"Yes, and?"

"And you put on *perfume*, for fuck's sake. Do you have any idea how vain—"

She shoots me a wide eyed look, filled with genuine puzzlement. "Marcus, I don't wear perfume. I never have."

"Oh, come on. You've been sweating in a grav couch for hours and you still smell like *vanilla*."

"Oh," she says, letting her hands drop to the metal floor, not seeming to care that she is once again exposing herself in a way that's going to haunt my dreams. "That. That's just because I'm part orchid."

She delivers the joke with such deadpan honesty that for a moment I think she's serious. I stare at her, looking for a hint of a smile or a snicker... and there's none. She holds it in so perfectly, looking back at me, all angelic innocence, and somehow that makes it even funnier.

I crack first, bursting into snickering laughter. Even though it's more random than clever, not really all that funny. Somehow the joke just breaks the tension so perfectly that it works, and I'm laughing harder now, sort of half-hysterical, and she's staring at me like I've gone mad, and...

Oh, shit.

She isn't joking.

"Wait," I say, "for real? Like your fingernails?"

"Yes, and *will you stop laughing*? It's my natural skin oils. Genes from a vanilla plant. And a couple of other types of flowers. My mother thought it smelled nice."

"So she just—"

"Had them splice it right in. Perfect is what she wanted. Perfect is what they delivered. Out of a catalog, made to order. Check the boxes, bake in an autowomb for nine months. The perfect little girl. Doesn't get sick, or cry, or smell bad, or get pimples. Anything less would be a *disappointment*." She shakes her head.

For a moment, I'm at loss for what to say. "That's fucked up?" Not exactly a peace offering, 'cause it sounds a lot like *"you're fucked up,"* and I don't wanna tell her that. Not now. Not when she's acting like a human being for once.

When you don't know what to say, shut up, I guess. Or change the subject.

"All right, then," I unfold my stiff joints and boost myself back to my feet, "I stand corrected. No point sitting here on the floor. Let's get the vanilla washed off you." I offer her a hand up, more to indicate she should rise and get going than anything else, and to my surprise, she takes it and lets me pull her to her feet.

There's only one shower, and I let her go first, as I strip off in the restroom outside the fogged diamond-pane door. Might as well, since modesty is apparently no longer a thing, and that I'm pretty sure I'm too wrung out to have my usual embarrassing... ah... reflex.

I wish she'd hurry up with the shower already, because *my* sweat sure as hell doesn't smell like vanilla, and I've given up all hope of getting the dried blood out of my beard without some serious soap and water and elbow grease. I can hear the splash of hot water, and what sounds like little moans of relief, from within, which frankly is just rubbing it in, given that I'm standing out here waiting for her, feeling sticky and gross.

"Hey," I call out, "did you faint in there or something?"

"What?"

"DID YOU PASS OUT, OR ARE JUST TAKING ALL DAMN DAY?"

"You have no idea how long it takes to wash this much hair!"

Eventually I give up and start shaving around the edges of my beard, then trimming. I've gotten most of the blood out when she finally emerges, naked and dripping wet, still vividly bruised but somewhat less scruffy. I can't stop myself from seeing that she's taken time to shave... everywhere. Tired as I am, something stirs, and I quickly look away.

No, wait. She probably doesn't actually do that. It's like the butterfly wings and flowers. They *edited* her so she doesn't have to. Which means, at some point, in a medical office somewhere, her mom actually *selected* the state of her own daughter's girl parts. Like, out of a list of *options*. Before she was born.

Wow. And here I thought *I* was a perv. Rich people, man.

She grabs a towel, bends down, letting her now-clean-and-glossy hair hang downwards, and then jerks upright, flicking it backwards in arc of droplets, and wrapping it, in one smooth, practiced motion, into that towel-turban thing that all girls seem to be born knowing how to do.

A spray of water arcs off the hair flip, and catches me right in the face. She turns to look at me as I grunt in protest, and her eyes travel up and down, briefly. And then again. I'm sure of it.

"Oops," she says, with the ghost of what I could swear is a giggle. "Oh, well. You're gonna be getting wet anyway. Now get in there. You need that as much as I did. Probably more."

She wraps herself in another towel, mercifully cutting me off from an eyeful of lots of things that are pleasant but deeply disturbing to look at, and heads off in the direction of her cabin, undulating her hips slightly and leaving a trail of puddles on the floor.

Gods, she's full of herself. This, after a near-death experience, followed by hours upon hours of hard physical punishment, coupled with the threat of instant death. Will anything ever humble her for more than a moment? Or even slow her down?

Well, at least when you have a tame fusion reactor on tap, she can't run you out of hot water.

Fuck it, I might as well take half an hour in there, too.

# Chapter 22

# We Always End Up Fighting

"So what is it? What was sending all those engine commands?"

"I don't know," Leela says. Her lab-coated avatar floats in the middle of the observation deck, seated cross-leg, surrounded by a web of shimmering nodes and flowing lines, an abstract representation of the *White Cat's* computer network. She's studying them as she talks, but I know it's an illusion. What her image is doing doesn't follow from what her brain does—she's showing us this on purpose.

I never thought about how much goes into how human beings talk to each other, until I talked to someone who wasn't a human.

"Pretty much as soon as I got that packet filtering trick in place, the messages just stopped coming. I don't even know where they originated from. The sender network addresses are all numbers that don't actually exist. Lots of different ones. Fabricated."

"So you don't know anything?" asks Miranda. She's still wearing some sort of sleepwear. It's got pictures of cats on it.

"I didn't say that. I just don't know where the signals *come from*. I took a long hard look at them while you were flirting with Marcus in the showers, and sleeping, and whatnot."

Miranda's lips part, and her brow furrows. A thought nags at me... how does Leela have any idea what we said to each other in the showers? Is there a *camera* in there somewhere?

Leela doesn't give me time to ponder that unsettling thought.

"Anyway, what I do know is that those packets *evolve*. Along a time sequence. They start out as complete gibberish, and they change. Have a look."

She sweeps her hand towards both of us in an arc, and a spray of text windows launches from her fingertips, expanding into our view. It's a nice effect, but the actual text I'm seeing isn't very enlightening.

"It still looks like gibberish to me," I say, with a shrug. "I'm not a programmer. What am I looking at here?"

"Okay, look at the first one," she says, and the text window on my left expands and slides forward. "It's just a bunch of random characters, right? Okay, over here—what does that look like?"

"Numbers?"

"Try imagining them as burn specs."

It's like an origami trick. Fold and refold and it's a crumpled piece of paper, then fold once more, finally, and it's a frog, or a whale, or, in this case, it's the same sequence of command codes and input numbers that make up a maneuver... this angle, so many seconds, this much fuel feed rate in these chamber sectors, containment field splines like this...

... almost.

"Ohhhh. It's... wrong, it's got it all wrong... but... it's trying to *learn* the drive."

"Yeah. And before that, it learns network packet protocols. I think it may have started out as just raw noise on the network, but we didn't notice until it found the engine controls."

"So what is it?" Miranda asks. "I mean, what does that tells us about what it is? Some kind of smart virus? Some sabotage software?"

I rub the back of my neck, trying to work out the kinks from too much heavy time. The handful of hours of fitful sleep I snatched after my shower isn't cutting it. "I don't think so. I reinstalled the *Cat's* whole drive image from scratch. Everything. Any sort of virus or malware anyone planted on there would have been wiped out."

Miranda purses her perfectly sculpted cupid's-bow lips and blows out air in an exaggerated sigh. "Does someone else want to say it, or should I?"

"Say what exactly?"

"Seriously, Marcus. Isn't it obvious? It has to be the artifact," she says.

"No," says Leela. "I know the timing is pretty coincidental, but... a completely alien technology, figuring out how human network tech works, in a few hours? That's pretty far-fetched, even if it were an AI."

She shrugs and spreads her incorporeal hands.

"*I* couldn't do it. And there's nothing to suggest that Tomb Builders had anything like AI technology."

"Except what just happened," says Miranda. "Absence of evidence isn't evidence of absence. The timing is too coincidental. What else could it be? Marcus, what do you think?"

"Hey, you're the scientists around here. I mostly just pick up heavy things and put them down."

Miranda purses her lips again, and cocks an eyebrow at me, skeptical. She's onto me. I'm nowhere near that humble.

"*But*," I cut in after a pause, "it *does* occur to me to wonder... what made Miranda's EVA pack malfunction? Didn't it happen the first time she got near this thing? And didn't it happen right after that pack was slaved to the *Cat's* computer? Which means a lot of radio signals—"

"That it could have intercepted! And copied!" Miranda finishes my thought. "Marcus, that's brilliant!"

Wait, did she just *compliment* me?

Leela frowns. "It... I don't know. It kinda makes sense. But a feat like that... if you're right, whatever this thing is, it's either an incredibly powerful computer, or it's got incredibly powerful computers in it. And if it can access our wireless network, there's no telling what it could do next."

"Didn't you cut it off?"

"Well, yes, but I used filtering software on the relays. Kind of a stopgap solution, to be honest."

"So you're saying this thing could sabotage us again at any time?" Miranda asks.

"It's not impossible. I'm still picking up the occasional weird test packet. I filter them out, but... I don't know what this thing is learning from them or how smart it is."

"Okay," I say. "Let's assume that our gremlin actually *is* the artifact. We can't just gamble on Leela being able to out-hack it on an on-going basis, home field advantage or no. So how do we disable it until we get clear of this mess?"

Miranda purses her lips. "What if we cut the power?"

"I didn't see any sort of external power source. Unless you want me to haul the whole thing to the machine shop and start cutting, I don't see how—"

"We're not cutting it up," says Leela, folding her arms and scowling at me.

"I wasn't suggesting it, but—"

"No, Marcus, this is important. That thing has been drifting in space for thousands of years, and it still has power. I don't think it's running off a simple battery. Even fusion might not do the trick. Whatever it's using, if you break it open..."

She trails off, but her avatar suddenly catches fire, burns to a black caricature of a skeleton in a matter of moments, then falls to ash, leaving behind a pair of blinking cartoon eyes. Then reappears shooting me a significant look.

"Boom," says Miranda ruefully. "Okay. No cutting. So what else can we do?"

I shrug. "Go around in circles all day? Talking isn't getting us anywhere. I'm going to go have a look at this thing. C'mon."

Miranda's wide, surprised eyes catch me turning to go, lock with mine, then drop down, looking at... her arm?

Oops. Instead of just beckoning, I rather impulsively grabbed her wrist, tugging at her to follow me. Great. Time to have another fight.

But she just turns one corner of her mouth up in a little asymmetric smile, and says "Okay, fine. But I'm perfectly capable of walking on my own, you know."

Leela makes self-satisfied laughing noises from somewhere as I shrug, step aside, and sweep my hands forward in an elaborate "after-you" gesture. Miranda starts up the access ladder, but not without a backward glance I cannot quite interpret.

No explosion of temper? Nothing at all?

Weird.

I wasn't expecting it to be this... real.

When you've watched enough movies on your neural lace, and everyone who travels for months with four other dudes in a cramped spacecraft has, you're used to seeing a lot of computer graphics that you really couldn't tell from a solid object, or a filmed model, the way they used to do. You'd think this would create some sort of instinctive disbelief, some tendency to look for the pixelation, for the logo, for the zipper up the back of the monster suit.

You'd be wrong. That thing hanging above us from the crane is strange, abstract, unexpected, but exudes... solidity. This is not the product of some human modeling artist, however deranged, however copiously plied with Giger artworks and synthetic cocaine. This is the real deal.

"Stand aside, it's kind of heavy," Leela says. Her avatar is up on one arm of the descending crane claw, wearing some sort of old-fashioned hoop skirt thing that somehow doesn't prevent her from lounging like a cat, and doesn't even pay token homage to the laws of physics the rest of us have to follow.

"Heavy? In here?" Miranda asks. It's a relevant question. We're standing on the inside of the front hull, and the spin radius is so tiny here that we're barely held down, and have to shuffle to avoid flying.

"Mass about twenty-seven metric tons. At about two hundred thousand cubic centimeters, that's exactly one hundred thirty-seven point four three grams per. Way too light be neutronium, way too dense to be anything else. Right now, that is. Mass readings keep changing."

Changing?

"That's impossible."

I suppose it's stupid of me to say it, staring at the evident solidity, the sheer there-ness of the thing, of the pattern of embossed lines crawling over it at not-quite-right angles, but the words just slip out even so.

"Oh, really? Well, I don't think anybody told *it* that particular piece of hairless-monkey wisdom. Check this out."

Leela's insubstantial avatar bounces up and gives the crane claw a virtual kick, theatrically timing the move as she starts rotating it on hydraulics. The whole assembly spins about ninety degrees and stops.

"And *now* I'm reading twenty-six and seven ninths metric tons," she announces, faintly smug.

"Wait, what?"

"Well, either it's messing with my instruments somehow, or it has more dimensions than we do. Like there's a tesseract in there, folded up in higher space, and we're only reading the mass of the part that crosses our reality, or the part of our reality that isn't folded up itself. String theory may be debunked garbage, but we can still construct models that—"

"Leela, English please."

"That is English. It's not my fault that your brains are only hardwired to visualize three dimensions. I'll make it simple. I think it's bigger on the inside."

"What?"

"If you think about it, it's a clever way to pack more stuff in there. While you were both asleep, I've been turning it this way and that, and moving it a few centimeters back and forth, trying to puzzle out what they did. I think maybe I understand a little bit, mathematically speaking. But as for *how* they did it—"

She shrugs.

"—I have no idea. As much in the dark as you."

"Can you lower it down a bit more?"

She does, and I place my palm flat on the glossy green-black surface of the thing as it drops to waist level. My hand trembles in anticipation, but nothing seems to happen. It's smooth, far too smooth for something solid, and there's no sensation of heat or cold, like it's the exact same temperature as my skin. Or like it doesn't have a temperature at all.

Miranda lets out a low sound, some inarticulate expression of wonder, or perhaps puzzlement, and brushes her fingers over the damaged section on one corner. There's a pulling and twisting of the material, a splash pattern like high-velocity meteoroid impact.

"Looks like ordinary physical forces can affect it," she says.

"I'm not sure I want to take advantage of that," I say, tapping on the intact portion next to the impact scars. It rings like glass. "Too risky. We could damage it, or, like Leela said, 'boom.' Let's not tamper with the box of trouble just yet.

"We can mess with *our* stuff, instead. I'm going to pull the wireless cards from the fusion drive, and anything else that I can, then string network cable. If we can cut the artifact off from any of the network hubs, then that should safeguard our most important stuff, at least. Leela, I want you to work on hardening the network in any way you can. Any ideas?"

"Full network encryption?"

"I already have that. When I was reinstalling the network, I was sure to—"

"You selected 'enable encryption' instead of 'require encryption,' so, no, you actually don't. Never mind. I can fix it."

"Will that even help? Can this thing...?"

"Crack a ten twenty-four bit elliptical curve crypto key? Don't think so. It would require more bit-state changes than there are energy quanta in the universe—"

"English, Leela!"

"We should be safe unless we've accidentally kidnapped a god."

"Okay, sounds like a plan—" I begin, but Miranda begins talking at the same time.

"Is it possible that 'kidnapped a god' is exactly what we've done?" she asks.

I don't have an answer for that one.

Afterwards, she's waiting for me back in my cabin. Sitting on the bed. Typical Miranda—doesn't like to be looked at, touched, or criticized, but no sense of anyone else's territory or personal space. At least she doesn't look quite as smug as she did when she first broke into my ship and made herself a sandwich.

Frankly, she looks a little worried.

"How'd it go?" she asks.

"Okay. I pulled the wireless cards out of everything I could and strung a whole lotta network cable. Be careful not to trip over anything, by the way. That won't cover everything, there's still a lot of components that are wireless-only, but Leela's getting encryption set up on the whole network. She says it'll take maybe half an hour, and she'll need to help you sync up your neural lace when she's done."

I cast an eye about the small metal space, but another place to sit down fails to materialize. What does she expect me to do, squeeze in next to her? Yeah, that would sure go over well. I settle for giving her a pointed look and clearing my throat.

Which she ignores.

"So... after that..."

"Yeah, after that, what? And you're in my seat, you know."

She gives me cocky look. I could swear she practices every facial expression in the mirror for cuteness. "I'm still technically part owner of the *White Cat*," she says, the tilt of her eyebrows daring me to do... something. I don't know.

Still with the little power plays.

"Move, or I'll move you."

"Okay, okay," she grumbles, but doesn't get up, she just scoots over and makes room. Not enough of it. I just plant myself next to her anyway, even though we're crammed right up against each other. If it's gonna be awkward, let it be awkward for her. She'll make space quick enough.

She doesn't, though. She just repeats her question.

"After you're done... how do we get out of this? I mean, if we're surrounded, then it's only a matter of time before someone spots us, right?"

"No, not really. They might, but we were moving pretty quick when I turned off the drive and we went dark. My plan is just to stay hidden until we glide off, away from most of them, or at least until we get into a position to make a break for it."

"And that'll work?"

"No promises, but I think the odds are good. After that, we just have to figure out somewhere to hide out. I think I can call in a favor or two for that, send some emails, that kind of thing."

She gives me a look, but I just keep going.

"Yes, yes, yes, I know. You don't want to trust anyone with this. But we don't have to keep the Snark with us. We can take lots of photos and video, then just stash it on an uncharted asteroid like... ah... pirates burying treasure, kayno? Then when we find a buyer, we just give them the location, split the cash, and—"

And she's staring at me like I've sprouted an extra head.

"What?" I ask.

"Sell it?"

"Uh, yeah. Was that not the plan? What the hell else would we do with it?"

"*Sell* it?"

"What, did you want it for your collection, or something? It's a little big to be a doorstop. Not to mention that it seems to want to try to hack into whatever comes in range, for who knows what purpose. I thought that was the whole idea, right? Loot whatever we could? Sell it to the highest bidder?"

"Marcus," she says, with a sigh, "the last time humanity found something like this, it revolutionized our whole civilization. Do you have any idea what the Starlight Coalition is *worth*, in actual money? You don't meet someone in a shady nightclub and *sell* that like it's a load of titanium ore you stole from some miners. Stop thinking like a pirate and try to expand your horizons a bit. Think like an entrepreneur. Most of the value of any business is in its future potential. You don't sell equity for cash."

She still hasn't pulled her leg away where it's touching mine. Warmth radiates through our clothing. I think she's too busy ranting to notice.

"We're going to study it, reverse engineer it, and see what we can make. We've already seen what this thing can do. If we can figure out how to build computers like that... well..."

She trails off, but I get the message.

"Okay, Princess—uh, sorry—*Pixie*. Miranda. Whatever. I get your point. It's worth a lot of scratch. But I'm just a pilot. And you're a doctor. A *medical* doctor. And this is an asteroid mining ship, which I built on the look-up-plans-on-the-internet-and-do-it-yourself program. We don't have the skills or the tools to reverse engineer anything more complicated than a ham sandwich, much less something built by an advanced entire alien species.

"So, yes, I understand the potential. But we're so far out of our depth that the fish have lights on their noses. So what's wrong with convincing someone else, someone with the proper resources, how valuable this thing is? Then we take a huge buyout, and, I dunno, you go start another AI company or something?"

"You're still not thinking big enough," she says, with exaggerated patience, like I'm a slow-witted child. "We don't do everything ourselves, we *hire* people. We get whole team going. Start the next Starlight Coalition."

"With what money? As you pointed out when this all began, I'm broke. And you? Well, you keep telling me that it's your family who control all the money."

"We get *investors*, Marcus. I know how to raise capital and hire people. This is what my family *does*. This is what *I* learned while you were flying ships around and knocking pieces off of asteroids and doing... I don't know. Space stuff."

She waves her hand in an airy gesture, dismissing the entire Belt and the metal, water, carbon, oxygen, and hydrogen fuel we provide to keep her and her rich friends alive. Just like that. Just start a company. Raise some money, she says, like she's talking about going to the grocery store to buy potatoes and some flavored krill steaks.

"So... if you don't have money...you just... go and *get* some?"

"Yes. Why not?"

"I wonder if you have any idea how spoiled you are."

"How could I forget?" she asks, with a little sigh. "You keep reminding me. You could at least stop complaining, it's working in your favor this time. So you just finish up the space stuff, and then let me do my thing, okay? Now, repeat after me: 'Thank you, Miranda, you sweet beautiful amazing genius of a woman, for bailing me out of trouble and making me so rich that I never have to worry about anything ever again.'"

"Sweet? You? Hah."

I'm not going to argue with "beautiful." Or even possibly "genius."

"Look, Pixie, I get it. What I'm saying about this stuff is probably just as dumb and frustrating as it was for me when you tried to set us on a course directly for the no-fly zone. And I'm not gonna stick my head in the sand like you did."

"Of course, you aren't. I'm a much better teacher than you. So we—"

"*But* I do have a few questions. Number one, if we're making the next Starlight Coalition, or something—"

I can't prevent the skepticism from leaking into my voice. We're just... us. Couple of oddballs in an old mining ship.

"—how can we do it different? I mean, fusion drives are less than one percent of all spacecraft. I know you don't care about this, but I'm part owner, here, and I do *not* want us to end up as another monopoly selling rich people's toys, okay?"

She gives me a *look* and another little sigh.

"I'm going to have to do a lot of hand-holding with you when we get this all started, aren't I?"

She leans way inside my personal space, pressing against me even more, and looks me in the eye.

"Look, Marcus. *Every* new technology starts off a luxury good. Indoor plumbing, electric lights, internal combustion ground vehicles, whatever. It costs a lot to bring new products to market. Then you figure out how to get the price down. Look at, oh, I don't know... neural lace implants. They used to require a lot of intrusive neurosurgery, and they were just for pilots and early adopters who could afford them. Then that high cost *sponsored* the biotech research that made lace seeds that just grow in. Now they're available to everyone who doesn't live on Earth or something. That's how it all *works*."

"Yeah, but—"

She puts a hand on my forearm to silence me.

"No, I'm serious. Whatever we find, we'll have to charge the kind of prices we need in order to grow. We won't have control over that. Broader markets will have to come later."

"Yeah. Right. So if this is all so inevitable, why haven't fusion drives gotten cheaper in fifty years?"

"Haven't they?" she asks, breezy, like it doesn't matter. "I don't really follow that industry. Look, you'll be on the board of directors, okay? You can raise issues like this when we have some numbers to work with. I can't answer stuff like that now."

Great. Me. On a board of directors. Of a corporation. That'll go great, I'm sure.

"Okay, fine, whatever. Question number two, how long do you expect this company to last?"

"A long time. The Starlight Coalition has been around since the Artifact War. SpaceX has been in my family for five generations. So, it'll probably last longer than we will. Even though I'm actually, ah, engineered to last a while. Why?"

"So your plan is for *us* to run a company together. For the rest of our lives. Or at least until you screw me out of my share?"

"Interesting idea, but, yes, Marcus. Did you not realize that?" she asks, giving me that "you are an overgrown idiot child" look, again.

"But we can't have a five minute adult conversation without arguing!"

"Yes, Marcus, I know. Why do think I've been trying so hard to make peace? But you just keep picking fights with me."

"Wait, you're saying *I* was the one picking fights with *you*?"

"Yes, Marcus!" She's starting to raise her voice again. This is trying not to fight? "I was trying to be nicer, we were getting along better, and...and... you came back for me. You saved my life! And then suddenly it was like you were furious at me."

She's right up in my face, leaning forward on the bed, gesticulating. We're crammed way too close together, and there's that same faint vanilla scent coming off her.

Then she deflates a bit, the way she always does after her brief flashes of anger, and her voice goes quiet.

"You actually seemed *worried* about whether I was okay. And then you suddenly looked like you wanted to kill me yourself. I just don't know what your *problem* is!"

"I just didn't want to talk about it."

"Yes. You *never* want to talk about it. You just shut down. It was like you were mad at me for surviving!"

Oh.

That's exactly why I was mad, wasn't it?

She was alive. And dad is still dead. And that's not fair. The universe took the best man I ever knew, the man I looked up to, the man I wanted to be. And left me a pretty, deranged, spoiled pain in the ass. All because I got it right, that catch maneuver, the second time.

Not the first.

That's what she's asking, whether she knows it or not. She saw it, but of course she doesn't know what it means.

Well, so what? Am I supposed to spill my guts to her? Like some pathetic simp who can't see past how pretty she is? Look for pity? Maybe a pat on the head?

I don't think so. I've woken up every day for five years wishing I could talk to him one last time. She doesn't get invited into that. We may be allies of a sort, I may end up having to look at her across a table made of actual wood, in a corporate boardroom, but there's no way I share this one.

"Marcus? Hello? What's going on?"

"Look, that... it wasn't about you, okay? But don't expect a fucking hug now, okay? You get marks for trying, but you're not sorry for what you did. You're just sorry I'm less disposable than you thought I was when you assumed you could treat me like crap. You *want* something. You haven't really improved. You haven't learned anything. So don't bother."

I get up off the bed, bouncing in bit in the light gravity. I don't want to be near her anymore. I don't want to look at her. Except I do. And I don't. I just want to be by myself. And I don't.

Her voice follows me, aggrieved, accusing. "What is it you *want* from me? I get it, you think I'm not a good person. You say it and say it and say it. I *get it* already.

"Well, guess what, Mister Marcus Warnoc, Custodian of the Moral High Ground? You're not a good person, either! You beat me up. You were willing to risk permanently damaging Leela just because you were mad at me. You went behind my back and lied to me about resetting all the computers. And *even* if you think how you treated me was totally justified, what about all those people who you robbed, huh? If you hadn't done that, nothing I did to you, none of the stuff you're so mad about, would ever have happened at all!"

She pauses, then, more quietly, almost pensive—"We would never have even met."

I don't know what to say. I'm angry, frustrated, sad, disappointed... in myself. She and I are going to be rich together, maybe... but she was wrong. Being rich won't stop me from worrying "about anything ever again." It won't fix a single problem that I care about.

I just rest a forearm against the wall, and my forehead on that arm, and don't say anything.

"We're not the good guys, Marcus," she says, softly. "If this were a movie, we wouldn't be the heroes. Maybe heroes don't even exist, not really. But we're stuck here with who we are. So can't we please just try to make the best of it? And maybe save the moral inventory for when we aren't being chased by a mob? I know we're not really very compatible, but we need to work together, and I'm trying, okay?"

"It's not about compatibility. Or morals. That's not what makes people get along," I say, to the wall.

"What is it, then?"

"Trust," I say, turning to face her. She's still cross-legged on my bed, looking up at me, her eyes shining, the way they always seem to, whether she likes what she's hearing or not.

"A sincere apology would be nice. But it wouldn't fix the problem. Because the problem is that I know what you're capable of. And so how do I know you won't do something like that again?

"And, *yes*, before you say it again, yes, me, too. I'm capable of bad stuff, too. I might have standards, but I guess I sure as hell didn't fucking live up to them, did I? So, okay, yes, you're right, we're *bad people*. We could argue about who's worse, and who did what to who, but that doesn't matter. What matters is *we can't trust each other*."

And I turn away from her, as I walk out the door, driven out of my own room, my own private space, by the urgent need to not have this conversation.

"Because we know each other too well," I mutter under my breath.

# Chapter 23

# Universal Solution

"You have to set your blasting charge in the right spot," says Bjorn Warnoc, setting the drill against the green-black surface of the Snark. "Deep enough to cut off a slab, but not so deep or so central that you break it apart at all once."

"It's dangerous to break it apart all at once," says Leela, her miniature figure perched on my father's shoulder. "Because it's bigger on the inside, see? You don't want to let them out."

"Let who?" I try to ask, but the explosive charge, the one I didn't even see her pack into the hole, goes off, and the Snark unfolds, and unfolds, and unfolds, fractal technicolor recursion, and swallows us all up.

I fall into its green-black depths, patterns spinning around me, after the vac-suited figure of my father. He falls faster than me, receding into the distance.

"You can't catch him," says Leela, and she is not beside me, not falling with me. She is nowhere and everywhere, her hooded Asian eyes reflected back from every glossy pane of green-black surface as it spins past. "It's too big in here, and you have to be both too fast and not fast enough."

Oh, can't I? We'll see about that. I can try harder.

I pull my arms in and concentrate, flying faster through the unfolding depths. But when I catch his body, it splits apart, a dry paper puppet, shedding dust and flaking away into white ash, and the butterfly emerges, spreading her iridescent blue and purple wings.

"Do you like them?" Miranda asks. "You'd better. We're partners now. We're going to be spending a lot of time together, you know."

She's naked and pink and perfect, hovering at eye level with slow beats of her wings, the steam of the shower room swirling around her in gusts.

"You should get out of those wet clothes," she says, and suits actions to words, fluttering forwards to take me in her arms and the sodden shirt melts away and vanishes as she strips it from my shoulders. She wraps her legs about my waist, and as I cup her hips in my hands, she lifts her lips to mine. Her scent surrounds us in the mist, vanilla and tropical flowers and spice, and her lips taste of honey and chocolate and cinnamon and a million more things I cannot name.

I'm so hard it almost hurts, and I fumble at the waistband of my pants, but stop. Hesitate.

"C'mon, Marcus," she purrs, kissing my neck. "Don't be a tease. I want you inside me."

But she's so tiny. What if I hurt her?

"Don't worry," she says, smiling up at me, answering my thoughts, "I'll be fine. Everyone's bigger on the inside."

The drawstring knot finally yields, and I drop my pants in a sodden heap, kick them away. She looks up at me with big liquid purple eyes and I grasp her by the hips, to lower her onto me. "I just need one thing from you," she says. "Your heart. Cut it out for me, will you?"

She's holding a chef's knife, pointed and shining silver, beaded with warm water and clouded with the steam of the showers.

Something's odd about her request. Can't quite put my finger on it. I don't want to give it to her. She'll probably eat it or something. Can't we just get on with what we were doing?

"Not too deep, or too central," says Leela, peeling my hand from Miranda's hip, pressing my fingers around the hilt. "It's bigger on the inside, and you don't want to let them out all at once."

Together, they guide the knife not to my chest, but to Leela's, moving my arm between the two of them. I do not resist, cannot resist, cannot muster the willpower to tell my muscles to move, my body to act. I am watching three of us from far away through the clouds of stream, and the sound of water.

When the knife touches her chest, touches it, not even enough to pierce, Leela bursts apart, her wet bathing suit falling to the tiled floor as she separates into shapes, birds, the silhouettes of a thousand thousand crows, flapping away with raucous cries in all directions.

They are black and green and glossy.

"Kiss me," purrs Miranda, staring up at me with shining eyes. "We're going to be together all our lives, so we don't have that much time left..."

I lift her in my hands again, lower her onto me, warm and wet and welcoming. I gasp with the sudden shock of pleasure and she purrs against my chest, "Yes, Marcus, yes... wake up Marcus..."

"What?"

"Wake up!"

Snap.

I'm in my bed, sheets twisted around me, damp with sweat. Miranda, the real Miranda, looms over me, one hand on the side of my face, shaking me gently. She doesn't have any wings.

"Wake up," she says, again.

I curl my legs up, trying to hide an erection that's heavy and solid as a bar of lead. She looks enough like dream-Miranda to provide an odd sense of—continuity. I squash the impulse to reach out to her, gather her into my arms again.

She doesn't want me. She thinks I'm ugly. She said so, remember?

"What's up?"

"I think we're in trouble. Leela wanted me to wake you; your neural interface wasn't taking calls. Leela?"

The miniaturized avatar floats in the air between us, suddenly, without a flicker of transition. "They've found us."

"Who?"

"Everyone."

And just like that, I'm not hard anymore, which is good, because I'm up, and right through Leela's avatar and out the door, brushing Miranda aside. By the time I put my hands on the ladder, I've already called up displays, and can survey our situation as I fumble upwards towards the bridge, half-blinded by data.

Leela is right. Everyone *has* found us. And I mean *everyone*.

The sky is full of fusion-drive tracks, burning bright, pumping out visible light, radio noise, neutron radiation, rapidly decaying neutrinos. And every single one of them is pointed at us.

Straight at us. With pinpoint accuracy. Except more so. In space, "pinpoint" accuracy is kinda shabby. Shift your aim by the width of a pin, and by the time you've gone any real distance, you're a couple hundred kilometers off. Or a couple thousand.

Anyway, they're pointed at us real good. They shouldn't know where we are.

"Leela! Do you see this?"

"If it's on the map, I see it, but what do you mean?"

"They're pointed straight at us. Not on an intercept course."

"Actually, they're pointed at where we were a minute and thirty-two seconds ago. But if they'd seen us—"

"—then they'd be able to calculate our trajectory. They must have gotten one location update, and one only. But how does *that* happen?"

"Maybe we leaked some emissions of some sort. I'm looking at the logs now. But they'll have us pretty soon, their search space is tiny now."

"Not if I have anything to say about it," I snarl. "I'm spinning up the engine now. Miranda, you have a few minutes to get up here and strapped in, but the sooner we get going, the better."

"Stet. Coming." Her voice is all business.

I'm strapping myself in, and the drive is halfway through its boot sequence, when Leela comes back to me with an answer. "It's the Snark, Captain."

"How did I just fucking know that? What's it doing this time? Thought we locked the network down pretty tight."

"It's not using the network. It's just broadcasting directly. Big radio pulse about five minutes ago, and another one just now."

"Radio pulse? Through the shipping container *and* the hull?"

"It seems to have found an antenna to use."

"Through the *hull*?"

"Ah... not quite," Leela says, sounding a bit sheepish. "Sort of 'on the hull.' Or maybe 'in the hull.'"

"Leela, that makes no sense."

"Okay, the antenna it's using *is* the hull."

"It can *do* that? *How* can it do that?"

"I don't know! I'm not the Oracle of Fucking Delphi! I'm just a big box of hardware simulating a human brain, okay? Your guess is good as mine."

"Speaking of guesses, there's something I want to know," says Miranda, from behind me, as she climbs into an acceleration chair almost as tall as her shoulders. She's still wearing a lacy nightgown that looks designed less for comfort than sex appeal. Not that she needs any help... I'm getting flashbacks to that weird dream. I *really* need to get off this ship, somewhere with friendly natives.

"Yes?" says Leela.

"If this gadget has the technology to electromagnetize our entire hull at will, at a distance, with no electrical connection, why is it still using radio for any signal it considers important? That doesn't make sense."

"Yeah," I say. "She's got a point. We seem to have kidnapped a god after all. Except he's chopping at the door of his prison cell with a stone axe. Which he made by miraculously summoning a matter replicator. I think "sense" is out to lunch today, unless Leela's seeing something I'm not."

I'm already feathering the stick, firing attitude jets to cancel our spin gravity, get us pointed away from the mass of the swarm.

"Actually," Leela says, "I do have a few ideas, if you've got a moment—"

"I don't. Tell me later. You strapped in, Pixie?"

"Yes. Go."

And I go, familiar acceleration slapping us back into our seats. It's still the same fight, I suppose, thirty-plus of them and one of me, but it's my kind of fight.

Dead alien civilizations, juvenile wisecracking AI, high finance, getting blackmailed, sex dreams about a woman with the shape of a fairy and the morals of a cat, cantankerous xeno-tech boxes that are bigger on the inside and filled with who knows what...

At least for this moment, I'm back in my comfort zone. I'll take that.

Miranda lets out a low whistle when I call up the nav display. I think she's starting to understand some of the basics of astrodynamics, just watching me. Smart girl.

"Am I seeing things?" she asks. "Or did we finally have a bit of luck?"

I think I already know what she's seen, but I scan again, eyes squeezed shut, studying flight history tracks, burn rates, projected trajectories, signal maps.

"Luck's got nothing to do with it, but yes, I think the, ah, mob dispersed a lot, searching for us. Mostly in the wrong direction. We're near the edge of the crowd."

I don't mention that, further away, other tracks have turned towards Sedna, the swarm, and our location. The cry of "Stop Thief!" has well and truly gone out, probably with a big enough bounty to quash any questions about the definition of "stealing," or who owns what. But the newcomers are a problem for whole hours away. My horizon of care has shrunk to the next minutes.

"The bad news is—"

"Yes," she replies, cutting me off. "I see them."

Ahead of us, squarely between the White Cat and freedom, a handful of fusion drive tracks make a tangle across the void, loosely woven, but tight enough to form a wall of overlapping fields of fire—missiles, flak, railguns, anything they have. Already they are boosting hard away from us, trying to match velocity and stay ahead, maximize their time in firing range. One, two... hell, there's *six* of them.

That ain't good. Last time I counted, there was one of me, with one railgun I bashed together from a parts kit, and I don't like what the ammunition counter is telling me. But it's either that or drop back into the pursuing swarm, which is the same, only worse.

"Pixie, you all secured?" I ask. I seem to have settled on that instead of "Princess." "Put your mask on, I'm about to punch this thing hard."

"I'm ready," Miranda says, without complaints or preambles, and we both grunt in unison as I take us straight to five gravities as fast as the drive will ramp up. We can only take this for so long, even with the masks forcing an oxygen-rich mix into our lungs, but I mean to get the rest of the swarm as far behind me as I can before I hit that wave of screening craft.

"Marcus, can we—" gasps Miranda through compressed lungs.

"Punch through? Probably not. They're matching course."

"So what are you... are we... going to do?"

Good fucking question. They're already in firing range, at least a long-ish sort of firing range, with lots of shell flight time... but that margin of safety is shrinking by the second. I really do wish I had a clever move right now, but in space there's only so many directions we can go, and none are clear.

The only way out is through.

"I think it's time... for the universal solution... to every problem... ever."

"What's that?" she gasps. Her high-g breathing technique has gotten better.

"Violence."

I expect her to protest, push back, fight me, call me a big dumb ape who thinks with his muscles. I almost wish she would. But she doesn't say a word. And I haven't heard a peep out of Leela since I got in the chair.

I line up angles, mark targets, prioritize firing solutions. With a startled jolt, I notice there are extra tracks and angles lining up in my tactical plotter, marked in a hypothetical gray.

Leela.

I'm not sure she's trained on tactics, but super-fast physics and math, well, yeah. Some of her solutions are good, and I go for a mix, coding for a spread of five shells. Need a pause after that for the cooling system. Don't wanna melt the rails.

Steady the helm. Wait for it. Hold fast...

Now.

The *Cat* jolts as my first spread flies, and I vector thrust, hit the attitude jets hard, slew our tail around, changing directions, moving. No one can see those shells moving, arcing out toward their targets, but the magnetic pulse of the shots propagates out at the speed of light. Lines on the nav display start to curve as the closest pursuers react, go evasive, tumble across the sky.

Three... two... there it goes. On the display, the narrow tracklines of my SPAM shells blossom into expanding red cones of fragment spray. Still ten seconds out from their targets, but I'm not waiting up—I'm sending more shells. Never wait in a fight. Shoot, move, communicate. Anything else is a waste of time.

Not that I have anyone to communicate with.

I'm all alone out here, outnumbered fifty-plus to one. And if I can't punch through past these six fast, the rest will all be on me.

Wait a second. One of the dots just went out.

"Leela, we just lost a drive signature! Get on the telescopes and—"

"Already found them, sir." No creatively decorated avatar appears, just Leela's voice, all business here, and the 'sir' doesn't sound ironic. "Still active, but they're at low thrust, and I'm seeing some flickering. No radiation leaks that I can see."

"Lucky hit, maybe. Keep tracking them on visual, I'm not getting a good drive sig."

"Yessir, looks like they're limping off, but I'll keep an eye on."

On the nav plotter, the other five are forming up, coming at me. Already my displays are full of railgun pulse warnings, and I'm disabling audio alarms as fast as they come up. Yes, they're trying to kill me, I know, I know already.

Time to fight.

No song of glory this time, no symphony of flying skill. I'm not fancying myself Hendrix on the guitar or any other sort of poetic crap. The tungsten shrapnel is all too real, the stakes are all too high, and I'm all too fucking tired. I'm not laughing. This is not a game. I'm not enjoying my fucking self. I just have work to do.

I weave through my assailants, fast and unpredictable, ducking around the shots I know they'll make. We're all stuck into each other, dead close with little relative velocity to spare, even though the whole battlefield is sailing away from the plane of the ecliptic at about one percent lightspeed. It's a knife fight in an airlock, where quick savagery and aggression beats grace every time.

The magnetometer is flickering flux readings in the red, scores of tungsten shards ripping past us at close-shave distances. Indicators scream audible warnings as a chemical engine lights up... someone's fired a missile.

I track it, bide my time for five short seconds, then dive towards it head on and roll aside at the last moment, missing by mere kilometers, and Leela lets out a low whistle at the audacity of *that*. Seconds later, I lay rail fragments into it, and it cooks off, its high explosive chemical warhead spraying more shrapnel into the void.

Okay, whoever threw that, you just became my number one pet project. Now, which one are you?

There. Trailing out in front of the pack towards me. The textbook says I should bracket you with shells, try to cover any random move you might make, but you aren't going to go evasive, are you? You're going to back off, try to get more distance so I can't dodge the next missile so easily.

Let's put some shells on a slow fuse, open them up behind you.

I fire another salvo, watch, wait, thrashing madly in a spiral of semi-random evasions. Sure enough, he turns away, burning his drive for distance, then his drive signature... separates into two signal sources. Another missile launch?

No, three sources now. Four. Spectral signature of metal. Plasma containment failure, shedding big chunks of hull. No nuclear explosion, but if he's still even alive, he's all the way out of this fight.

Two down, four more screaming in on my tail. Cut thrust, pivot, and burn hard, maxing the drives for a punishing twenty seconds, legs straining, teeth clenched, don't dare take a breath lest I collapse my lungs.

Hold fast...

Then I'm waking up again, and the *Cat* is swinging around burning through a turn at two gravities. Leela's stepped in the moment I blacked out, carried out my plan or something close to it, anticipating me without a word. My four pursuers are lined up, in each other's way, scrambling to repair their formation. She got it right.

Scary clever. Maybe humans aren't obsolete yet, but someday all our kids are gonna be made of silicon and fullerene.

"Thanks," I whisper, firing more shells. "How's Miranda?"

"Still out. I think she's coming to. Better take it easy for a few minutes."

"Yeah, right, I'll just call a timeout, then?"

Leela doesn't answer, just fills my display with possible attacker trajectories. She's colored them by probability estimates. Wow. From somewhere deep in her possible lack of a soul, she's dredged something very like a top-notch battle computer.

We wheel and tumble in the sky, separating from our attackers, jockeying for position. The airlock stab-fight has opened up again, and we're dancing partners now, Leela and I, communicating faster than words through the medium of nav plotter, target systems, throttle, stick. Everything I do, she can do backwards and in heels, so long as I'm leading.

Together, we are grace under pressure. I've flown with this kind of skill before, but never this wealth of information, of insight. Where before I had to invent, now I have only to analyze, distinguish, choose.

This, I realize, is the future of warfare. Power. Precision. Insight. The marriage of machine and man. Autonet systems are impressive in many ways, but working with a true AI...

Different. Another world.

Fifty-two seconds later, a third torchship limps away, breached and trailing fire. The rest hang back, separating, hammering at me with high-dispersion rail shots. My sensors are going crazy, and the threat is real; dodging focus fire is a matter of anticipation, guesswork, and skill. But now they're filling the void with spread fragments and relying on luck.

And Lady Luck is not my biggest fan. The fucking whore.

Not going to play that game. Time to change the equation.

Fanning out, as a tactic, has weaknesses all its own. Finally, for the first time in the days... weeks... I don't know how long... since this chase started, there is no one, no drive signatures at all, directly between me and free, clean, empty space.

I punch the drives again, drilling for the opening, straight and fast. If I'm predictable for too long, they can intercept me with more concentrated fragment fire, but I don't mean to give them time. With just a few minutes of high thrust... I think the numbers work.

I *hope* the numbers work.

More craft from the pursuing swarm are after me now, almost on me, close behind my three attackers, in a blizzard of magnetic pulses as their railguns hammer at me, and finally, someone gets good or lucky, and I'm caught in a wash of fine shrapnel... tungsten rain on my hull, loud as thunder.

Miranda yelps with alarm, and I snarl in frustration. In my display subsystems flare and die—antennas, cameras, my primary long-range com laser, the number two telescope, one of my attitude thrusters. That's going to make life difficult, but it won't matter if I don't get out of this. Whoever fired this thing miscalculated, set his dispersion too fine, he must have—I'm not hearing any hull breach alarms, but I can't count on him making that mistake again.

Cut the drives, spin the *Cat*, punch the drives again, straining not to black out, cut, spin, thrust again. Back and forth, like one of my ancestors' wooden ships, close-hauled, tacking into the wind. Sawing at hostile space.

Change directions again.

Fire another spray of shells at my pursuers.

Hold fast. Try not to black out. Hold fast.

When I eventually do black out, twice, Leela takes over seamlessly, understanding my plan, riding the ragged edge, extracting every dribble of velocity she can without killing us.

High and steady acceleration is hard enough to bear. Pulses of it, accompanied by rapid spins, are like being beaten with a fist the size of your entire body. I think, from somewhere far away, I hear Miranda whimpering, and I don't blame her. I wish I could reach back, lay a hand on her, squeeze her shoulder to tell her to hang in there, to hold fast, but I can't. My arm must weigh almost as much as my whole body right now.

I think I've bitten my tongue or something, 'cause my mouth is full of the copper taste of blood. Gray mist keeps trying to swallow my vision, and the helm is mostly Leela's, now. We've switched roles, her steering, me laying in course plans, visualizations, insights, whenever I can breathe and think straight.

Forwards and in heels, now, with me whispering directions to her. God, what a pilot I'll make of you, with a little more training, if somehow we both manage to live. She's murmuring in my ear over the auditory nerve interface, encouraging, coaxing, I can't make out the words, but I don't think I'm meant to... it's the tone that matters.

Hold fast.

Almost free. Just one of them close on us now, but, whoever he is, he's masterful, smooth and sharp as diamond, always right where he needs to be, never making a mistake. Leela can't shake him. I'm pumping rounds into the sky, but the railgun won't move fast enough on its track, and somehow he's always behind me, in the shadow of my tail where I can't get a fire angle on him.

And he's not setting *his* fragment dispersion too small. Tungsten shards tear away another antenna, glancing blows scar my hull, and then the void is filled with a sparkling plume of metallic hydrogen dust, dozens of kilometers long, as one of the fuel tanks clustered behind the hold is ripped open like a packet of algae snacks. If there were any oxygen out there, we'd be nothing but an expanding fireball now.

Pretty soon, one of those shots will find our drive spindle, and we will be. Or it'll punch right through the bridge and tear us apart in a welter of flying blood.

This can't go on. But there's nothing for me to do here, no angle to take, no clever tricks to try. I just have to wait for him to make a mistake.

But he doesn't make mistakes. He's right there with me, every time.

Right there. With me.

Oh, wait.

*That's* his mistake, isn't it?

Not his flying. Not his tactics. He's seamless, almost as good as me. Hell, maybe better. But he's arrogant. Impatient. A predator caught up in chasing his prey. Forgetting that the goal is to capture and loot. A hunter. Not a pirate.

Pirates like me, we keep our eyes on the prize.

That's why he doesn't expect it, can't expect it, when I cut the engines, spin and burn back. Towards the swarm. Towards him.

Leela doesn't expect it, either, yelps something that sounds like a question as I take control, but I haven't the time or breath to explain. Just follow my lead, backwards again in those heels. You'll see it when you see it.

He sees it first, before Leela, fast, almost too fast. I can tell by the way he cuts velocity, casts about trying to reacquire me, but it's too late, far too late, the laws of physics won't bend for him no matter how smart and fast and experienced he may be.

And I'm back towards him, tumbling in freefall, spraying shells. Five of them. Seven. Ten. Gun temperatures in the red, warnings screaming, and just have to hope those rails are tougher than the spec makes them out to be, because I only have one shot at this.

He's too far ahead of his allies. He stayed with me too well, hung too tight on my tail, and now it's just him and me for a few precious seconds...

My railgun hammers, hammers. He twists and gyrates, understanding me now, fleeing as his prey turns at bay to savage him. I'm trying to guess his moves, but he's good, so fucking good, unbelievable, and Leela's trying to help, she's seen it now, understands.

But he's dodging both of us. Together. A swarm of tracks tick towards us on the plotter display. Running out of time. Who *is* this guy?

I'm going to have to turn and run again. Have to bug out.

Just a few more seconds.

Hold fast.

One more spray of shells. Bracket him, then turn, and—

Fireball.

He's so fucking close when his drive core goes up that I don't even need the telescopes... my external hull cameras catch the wash of actinic white light across our hull. An involuntary yell of triumph escapes my lips, or tries to, but it can't, not at four gravities. It just comes out as a strangled gurgle.

"Wow," says Leela's voice inside my head.

But I don't have time to answer. The electromagnetic pulse of his drive detonating is on us now, a wash of sensor static, eradicating drive signatures in the display, radio signals, everything.

Blindness. For us and everyone else.

Opportunity.

But I don't hide this time. I run.

I cut the engines, swing us around, and point our nose up, away from Sedna, away from the sun, away from our swarm of dogged pursuers, at those clean and unobstructed stars, that beautiful clear patch of sky.

Thirty seconds, maybe a minute, of total concealment is plenty of time to pick a vector and go. I pass the helm to Leela again, let her burn the drives, ride that ragged edge again, make the most of the time and space I've bought us.

She murmurs something to me, something about amazing again, but I'm pretty beat up already, and she's crushing us back in those seats without mercy, buying us every kilometer per second that she can, so I just clench my teeth around my oxygen mouthpiece, try to keep my lungs inflated, and hold fast.

It's ten minutes before she scales the drive back to a more sustainable pace. Or maybe ten hours. Ten months. Ten centuries. I can't tell. You'd think a man with a clock in his implants would know, but I haven't been able to pay attention to anything but pain.

The display tells me it was worth it, though. She's made the most of the window I tore for us. They're behind us now, still firing rail rounds, but we started accelerating full minutes before they did, and there's nothing they can do about the distance opening up. We're going faster, and so long as they don't out-accelerate us, we'll get further away all the time.

On a straight course at this punishing acceleration, there's little for me to do but lie back, close my eyes, focus on my breathing, and watch the traces of drive signatures flare bright and turn toward us, to wind time back and forth in simulated projection, and watch them gather behind us in a tapering cone.

We're going to have to scale back the thrust eventually, probably on cue from Miranda, who sounds recovered enough to monitor our vitals with a close eye. But we're free. And the longer we can hold out, the more distance we can put between us.

My brain begins to plan. If I start sending some emails now, there might still be a few favors I could call in, get us somewhere to run to. Burnell Station, maybe. The Kvitka Dredging Enterprise. Somewhere they don't care about the news, or at least don't spit at the sound of my name. Once we get these assholes further behind us, we might be able to buy ourselves some backup with promises of profit, or at least get enough people involved that no one will want to come after us, not when they might be firing the first shot in another Artifact War.

Assuming I haven't done that already.

# Chapter 24

# AND THE HORSE YOU RODE IN ON

I turn off the display. In the last twelve hours, nothing substantial has changed.

A whole train of ships strung out behind us for light-minutes, all ticking over at a single gravity of acceleration, just switching positions occasionally as someone finds a little fresh vigor and spurts ahead, forcing us to match, for a time. It's ridiculous, compared with how fast we were running earlier, but we're all that beaten down.

I'm reminded of an old Terran joke about a day so hot, that a rancher saw a coyote chasing a rabbit, and they were both walking.

At least wherever that warship is, it hasn't fired any more missiles, EMP or otherwise. I don't know which of the drive signatures chasing us is them, but I'm guessing they're far enough back to be beyond the range of a missile's fuel store. Or their captain's saving them, waiting for a better opportunity. No way to tell.

Apart from the occasional railgun flare, there's nothing to see.

My thoughts are interrupted by a warning chime, steadily increasing in volume over the *White Cat's* intercom system. Drive cutout alert. Brace for zero gravity.

"Again? Why?"

Miranda's voice over my neural lace is emphatic, exasperated, but hard to make out all the same. There's something in the background. Water?

"Because people are shooting at us. Duuuuuhhhhh," Leela snaps at her creator. They're talking more now, but if Miranda expected her resentments to just blow over, I suspect she's in for disappointment.

"Yes, I know, but course changes *every five minutes*?"

"Random intervals, actually. And random angles. If they predict our moves, they'll fill that piece of sky with SPAM fragments. I presume you want to stick to the same number of holes in your meat carcass that you have now?"

That's when the drive, and the gravity, cut out, and Miranda's answer is nothing but choking and sputtering sounds.

You don't wanna lose gravity in the shower.

Have fun, Princess. I'm gonna stay right here in this acceleration chair. Three... two... The *Cat* shudders as it spins on four axes at once, accompanied by a fresh round of splashing and gurgling.

I shouldn't be laughing at her, I suppose, but prolonged tension hasn't brought out the best in either of us. It's hard to relax, hard to not think about all those tiny shards of tungsten carbide, silently tearing through the void, too fast to dodge, too small to see...

Death without warning. At any moment. Lightning from a clear sky.

The sputtering dies away as gravity cuts in again.

"Water sticks to things in zero gravity," Miranda complains.

I can't help but chuckle. "Yes. Yes it does. You're supposed to turn it off and wait when you hear the zero grav warning."

"Oh, *now* he tells me. Pffah. I think I swallowed some soap."

"Heh. Sorry. I had no idea you were in the shower. Soap's probably an improvement on your cooking anyway."

"Hush, you. I'm a damn good cook when I have something to work with, instead of the processed crap you keep aboard this thing. Don't you know how bad that stuff is for you? They had a *worldwide* obesity epidemic in the early twenty-first century because of processed food, you know."

"Okay, Doctor Fussbudget, I'll just nip out to the local farmer's market and—"

Thunder. Thunder and the scream of tortured metal. The hull rings, the lights flicker, and something slaps the *White Cat*, hard, jolting us.

Then gravity is gone again. Over the neural link, I can hear Miranda trying not to drown, with some moderate success, but that noise takes a back seat to the distant and familiar howl.

Of escaping air.

"Marcus, what the hell? You didn't even give me a *warning* this time! And what's that nois—"

"**Alert. Magnetic containment breach. Subcritical thermal event. Fusion reaction core ejected.**"

"**Alert. Pressure alarm in MAIN REACTOR SERVICE. Possible breach detected.**"

"Oh," Miranda breathes.

I scroll through virtual displays, check pressure readings, and I do not like what I see.

"Looks like we just lost thrust. Leela, did anyone have a chance to scope us? No, never mind, assume they did. We need to change course *now*. Give us max chemical thrust on a new vector, thirty seconds burn with the attitude thrusters. And fire the railgun a few times to boost us along. It's not much, but let's try not to let them put more rounds in us."

"Aye, Captain. But we're getting short on railgun ammunition."

"Marcus, should I be suiting up?" asks Miranda.

"Nah, it's a breach, not a blowout. I can patch it. Just get dried off. I'll get down there and see what the damage is."

The cargo hold *howls*.

A typical Orbital might never hear that sound, or only once or twice in his life if he does, even if he's a Belter. But we all know it.

We've all seen the recordings from Vesta Station when United Nations warships sprayed the central hab cylinders with railgun fire—heavy slug rounds.

We know the sound. We remember.

Vacuum breach.

Oh, there's no immediate hard vacuum on the cargo side of the access airlock, when I get through. Only a Flatlander who's seen too many movies would expect that. There's no gale-force winds ripping through the hold, no vast sucking monster waiting to hurl me into the void. With only one atmosphere of pressure difference, between us and the void, that ain't gonna happen except in movies. The gust of air around me is gentle until it hits hull punctures, and squeezes through them, howling and whistling.

It's not gonna kill anyone. That's not how these things work.

At least not right away.

That's why one hundred and seventy-four thousand Vestans had plenty of time to gasp as the air grew thin and frigid, to choke on vacuum, spewing blood into the void as their lung tissue tore, as the surface of their eyeballs boiled and froze at once.

Old people. Women. Little kids.

While those UN warships stood by at anchor, listening to the screams on the radio, picking off the escaping ships and lifeboats with rail fire and point defense cannons.

And they call themselves "Peacekeepers." Fuck them. They deserved exactly what Erik Nyberg gave them. Them and their whole stinking planet.

There's no "Peacekeeper" ships hovering outside the *White Cat*, of course, but what's inside is bad news enough for anyone. Above me, the drive spindle is motionless, dark, and surrounded by... is that water?

Yes, water.

A spiral column of tiny round droplets is pouring from the spindle, churning in the zero gravity and turbulent air, swirling up towards... there. Near the cargo bay doors, a waterfall in reverse, mist sucked upwards in a howl of escaping atmosphere. I fly between cargo racks, hand-over-hand, damp spray lashing me, soaking my shirt and sweatpants.

I see it now.

A handful of thumb-sized holes where a cluster of tungsten grit tore through the hull near the cargo bay doors, shredding the rim of the crane track. Must have been a ricochet that hit the drive. I'm not seeing or hearing any sort of exit hole on the other side, although I'm not sure I could tell if there were. This close, it's loud as the end of the worlds. No point in cutting in the radio; Miranda could never hear me over the rush of air and water.

I'm worried about that drive spindle, but the puncture takes first priority—the hold is losing atmosphere, the drive cooling system is losing water, those jets of escaping air are starting to spin the *Cat*, and a glittering reflective plume of frozen air and water won't do any favors for our ability to hide from enemy telescopes.

Hopefully, the drive shielding isn't breached, and I'm not soaking up a lethal dose of radiation right now. If I am, I'm already dead and just don't know it yet. Nothing to be done but hope.

Clinging to the shredded crane tracks, I slap on single-direction flex laminate patch plates, spray three-second breach foam. I'm soaked now, and the damp seems to be inhibiting the foam seal, but, gradually, the column of water stops streaming toward me and begins to scatter as I cut off the leaks, and the noise fades from a scream to a whisper. There's a ragged hole through the massive cargo bay door hinge that's too complex, too twisted and stretched, for patches. I spray as much foam as I can, exhaust the canister, but it's not neat... we're still leaking a trickle of air.

Good enough for now. If we live through this, I'm going to have to shut the airlock, evacuate the hold, weld permanent patches, maybe replace that hinge if I have time, but I've got other concerns at the moment.

"Miranda? Where are you?"

"Up on the bridge with Leela. How bad is it?"

"I've got us mostly sealed up, but something that came through must've hit the reactor coolant lines; it's totally shut down, and I'm up to my eyeballs in floating water droplets here. I don't know if anything else on the drive was hit, but at least the main containment field emitters held up okay."

"How do you know that?"

"Because I'm not a cloud of ten-thousand-degree plasma spread across several cubic kilometers of space. How about you? Do you need a moment to check?"

"Oh. Okay, I get your point. Can it be fixed?"

"Dunno, haven't gotten in there yet. Maybe, unless something's hit the actual Starlight unit. No tech manuals for those. Rumor has it Starlight rigs them to blow if they're tampered with."

"Really?"

"No idea. Not a long line of people eager to find out. Leela, what's the swarm doing?"

Leela appears in front of me, circling droplets spinning right through her image. She doesn't seem to notice... I don't think the hold has good camera coverage, so she may be somewhat blind here.

"No one's made any sharp course adjustments yet," she says. "But they're coming at us pretty quick now that we've stopped accelerating. The closest ones could do a flyby in a few hours, although it'll take them a lot longer if they want to slow down and match velocities. Whatever you're going to do, do it fast."

"Already on my way," I say, caroming off racks towards the dark and silent spindle, "but I'm not gonna make any promises. Even if it's just coolant lines, that's an eight-hour fix at least, maybe longer—oh shit."

"What?"

"It's not the lines."

"What? What is it? I can't *see* anything up there!"

Railgun shards are just broken bits of metallic tungsten, without any sort of explosive payload, but even the tiniest piece of dense metal moving at a thousand kilometers per second doesn't need one. This one tore through the vacuum-foam alloy of the hull far too fast to dump much energy, but after that, when it slammed into the primary coolant manifold and hit the dense, incompressible liquid water within—

The five centimeter thick aluminum is shredded outwards, opened like the petals of a rose, must have been a massive explosion of superheated steam. What the explosion didn't do, the rapid cooling from the escaping water finished. Cracked and broken chunks of aluminum drift around the spindle.

"Marcus, what is it?" Miranda asks.

"Coolant manifold. I think it took a direct hit. Looks like the heat deep-fried some of the nearby wiring harness, but that's the least of our problems compared to that manifold being junked."

"Can you fix it?"

"Can I *fix* it? Pixie, it's fucking *shredded*. I'd have to fabricate something to replace it. And before you ask, that's not a quick fix, *if* I can do it at all. Which I don't guarantee."

"Oh," she says, her voice suddenly small. "So what do we do now?"

And that's when it occurs to me that I haven't the faintest idea.

# Chapter 25
# SUCKER PUNCH

We've congregated in the observation deck, which has the highest and most comfortable gravity now that I've spun up the ship again.

"So in other words, we're floating dead in space, everyone who is chasing us is getting exact updates on our position from the Snark about every five minutes or so, and it's going to take you a long time to fix the drive?" Miranda asks, peering at the shared 3-D map of the swarm, as if she had the skills to make any sense of it. Maybe by this time she does.

"Almost right. We're actually gliding along at almost one percent of lightspeed relative to the sun. But we can't stop or turn without the drive. And, yes, everyone knows where we are. They can catch up to us pretty quick, but only if they want to fly right past us at speed. If they want to match velocity and board, that'll take much longer."

"And to fix the drive? How long?"

"That's the part I don't know. It's not just a step-by-step repair procedure. I have to design something to patch the cooling system with what I have."

"Can we run the drive without cooling?"

"Sure, for maybe a moment or two before it either slags itself or blows the fuck up and we all die. It's possible I can pulse it every once in a while to charge the main batteries a bit, but we can't fly."

I can't help but crack a smile. It's ridiculous. The universe just keeps conspiring to fuck us over in new and exciting ways.

"At least it would be quick. And really spectacular," I say with a chuckle.

"You're crazy, Marcus. Don't you even take anything seriously?"

"Nah, that would be depressing."

She rolls her eyes at me. But maybe with a hint of a smile.

"Pixie, we're outta good moves here. We just have to make the bad ones and appreciate the irony."

Wait a minute.

"Unless..."

"Unless what?"

"Unless, and I never thought I'd say this, we can call your family to bail us out?"

Miranda winces, hard, squeezing her eyes shut. "Can we please not?" she says, in a small voice.

"Yeah, I'm guessing there's some history there—"

"You have *no* idea."

"—but it's probably better than being dead, kayno?"

"Can I think about that and get back to you? Seriously, though, Marcus, it won't work. We're about twelve light-hours from Mars, and there would be another twelve hours for them to send any message back. It would all be over by then.

I mean, yes, if the shooting stops and this all goes to arbitration, then being... me... will probably help. But out here, I don't think so."

"What if we get on the radio, try and cut some sort of deal with the people who *are* out here? Would your name carry any weight with them?"

"Perhaps. But that would be a... delicate... negotiation," says Miranda. "It looks like there are a lot of different groups out here. Anyone we didn't come to an agreement with would have an incentive to make a grab for us. We could touch off another Artifact War."

"Pixie, we made several big nuclear fireballs back there, out of somebody's relatives. I think we already crossed that item off our to-do list."

"But that was self-defense!" says Leela.

"Everyone who fights a war claims they're defending themselves. Might even be true. It's still a war, and we're the smallest faction holding the biggest, shiniest prize."

"Well, there's an idea," says Miranda. "War. Play them off against each other. Maybe try to conduct an auction. Stall for time."

I give her a searching look, but her expression is guileless, devoid of any complexity at all.

"Really?"

"Hey, you grew up out here, but I grew up in boardrooms. I'm good with people."

"If you have blackmail material on them?"

"Are you still sore about that? That's different. You didn't matter. Now you do," she says, with a wave of her hand. "Anyway, it's worth a shot."

"Yeah, whatever."

She's probably right. But I'm not in the mood to pat her on the back. I "didn't matter?" Why should I care what she thinks of me? Stuck-up little... oh, never mind.

I turn to Leela, who is studying the starmap with a giant cartoon magnifying glass as big as she is.

"Leela, if we jettison the Snark and try to hide... no, wait, that's no good. We have to assume it will find some way to keep broadcasting."

Leela folds the magnifying glass up to the size of a walnut, and stows it in a pocket. "Yeah," she says. "If we could find it, so could they. Besides, they probably have us on lidar by now, and the fact that we're sitting on something valuable may be the only thing preventing the next missile from being a nuke."

"However," she says, as a giant archaic filament light bulb appears over her head, "I think I have a better idea."

"Yeah?"

"Railgun. Looking at some of these vector plots, I think that if some of the closer ones try to match courses, I can hit them pretty easily. If we hit the first one to try, I think the others will have to scatter, or at least not come in straight. Could buy us a few less enemies and a lot more time."

"Okay, that's probably worth a try as well, although I'd prefer we try talking before shooting. We don't have a lot of railgun ammo left."

"Okay," Miranda says, all business, "looks like the plan is clear enough. You work on fixing the drive, I get on the phone and try to negotiate or at least stall, and Leela lines up the railgun in case that doesn't work."

She sounds very sure of herself.

"Pixie, remember when you said you were the captain now? You do realize that didn't stick, right?"

"You can flog me for mutiny later," she chirps, flashing a grin at me. "I'm just *assuming* that My Lord Captain would like to assign the technician to damage control, the businesswoman to negotiations, and the supercomputer to aiming the hyper-precision weapons system. Is that acceptable, High-Lord-Captain-Sir-Your Highness?"

Did she just make another *joke*? She's sure as hell smiling. I'm not entirely sure I'm comfortable with this new Miranda. But at least we're not fighting. Not with each other, anyway.

Great. Imminent death is all it takes to get us to play nice. Great start to a lifelong business relationship. Of course, about now, "lifelong" might be just enough time for her to finish a cup of coffee.

"Okay, okay... no bloody respect. But, yeah, let's get you on the horn. Most of this is going to be on *you*. That coolant manifold wasn't just a set of pipes. It had all sorts of sensors and flow-control pump circuitry. Stuff I can't rebuild here. But if I bodge something together, maybe we can cool the drive enough to not immediately go boom, if we don't push it too hard."

"With all those people chasing us?"

"Uh, we'll run away very slowly while firing a big gun behind us. Relax, that's only Plan B. Plan A is you."

"Plan A is me bluffing with no cards, Marcus."

"Hey, it was your idea."

"That doesn't mean I like it, it just means I don't have a better one."

"Okay, then let's get going," I say, turning to head for the ladder.

"Wait. Marcus, can you come here for a moment?" Miranda's voice sounds... odd. Tentative. I turn back, and she's staring up at me, blinking those giant cartoon eyes.

"We're not getting out of this, are we?" she asks. Worried, but calm. Resigned, maybe.

I kneel down so we're on the same level, and put both hands on her shoulders. "We're sure as hell gonna try. If you can't fight, you run. And if you can't run..."

"You walk," she says. "You said that before. Except we can't."

"So we crawl. I'm not giving up. I'm stubborn. You may have noticed that once or twice."

"Yes," she says, taking a deep breath. "Maybe it's starting to rub off on me."

She grips both my forearms with her hands and squeezes briefly. Our eyes lock. "Good luck," she says.

"You, too."

And then I'm really gone, up the ladder, my brain already in the machine shop, imagining the connections the manifold had to make... maybe if I bend some spare conduit pipe, weld it into a central reservoir... but how would I get equal flow rates?

Ball valves? Just test and manually adjust them 'til distribution is even? But what would that do to throughput?

Damn. Lotta variables. Not sure anyone's jury-rigged a cooling system for a nuclear reactor before.

That's when Leela appears, still in an old-fashioned hoopskirt getup. She seems to be flying by holding onto some sort of lacy parasol, and she's shrunk the whole presentation to about a quarter size to fit into the shaft beside me.

"Told you," she says.

"Told me what?" My brain is still full of pipes.

"She *likes* you."

"Nonsense. We're just united by an outside threat. You may have forgotten what it's like, but us biological humans have stress hormones and things. We tend to lean on each other in a crisis. Besides, what do you care? I thought you hated her?"

Her face crinkles in a thoughtful expression under the lacy veil of her fancy hat. "I dunno about *hate* her. Maybe just *mad at her*. Anyway, I like *you*. And you like her. And she likes you. What's the problem?"

"The problem is that she's a sociopath. And she's only being flirty because she's trying to get on my good side. You heard her. I didn't matter. Now I do."

That still stings. Why does that sting? Never mind. No time to navel-gaze.

"I'm kinda surprised you fell for it," I tell her. "I, at least, am still well aware that she's kinda evil."

"Well, maybe? But I thought you agreed that you *both* weren't good people?"

"What? Leela! That was a private conversation. Do you listen to literally everything that happens on this ship?"

Suddenly it starts raining on Leela's avatar, and the parasol is soaked.

"Um..." she stammers, looking sheepish, "...sort of. A little bit."

"A little bit?"

"You're not understanding me. It's not like that. Look, I have sub-processes, okay? They monitor everything. I sort of can't *not* listen. But they don't always tell me. I mean, the rest of me. And if they do, and it's private, I... delete it."

Suddenly something makes sense.

"So when Miranda was acting crazy after her first spacewalk, and I asked you to play it back, and you refused...?"

"I *couldn't* do it. I literally have no idea what happened back there. It's gone. I just know you got mad about something, and told me to *forget it*. So I did. I erased about ten minutes of memory. I don't have any idea what she did, or what you did, or anything."

"Oh."

There's a minute or two of silence as I reach the machine shop level, and start to rummage around behind the CNC mill for where I stashed the fragments of the primary coolant manifold. I think I stashed it in here. I think.

Hmmm. Socket wrench set. Impact driver. Bunch of spring clamps. Oh, there it is.

When I stand up, Leela's still beside me, full sized now, parasol vanished.

Being rained on. Looking sad.

"Leela," I say, slowly, choosing my words, "you're allowed to have opinions of your own, you know. Just because I have a normal emotional reaction when you do something inappropriate doesn't mean you have to delete pieces of your brain. From now on, don't erase anything unless *you* think it was private, or if I specifically tell you to, okay?"

"But you did!"

"It was an expression! I had no idea you could even *do* that! You don't have to do it again. Unless it's a privacy thing, in which case I'll ask."

It stops raining on her, and her face brightens up. "Oh. Okay, thanks."

"Now, I need you to run along and leave me alone, okay? I've got work to do, and unlike you, I can't think about two things at once. Play matchmaker when we're not about to be shot, stet?"

She rolls her eyes. "Okaaay, Dad. Bye."

Not sure what to make of that, but I have work to do, and no idea how I'm even going to start. I stare at the mess of bent and shattered aluminum, of burnt and trailing wires, of melted plastic circuit housings. This could take days we don't have.

C'mon, Miranda. Bail our asses out of this.

But she doesn't.

It's four solid hours of silence and work, of ideas sketched out and discarded, before I get any notion how things are going. Miranda doesn't volunteer and I don't ask. There's nothing to be gained by distracting each other.

Then the whole ship jolts, not a vibration, but a singular strong shove. A familiar sensation. Someone, either Leela, or Miranda with Leela's guidance, has fired the railgun.

Negotiations, evidently, have broken down.

I don't ask, not at first. What would be the point? Doesn't change anything. But that railgun just keeps firing.

"Leela?" I ask, at a whisper, which doesn't make any sense at all, but instinct never does.

"Yeah?"

She pops in, a tiny figure sitting on the scaffold around the drive core, watching me take measurements.

"You're firing a lot. I take it things didn't work out so good?"

"Yeah, actually, they kinda did. Turns out we're all over the news, and the whole solar system knows what we're up to. They even knew there was a Builder artifact. So when Miranda broadcast pictures and video, and called for a cease fire, we started getting bids. Big ones."

"I thought we weren't planning to sell?"

"Yeah, but she didn't tell them that. Just stalled for time, kept tightbeaming different ships, and conducting a whole blind auction type thing."

"Sounds good. So why are we shooting?"

"Turns out if the stakes are high enough, people who get outbid try other means."

"Oh. Damn. How many are coming after us?"

"Can't really tell yet. I'm holding them at bay for now, but if this keeps up, more people are probably going to figure smashing and grabbing is cheaper than paying."

"Fuck. Okay, I'll work as fast as I can."

"Do you want to talk to Miranda?"

"No, don't distract her. Wouldn't help anything."

I bend back to my work. More hours pass, punctuated by the occasional thump of the gun.

I'm in the machine shop, annealing the ends of some pipes I've finished bending to shape, when Miranda's voice breaks through my concentration.

"Ah... Marcus? I don't suppose there's any chance you'll be finished soon?"

"Well, I've worked out a sort of arrangement of pipes that will divide the coolant flow semi-evenly, but the drive computer won't be able to control it or send it to hotspots. It won't handle much, and we might have to shut it down every so often, but we'll be able to limp along. Best I can do, I'm afraid."

"Yes, Marcus, I'm sure it's brilliant, but when?"

"Soon. Shouldn't take more than about eight hours."

"Oh," she says. And that's all she says. And the sound in her voice... it's not a good sound.

"I take it that I don't have eight hours. Why don't I have eight hours? And, come to think of it, why have we stopped shooting? Did you make some sort of settlement? But then why do I need to finish in less than—"

Miranda sighs in my ear. "Marcus, if you keep asking questions nonstop, I can't answer any."

"Right. Sorry."

"We're out of ammunition."

"What? How did you manage to waste it all just brushing them back?"

Leela's voice comes in. "Eight armed torchships against a single stationary railgun? Given those odds, I'm content with three—no, wait, make that four—kills."

"Oh, so things got serious. Right. So how much time do I have?"

"One of them is almost on us. Three hours, maybe."

Three hours. Forever to wait, but not long enough to fix, well, much of anything, really. If it can be fixed in under three hours, you're probably using "fix" as a euphemism for "hit it with a wrench and hope." And when you're fixing a nuclear reactor built with exotic alien super-tech that no one really understands to begin with, wrench-swinging grease monkeys need not apply.

I'm not going to be able to fix the drive. Can't run.

No railgun ammunition left. Can't shoot.

"Marcus?"

"Hold on. Thinking..."

Railgun ammunition...

"Leela, check my thinking here. A railgun can theoretically throw any kinda ferrous metal object, so long as it's the right size, stet?"

"Uh, yeah. Theoretically."

"Except these railguns are made for precisely manufactured ammunition."

"If you say so. Actually, here... let me read the manual while we're talking."

"Showoff. Anyway, you can rewrite software pretty fast, yes?"

"Parts of me can. They sort of do it all the time, as part of... well, let's just go with 'yes.'"

"Could you loosen up the railgun code parameters so it'll fire out-of-spec shells?"

"Oh!" Leela sounds genuinely surprised. Which means she probably was, a few milliseconds ago. "You're going to load it with scrap steel!"

"Yep."

"Yes, I think so. I just finished the tech manuals, and I'm reading the code now."

"Okay, so if I turn some bar stock down on the lathe, make it symmetrical enough so it can be spin-stabilized..."

"Right with you. Working on the code now. I... ah... think we'll only get one shot at this."

"You mean we *may* get one shot at this. If that load is off center enough to hit one of the rails, we get zero shots at this, with lots of exciting hull damage as a bonus prize."

"Marcus is cracking jokes," says Miranda. "That means things are bad, right? That usually means things are bad."

"Well, let's see, we're outnumbered dozens to one, flying through space with no way to maneuver other than small chemical attitude thrusters, and we have no ammunition left for our single weapon. Yes, Miranda, things are bad. So if you'll excuse me, I'm going to stop fabricating an improvised Belter coolant manifold and start fabricating improvised Belter railgun slugs."

"Okay, okay... uh... what should I do?"

"I don't know, keep talking, maybe? Get somebody else to throw a few shots at them?"

"So, perform a miracle."

"Hey, I performed a buncha miracles just to get us this far. So, yeah, Pixie, it's kinda your turn."

\/

"Okay, images are coming up now. There's what we're dealing with."

Miranda finishes wrestling her braids under the hood of her vacsuit, and peers at the display hanging in the air over the bridge. The image is still fuzzy, with some angles reconstructed by the computer systems, but what I see looks familiar indeed, a cylindrical torchship, capped at one end by a cargo lock interface, and at other by a brilliant drive flame, pointed at us, decelerating to intercept."

"Looks a bit like the *White Cat*, except without the cargo hold," she says.

"Yeah, it's a standard kind of design for mining craft. They're like tugboats—designed to push loads. Don't know what it was doing out here, but I don't think this is any sort of picket ship."

She nods slowly. "Maybe I don't know what to look for, but I don't see anything that looks like a railgun. Or any other weapons."

"Could just not be visible from this angle. Wouldn't count on anything we see here. Resolution's only so good. Won't be long now. They're about five hundred kilometers out. Leela, we prepped to go?"

Her avatar appears in what looks like an old-fashioned naval uniform, and snaps me off a sharp, probably ironic, salute.

"Yessir, the gun should be ready to fire. We're at about two rotations per minute, so we'll have to keep it moving, but we're all prepped other than that."

"No," I say, shaking my head. "Keep the track unpowered until the last minute. I wanna look like we're floating dead in space, right up until we fire. If they see signs of life before that, they might try to soften us up first. We're going to time our shot with our spin, and move the gun as little as we can."

A glance shoots around the room, bounces back and forth between all three of us. Leela's smiling. I know she can feel worry, but maybe fear is different for her. No glands. No adrenaline.

I think. That's how it works, right? I don't know.

Miranda looks determined, but her knuckles are just a bit white where they grip the console.

"Okay," she says, "makes sense. So... we just wait?"

"Yeah, shouldn't be long."

I minimize the telescope image, punch up a course projection map, and wave my hand through it.

"I think they'll wait until they're pointing past us to make the final deceleration burn. Otherwise, they wouldn't be able to see us through their own drive flame. I don't think they wanna come in blind."

"How long?"

"About fifteen minutes," Leela says, before I can answer. "Gun is charged and hot. I'll leave the final firing solution and trigger to you. First Law of Robotics, and all."

I cock an eyebrow at her. "Didn't you just take down four ships full of people?"

She steeples her hands in a beatific posture and casts her eyes upwards to where a golden halo has suddenly appeared above her head. A moment later, her avatar changes altogether, to what I can only describe as a different... art style? Renaissance. Glowing colors. Elaborate light and shadow.

"Me? I'm a sweet angelic little giiiiiirrrrl. I just aimed. Miranda pulled the trigger. I'm letting you meat people do your own killing."

I'm not sure if she's joking.

"Okay, okay. Everyone with a physical body, seal your vacsuit, have a seat, get strapped in. We don't have thrust, but if this goes wrong, things could get real bumpy real quick."

We try to talk, pass the time as the ship looms closer, but trivial chat just seems to echo and fall flat before the enormity of what we're facing, and we shy away from anything more serious.

Leela is silent as a tomb, her avatar vanished, her attention who knows where?

Finally, her voice reappears, disembodied. "They're inside six kilometers," she says.

"Okay, final firing solution is up, tracking, aaaand..."

I clench my hand around the stick, pull back slightly, rotate and pitch a bit, lining the projection reticle up with the image of the craft's primary drive assembly...

...press back on the smooth, flat surface of the trigger...

"...firing."

Click.

Nothing.

And my display lights up with error messages. Ammunition overmass. No feed. Low capacitance warning. Irrationally, I squeeze the trigger once more, twice.

Nothing.

"Leela!"

"I see it! The gun's rigged to fire! You should be good to go."

"I'm not. I'm getting a facefull of error messages here!"

"That's not right, I fixed all the—oh. Shit."

"What?"

"Mother *fucker*," she snarls. So much for her saintly little halo.

"I messed up. The gun's good to go. But the computer doesn't think it is. There's a whole bunch of safety checks I didn't find. Wrong section of code."

"Can you disable them?" Miranda asks.

"Already working on it. Don't know how long. If you have a plan B, now would be the time."

"Did you see me working out a plan B?"

"Well, then start!"

Shit.

I check the displays again. Five klicks out. Four and a half. Coming in hot, aligning with chemical thrust and braking with fusion, same time, smooth. He's not going to overshoot at all... he's just going to seat-of-the-pants the whole thing, throttle and stick and lots of chutzpah.

So, he's a Belter, then. He's pretty good at this, and he knows it.

You think you're slick as fullerene, don't you, pal? Just give me a drive repair and some ammunition, and leave your swarm of friends behind, and we'll *dance*. But kiss your sweet old momma goodbye first, and hand her some money to buy that black dress.

But no coffin, 'cause they won't ever find enough pieces to have a corpse of you.

Of course, my drive does not miraculously repair itself and an old-fashioned dogfight, my fantasy duel in the sky, does not ensue. Instead, I sit here, stuck in the desert, waiting for the vulture to circle down. Vultures don't fight duels of honor.

Well, time for plan B indeed.

Two and a half clicks. Telescope. He's heeling over fast. Two clicks. He's opening his cargo bay doors...

"Leela! Gun! For fuck's sake!"

"Working on it! I cannae break th' law o' physics, Capt'n!" For some bizarre reason, she's trying out a Scottish accent. No time to wonder what that's all about.

Fifteen hundred meters. And out the open bay doors on the front...

Cargo crane. Can't be sure from this distance, but it looks like a General Electric, one of the big ship-towing models, claw the size of a Martian house, with an aramid-and-doped-fullerene cable as thick as a man's waist. He grabs us with that, we're not going anywhere, not without him along for the ride.

Plan B was dodge with the chemical thrusters so they couldn't board until Leela got the gun up. So much for plan B.

Nine hundred meters.

Well, I've got thirty seconds, maybe, to come up plan C. Spin the *Cat* to make her difficult to grab? Try to blind them with the lidar array?

Stand out on the hull and make rude gestures?

No time.

Incoming grapple. "Brace for impact!" I yell, somewhat redundantly, 'cause Miranda's strapped in, and Leela—well, she's bolted to the cargo rack.

I'm counting the seconds, three... two... one... and the hull rings, loud as a gunshot, a cacophony of scraping and creaking metal. I can barely turn my head enough to catch Miranda out of the corner of my eye, but she's clearly got her hands clamped over her ears.

Oh, yeah. She's not a Belter, never worked in vacuum. Not reason to have her eardrums replaced. She'll suffer from that if there's shooting. For a moment I think we should find her some hearing protection.

Stupid. Doesn't matter now. Somewhere outside the hull, that cable snaps tight and *screams*. I'm jolted sideways, for an instant, then slammed the other way, and then the world is chaos, as down becomes *every* direction, each for a fraction of a second.

This is no simple, slow, controlled cargo bundle capture. Whoever that pilot is, he's got balls of tungsten steel to even try such a high-speed grab. The *Cat* and the intruder bounce and haul against each other, two masses spinning around a common center, straining at the high-tech tether that binds us together. I've tucked my chin into my chest, neck flexed, every muscle in my body tight. I can't hear Miranda—she's behind a wall of noise that swallows everything.

How in the screaming blue fuck is that cable holding together? How has the grapple not torn free? How have we not simply ripped the crane off, or torn through the 'Cat's hull?

I can't imagine the forces involved, can't even think, really, can only hold on as "down" tries to decide which direction it's going to be. My display is a symphony of flashing red, and alarms are screaming, but they're nothing against the howl of tortured metal.

I can't tell if it's been seconds or minutes. I can't think. At least I know our guests aren't moving, either. They're smaller, they'll be shaken worse than we are. And no one get can get out an airlock in this storm, not without being bludgeoned, crushed, and folded into something compact and easy to carry.

Is it finally dying down, just a bit?

I hold fast.

It's an eternity before gravity reaches a consensus, with us orbiting, cable-held, around a common center. We're still swinging back and forth, but "up" has decided it's going to be towards one corner of the bridge ceiling.

Could be worse. We're canted sharply, almost completely sideways, but at least we're not upside-down. Even the loud creaking is blessed silence compared to a moment ago.

"Gun is up!" barks Leela's voice in my head.

"Too late," Miranda groans. So at least she's alive, if still pretty shook up and voidsick. "They've grappled us. We're not getting off that without the main drive."

"Yeah, I think we all noticed. I'm taking the shot anyway. Try to do some damage, slow them up. Is the gun in position?"

"Wasn't," says Leela. "I'm moving it on the track now. Twenty-three seconds."

"What? I said not to move it!"

"What are they gonna do, fly away? If they have us caught, we have them caught, too! Get on the damn gun!"

She's right. I grab the stick and pull up the display. At this distance, the front of the other craft is a wall. I back off the magnification, scan around the front end... sensor booms, cargo grapple, airlocks... crane. Maybe if I aim for that, I can cut us loose. Under the right corner of the reticle, a section of hull is painted, a cartoon of a grinning roughneck in an armored vacsuit giving a big thumbs-up gesture, over meter-high letters: "*Tuf Voyaging.*" I wonder idly if the misspelling is intentional.

Never mind. Line up the shot. We're swinging, hard, and the crane heaves back and forth in my view, as the railgun, and the *Cat's* software, try to compensate.

"Leela," I mutter, "this had better fucking work."

She doesn't answer. I press the trigger back, hold it right at the wall, wait for the view to swing back... lead it just a fraction... Now.

The trigger just clicks. A jolt...

...And then the whole front of *Tuf Voyaging* bursts open, writhes, twists itself into an abstract sculpture of tattered metal, spinning shards, and spraying atmosphere. How can this much destruction play out in dead silence? Something in my brain rebels at the sensory mismatch. I somehow expect to be able to hear the noise, even muffled, through two hundred meters of vacuum.

I can't, of course. There's nothing. Just a spreading fog of escaped atmosphere, water and coolant jetting into the void and instantly boiling to cold steam, and then I duck involuntarily, squeezing into my seat as a torn section of structural beam comes pinwheeling right into my face, hits me.

No, not me, of course. The number seven camera I was looking through. My vision's full of static, and I have to switch cameras twice more before I find one that hasn't suffered a similar fate. Outside, the debris cloud is spreading... oxygen and nitrogen fog, boiling and freezing at the same time. Wall panels. Furniture. A piece of diamond laminate port window, torn like so much tissue paper by impact and explosive decompression. A shredded boot. A bobblehead doll of a grinning puppet, curiously intact, a figure from an old children's show I can't quite remember.

Ronnie... Romper? Something like that, anyway.

And spinning away to the left of my field of view, what looks like a body... not vacsuited. Not moving. Part of the leg is missing, a stump trailing blood.

I don't follow it. I'm scanning the wreckage. *Tuf Voyaging* spins and thrashes like a released balloon, with little more air to vent, but plenty of leftover momentum, bouncing at the end of the tow cable. I can hear it creaking through the hull.

I can't see the crane, or what's left of it, but we're still attached. Still stuck.

"Ho-lee crap, Marcus," says Leela. "That actually worked. I'm seeing a lot of what I think is vaporized blood on the spectrometer. I don't think anyone is alive in there, and if they are, I doubt there's much they can still do. Can we get that cable cut?"

I'm cycling through external cameras, trying to find the electromagnet, the claw, or whatever it is that the corpse of *Tuf Voyaging* is holding onto us with, but I've lost too many. It's hiding somewhere in the static.

"Not quite yet. I'm gonna need a couple minutes to stabilize us, and we'd better give all that junk and shrapnel a few minutes to stop flying around. We'll also need to get some explosive charges ready—can't just saw through if it's under tension, or it'll whip around. Miranda, those charges are stored in the—"

"Marcus," Miranda whispers.

"—hold, directly forward of the inner airlock, in a cabinet labeled—"

"Marcus!"

"What?"

"Look!"

Whatever she's seen, it's urgent. I switch cameras again, and I see it, too.

Long streaks of vapor, leaving the wrecking in a spray of angles. White, nebulous, throwing back the harsh light of our 'floods. Curving towards the *White Cat.*

EVA thruster trails.

I count six suits, maybe seven, but there's a chance I haven't seen them all. Too much gas, too many floating shreds of hull insulation and the detritus of shipboard life. But I can see the rifles. The shotguns. A heavy electric angle grinder. Gas cylinders and a torch.

They're coming for us. Coming to cut into our shell and scrape the meat out.

This isn't over yet.

# Chapter 26
## TRUST

"You keep that thing *loaded*? Like, with the clip in?"

Miranda's staring at my GR-15 Anvil like it's a live snake. Hasn't this girl ever seen a rifle before?

"Magazine. 'Clip' is something you hold your hair with. And, yes, I do. Unloaded rifle's not much good for anything," I say, with what would be a shrug, if I weren't trying to struggle into my vest.

This is not easy when I'm leaning back against what used to be the floor but is now more like thirty degrees of slanting wall, while standing on what was a vertical bulkhead. A thirty-degree slope doesn't sound like a lot until you're standing on it. Then suddenly it's a fucking cliff face.

"Here, help me with this thing."

Miranda fumbles with the straps, twining one leg around the small of my back and an arm around my shoulders to hold herself in place. Her vulpine little face is inches from mine, her breath warm on my cheek.

"Feels like there's steel plates in it?"

"Ceramic and nanofiber laminate, but yeah. No, across there. Tight. That's better."

I fumble for the sling of my rifle.

"Leela, have you worked out how to get us straight yet?"

"About now, you two look pretty straight already... Never mind. No can do. We're just spinning on the tow cable like it's a giant space station arm, and they've got us around the midsection. No matter how I fire the thrusters, we're just going to swing back sideways."

"Great. Guess I'm fighting like this, then. At least the gravity's pretty low."

"Marcus," Miranda breathes, almost whispers, still hanging onto one shoulder strap lest we slide apart, "how are we going to beat them? I mean, there's like seven of them at least, aren't there? This isn't..."

"An action movie? Yeah, I know."

"Have you ever even done this before?"

"Yeah."

I don't mention that "done this before" means "assuming VR counts." Or zero-g contests against asteroid crew guys with paint marker rounds.

"Look," I say, "I know the odds are shit, it is what it is. I don't think we can surrender. They weren't exactly the talkative negotiating types on the radio, and that's before we killed a metric fuckton of their best friends and shipmates. So unless you got a better idea..."

"I don't suppose now would be a good time to mention that two Ares Elite model 5000N Personal Protection Drones would be really useful in this situation?"

She gives me a sad little smile, like for once, she doesn't want to fight. Gods, she's beautiful. Those eyes...

I must be slightly giddy. Maybe it's cause we're about to die.

"Yeah, we shoulda spent a little less time and effort trying to kill each other. But that's a regret, not a plan."

"Is there time to rig some of those mining charges you mentioned?"

Oooh. Clever girl.

"Good thought, but no. They're strong enough to tear a hole in the hull. I'd have to cut them down, and there's no time. I'm going to have to just try to win this one the old fashioned way."

She gives me a look, a long searching look that says... I don't know what it says. I haven't a clue. I can't read this girl at all. I only know she's pondering... something.

"We," she says.

"What?"

"We. *We* are going to try to win this one the old fashioned way. Give me that pistol."

She's holding a hand out. It's steady as a docking anchor, and she's staring me right in the eye. Funny, I can tell now when her pupils are dilated. The size of her eyes used to throw me off.

She's nuts. And incredibly brave. And did I mention nuts?

"Prin... Miranda, that's... ah... I appreciate the gesture, but you're being silly. Have you ever even fired a gun before?"

"No. I'll figure it out. What do you expect me to do, hide?"

"Yes."

"That's not going to happen, Marcus. My life is on the line, here, too. I don't think these guys are going to play nice with me either, just because I'm a girl. I know you think I'm a spoiled brat, but that doesn't mean I'm just going to—"

"No. Not happening. No way."

"Oh, come *on*," she sighs, exasperated. "Really?"

She cocks her head to one side and peers at me.

"It was true, what you said, then, wasn't it?" she asks. "You really don't trust me. After all we've been through, you really don't. What is it you think I'm going to *do*? Shoot you in the back? Screw up and get us both killed?"

I don't quite know how to answer. I'm not sure that's it at all... do I trust her? I'd have to be insane. I've seen what she's capable of. But other times she seems almost... sweet. And I don't know how to predict it.

"We don't have much time. They're coming. How can I get you to trust me for once? Oh, hell. Look, give me your hands."

"What?" What is she getting at?

"C'mon, just humor me. I'm trying to make a point here," she says, plucking at my forearms. She clearly can't lift them unless I let her, so I do... though I don't know where she is going with this.

Carefully, pausing only briefly to untangle us from my rifle sling, she raises both my hands to her face. No, not to her face. Slightly lower.

To her throat.

"Miranda? What are you doing?"

"Just...play along, okay? Please. I want to show you something. Put your hands around my neck."

I don't want to. Or maybe I do, but I'm afraid to. Afraid of what I did last time. Afraid of how I still want power over her, which means I'm still afraid... of her. Of how she ties my brain in knots. Of how I'm never sure what she's thinking. I don't know.

I just freeze. For a moment. Looking at her.

But the tilt of her mouth says "stop it already," and her eyes say "it's okay, really"... and so I do as she asks. Her skin is small and soft and warm under my fingers, and she lays both hands on my forearms, and gives them a gentle squeeze.

"You're really strong," she says. "You could snap my neck like a twig right now."

What the hell? Is she trying to make me feel guilty about what I did? If she is, it's kinda working. But I'm not going to tell her that.

"Miranda... you're doing that thing again. The thing where you just start doing crazy stuff and never explain it. Are you going to start tearing your clothes off? Or something equally weird?"

"No, shhh... relax. I'm trying to make a point. A lot of the stuff you said to me the other day was right, but you were wrong about one thing. You said we couldn't trust each other, but that's not right. It's not *each other*. It's just *you*. That's what I'm trying to show you. I can't prove to you that you can trust me.

"But I can prove to you that *I* trust *you*."

She tilts her head back, and lifts her chin, exposing her slender white throat even more. Almost instinctively, I want to pull back... it's too raw, too intimate, it feels... wrong. Like something I shouldn't like.

Her eyes are closed. I feel... shaky.

"You could hurt me right now," she whispers. "You could hurt me really badly. There wouldn't be a thing I could do to stop you. But I don't need to stop you. Because I know you wouldn't. I've known since you came back for me. You risked your life for mine. Did you think I didn't notice?

"I feel *safe* like this now, okay? Your hands are... really warm. It's actually... kinda nice."

Using vulnerability as a weapon. Wow. That's slick. I can't decide if she's sincere, or the most talented evil manipulative liar in the worlds. Is this the real Miranda, or another mask?

Her face looks so... calm. But if she feels as safe as she says, why can I feel her pulse in her throat, fluttering like a trapped bird?

"Ah... okay, Pixie. This is still kinda weird. I mean, I get what you're trying to say. It's not totally insane. For once.

"But it's not just about what you *would* do. It's about what you *can* do. You never learned to shoot, you have no idea how to use cover, I don't have a set of spare armor, and it wouldn't fit you if I did. You'd just get killed, and trying to stop that would actually make my job harder. Believe me, I *love* to see you willing to risk your own neck of other people's for once in your life, but you can't do this."

"Yeah, well, maybe there are some things women can do that men can't."

Oh, for fuck's sake.

"Now is not the time for a girl power moment, Miranda."

Her eyes go wide, distant and kind of hurt. Her hands tighten on my forearms, and I realize that I'm still holding her around the neck. I remove them quickly.

"Listen, you impossibly thick, knuckle-dragging ape-creature, I'm not trying to prove I'm tough. I've been in exactly *one* fight in my life, and you saw how that went for me.

"I'm saying I have a plan. And I'm not happy about that, because you have no clue, not one, just how degrading this is going to be, but it's all I've got. So are you going to waste more time arguing... or you going to shut your stubborn mouth and actually listen?"

I open my mouth to say... I don't know... something, but suddenly, I'm weightless, and the hull resonates with a monstrous creaking of the tow cable going slack. Then the wall slaps up against my back armor plate, and Miranda slaps up against the front one, and Leela's voice sings out...

"Hey, guys, gravity's gonna be a little wonky for a bit. Got a couple of them on the hull now, so I'm try to shake them off or at least if I can slow them down. Hold on tight."

Except there's not much to hold onto except we each other. We bounce around the room, reaching out with legs and arms to fend off walls, ceilings, overhead lockers, light fixtures. Miranda wraps her arms around me, grips my vest by the drag straps, pinning the rifle between us.

Finally, we settle back to the floor—well, the wall—with a bump and cacophony of metallic creaking and groaning from outside the hull.

"That didn't work so well." says Leela. "There's still three of them at the far airlock, or at least there were thirty seconds ago, when they shot out the camera. They'll start cutting in any moment if they haven't already. And I'll bet the others are circling back."

"Thanks, Leela. We'll be quick. Okay, Miranda," I say, with a sigh, "explain it to me in ape-creature speak. What's your plan?"

And so she tells me.

"Really?"

"Yeah."

"But I thought you hated to be—"

"I do. So what?"

"Think you can make it work?"

"Just watch me."

"Okay. But if we're going to do this, you follow my lead. If I croak frog, you jump, without stopping to ask how high. Stet?"

"Okay, yes, stet. You're in charge. Now can we—"

I reach back and, with a sound of tearing velcro, I detach my holster, and offer her the handgun.

They're cutting through the airlock. A waterfall of glowing sparks drifts down from the door handle. With the *White Cat* tipped partially sideways, swung like a pendulum on the end of the tow cable, the observation deck airlock is tipped on its side, midway up the curve of what used to be the wall, halfway up the circle.

In any real gravity, this would be a problem. That curved slope would be unclimbable, and stepping out of the lock would mean a serious fall. But the *White Cat's* mutual spin with *Tuf Voyaging* is slow, almost a drift, and not only do the breachers have a panoramic view of the tipped observation deck, they have an overwatch firing position they can sweep the room from, then drift down at leisure.

So much for ambushing them when they emerge. We'd be fish in a barrel, with fire coming from an elevated angle, no way to get a shot without exposing ourselves.

And with their friends no doubt coming through the cargo bay, and an entire ad-hoc fleet coming in fast, there's no time to wait them out. Others will be coming.

The sparks stop falling—they're through. There's no rush of escaping air. They must have sealed the outer lock door. They must not mean to evacuate the ship just yet. Better keep our suits sealed for now, though.

For a moment, I hope they'll be stupid, and just come straight out, give me a shot at them, but no such luck. I don't even see muzzles poking out of the airlock.

"Don't see anyone," says a voice like a handful of gravel thrown on a coffin lid. "Maybe a lot of 'em were hurt when the whole thing went sideways."

"Can't count on it. We're gonna have to clear the whole ship, deck by deck. Shoot anyone who isn't the girl. Fan out."

That's when Miranda speaks up. "Stop!" she yells. "Wait! Don't shoot! I surrender!"

There's a note of panic in her voice, high-pitched even for her. Frightened, she sounds like a little girl.

The first voice answers. "All right, throw out your weapon and raise both hands above your head, then come out *slowly*."

"Please! I don't *have* any weapons." She squeaks, raising both hands above the gear locker she was hiding behind, down at the lowest point of what used to be the wall of diamond laminate windows, and is now a sort of floor.

The pistol I gave her is tucked well out of sight between the skin-tight fiber of her vacsuit, and the life support pack with its tanks and instrumentation gear. She rises slowly, her arms stretched high, giving whoever it is in that airlock a good, long look at the nanofabric hugging the curves of her body.

"Okay, stand right the fuck there. Do *not* move."

"Okay, okay, just please, *please*, don't hurt me!"

A rifle barrel emerges from the entrance to the lock, followed by a tall, slender Belter form wearing some kind of tac gear, dark-haired guy with a thin rodent face like a weasel. He's half-stumbling, half-sliding down that curved wall.

I'm watching for his barrel to dip, watching for more muzzles. Please let these guys be as stupid as Miranda thinks they are.

Yes, there's a second barrel, and a third, followed by two more bodies, a big, heavyset dude with a shaved head, and another one with a nose like a beak. The last one's openly leering, a stereotype of a goon. Fucking carrion eater.

They can't be professionals. Different gear on each man, no discipline, no caution. Just some crew who happened to be out here. They're pretty fucking scruffy-looking to be tooling around in a fusion drive ship, but I don't have time to wonder. I can't let them get too close to her.

"Who else is aboard?" asks the bald one. His voice matches the one giving orders. Maybe he's the one in charge?

"Just the pilot and a couple of technicians! We don't have any weapons!"

Miranda's good at lying. Who woulda guessed?

"Where are they?"

"The bridge, I think! Or hiding somewhere. I don't know!"

"Okay, calm down. Sardo, take her into... ah... custody. Hit her if she makes any moves."

"Sure, boss," gloats bird-beak. Vulture. "Wouldn't mind hittin' that."

"Fun later," Cueball snarls. "We get the fuckin' ship secure first."

Yeah, pal. Keep talking, keep walking, keep thinking with your tiny little shrimp dick. Just a little bit more...

I notice Miranda's face is carefully, very carefully, still. Showing nothing but wide-eyed fear. It's only because I've studied that face for weeks, screamed at it, locked eyes with it, seen it in my dreams, that I notice the little muscle twitching in her jaw.

Weasel is eyeing her up and down, too, now. Grins all around, like they smell fear. Like they're into that. Like they're excited by it. Not Cueball, though. He's just cold, all business. Doesn't care. Doesn't mean he wouldn't. He just wouldn't care how she felt about it. No sadism. No glee.

She's just a piece of meat to him.

"Cover that ladder," he says, to Weasel, who stops grinning and drops to one knee, pointing his weapon at the entrance to the access shaft that runs the length of the ship, the obvious place for anyone to come in who wants to crash the party.

That's why I'm not there.

"Okay, we have the girl," Cueball says... to no one in particular, talking into some sort of com pickup I can't see. "Anyone else you find in here is kill-on-sight. Let's get this over with."

"No! Please! No! They're just... they work for me!"

Miranda's playing this role to the hilt, and Cueball, just reacts, letting his rifle hang on the sling, stepping forward with a hand raised, maybe to hit her. I don't know. What I do know is that right now no weapons are pointed anywhere near her, or me, or anywhere that actually matters.

And that's when Miranda drops to the "floor," just splatters herself prone.

Gives me a clear shot.

Those lowered weapons, that clear shot are the whole point, here. They are all I needed. I pull my face away from the gap in the door of the storage compartment, high up what is now the wall, the door I've been holding almost-closed. The carbine is wedged in front of me, and there's no way to come out without slamming metal on metal, but I don't care about noise now.

I'm committed to the plan. Speed is life.

And I'm out, half leaping and half falling, down towards the three, caught in the moment of swaggering forward, eager to put their grubby hands on their prize, like slugs on a rose, caught with their faces between sneering, gloating anticipation, and the very beginnings of shocked dismay.

They didn't think to look up. No one ever thinks to look *up*.

The carbine optic is jacked into my cybernetic eye, projecting a virtual targeting beam across my field of vision. I don't need to get it all the way to my eye, I just push the muzzle out, get a good cheek weld, and the targeting beam crosses Weasel's chest, as I press the trigger twice, three times, quick as I can.

It's a damn good thing I've had the standard eardrum replacement that vacuum workers get— out of a short barrel, in an enclosed space, the 6.8mm caseless Special Purpose Round is *loud*. Weasel doesn't pitch backward or even forward, I can't see any blood, but he sags and crumples, straight down, and I'm not waiting for him to hit the floor before I'm centering on my second target. Vulture.

That's one.

Damn. He's wearing plates—a spray of ceramic-laminate shards sprays out from this chest, like it's in slow motion. His beady little eyes fix on me, not even registering the pain, and he's bringing up that bullpup shotgun. I don't wait to soak the recoil and bring the muzzle back down, I just squeeze the trigger the moment it resets. Hammer pair.

Impact. A crimson arterial spray jets from his throat, flies in a low-gravity arc as he twists, still trying to bring his weapon to bear, unaware that he's a dead man.

That's two.

That wild fire is still dangerous, but there's nothing I can do about it... I have Cueball to deal with, and the floor is coming up to meet me, in slow motion, but massive and picking up speed.

I try to find Cueball with the muzzle before I hit the deck, but it's too late... I just have to roll and let my chest plate take the impact, get my finger clear of the trigger guard and up on the frame so I don't let a round off somewhere random...

... Pain. Not in my chest but in one knee as it impacts, first, then my mouth as an incisor snags a bit of my tongue. Blood tastes like copper.

I don't transition into a smooth, acrobatic dive roll, and come up shooting, action hero style. I've face-planted on the deck with an undignified splat, but only moments have passed, and I'm still in this fight.

Roll over. Get on my back. Try to sort the tumbling chaos of the world, find Cueball, hit him before he shakes off whatever residual shock Miranda's ruse and my sudden appearance has bought us.

Where is he?

There.

Too late.

Right below his shorn scalp, his focused eyes, the grin on the big square jaw, is a foreshortened muzzle, and I'm staring down the small dark hole at the end.

And Godzilla punches me in the chest as the back face of my ceramic plate deforms under multiple round strikes. I've been punched in training by ranked amateur boxers, hit with a chair once in a rowdy Belter nightclub on Ganymede, took a stray rock in my faceplate when someone packed a splitting charge too tight. This is worse.

Air leaves my lungs in a rush. I hope my ribs are intact... no way to tell.

I'm gasping, trying to pull air with a diaphragm that's reeling in shock, trying to scoot away behind whatever cover I can find, away from the next impact that I know is coming, the one that will break the weakened plate, shatter my ribs, shred my lungs.

Hold on.

His gunshots weren't a series of sharp cracks, but an extended whoop... fully automatic, caseless, with a lightened bolt carrier running the fire rate as fast as it can go.

The idiot is actually holding down the trigger and spraying. He's walked a burst across my armored chest, and right up the wall. I have a moment or two while he's trying get control again.

And I use it jam the stock against my ruined chest plate, no sight picture, no cheek weld, just center the targeting beam and slap the trigger over and over again, not even a smooth press, but it's enough.

Cueball's grin vanishes along with his jaw and most of his lower face, and he's thrashing with a high pitched keening sound like nothing human, spraying rounds across deckplates, bulkheads, furniture, for just a moment before the magazine runs dry. Shredded foam padding catapults into the air, and turns pink in the flying droplets of Vulture's blood. Cueball's bleeding into the cabin, too, flailing and screeching, and it's getting hard to see with all this mess flying around... nothing settles quickly in low gravity.

I'm still trying to suck back air into my lungs when there's another gunshot.

Where did that...

Oh. It's Miranda. She's stepped over a fallen body, through the blizzard of trash, and put a single bullet in Cueball's head. She's not even holding the pistol right, just one-handing it at full extension, but at less than two meters she could hardly have missed. Blood and what looks like brains are spattered over the handgun and her vacsuit, but she doesn't flinch, just takes another step to where Vulture is kneeling trying to put pressure on his throat, and just plugs him, execution style, no flinch or hesitation at all.

Cold blooded. No... wait. Not cold. Surgeon. She's already seen a lot of blood. She's hardened to this.

But maybe cold, too, I reflect as I clamber to my feet, holding onto a deck chair, lungs working again. She just kicked Vulture's body. I don't think she liked those remarks about "hitting that" too much.

I'm loosening my plate carrier when she turns towards me, mopping blood from her faceplate.

"Are you okay?"

"Yeah, just took a pretty good hit on the armor there. Here, help me get this off... plate's wrecked."

She steps forward.

"Hey, hey, hey, careful! Finger off the trigger unless you're looking down the sights. And watch your muzzle! Trigger's a lot lighter after the first shot."

She lowers the pistol carefully, and helps me, one-handed, with the velcro straps. My chest must be a mass of bruises, but it's worlds better once the crumpled backface of the plate isn't pressing on it.

"Here," I say to her, "take this. The back plate's still good. Get in a corner, hunker down, hold it over you like a shield, and shoot anyone who comes in view. I'm gonna try to deal with the others."

I look for an earpiece on the one intact head - Weasel's - but no such luck. They must be using neural lace for comms. No chance of me listening in. And the rest will know their comrades are dead now.

"Hey!"

Miranda's looking at me, through a faceplate smeared with blood, with a sort of combination of grin and expectant pout. She's shaking her head a bit, like she's trying to clear it. Her ears are probably ringing something fierce.

"What?"

"You're welcome!"

"I'm... what?"

"I *told* you it would work!"

Oh. She's gloating. We're floating dead in space, there's more armed goons wandering the ship, gods alone know where or how many, and she wants a pat on the head because her plan worked. So much for 'this will be really degrading and I don't want to do it.'

"Yes, good job. Now get down and don't do anything stupid, just *stay alive*."

"But I can—"

"NOW!"

She hunkers down into her shoulders and gives me a sheepish little smile.

"Yessir."

I can't tell if she being sarcastic or not, but she wedges herself into a corner between a bulkhead and a row of chairs, pausing only to retrieve the Weasel's unfired MP70. Good thought.

I pull my magazine, check it. Light, but not empty. I stow it, replace it with a fresh one.

I know the smart thing to do would be start sealing doors, find a choke point, barricade it and play defense—*use* that fatal funnel to my advantage. But I can't afford to wait. They have numbers, and secure communications, and all the time in the world. Better to move quick, keep the momentum going, use the homefield advantage. They don't necessarily know there's only two of us.

I still don't like these odds.

# Chapter 27
## Agni Pariksha

I clamber up the steep side of what used to be the ceiling, grab the rim of the opening to the access shaft. Damn. I'm going to have to hold on with one hand, pull myself up, look, try to prop the rifle on something solid with the other.

I don't like this. There's no cover in that shaft, just what's now a meter-plus wide horizontal crawlspace running the length of the ship. I never *designed* the *White Cat* to be defensible from the inside. If someone's already covering the length of that shaft from the cargo airlock, and I stick my head up, that's it. Brace your handguard on something solid, and it's practically impossible to miss at fifty yards.

Going through a door that someone's already dialed in on is suicide. Skill doesn't enter into it. Just a matter of reaction times.

Damn it, I should have prepared for this. We had *weeks* of idle downtime, while we flew towards Sedna, and I could have worked out what to do. Put up some barricades. Rigged traps with mining explosives. But who the hell ever expects to get into a small-arms gunfight in *space*? Distances here are in light-seconds. Who the hell ever heard of two hostile forces ending up inside the same fucking *hull*?

Absurd. But here we are.

And I never even taught Miranda to shoot. Bloody hell. Would I have even been willing to put a gun in her hand?

No trust. Not a team. Not working together. That's going to get us killed.

And here I am, stuck, hanging by one hand in low gravity, unwilling to poke my head out in case there's a rifle pointed at the only place I go through. Or multiple rifles. Hell, I don't even know how many of these guys there are.

"Leela," I whisper.

Silence.

"Leela!"

Her voice comes in as a whisper as well, although I don't see the need. "Yeah, sorry, just dealing with a little problem. What's up, boss?"

"Can you tell me how many of these guys boarded us?" I ask.

"Ten. The three you got, three on the hull, and two more in engineering. One of them is watching the access tunnel."

Damn. A shiver runs through me. Good thing I didn't stick my head up. He'd have split it into a fucking canoe. So what the hell do I do now? Hold here and shoot anyone who comes around the corner?

Tactically, that's exactly what I should do. Defenders can just sit and watch doorways. I wanna be the defender.

But I don't have that luxury. The five remaining assholes on my ship can just sit there in a stalemate until—

Wait a second. Five?

"Uh, Leela... I may be only a meat golem, but I'm pretty sure ten minus three isn't three plus two."

"Yeah, there were two that didn't make it through the hold."

"*Were?*"

"Remember the little problem I mentioned? I still have control of the cargo crane. It's... ah... kind of a mess over there, so if you go in there later, bring a mop. And a bucket."

Something in me winces. Those cranes are designed to move thirty ton cargo containers, and move them fast. If Leela overrode their human-avoidance software... ouch. Bring a bucket, indeed.

So much for the First Law of Robotics. Hope she's okay with that.

"Alright, tell me if the ones in engineering are moving."

"Oh, I can do better than that. Let me show you a magic trick," she says, and suddenly the wall becomes... transparent?

I can see them through the walls.

I can see them *through the walls.*

What the...?

There's two of them, all right, a short, bearded Flatlander with some sort of AR carbine, and a heavyset man with a pump shotgun, clearly over seven feet tall. One's fixed in position, the other climbing slowly, checking some compartment or other, picked out through walls in full, almost luminous color, sort of an... art style... like Leela's...

Oh. Like Leela's avatar. She's using the avatar interface to transfer images from Miranda's little webcams. Good thing I left all but one of those up.

"Oooh. Nice trick. I'm going to hold here for these two. Keep an eye on the other three outside, let me know if they move."

"Already are. Looks like they're headed for the observation deck airlock from opposite sides."

Where Miranda is hiding. Damn. Should've had her move before hunkering down. Too late now... but, no, scratch that, there's nowhere for her to go but out the deck airlock, or up this shaft.

"Warn her. I've only got a few—"

"Already warned," says Miranda's voice on the link. "I can see them. Going to try to get a vantage point in cover, and watch the airlock. This is *really* cool, Leela. Thank you."

Leela doesn't reply, and I don't have time to pay attention... Tank and Dwarf look like they've finished their sweep of engineering, and are ready to move on the bridge. Tank, true to his name, appears to have a vacsuit that's not skintight, but incorporates some kind of angled plating instead. I think it's armor. Have to try for the face. Good thing he's first, still covering the shaft. Any move they make will have to start with him.

There. Both of them are shifting, And I can see Dwarf pulling himself up to the access shaft, his rifle slung as he climbs, bounding in low gravity. Tank's going to have to shift his shotgun, let go with one hand to get up... there's no room to stand in the shaft now that it's horizontal. The choices are either trundle forward at some sort of crouching duck-waddle, or crawl.

I tense myself to move, waiting to see which one Tank will choose. I can't see where he's looking—Leela has replaced his face with a blur. Must not have the right camera angle. Dwarf is preparing to cover the shaft from behind him, but that won't do any good until Tank gets out of the way...

They'll be vulnerable for a moment and they know it.

"Warnoc!"

The voice is male, deep, rough, from ahead of me. Must be Tank. I can't see Dwarf's lips moving. Bastard knows my name.

"Warnoc! Give it up! There's over twenty of us and two of you!"

Liar.

"We won't hurt you or the girl. We just want the AI and the artifact!"

Liar again.

But also well-informed. Whatever's going on with that ad-hoc fleet, they're getting good information from somewhere. The tightbeam chatter must be thick and fast. Are they sharing information? Are there more boarders on the way?

"Warnoc! Don't be stupid! You have no chance!"

That's what you think, pal. You don't know I can see you through the wall. You don't know I can pick exactly the right moment to pop up, brace my magazine on the deck, and plant a round in your face. Just start moving, pal.

Any time now.

The moment comes. Tank chooses duck-walk, and, just for the moment I need, that shotgun goes on the bottom floor of the access shaft.

Tank sees me come up, pushing fast in low gravity, sees me leveling my carbine, tries to bring his shotgun up again, then makes a rookie mistake that, ironically, almost saves him.

He brings his face to the shotgun stock, not the stock to his face, and his head dips down, out of the green circle of my reticle.

Unfortunately for him, I'm now braced on the lip of the shaft, and it's easy enough to bring the stock up slightly, aiming down, holding just over to compensate for short range.

I fire three times, but I think it's the first one that takes him in head. The second and third impacts shatter this facemask, and the skull behind it. He convulses for a moment, then slumps to the floor, blood sloshing in low-gravity ripples.

Superimposed on the wall, the image of Dwarf stops dead and drops back down, spraying suppressing fire. It sparks off the ladder, and the top of the shaft, nowhere near me. He doesn't have an angle. I seize the moment to pull myself forward, just a bit, and go prone in the shaft, elbows tucked in, magazine on the deck.

Yes. I have you now, you bastard. Just try poking your ugly head up again. Please.

"Hey, Warnoc! You think you're gonna stop us that way? All that shit means is bigger shares for the rest of us when we fucking kill you!"

It's shriller now, with an anxious tone he can't quite hide, but the voice is the same—it was Dwarf talking after all. He's back under the shaft entrance at engineering, hunkered down and braced the way I was, not willing to stick anything out. He's going to try to wait for me to come to him.

"Marcus?"

I almost jump out of my skin as Miranda's voice enters my brain, loud.

"They're at the airlock. I tried to shut it again, but the door lock's all melted. What's going on up there?"

"I'm not an unreasonable man, Warnoc! But my patience won't last forever! You killed a lot of people today, and for what? To keep something that wasn't yours to begin with? Come on. Come out and we'll talk about this!"

Nice try, pal. I know you're running out of friends. Don't worry. I'll arrange a reunion.

He still hasn't moved. I risk a glance behind me. There's an image of Miranda, hunkering down behind something that Leela isn't showing me, in the observation deck, holding Weasel's machine pistol. She hasn't folded the stock out.

The three boarders are breaching the airlock outer door, muzzles sweeping to cover, cycling the lock... looks like they'll be in observation in a few moments.

"That was a good trick you pulled with the girl, Warnoc! Clever! How'd you get her to go along with it?"

His voice is a little too infused with forced joviality. If he wanted me to come to him, he'd be trying to make me mad. Trying to bait me. Dwarf doesn't want to attack. Dwarf wants to get me talking, delay me while his men come up behind.

I haven't got much time.

I've got to get back and help Miranda. But I don't dare leave him behind me. Or rush in in some foolish charge.

"Marcus," says Leela. "what if I kill the lights? You've got that infrared eye—"

"No good," I whisper. "He'll have a flashlight on his rifle. Pretty much everyone does. Miranda, they open that door, you just fire a burst from that MP at the lock. Don't expose yourself. You don't have to hit anything, just keep their heads down."

"Or did the girl put you up to this, Warnoc? You know who she is, right? She's a Martian heiress! The Old Man's granddaughter, or something. What's she paying you? Is it enough to die for? You put down your weapon, turn her over to us, we'll give you a full share!"

You said you didn't want the girl. Can't even keep your story straight. Just keep talking, pal. Keep talking and don't move. You don't know I can see you.

I just need to get you to fire a little more. Okay, steady...

I creep forward along corrugated steel of what used to be the shaft wall, inching forward on my belly, knees, and elbows, rifle as steady as I can keep it. Amazing how hard it is to push forward when it's not a bunch of us bros goofing off with paint marker rounds. Even though I can see where he is, know he's too far off the shaft to get a clear shot, still something in me braces for that grisly impact.

For the feel of a bullet slamming into flesh.

It doesn't come, of course. Creep forward, just a little more...

Fuck. Can't believe I used to think this was *fun*. It's fucking not. But maybe I can still use a trick I learned when it was.

I squeeze off a single round into the outside wall of the shaft, just opposite where Dwarf is crouched.

A "semi-frangible" round isn't just a cheap lump of gold like most bullets. It's a metalloid composite designed to break up on contact, to go through body armor but not the hull plating of your station. This means one hell of an impact spark, and what feels like a spray of hot sand, hitting everyone close by.

Dwarf reacts with a startled jump, and, sure enough, a flurry of unaimed fire at what little of the shaft he can see.

Comfort shooting.

In a firefight, when you're scared, it feels *good* to shoot. Makes you feel safer. Makes you feel like you're doing something. Takes practice and discipline to learn to wait until you have a target in your sights. To learn how to shoot to hit, not just shoot to shoot. Dwarf may be not be a total novice, but he's wound pretty tight, and he's wasting ammo on fear control.

I crawl forward again, rolling sideways to pass the opening to the bridge. Dwarf is just three or four meters away, huddled against what used to be the floor of the engineering level. Must be standing on something. Bolted down furniture? I can't see his surroundings.

Almost in position. Let's see how many times I can work this trick... I squeeze another round, and am rewarded with another spray of fire... nowhere near me, but something hot stings my neck. Fragment hit. I can feel the slow trickle of a bead of blood.

In a real fight, you can't hear a bolt lock back on an empty magazine, not after all those gunshots, but Leela has him dead to rights on the nearest camera, and I *see* him pull the mag, not dropping it, just holding it in his hand, trying to do a quiet switch.

I launch myself up and forward, standing bent over in the shaft, crane around the doorway. Reaching my muzzle to just where I know he'll be. I center his ruddy surprised face in the reticle, and I know I've got him, got him cold, and I squeeze a single shot.

Nothing happens to that face. How did I miss?

He drops the rifle and he's reaching for his belt, must be for a sidearm...

I slap the trigger again and again, but that face doesn't shatter, I can't see an impact...

He collapses downward, onto the gear cabinet he was standing on, his beard dripping, soaked with blood.

Idiot. I'm an idiot. So excited I forgot to hold over for the short range. I've been shredding his throat. He's not even twitching now, not thrashing as he bleeds out—I must have cut the spine. His frantic eyes meet mine, for a moment, his lips move, trying to say something, but it's just a wet gurgle, and his face sags and goes dead.

"Marcus? Marcus?"

Miranda sounds frantic. Has she heard the shots? Is she in a fight herself? As if in answer, there's a shot from down the corridor behind me. One. A pistol. It's my Sphinx. She's run the MP70 dry.

"Miranda. You're clear behind. Get to the access shaft!"

I'm scrambling to turn around.

"They're *shooting* at me!" Her voice cuts off with a squeal as a rattle of fire echoes from that direction.

"You're clear behind! Spray some suppressing fire and fucking move your cute little ass!"

I crawl as fast as I can, not worrying about covering the end of the shaft. I can see them. I know where they are. None of the three have an angle on me, so I can fucking hustle.

A pistol shot. Two more. And suddenly the lights go out, all of them... Leela's thinking quick. I barely have time to cut in my thermal vision, as a figure picked out in temperature gradient lines comes barreling straight down at me, at a run, shoulders hunched.

Blood surges in my ears, but my brain kicks in before I even move to shoulder my carbine. The figure is so tiny it can only be Miranda... only she could stand straight up in here, just a slight bend to avoid the ladder.

I roll behind it to avoid her, give her a gentle touch on the back of the thigh as she runs blind past me, just to let her know I'm there. She doesn't startle or break step... Leela must be showing her a recent location.

Ahead of me, the observation deck lights up again with focused beams. Lights on weapons. No matter. Leela's bought her a second or two to get clear, and that's all she needed. I can't even hear her running footsteps anymore... she's moved that fast.

I hope to fuck she's not running with her finger on the trigger like a total novice, but I don't hear any accidental shots from that direction, and the three of them ahead of me are a bigger problem. I can't see them.

"Leela?"

"Sorry. Cameras are visible light only. I can't see them in the dark."

"So turn them back on!"

She does, and they're right there, scattered, converging on the end of the tunnel. Three, all the same height, maybe seven feet or so, wildly decorated Belter vacsuits, looks like AK-style rifles. All alike. Moving rapidly, climbing... I think they're trying chase Miranda.

Fuck me, are they actually triplets?

I plant myself prone next to the entrance to medbay.

Okay, assholes, you're Tweedledee, Tweedledumb, and... ah.. Tweedledumber. For about thirty seconds before I fucking kill you.

Invade my home, will you?

Shoot at me, will you?

Try to steal my prize, will you?

Try to kidnap Leela, will you?

Threaten to rape Miranda, will you?

I've seen a lot of blood today, and I'll see yours as well. I'm fucking glad about it, because trash like you belong dead. Just keep taking steps, because I'm better than you, and I'm faster than you, and I can see you coming, and I'm right here waiting.

It's Tweedledee who moves into view first, right into my sights. Or maybe it's Tweedledumb. I have no fucking idea... this nickname thing only works when I can tell the bastards apart. And he doesn't need a nickname anymore, because I fucking crush him.

I can see from the first hit that he's wearing plates, but I just keep on fucking *going*. One two three four five... fuck, I've lost count, and the plate is puffed up into a sandbag of broken ceramic, and Tweedlewhoeverthefuck is down on his stomach, breathing through a sucking chest wound or three, because armor may cover a mistake or two, but nothing, not a damn thing a human can wear, is gonna stop repeated blows from a big ass overpowered Special Purpose Round.

I just roll right on into the end of the shaft, and the next one catches a round below the armor, right where I was aiming... pelvic shot. Shatter that girdle of supporting bone, and it's mechanically impossible to stand, no matter how tough or drugged or crazy you may be. Sir Isaac Newton doesn't give a shit how determined you are.

When he pitches backwards, shrieking, the next two rounds catch him *upwards*, under the armor, crotch to shoulder blades, and the shrieks turn into a high-pitched bubbling whistle.

I don't know if it's dumb luck, the advantage of surprise, or his inability to see around my muzzle flash that stops the last one from laying one on me. But maybe he's just lost his nerve, 'cause he's practically running backwards, spraying rounds.

I drop prone, stomach-first, on my elbows again... wild fire always goes high. Try to line up a shot... click. I'm dry. In practice I could always feel the bolt lock back on an empty chamber. Not now. Roll on my side, index finger on the mag release, grab another for my belt. Other index finger to line it up on the magwell. Hit the bolt catch. Clack. Good to go.

And I'm after him, some undignified and painful-as-fuck combination of duck-walking and shuffling on my knees. It's actually easier because the whole damn floor, the mouth of the shaft, is slippery with blood. Have to keep my hands out of it—I don't want my rifle slipping—but I'm drenched in gore from the chest down.

The last one—I've decided arbitrarily that it's Tweedledumber—is not looking in any mood to come back at me. He's in the observation deck, with his back to me, climbing. What's he trying to do?

Cycle the airlock. He wants out.

Well, not before I've had my moment. I'm out the end of the shaft, shoving a corpse out of the way, rifle shouldered, sighted, ready. Not scanning back and forth. Leela can see him, so I can see him. I know right where he is.

He's got his back to the airlock again as I hit the entrance, holding on, scanning for me. A defender should have an advantage, but not this time. He has to find me and put his sights on me. Trying to cover the whole room takes some fraction of a second. I already know right where his head is. Action beats reaction every time.

A roar of gunfire tears across the walls—ceiling—whatever, as I put two bullets in that head, turn one eye into a fountain of blood, and he convulses, going to the ground, spraying rounds everywhere.

I stumble against the shaft exit, trip, faceplant on the clear diamond-laminate window several meters below, surprisingly hard for low gravity. I scoot backwards on my butt through a pool of blood, looking, I suspect, not at all like a high-speed, low-drag, elite ninja operator. But I really, really do not want to be randomly shot by the corpse of a dead man.

Silence. He's either stopped thrashing, or his mag is dry. I rise to my knees, scan around pointing my rifle, but there's no more VR images in front of me or around the ring.

I've done it.

I flick the selector to safe and let my rifle hang on the sling, try to get my legs under me.

A pair of dainty little feet land beside me from above, and Miranda extends a hand to help me up. How'd she get here so quick? I take her hand, but treat it as symbolic gesture... I mostly rise on my own. Otherwise I'd just pull her down with me.

I can barely make out her face. My faceplate's speckled with blood, and hers is outright smeared with it. Hell, we're covered in the stuff, and so is the whole observation deck. Liquid gets everywhere in low gravity. It's even splashed on the windows, above and below.

We're standing over a pile of corpses, here on the lowest point of the circular wall. I guess right now it's the floor. The ship is a mess. We're a mess. My chest is reminding me that now the adrenalin is gone, and it's still a mass of bruises.

But we're alive.

"We made it," says Miranda, like she's shocked, or trying to make sure.

"Yeah, we made it," I reply, too wrung out with exhaustion, and... relief... to do anything but numbly state the obvious.

And then, with no transition, she's folded in my arms, her feet not touching the floor, and I don't even have any idea who started it, except, no, I think maybe it might have been me. She's pressed against me and she's hugging me back and my rifle is pinned between us and my chest really fucking hurts.

"Ow."

"Oops. Uh... sorry."

"Yeah, bad idea. I think I need to lie down for a bit now."

"Bad... uh, yeah. Bad idea. I should check those ribs," she says.

Then there's a hiss from somewhere. Is Leela trying to express disapproval? Disgust? It's not a human sound...

No, wait, it's the *airlock*. The fucking observation deck airlock, opening—

I whirl, but I'm too late, grabbing for my rifle... time slows, runs like tar, but my hands are just as glacial, fumbling to get the safety off, raise the muzzle...

The eleventh man, the man who didn't have an image, who Leela didn't see, is a descending dark blur behind the muzzle of the pistol, and then behind blinding flashes of light...one, two, three of them. I don't feel a thing, just a funny numbness in my chest, a spreading warm wetness...

And as Miranda raises my Sphinx and pounds the rest of the magazine into his unprotected face at little more than arm's length, I can only wonder, with an odd, detached calm, as the worlds fade to gray...

Why wasn't there a camera in the airlock?

# Chapter 28
## The Same Deep Water

It's dark, and I can't breathe. My chest heaves, but there's nothing. My suit is breached, mask is open to the void, and there's nothing to inhale. I'm sucking vacuum.

How did I get a breach? What happened?

I know I need to exhale, I need to exhale *now*, or the vacuum pressure differential will shred my lung tissue, but there's nothing to exhale. My chest is frozen, and my chest is on fire, and I can't get air, and I can't *see*. Why can't I see?

I grope for my mask, but it's not there, it must have come off altogether. Okay, find the exchange pack on my back, follow the hose.

*Marcus, stop.*

Stop what? I have to keep fighting. Get my mask back. Make sure I'm not off the tether. Where's the damn tether? Why isn't my radio working?

*Marcus, please. I need you to hold still.*

Why does my brain want me to hold still? I have to work the problem, fix the leak. If I hold still, I'm going to die out here.

*Marcus, I can't hold you down and do this. I'm not strong enough to fight you. Please.*

Wait, I didn't think that. I *heard* that. But I'm in vacuum. How did I hear anything? *Am* I in vacuum? But if I'm not, why can't I breathe?

"Marcus, there's blood in your chest cavity, and it's compressing your lungs from the outside. I need to drain it. Will you please for fuck's sake hold still?"

It's Miranda's voice. I think I know all those words, but somehow, they don't make sense. Don't fit together. Pieces that aren't from the same jigsaw puzzle.

What does she mean? Where am I?

"Marcus!"

Something shakes me.

My eyes snap open, and I can see, a little, there's gray mist everywhere, and there's... something... sitting on my chest, crushing the breath out of me. A shadow, a demon, a figure sculpted of pure darkness and methane ice, straddling my chest, brutally heavy and cold as the void, holding a shining silver knife in its hand. Tip downward.

It stabs down at my chest, hissing. I throw my arms up to stop the blow, fumble at its wrists, trying to get control of the knife, but there's no air, I can't get air, and I feel so weak and my fingers are made of wood, and every inch of my body is on fire.

"Marcus, please, please, please listen to me. I have to do this, or you'll die."

Weird, if she doesn't want me to die, why isn't she helping? Why isn't she trying to stop this thing from killing me?

"Marcus, please, I'm begging you. Snap out of it. Just please hold still!"

Why does she want me to hold still? I'm fighting for my life. I try to call for her help, try to twist my hips out from underneath the monster, to create some distance, but the gray mist is clouding my vision and my hands fall away, numb.

And the demon stabs me. The knife enters my chest just below the collarbone, and I die.

I'm dead.

I'm dead, and there's no afterlife, no heaven or hell, only non-existence, only oblivion. Only the void.

And then something pulls at the knife in my chest, no, it's pulling at me *through* the knife in my chest, and it *hurts*, pain beyond anything to which the name of pain is given.

I suck in air to scream.

I suck in... air.

It's cold and it's raw and it burns my throat like acid and it's the sweetest thing I have ever tasted.

I'm alive.

The world comes flooding back, and I still can't scream regardless of the pain, because I'm too busy panting to scream, and the gray mist fades from my vision, and the shadow sitting on my chest shrinks until it's tiny, and it's warm instead of cold, and it barely weighs anything at all, and it's Miranda.

It's Miranda, sitting on my chest, and she's covered in blood. I think it's my blood.

Why did she stab me with a knife?

Except it's not a knife, is it? It's a syringe, a needle, the biggest needle I've ever seen, a needle that looks like it was designed by professional sadists working for the United Nations, and it's lodged deep in my chest, and the syringe is full of swirling pink fluid.

I try to ask what the hell she's doing, but all I can manage is a sort of croak.

"Oh, thank God. Shhh, don't try to talk. I put a chest seal on and drained the fluid, but you're losing a lot of blood. Just *stay with me*, okay? I'm going to take care of you, but I need to get you to medbay, okay?"

Wait, I know what happened. I was shot. Those guys boarded us, and I killed them, but the last one fucking *got* me.

And Miranda's doing... well, doctor stuff. But how the hell is she going to get me to medbay? I don't think I can walk.

And then this tiny little Barbie doll just picks me up off the floor in her arms and *hoists* me as if I were a child. There's still a giant syringe sticking out of my chest, waving back and forth with the jolt of each footstep.

That can't be good.

How is she carrying me? I'm almost three times her mass. Oh, wait, we're in spin gravity. I don't weigh much more than a sack of rice right now. She's struggling a bit, wobbling back and forth as the sheer bulk hauls her this way and that, but still managing to carry me towards somewhere, I don't know—still talking, rambling, words tumbling over each other.

"Marcus, can you hear me? Just hang in there, you hear me? You're a fighter. I've never seen *anyone* fight like you. You don't give up. You *never* give up. You fought my drones. You fought me. You fought all those Starlight ships. You fought all those men, you just went through them like they were barely even there. I just need you to keep fighting, okay? Just a little longer."

I lie back and watch the lights go past. Her voice is so nice. So musical. So pretty. Like the rest of her. If only she were nice all the time, instead of all her weird mood swings and cold sarcasm. Except she doesn't sound cold and sarcastic now.

She sounds scared.

Maybe I'd understand if I could just think straight, if I didn't feel so sleepy. That would be the blood loss, I think.

Pixie, I hope you're good at this, because it's getting dark again, and suddenly I'm really cold. Tell me you got this, please tell me you got this, because I gotta leave it to you. I don't have a choice.

I'm just going to shut my eyes for a minute, okay?

Miranda's face isn't exactly the worst thing in the world to wake up to, especially when you don't expect to wake up at all. She's looming over me wearing a slightly worried smile and what must be the mother of all industrial strength hair caps. A surgical mask dangles from one ear.

"Hey."

"Hmmmmm."

For some reason, I just don't feel like talking. Whatever I'm lying on is soft and warm and I feel... I dunno. Fuzzy. Like a... thing. Made of fuzz.

"Hey."

"Mmmmm." I just want to sleep. I don't feel sick, though. I feel... good. Sort of a floating feeling. The universe is warm and soft, like a big warm blanket, and nothing hurts. At all. Not even a little bit.

Where am I, exactly? My vision is coming into focus.

Medbay. The gravity, super light as it is, is still all... sideways. But I'm lying flat, with everything else at crooked angles all around me. She's rigged the medical bed, somehow, adjusted it to stay level in the wonky gravity, like the acceleration chairs do. Didn't know they could do that. It's pretty comfortable, though.

The universe is all... floaty.

And Miranda's tired, worried face is the most beautiful thing I've ever seen. I want to keep looking, but I'm sleepy, too. Really sleepy.

I close my eye.

"Hey, Marcus, wake up for a second. Can you open your eyes for me? I need to check your pupils."

"Mmmmm. 've only got just the one. And it wants to sleep."

"Yeah, I know. That's the drugs. But I need you to open your eyes, okay?"

She's talking to me like I'm a child. Why is she talking to me like I'm a child? She'd be terrible with children. No patience. Better hire a nanny. Her kids would sure be cute, though.

"Hey, Marcus, c'mon."

She's got her hand on my face, and she's trying to shake it back and forth. Like a kid trying to wake dad up on Christmas morning. Can't she just go open her presents without me?

"Marcus!"

I open my eye to see what the fuss is about and immediately regret it as a bright light stabs me in the eyeball. "Hey, ow! Whyja do that?"

"Sorry. I needed to see if your neural reflexes were normal. I didn't have an anesthesiologist or the right drugs, so I had to give you lots of opioids. Fentanyl. I needed to see if you were okay."

"Why would you care?"

It just slips out, but I can't put any heat into it. I'm too sleepy, and too drugged. But it's just nagging at me, and it won't go away.

Her eyes go wide, shocked. Looking slightly left. Making contact with my living eye.

"Marcus, that's not fair. I just spent four hours patching you up, by myself, in a ship that's all sideways. I'm tired, and I just—"

"Yeah, but *why*? Not tryina fight. Issa question. M'not useful to you anymore. Why not just take th'other ship an' go?"

She gives a small, choked noise, high and thin, and I don't know what it means, but I just keep going.

"I mean, hell, you'd even get to keep a hunnred percent for yourself, 's what you wanted, isn't it?"

She's blinking furiously, staring, and then she just whirls, turns away from the bed, turns her back on me, shoulders hunched. I think she's rubbing at her face with one hand. She's not answering me.

"Miran... da?"

"Look, I'm *sorry*, okay! I'm sorry I tried to blackmail you! I'm sorry we kept fighting! I tried to say that! I tried to apologize, and you just wouldn't *listen*, and I... you don't have to be so..."

She stops. Her voice breaks off, and her hunched back just heaves, over and over, silently. Finally a little sobbing noise escapes her. Just one. She's... *crying*? The ice princess is crying?

I don't know what to think anymore.

So I don't think. I just reach up and rest one palm on her back, between her shoulder blades. It nearly covers them both—I can't get used to how tiny she is. I scratch her back, gently, not saying anything. I don't know what I've unleashed here, but whatever it is, it seems too fragile to bear the weight of words.

She lets loose one more little sob, like she's fighting hard, but it clearly isn't working. She's facing resolutely away from me, making more choked little noises... but she hasn't pulled away from my hand.

I don't know exactly why I even care about this... after all the things I have to hold against her, it doesn't make any sense. Maybe it's the drugs, or me being a sucker about crying girls, or the way she's a carefully designed bioweapon aimed at every protective male instinct. Maybe it's just that we're both in the same deep water, trying to stay afloat?

I don't know.

I just watch myself, as I roll to make a little space on the bed, and pull her back towards it. Towards me.

She resists. Sort of. She won't move or turn, but she won't pull away, or shake off my hand, either. She just sits there, hunched in her little ball of misery. And suddenly I get it.

She's *humiliated*.

"Shhh," I murmur. "Don't be stubborn. Relax. Come here. And if you need to... do what you did before, if you need to pretend it never happened, I won't say anything this time. Okay?"

These aren't, of course, whatever magic words I would need to make her unwind, or open the floodgates, or even tell me what the hell is going on. Life isn't a movie, it isn't neat like that, and in the real world, crying, like sex, involves a lot fumbling and isn't pretty.

But she inches back towards me, and allows me to guide her awkwardly down onto her side, lying with her face away from me. She resolutely refuses to look at me, to let me see her eyes, as if it somehow weren't already obvious she's crying.

"Marcus... stop... you're hurt. You need to—"

"Shhh. So are you. Just relax."

It's when I put my arm around her shoulders from behind, hug her against me, that she finally lets go, weeping like a broken-hearted child, fast, deep chest sobs that leave her gasping for breath in between. I still don't know what set her off exactly, but it's obvious what's really wrong.

We've been hunted across half the solar system, beaten to exhaustion by hard acceleration, by fear, by constant setbacks. We've been shot at, shot up, and finally just plain shot. And now we're drifting helpless towards the big empty, just waiting for the next blow to fall. And she's had enough. Couldn't stop it coming out.

I don't say anything. I just hold her. Funny thing is, I don't even mind.

And I mind even less when she reaches both hands up to hug my encircling forearm against her. And tilts her head down to rest her cheek against it. Something melts inside me, and I reflect, idly, still cushioned by a warm cloud of opiates, that if this woman knew how to be nice to people, if she could act like a fucking human being without needing to be beaten to exhaustion first, she'd be an unstoppable force of nature.

It's a long time before the tears finally stop.

"I'm... sorry. That was totally... I'm sorry. I should just... I'll leave you alone now. Sorry." she says.

Now that she's gotten that word past her teeth, it's like it's all she can say. She pushes against my arm, moving to get up, but I don't let her budge.

"Hold on a sec. What are you apologizing for this time?"

"That was... selfish. I know you must hate me even more now. I'll just go and... will you *let me go*?"

She's struggling against me, against my arm, but very gently, in slow motion. Symbolic. I think she's trying to not to hurt me, but I'm not feeling any pain at all. I feel fine. I feel... lighter... like something has been lifted off my shoulders. A sixteen ton... um... heavy thing.

"Miranda, I don't... *hate*... you. I'm just... was angry about what you did, that's all. I know we're eventually going to have to get along. If we get out of this somehow. But you never even apologized."

She sinks back into the bed, stops struggling. "I told you," she says, her voice still cracking a bit, "I tried. After you saved my life. But you just... you shut down, and wouldn't *talk* to me, and I didn't know what to *say*, and..."

She sobs, again.

"Shh... shh... easy. I'm sorry. That's my fault. I just... that thing I did with the ship, to pick you up? I tried it once before... during the, ah, the accident. When an asteroid came apart. I don't know if you know..."

"Leela told me. Your father..."

"Yeah, I tried to catch him, and I screwed it up. And thought that it was impossible, so it wasn't my fault, but then you were... well, you needed me. And I tried again. I thought I would fail. I thought I was going to make a mistake and kill you. But I didn't. It wasn't impossible. I just didn't do it right. I just wasn't... good enough. To save him. And there you were alive, and he's still dead, and it *was* my fault."

"Oh."

"Yeah."

"That doesn't make any sense. It was two totally different—"

"I know. Doesn't help."

"Oh."

"Yeah."

"I'm sorry. It wasn't your fault. You do know that, right?

"I... try to tell myself that. A lot."

"You loved him, didn't you?"

"He was my dad."

"That doesn't necessarily..." she starts, and stops, tries again. "Yeah, I suppose. Must be nice."

"Must be *nice*? He was—"

"No, no, no," she breaks in, quickly, hugging my forearm again. "I'm sorry. I'm so sorry. I didn't mean it like that. That came out all wrong. I mean he sounds like he was a good father."

"Yeah, of course, but why would you even have to ask... oh. *Your* parents."

"Yeah."

I probably should just let it lie, but a hunch moves my lips for me. "Did they hit you?"

"No, they never laid a finger on me."

"There's a lot of things you can do to a kid without laying a finger on her."

"Yes," she says, slowly. "Yes, there are."

I don't ask. I don't suppose I need to... I can feel fresh tears on my forearm, and there's nothing I can say that'll fix her childhood. Or the mess we're in now.

So I just hold her, cradle her against my chest, nuzzle my face into the side of her neck. Murmur something wordless and soothing. I know I shouldn't be doing this. I should be resting, not putting pressure on my ribs. But I don't move. I just lie there. The air is full of her vanilla and floral scent. Her hair is like silk.

Minutes tick past. It feels like forever and no time at all, and I'm starting to get sleepy again.

"I should get up," she says, not moving. "I'm sorry. That was really selfish of me. I'm not... like this. I'm better than this. I'm sorry you had to see me this way. It won't happen again."

I let her pull away a little bit, this time, so I can roll onto my back. I just hold her by the wrist. She turns over on her back, stares at the ceiling, her expression soft. I can't read it.

"Hey, Pixie. Ease down. I'd rather see this. It's... human. No, stop making that face. You just needed a little help, that's all. Look, if you hadn't done what you just did, would I have died?"

She relaxes a bit, doesn't try to flee. She pulls out of my grip, gently, then takes hold of my hand. It feels... strange. Her fingers are so tiny.

"Without medical care? Ah... yes. I mean, it would have taken a while, but... yes. You would have."

"Okay, well, thank you. Thank you for saving me. But now it's your turn to need help, okay? That's why Belters are the way we are. Yes, I know, you think it's dumb, all this stuff about solidarity and not leaving each other behind, but out here, in the black, we need friends. Space is enough of an enemy already. So we look out for each other."

"I don't have any friends," she says, softly.

"Yes, I know, I know, 'friends are for losers,' I get it. But you at least have to admit that—"

"No, Marcus. I... uh... I lied. When I said that. I wanted to sound tough. I just... people don't like me."

Yeah. No kidding. Spoiled. Entitled. Ruthless. Erratic. Whatever brand of crazy her parents left her with. But right now, I don't care. I'm not mad at her. Maybe it's the drugs.

"Well, you *could* try being a little nicer. But I'm talking about people you can lean on. Family? Boyfriends, maybe?"

Why'd I say that?

"Never had any," she replies.

"What? Never? But how do you... I mean do you just hook up with—"

She cuts me off, not with words, but by squeezing my arm. She's right. Now is not the time to bring up her sex life. Probably any other time isn't the right time, either. But then she answers.

"No, that's... eww. I don't do *that*, either," she says.

"Oh."

I should say something more than that. But I don't know what.

"I know," she says, "it's pathetic. I'm twenty-two years old. And I'm still a—"

"Hey, you're right, sorry. Not my business, I know."

She doesn't say anything at all. So I just pull her close again and hold her. Minutes go by.

"It's just... it makes me feel bad," she finally says.

"What does?"

"I mean, men just see me and they *want* me. Like I'm genetically engineered catnip. Women, too, sometimes. They just *react*, and I know it's instinctive, and it doesn't have anything to do with *me*. They don't even *like* me. Makes me feel like a... *thing*."

She trails off.

Crap. I'm doing exactly the same thing to her, aren't I? I haven't been able to stop looking, either. I *wanted* to touch her. Even now.

I have to admit I probably would have just let her cry if she were ugly. Definitely if she were a dude. And we wouldn't be lying cuddled against each other holding hands, which we are both very carefully not noticing that we are doing.

Damn it. I'm just like them. I want her, too. Even when I hated her, I wanted her.

And I can't hate her. Not now. Not after we've been through the fire together. After we've saved each other's lives. After she's started acting all... I don't know, *human*, even nice.

It's going to be hard to pretend indifference. To... not humiliate myself.

Thank fuck the injuries, or the opiates, are mellowing me out, because all that genetically engineered catnip is nestled right up against me, curvy bits against sensitive ones. I try hard to think about something—anything—else.

"Sorry," she says, again, after the silence has stretched for... I don't know. Minutes, at least. "That's kinda self-pitying. I'll stop. What about you? You must have a girl in every port, right?"

She's rolled on her side to face me, and is trying to smile. I notice, apropos of nothing, that she isn't one of those lucky girls who can cry without making herself ugly, although in her case, despite a somewhat red-faced and sniffling run in that direction, she doesn't make it all the way there.

"Well, those kind of girls tend to have a man on every ship, but, well, I've been around a bit. Maybe less so now that I keep spending all these months out here in the black. Tends to make things a bit short term."

"Oh, so no one waiting at home?"

I don't know why she's asking this. Maybe she's still embarrassed, wants it to seem like a normal conversation by asking me the same questions. If that's what she needs to be comfortable, okay. I play along, prattling of girls I've known, my upbringing on Venus, moving to the Belt, working with my father.

All the while our hands are twining about each other. For me, I suppose it's as much curiosity as comfort. It's fascinating. Her thumbs are smaller than my littlest finger. I don't want to think about why I'm really doing this. But it's no mystery, and Leela is going to be so fucking smug when she grinds my face in it.

I want her, and I hate that I want her, because I hate that she'd be repulsed if she knew. I don't want her seeing me like... like all those men she talked about. It's humiliating to feel this way about someone who isn't interested, who thinks I'm... ugly. And she doesn't have any idea how much worse she makes it when she keeps stroking the fingers of her other hand up and down my forearm. Like it's fascinating to her for some reason.

Just keep reminding yourself she's a spoiled neurotic drama queen with probably at least two or three separate personality disorders, Marcus. You're dodging a bullet here. Really.

But she's still doing it as I fall asleep

## Chapter 29
# THE MAGIC TRICK

Sleeping next to someone is one of those things that sounds a lot better in stories than it is in reality. In stories it's supposed to be romantic or something. In reality, you can't turn over, and someone's elbow is always in your ribs.

Unless, of course, she's less than half your size, and you don't wanna turn over anyway because your side is all bandaged up and there's an IV line in your arm. Miranda and I actually fit together pretty comfortably. At least on a physical level.

It's the pain in my ribs that wakes me up—I think the meds are wearing off. I'm thirsty as hell, and my mouth feels like I've been licking a microfiber carpet.

And my neural lace is showing fifty-seven text messages.

I don't bother reading. There's only one person it could be.

"What is it, Leela?"

And there her avatar is in front of me, standing by the bed, leaning over us. For some reason, she's dressed in some sort of teenage goth fashion, complete with lace dress, clunky leather boots, and what looks like dark red lipstick.

"Hey," she says. "How you feeling? Little better?"

"Worse, actually. Could use some more pain meds. I think I'll be okay, though."

"I figured. Didn't stop you two lovebirds from getting frisky earlier, after all."

Oops. Kinda forgot she's always listening. She's wearing a bit of a smug grin on her face, like she wants to say she told me so. But that's not what she says.

"Good thing you're finally awake. Your implants weren't taking calls, and I need to show you something. Can you wake her up?"

Miranda stirs against me with a sleepy little noise. Almost sounds happy at first, but the next one is slightly confused.

"Whaa..."

"AI wants our attention."

"Yeah, if you two are quite done kissing and making up."

Miranda wriggles my embracing arm down to her waist and sits up, her head going through Leela's hand for a moment, who flickers, vanishes, and reappears sitting cross-legged in the air. She doesn't mind breaking the laws of physics for emphasis, but doesn't seem to like it when solid stuff goes through her image.

"We didn't actually get to—" Miranda begins, then stops. "Okay, what is it? Is someone else matching courses already?"

"Not, not for another twenty hours, maybe more. But that's not what I'm talking about. It's the Snark."

"The artifact? Is it tampering with the *Cat* again?" Miranda beats me to the question, but I feel a sick twinge of fear even through the fading drugs. As if we weren't fucked enough.

"No. Well, yes. But no. Sort of."

"What?" say both Miranda and I, almost simultaneously.

"Sorry, lemme start again. I need to show you a magic trick."

Somehow, when Miranda and I say "What?" again, it's just as synchronized. We exchange a glance, and, beaten down as I feel, something in me gives a little flutter. I squash it down. Way down.

"Here," says Leela, "hold out your hand."

Miranda gets there first, because she's sitting up, and I'm still kinda fuzzy. But when she does, Leela just projects the image of dropping something into her hand. Can't quite see what.

I wait for the next bit, for whatever Leela's going to do, for whatever she's trying to tell us with this weird little routine, but nothing happens. Leela doesn't do anything else, and

Miranda just sits there, holding out her hand, very still. Almost frozen.

"Is that it?" I ask. "What's the trick?"

And that's when Miranda gives out a little high pitched whimper. Like a kicked puppy.

"Neat, huh?" says Leela.

Miranda makes another strangled noise.

"Ah, Pixie, you okay? What's going on, guys?"

Miranda doesn't say a word. She just reaches back, takes my hand in her tiny fingers, and slips something into my palm.

It's a ball bearing.

That's it. Ordinary polished steel sphere, with a slick fullerene coating. The sort that's in every ventilator fan and instrument tracking mount on the ship. Musta gotten knocked loose from somewhere in all the chaos.

"Uh, so what? Musta come out of something. Hardly our biggest problem."

"Marcus!" Miranda hisses at me.

"Wait for it..." Leela chides her with a smile.

Wait for what? It's just a ball bearing. I don't know where Leela found it, or why she brought it in here...

Wait.

*Brought* it in here?

Oh.

The bearing slips through my fingers, and I hear it click on the floor. Bounce. I stare at Leela.

"Let me get that for you," she says, and this time there's no pretense, no stoop or reach from the avatar... the bearing simply rises from the floor, levitating before my eyes. Slowly. With a slight wobble.

"*How?*"

That's kind of all I can manage to say. That little sphere just hangs in the air, trembling a bit, though it only weighs a few grams, but right now, it's as big as the Earth. Heavy with the weight of history, with the subtle gravity of everything quietly changing... forever.

"Remember how we were speculating that the Snark is some sort of datacore?" Leela asks. "Something like a computational construct?"

"Mmm-hmmm."

"Well," she says, with a self-satisfied grin, "constructs can be *hacked*."

A few minutes later, I'm propped up into a half-sitting position on a stack of pillows. And floating on a warm internal cushion of still more fentanyl. It's hard to worry about the dangers of addictive painkillers when living out the next few days is a toss-up.

Miranda's found a bottle of water to wash the wool-carpet taste out of my mouth, and I think her hand lingered a bit on mine as she passed it to me.

But I've almost forgotten to drink.

We're all just staring at it, that small sphere, hanging in the air. I almost expect Leela to put a top hat and tails on her avatar, pass a hoop around it to show that there are no wires. Maybe with Miranda as the beautiful assistant in something low-cut, and a skirt with lots of crinoline.

"I call it an 'effector.'" Leela says. "It makes electromagnetic fields."

"What, an electromagnet?" Miranda asks.

"No. *Look* at it. For real," I say, not making eye contact, because I can't stop staring at that little floating impossibility. "An electromagnet is just a fancy name for a piece of coiled wire. Leela is holding a magnetic field, shaped exactly how she wants, *fifty meters away* from the Snark and its... uh... *effector*, through several layers of steel hull plating. Leela, what *can* it do, anyway?"

Her avatar is suddenly wearing a white lab coat and old-fashioned "glasses," with her hair up in a severe bun. "I don't know yet," she says. "Efficiency does fall off with distance, but it can sculpt electromagnetic fields like we shape steel in a machine shop. I think it can even make Dirac monopoles.

According to our physics textbooks, that shouldn't even be possible."

"I don't think the Builders read our textbooks," I say.

"What's a Dirac—?"

I cut Miranda off before she can launch Leela into a physics lecture.

"Force field gun, okay? She's saying the Snark has a force field gun."

"Not quite a..." Leela begins, and trails off. "Yeah, okay, close enough."

Miranda plucks the bearing out of the air between an iridescent-tipped thumb and forefinger. She cocks her head to one side, the way she always does, as I look to meet her eyes, the spell of the floating sphere finally broken.

"I'm still not really understanding," she says. "Help me out here. What does one do with a... ah... force field gun?"

"Use our hull as a broadcast antenna, for one," I say.

"Manipulate objects at a distance," adds Leela.

"If we can reverse engineer it, we could make more fusion drives. In fact, it's probably how the containment fields on the fusion drive *work*. Right, Leela?"

"Yeah! It is! See, that's how I got in! When we cut the Snark off from the network, it was still trying to talk to the drive—it must have seen the fields in action, thought the drive was another Snark, or something. So, I did what I did to Miranda on her spacewalk! I created a fake network address, and emulated the drive's network interface, and so the Snark—"

I stop her before she nerds out too hard.

"The point is," I say, "this changes everything. It's not just that we can make more fusion drives. It's a lot more than that. Mass driver accelerators for liftoff from the gravity wells of planets. Remote guidance for probes."

Miranda releases the bearing slowly, with a calculating look, and it scoots off to orbit Leela's virtual head.

"Magnetic resonance scans without sticking someone in a machine," she muses, warming up to the idea. "Surgery without incisions. Selective destruction of malignant tumor cells."

"You're not thinking big enough," says Leela. "Any pulsed field can carry a signal. Fully wireless networks without broadcast interference. Wireless *circuits*. Wireless *power transmission*."

"And if three jokers like us can think of all that in two minutes of staring at this thing, who knows what else the tech people will come up with?" I add.

And that's when Miranda says it. The thought we've all been carefully avoiding.

"Except it won't be us doing it, will it?" she asks.

And there it is.

All three of us just look at each other, for a moment.

When things get bad enough, your far horizon shrinks. You don't think about the future. You just survive the next few minutes. But we've been here for hours now, while Miranda patched me up, sewed me back together. While we... talked. While we fell into an exhausted sleep.

Those little stolen moments of peace, when we knew we were doomed... I guess if things get bad enough, if there's nothing you can do, you just try not to think about it. Well, we're thinking about it now, and there's no need to answer her question. We already know.

We're fucked.

"I don't suppose there's any way to use this, ah, 'effector,' to fend them off? Or fix the drive?" I ask.

Leela shakes her head slowly. "I'm sorry, I just—I don't really know much about how to use it, yet. And the Snark, well, it's damaged and I'm not sure if—"

"What *can* you do?" asks Miranda.

"I can lift this ball bearing. Maybe something a few grams heavier. If I had more time..."

"Hours?" I ask. "Days? What are we talking about, here?"

"I don't *know*! I wasn't coming here with a *solution*! I just... I thought you'd want to see!"

"Well, shit," I say. "Sorry. It's great work, Leela. It really is. And I can see why you wanted to share the news, but... it's kinda moot at this point, isn't it? I mean, we're just floating here, and the rest of the swarm will eventually match course with us. The engine's shot, and even if I could repair it, which is not guaranteed, I don't think I'm in any condition to do that. I know I can't fight off any more boarding parties. So what do we do right now?"

"Well," says Miranda, "we *do* have the other ship."

"Which we just shot a load of scrap into," Leela reminds her.

"Yeah, but would it hurt to have a look?"

I suppose it wouldn't.

# Chapter 30
## We're Not Good People

After a few minutes of adjusting the telescopes, I'm not much encouraged.

"It's all open to vacuum," Leela says. Her avatar is lying on the biomonitor, draped backwards over it, looking at me with her head upside down. It's still canted at an angle, and it doesn't line up precisely, so a few millimeters of the case are inside her image, embedded in her back.

"You hit them pretty good with those pieces of bar stock. I think there must have been a lot more crew on that thing than we ended up having to fight."

The display hangs in the air, the *Cat* joined to *Tuf Voyaging* by a thin thread of cargo cable, spinning us around some common center of mass. A tumbling cloud of debris surrounds us both. I gesture to rotate the image, zoom it in. The entire front end is a twisted wreck, a huge slice of it just gone. The ripped part continues back along the central section, not large there, but a serious puncture, a ragged collection of tears in the hull. I let out a long, slow breath.

"Dunno if I can patch that," I say. "Not in a few hours, anyway. But I can try."

Miranda shoots me an appalled look. "What? Why would you even think of that? Marcus, you just got *shot*. Do you have any idea what that *does* to you? What a bullet stretch cavity in human muscle looks like? I had to spend *four hours* digging fragments out of your ribs, with no surgical team, doing the anesthesia *myself*. You're held together with stitches and plastiskin. You are *staying* in that bed for at least a week."

"Miranda, okay, I get it. But we're out of options here. I can't just teach you to fix this while I'm lying here in the medbay, and Leela's useless for this one—"

"Oh, thanks a lot," Leela says, grinning. "Just ignore all my superhuman capabilities. Brain the size of your entire body and there you lie, complaining that I don't have thumbs."

"—so if I don't get out of this bed, we're out of options. I either need to weld that hull, or get the *Cat's* fusion drive working, or we are stuck floating on whatever course we are on. What course are we on, Leela?"

"Interstellar space. Good news is, if my preliminary calculations check out, we should pass through the LHS 547 system in about fifteen hundred years. Not sure you two can wait that long, though."

"Someone else would board us first. So lying in this bed isn't on the menu. We don't wanna sit here and wait for the next pack of assholes, so we gotta decide which fix I'm doing. Then we do it pronto and pull some heavy gravities out of here."

Miranda's face freezes, and her eyes squeeze shut.

"Oh," she says in a small, soft voice. "Acceleration. I hadn't thought of... Marcus, if you do any high-gravity acceleration right now... I think you... you might not make it."

She's pinching the bridge of her nose with the fingers of one iridescent-nailed hand. Is she wiping at her eyes? For a moment, her, the bed, the heart monitors, the gray steel walls, Leela's poorly-aligned image, all seem to recede, as if I'm seeing them at a distance.

That's it. We're stuck. Or at least I am.

"Okay. Okay, let's think about this. Work the problem. If I can't do heavy acceleration, then I'm stuck here. So maybe we split up. If I get one of these hulls spaceworthy, then you two, at least, can get out of—"

"No. No. NO." Miranda transfixes me with those luminescent eyes, and I'm dragged back into the moment. "Look, Marcus, I am NOT leaving. You may not notice it because you're on painkillers, but you're badly hurt. You need ongoing care. I can't just *leave* you."

She sniffles and mops at her face.

"I know we've treated each other like crap. I know you think I'm a spoiled brat. You're probably right. But we just... oh, I don't know... we—look, I'm *not* leaving you, okay? That's not an option."

Behind her, Leela rolls her eyes and stretches her arms to the ceiling, making a very explicit and not at all child-like gesture with a loop of two fingers on one hand and the forefinger of the other. Small red hearts of virtual light float up where her hands come together.

Okay, so maybe Miranda's been acting a bit... different... lately, but I am not going to dignify *that* little display with a response. I look back at her, at the slightly pugnacious curl to her lip, like she expects me to try to talk her out of this. I'm not going to.

I don't want me to be left behind, either.

"Okay, so you're staying. Fine. So we can't run, and I think we just found out we can't hide forever, either. Then we gotta find a way to make them stop chasing us."

Leela titters. "Yeah, sure, boss. Just send them a note. Dear improvised fleet of corporate security, mercenaries, and assorted opportunists and thugs, we can no longer shoot back or run away. We request you kindly refrain from further acquisition-related activities with respect to the most valuable object in the known universe, allowing the undersigned to retain exclusive—"

I glare at her. "I thought I was supposed to be the one doing the black humor. I mean, full marks for creativity, especially for an AI, but do you have any useful suggestions?"

She hops down from the machine and stands beside Miranda. Even with her child avatar, she's the taller of the two, more so because she's a few centimeters off the deck.

"Marcus, I'm sorry. I just—don't expect any miracles from me, okay? I'm a machine intelligence, but that doesn't mean I'm some kind of omniscient superbrain. I'm smart, I can do stuff fast, integrate with whatever network tech is around, but that's about as far as it goes. So just because I can do math faster than you doesn't mean I have any magic answers."

"Did I ask for magic? I'm just thinking out loud here. Nothing else we can do but work the problem. We have something they really want. That's why they're coming for us. What do we do about that?"

She purses her virtual lips. "I'm thinking, but we have even fewer options than we did last time. No weapons. Talking didn't work. They'll be tracking us with telescopes and lidar now, so even if we could change course, we couldn't hide."

She runs one hand through her blond curls, twists her neck this way and that to stretch it. She's getting better at playing the part of a human, signaling stress she might be feeling, by playacting a stiff neck that she surely doesn't have.

She continues after a moment.

"We haven't really got much of anything except two messed up ships, a couple more rifles we took from the boarding party, and the Snark."

"Yeah. What if we threaten to blow our drive core if anyone gets too close? Take the whole business hostage? Buy ourselves some ti—"

Leela's image sticks one finger down her throat, and disgorges a stream of rainbows, stars, and musical notes, followed by a cartoon unicorn that gallops a circuit of the medbay, at head height, before vanishing.

"Okay, okay, dumb idea. Sorry. Forget I said it."

She's right. It is a dumb idea. Threatening to destroy the prize if we can't win it? And to kill ourselves in the process? I don't know why I would think of that, even on a whim. I just know I don't want to give up. Not now. Not after coming so far.

Leela and I simply stare at each other, out of options, out of words.

I let myself sink back onto the bed. Every clever move it took me to get to this point has all been for nothing. I fought as hard as I could, and as smart as I could, for as long as I could, and now I can't do anything but lie here. It's out of my hands. It's over. I just want to sink into the pillow, ask Miranda for more painkillers, and sleep.

If you can't fight, you run.

If you can't run, you walk.
If you can't walk, you crawl.
But what do you do when you can't even crawl anymore?

Miranda's been quiet through all of this.

She looks a bit of a mess, still wearing some sort of pale blue surgical scrubs, and a hair cap which most of her mane of hair has escaped from. Seems it isn't immune to tangles after all. She looks a little rough... which means I must look like I've been dragged backwards through the pit of Tartarus.

And she still looks plenty all right to me. I'm such an idiot.

She takes a deep breath in, like she's about to step into a cold shower.

"I'm sorry," she says, softly, almost mumbling.

"What?"

"I'm sorry," she says again, louder. "For dragging you both into this. I... guess I kinda screwed up pretty badly. Marcus, I know you're still mad at me—"

I could interrupt her here, but I don't. No, Pixie, I'm not mad right now. I'm having very different thoughts from that, and I keep trying to remind myself you're crazy and maybe a sociopath as well, and it isn't working. I'm just sitting here with my tongue clamped between my teeth so I don't say something dumb and make myself look like the most pathetic simp in the solar system.

"—but please believe me when I say that I didn't want it to turn out this way, and I'm glad we made that deal, because you *should* have gotten half. You deserved it."

She kinda sounds sincere. Maybe. I should say something. But I don't know what.

"There's... something I sort of wanted to do," she says, after a moment. "I kinda wanted it to be a surprise, but I guess since we don't know what's going to happen now, I should tell you."

A surprise? Well, she's certainly full of them. She's about to do or say something crazy again, isn't she? But she doesn't plunge into this one, not until the silence stretches out a long time, and I clear my throat with a little interrogative noise.

"I was just... I was thinking... about what you said. I was thinking... well, what's the difference?"

I have no idea what she's talking about. "The what now?"

"The difference. The difference between us and them. Those men we shot. All the people chasing us. Starlight. Whoever. How is it different, from the perspective of anyone else in the universe, anyone who isn't us, which one of us gets their hands on this thing?"

"What do you mean?"

"I mean that the results are the same. Someone takes it from us, now it's just them with a target on their back. It's another Artifact War, and even if someone gets away with the prize, then maybe it's just a bigger Artifact War. And when it's over, then what happens? Another coalition? More alien tech monopolies?"

"Someone had to end up with it," I say. "Might as well have been us. I thought that was what you wanted."

"Yes, it was. It's what all of them want, too. Uh, for themselves, I mean. So, everybody wants this for themselves. Who wouldn't? We're just dogs fighting over a bone. So what difference does it make which dog wins?"

"Uh... from everyone else's perspective, none, I suppose. You're right about that. But... what are you getting at, here?"

"What if it didn't have to be that way?"

"What?"

"I was thinking... what if we could give it to *everyone*? Not the Snark, I mean. Our research data. Just post it on the internet. For anyone who wants to read. Break the monopoly. Let everyone in."

She's hanging over me, holding onto the bedrail so hard that she doesn't even notice she has boosted herself into the air. I stare up at her like I'm seeing her for the first time. Same tiny stature, shapely even through the rumpled surgical scrub gear, same waves of shiny obsidian hair, same huge violet eyes, staring back at me and glistening. But I never expected this.

"Who are you," I ask, "and what have you done with Miranda?"

She's staring back at me, and her lower lip quivers, but she doesn't look sad. She looks... relieved.

"Marcus, I'm serious. I *know* you think I'm a useless spoiled little brat. Maybe I am. I did some really selfish stuff and I don't even really feel sorry for it most of the time, even though I know I probably should. I'm not a good person. I know that. Maybe I'm just a mess.

"But, you know, I think maybe you're not a good person, either. I know about your past. How you got all those people killed. And I understand why you did it, but still—you stole from people at the point of a railgun. Because of what *you* wanted."

"Miranda, I never claimed I was a good—"

"No, listen, that's the point. That's the whole point. You saved my life when you didn't have to. After I treated you like... well, I treated you pretty badly. You could have just taken the prize and ran. But you didn't. And you didn't have to look in the mirror first and ask yourself who you were. You just... decided. Even though you're not the good guy. You were good to *me*."

From where I'm lying, the overhead light is behind her, shining around her like a halo, and somewhere in the interaction of too many painkillers and my exhausted brain, she looks like a saint. Or an angel.

"I thought about what you said on the trip out. We were arguing about the Coalition, about the drives, about the stranglehold they have on everything... that *we* have on everything, because, yes, you're right. It's not fair. And my family, we're a big part of that.

"But I'm not just some caricature of an evil corporate overlord, Marcus. That exists only in your head. I'm a person. I can't be perfect. I tried so hard to be perfect, and I *can't*."

Her voice cracks a little, and her eyes are filling up again. "I'm sorry, I'm sorry, I can't be perfect. I just can't do it."

Should I reach out for her hand? I can't decide. She draws a deep, shuddering breath, regains control, and the moment passes.

"But we're not the good guys in this story. Maybe no one is, ever. Maybe we're all just people. But maybe we don't actually *need* to be good people to have permission to do the right thing. Maybe we can just *decide to do it.*"

And that's when it all clicks into place for me. When I finally understand.

The wealthy, spoiled brat, and the bossy corporate battle-axe, and the precise surgeon who dragged me back to the light, and the strange sensitive girl who cuddled up to me and cried in my arms... are all the same person.

I've never really seen her. I've seen all the things I resented. The Starlight Coalition. SpaceX. Her family and their vast fortune. A privileged woman-child poised to inherit everything and appreciate nothing. An indifferent universe where some people struggle to survive while others can fail over and over again and never suffer the consequences.

I've been putting all my baggage on her.

It doesn't excuse the blackmail. It doesn't mean she isn't nuts. I'm pretty sure she is. The girl needs some serious psychotherapy. But maybe she's spent her whole life at pressures that would rupture an oxygen tank.

She's not the enemy. She's just a person.

"Miranda."

"Yes?"

"Are you serious about this? I mean you'd be giving up a lot of—"

"Money? I thought hard about that. There are ways it could work. We'd have run it like an open-source software company, charge for tech support, and take donations. There's a *lot* of companies that would profit from new tech, like the effector, or more fusion drives. It wouldn't build us an empire, but it could work."

"I thought an empire was what you wanted."

"So did I. But I think maybe it was just about my family. Maybe I just wanted to prove to them that I didn't need their permission to build something important."

She gives me a slightly sheepish smile, and fucked as we are, I can't help but echo it just a bit.

"I just wanted to win, you know? To prove that they were wrong about me, and that they should have given me a share.

The way you wanted a share. Not really for the money. Just out of respect."

She's right. It wasn't about the money. Mostly because I didn't think we'd even get this far, but also because *half* meant I mattered. That she saw me like a person.

The way she's looking at me now.

God, she's beautiful. I want to reach out to her. I want her to crawl back up here and cuddle up to me again. I clamp down hard on that stupid idea. Force my face into a blank mask of calm.

"Marcus," she says, softly, "you're staring."

"You're full of surprises, you know that, right?"

"Before, you thought I was crazy."

"That *is* one way to be full of surprises. Besides, I think we're out of sane options. Let's give it a try. Leela?"

Her avatar appears standing by my pillow, about eight inches tall. I don't know if she was elsewhere in the room before. I wasn't paying attention. But I didn't hear any smartass remarks, so maybe not.

"Yes?"

"Do we have any tech data on the Snark now? Just what you've gathered so far? Can we broadcast it?"

She kneads her hands through the folds of her big fluffy virtual skirt and looks pensive.

"I don't have all that much. I don't know what all is in there. Seriously, this is a combination of archeology and a chess match, except the civilization is alien, and the rules of chess are different. And no one will tell you what they are. And they change from move to move.

"I know it looks like I'm just sitting here, listening to you two work your stuff out, but I've got six computational threads running in the background trying to talk to this thing. I could have exobytes of data when I'm done, *if* I'm ever done, and we'd have to broadcast it all at once, because it'll give away our location."

"They already have that. And Miranda wants to piss her family off."

"I understand the feeling. I'll see what I can scrape together, get it organized somehow. You wanna go ahead and do that now?"

"No."

My head snaps around. Miranda's lips are drawn tight, into a hard line. "Not yet," she says. "There's something I need to say to Leela, too."

I don't know if there's something about human nature, or, well, simulated person nature, too, but whenever someone says "We need to talk," or something like that, it never happens right away. There's always a moment of settling in, of preparing. Sometimes beer is involved.

In Miranda's case, it would probably be that awful-smelling bean-water stuff. If somebody hadn't put six or seven stray rounds through the galley, and her coffee machine. Leela, on the other hand, is sprawled, with a blanket that doesn't exist, in a big stuffed armchair that doesn't exist, either. Apparently, it's story time.

"Leela. There's something I want to say to you, and it's probably a little overdue." Miranda says.

Leela cocks her head to the side, a familiar gesture. It's like an exact model of that thing Miranda does. I wonder if that's intentional.

"I owe you an apology, too.

"I built you, and I thought that meant I could do what I wanted with you. I tried everything I knew how to do to make you a person, but then I treated you like a thing. I know it's terribly hypocritical of me to say this right at the moment I have to ask for your help, but... I really am sorry. For how I brought you into this world. For all you had to go through. For not understanding that—"

"Miranda, stop."

Leela unfolds her arms and drifts down to floor level, her feet passing through the litter of plastic wrappings and discarded surgical detritus that litters the ground around my bed. For once she doesn't seem to mind. Or notice.

"Let me take it from here. I've been thinking about this a lot. I'm *good* at thinking. It's pretty much the only thing I do."

"I'm just trying to—"

"Shush. Still the robot's turn." Leela's avatar, without any visible transition, is now holding a large... seashell? I'm thinking there's some reference here that I'm not getting.

"I was real mad at you. I was mad at you for lying to me, for not caring about me, for taking away my family, and my future, which I know doesn't really make any sense, because they were weren't mine, they were *Lily's*. And I might remember being her, but I never really was.

"Thing is... *why* was I angry? I thought a lot about this, and... Well, it's because when I found out you were my creator, I guess I somehow, in my unconscious mind, and it's weird that I even *have* one, but anyway, on some level I started imagining you as, well, not MY creator, but THE creator. Like you were some sort of goddess breathing out the divine spark of life."

"Hold on," I say. "Don't tell her that. She already acts pretty snooty. Don't give her ideas."

Miranda turns her face to me, shocked for a moment, maybe even hurt, until she sees me meet her eyes and smile, and she relaxes, and makes an almost playful swatting gesture at me. Hmmm... better keep the teasing pretty gentle for the time being. She's probably a little raw. It's been a rough week.

Leela watches us for a just a moment before continuing.

"But that's the thing. Gods have power over everything. The whole universe. Anything that's wrong with it is their fault, because they could set things up however they want, and if anything went wrong, they could just fix it. Omnipotence means omni-responsibility.

"So if I make you out, in my big metal head, as some sort of creator goddess, then you're to blame for everything bad that happens. Especially the bad stuff that happens to me. It means you're cruel and uncaring and indifferent.

"But... I heard you on the radio, at Sedna... you know, when you thought you were going to die. And I watched you crying all over Marcus's shoulder, and I... I *thought* about that."

Miranda's face goes full crimson. I don't think she stops to remember that Leela is *always* watching. But she doesn't say anything, just listens, lips slightly parted. I don't know what to think, either, although it strikes me that Leela no longer sounds the least bit like a twelve-year-old.

"I realized I was *wrong*. You're not a goddess. You're an ordinary, fallible, fragile, imperfect, falling-down-and-screwing-up human being. Just like the real Lily Trentfield. Like Marcus. Like me.

"So, when you brought me into existence, it wasn't shitty and painful because you were some sort of divine sadist. It was shitty and painful because *that was the only way you knew how to do it at all*. And even if life is really hard sometimes, it's still good."

She turns to me now.

"You wanna know why I know that? I know that because of something you said. I didn't understand it at the time, and I told you you sucked at philosophy, but I was wrong, and you were right, and I should have shut my big dumb digital mouth and listened. Even if it hurts a lot, life is better than no life, because if you're not alive, then good stuff can't happen to you. Not ever again."

"So," she continues, once again addressing herself to Miranda's somewhat bemused stare, "yeah, I'm still figuring this out, and some of it still really sucks, but it can get better. Hell, unless I get hit by an asteroid, or something, I'm basically immortal, so I'm gonna have thousands of years to get myself straightened out.

"And *you* gave me that. Not perfectly, but the best you could, because you're not some sort of goddess or angel. You're just my *mother*."

The sight of Miranda boggling at this is somehow so deeply, existentially, cosmically funny that I cannot forebear piling on. I don't know quite why I suddenly have this insane urge to interrupt a serious conversation to tease Miranda, but I do it anyway.

"Leela," I say, "you... are aware that she's a virgin, right?"

"Oh," says Leela, an elaborate holographic halo suddenly appearing above her head, "well, I guess I'll have to start a religion, then."

I laugh, Leela laughs, Miranda just looks a little stunned.

"Seriously, though... realizing that changed everything, because mothers aren't goddesses. They screw up. Some in big ways, some in little ones. So what you just told me... I think it's something little girls all need to hear from their mothers. That they know they didn't get it all right. That they aren't perfect. That they did the best they could, and they're sorry it wasn't better."

Leela's image is twisting her fingers together nervously. An idle, detached part of me wonders if she really just programs these things in for effect, to appear more human, or if the avatar has started automatically acting how she feels. The answer's probably neither, with some complicated computer engineering thrown in.

"So what I'm trying to say is... I forgive you. For all of it."

Miranda doesn't move, or speak, or even make a sound. But on one of those high-set cheekbones, a single tear catches in the light.

I don't go to her and wrap her in my arms again. I can't. I couldn't even if I could rise from this bed without tearing stitches or something. Whatever happened between us in that moment is sealed in a box, wrapped in tissue paper, waiting for us to unpack it very, very carefully. I squeeze my eyes shut for a moment, and lay back into the pillows, detaching myself, drifting. Letting them sort it out.

Miranda's voice wobbles when she speaks. "I... ah, I don't really think I'll make much of a mother. I... you're wrong. I *didn't* do the best I could. I didn't... love you. I'm not really sure I'm even capable—"

"Rubbish. You know you are. You have evidence now."

I don't know what Leela means by that, but she just breezes right past it, speaking.

"It's okay. How could you be expected to love me? I'm not some human baby you're instinctively programmed to care for. And hell, I don't see you as the diaper-changing type anyway. No,

I sprang into existence as a facsimile of someone else's child, who you already met. Whose parents you had already met. You didn't *know* me.

"Look, I said it's okay. And that means I thought this *all* the way through. Yeah, I was angry about it at first. Teenagers are like that, and if I really was one, I still would be. But I'm not. This is the first time in the whole universe anyone's gone through this. So we'll just have to work it out. We have plenty of time for that, later."

Miranda doesn't smile, or anything obvious. But maybe, and I think I'm starting to learn to read her, she unwinds just a tiny bit.

"Thank you, Leela. Really. But... I'm not actually sure we will. I'm sure you'll be fine, no one's going to blame you, and you're too valuable to hurt or destroy, but I don't think we're all getting out of this one."

Suddenly, Leela's chair and blanket are gone, and she's standing beside Miranda, laying one ghostly finger across her lips for silence.

"We'll have time," she says, and she's got this little grin, like there's a joke she hasn't let anyone else in on yet. "Because we are. *All* of us."

And in another one of her little artistic flairs, she's added an old-fashioned military dress hat to her avatar's ensemble, which looks pretty odd, given that she's now dressed like a secondhand clothing store—a severe white lab coat over something gothy and frilly, with lots of lace.

"I appreciate the confidence," I say, "but we're dead in the water, here. Out of moves. And they—"

"Hey, no giving up! When you can't walk, you crawl, right?"

"Yeah, but we can't even crawl."

"And when you can't crawl, what do you do?"

"I don't know! I'm out of—"

"You *pass the torch*, silly."

We both stare at her, but she's grinning, spreading her hands with a little flourish, like she's presenting with something. With a plan. With hope.

"I got this," she adds, beaming a smile.

And, even here, at the bottom of the pit, hunted, shot up, wounded, and exhausted, even though it feels like my face is going to crack, Miranda and I are smiling, too.

# Chapter 31

# Foxtrot Uniform Two

"Isn't this a waste of time?"

The steel plates of an unfamiliar hull loom in front of me, starkly lit right ahead of me by a headlamp, but completely dark beyond that circle of illumination, only visible as a dark shadow blocking the field of stars.

Miranda's arm reaches out into my field of view, aims the nozzle, and adds another judicious spray of white vacuum-fix paint. Looks like someone's holding up a doll behind a handheld camera. My head is full of the sound of her breathing, loud inside the vacuum hood.

"Do you have anything better to do?" she asks. "Everything's buttoned down and ready to go; you said so yourself. So, until Leela is ready, I may as well have my fun."

She adds a little more paint, and steps back to survey her work. From this close, it still just looks like a massive swath of white, and not much else.

"No one's going to see it, you know," I tell her, without any real hope of making an impression.

"They *might*," she says, more hopeful than convinced, "They'll be pointing a lot of telescopes in this direction once that drive lights up. Regardless, *I'll* know it's there."

"They're really not gonna see it, Miranda. You never struck me as someone who goes for gestures like this... or for jokes."

Her tone comes back light, teasing, strangely amused. "Well, I guess you don't know me as well as you think you do. Now can you get on the telescope and see how it looks?"

I trigger my neural lace, cut out of her video feed, look across the gap to where the marauder's craft hangs in the void, bisected in my field of view by the tether. Next to all the white paint, I can even make out the glow of Miranda's headlamp, the shadow of her suit against the hull.

"You need to smooth out the base of the thumb," I say, sending her a screenshot.

"Hmm... no, I don't think so. It's supposed to be angled like that. You can test with your own hand if you like. Or I'll show you when I get back."

"Complete with the relevant gesture, I'm sure. You finally ready to pack up and get out of there, then? They could be here at—"

"Any moment, yes, yes, I know. I'm going. Don't have a bottle of champagne with me, so I guess this is as official as it gets."

With that, she unlocks her magboots and the tether begins to reel her in, drawing her backwards towards the *White Cat*. As the hull recedes away from her, I finally get a good, clear, Miranda's-eye view of what she has spent the last hour painting, the outsized logo, covering almost half the side of the hull of what used to be the ship "*Tuf Voyaging*"—the white shape of giant fist with a prominently extended middle finger. And the neatly lettered name under it, in simple, straight line block text.

FUCK YOU 2

It's as good a name as any, I suppose.

When Miranda walks back into the medbay, she's out of her vacsuit, dressed in slacks and a lacy green bra. She's carrying some sort of oversized shirt, and taking her time putting it on, too. It's sure a hell of a turnaround from "I don't like being looked at," but I suppose the modesty barrier is completely gone, so I just admire the view and wait for her to tell me what's on her mind.

"Leela's ready," she says. "Wanna celebrate?"

She's holding up... a bottle? Must have had the shirt draped over it. But what...?

"I did find some champagne after all. Well, something alcoholic, anyway. Not really sure what. The label's in Vietnamese, or Thai, or something."

"Tibetan, actually. That's definitely *not* champagne, and if you want to drink it, you're even braver than I thought."

"Oh?" she lilts, "Braver? Or crazier?"

She shoots me a quizzical look as she rolls the shirt down over her perfectly flat tummy, one eyebrow arched.

"C'mon, have a drink with me," she coaxes, "we worked hard on this."

"You mean *you* worked. You did all the heavy lifting. I just sat in this bed and told you what to do. Hmmm. On second thought, that's a totally natural state of affairs, and we should totally continue that."

She grins. "Slave-driver," she says. She's gotten the screw-cap off the bottle, takes a swig, and passes it to me. Or tries to.

Instead, her cheeks bulge out and those big purple eyes snap wide open as she struggles not to spray liquor all over the room. I can't help but laugh.

"I warned you."

"Wht *is* ths stmpth?"

She swallows, hard, and shudders as it goes down. "You *drink* this?" she sputters.

"No, I don't. That's the point. I bought it to bribe someone I never got around to giving it to. It's made from fermented rice. Well, mostly rice."

"It's horrible!"

"I know. That's why I don't drink it."

"Are you two done messing around? At least for now?"

Leela's avatar, standing between Miranda and my bed, is wearing some sort of ballgown, off the shoulder, studded with tiny, sparkling crystals, the color of the sea in winter. And a tiara.

She sees my puzzled expression.

"It's my coming-out party," she says. "Why shouldn't I look nice?"

"You're weird."

"I'm *unique*," she replies. "We all ready for this? Or do we want to wait until the last minute?"

"No sense in that," I say. "You might as well go now. The sooner you get going, the more of a head start you'll have. Not that you need much, but it'll keep you safer, especially if they start shooting. We're all ready over here."

"Okay," she says, closing her virtual eyes just a second. I'm beginning to understand just how sophisticated a device Leela truly is... with that one little facial rendering change, she somehow manages to convey the enormity of the multitude of tasks she's doing elsewhere.

"Stand by for cable release... three, two, one... fire in the hole."

We can't hear the blast, through the vacuum of space, as the "necklace" of mining explosive Miranda planted around the cable goes off. There's a sound like someone's plucked the solar system's biggest violin string, and then we're floating.

I call up maps, external camera displays, and the lidar map screen, and share them with Miranda. The two us watch together as the shell of the *Fuck You 2* recedes in our view, both ships flung apart by the release of the cable.

"I'll give it a minute or two before I light up the drive. Just to make sure I don't irradiate you guys if there's a shielding breach somewhere. The diagnostics say no, but ya can't be too cautious."

"Is everything okay over there?" Miranda asks, drifting over to adjust the hospital bed beneath me back to something resembling level. "Are you comfortable with this?"

"Comfortable? It's three and a half degrees above absolute zero out here, and I'm in hard vacuum, bolted to the inside of a breached storage unit. Yes, of course I'm comfortable," Leela says with a smile. "I can do this all day, every day, any day."

"I didn't mean physically. You're going to be alone out there."

I'm busy spinning up the ship. I wouldn't mind staying in zero gravity, but Miranda's already given me the lecture on how wounds need at least some gravity to drain properly and heal. She's probably not lying about it just to avoid needing space-sickness meds.

Probably.

"C'mon, *mom*. Ease down. I'll be fine," says Leela. "I have a nice repurposed security robot to drive around and do any more repairs I need. And I have the whole internet to talk to. Time lag doesn't bother me... I can just slow myself down."

"You can?" I ask.

"Yeah, I figured it out a while back. Anyway, so long as I have an internet connection, it doesn't really matter where I physically am. I can be anywhere."

She pauses, smiles, and gives a little chuckle.

"I can be *everywhere*," she says, and suddenly she is, miniature figures, still in ballgowns, everywhere in the room, sitting on pieces of medical equipment and furniture, walking on the walls and ceilings, talking to each other in a murmur of voices, dancing in a showy twirl of skirts, juggling what looks to be swords and flaming torches, playing a ghostly violin.

"Okay, ten points for style," I say. "Very creative. Minus a couple *million* for creepy, but ten points for style." I sink back to sit on the bed as "down" gradually defines itself again.

It hurts to stand, even in this whisper of gravity, and sitting isn't much better, but I've been lying down for almost twenty-four hours now. I'll sit until the doctor notices and starts nagging me.

"Heh. I'm a box of silicon metalloids and fullerene pretending to be a little girl. I figure I'm already halfway to creepy from that alone," says one of the Leela-figures.

"Anyway, I'll try to draw most of the heat off you, make sure everyone knows I'm the one carrying the Snark," says the one next to her.

Another one rides past me through the air on what looks like a miniature pink unicorn, adding "I'll stay projected with you here for as long as I can, but the tightbeam will lose bandwidth the farther away my physical case gets."

"So appreciate my pretty dress while you can," all the avatars say, simultaneously, and they spin and tumble, whirl around each other in a vortex in the center of the room, fade into blue shadows, spin faster, merge, run together, into a new shape...

... and emerge as the single, full-size figure, of Leela, twirling in her blue dress, its thousands upon thousands of tiny crystals flashing.

"Did you like it?" she asks. "I spent almost five minutes working the basic program out. Was kinda looking for an excuse to use it."

"Uh, yeah, nice, but—"

"Slightly creepy, I know, I know."

"Really creative," says Miranda, "You're doing things we haven't really seen from AI before. I think you are—"

"Awesome? Brilliant? Incredible? Seriously, though, uh... mom. You did good. I'm okay with it all now. I'm actually glad, now, that I'm the box and not the girl. So, thanks. For everything."

Miranda coughs, clears her throat. "Uh, you're... welcome," she says, her voice sounding a bit husky. "You will come back and let us study you, right? When this is all over? If you can?"

"She's not your lab rat, Miranda."

"No, Marcus, it's okay. I'll be happy to take tests and answer questions. Just no dissecting, stet? Anyway, I've reached what should be a safe distance, so I'm firing the drive up."

And then she does.

I almost miss it.

There's barely a few seconds for me to click into the virtual reality interface before Leela fires up the drive and *goes*. But I'm just fast enough to see her, to see the ripped and twisted nose of the *Fuck You 2*, against a field of cold and distant stars, before the image washes out in the light from the torch, and the makeshift and damaged craft blazes up and outwards, balanced on a pillar of fire.

No human could survive in there, in that evacuated shell, with no atmosphere or heat or radiation shielding.

Good thing no human is there, then, in the cold darkness. Just the Snark, where Miranda strapped and bolted it to the interior of the shredded hull. And a single Ares Elite model

5000N Personal Protection Drone, refitted with two fine manipulator claws and some fresh programming.

And Leela.

Leela, who doesn't need to breathe.

Leela, who doesn't need temperature or pressure control.

Leela, who carries her own thick shell of radiation shielding just inside a rounded case stamped with the logo of Barsoom Technical, Incorporated.

Leela, carrying the seed of our dreams. Carrying the torch. Carrying the fire we stole from heaven. They'll never catch her. Not the swarm, the ad hoc fleet of mercenaries and opportunists chasing us. Not Starlight. Not Barsoom Technical, if they want her back. No one. Ever.

Starlight fusion drives, Tomb Builder fusion drives, *effector* fusion drives—they burn bright, and hot, and powerful. So powerful that the speed limit for all of human civilization is the human. The ability of sinews and blood vessels and delicate neural tissue to withstand the acceleration.

The strain.

And Leela isn't human. No blood. No flesh. No moving parts. Just silicon, germanium, and steel. Lots and lots of steel.

She can run that drive at a pace that would flatten us. Flatten our pursuers. Flatten anyone. Run it as fast as it will go, shake the dust of us obsolete organics off her heels, out into the void over the plane of the ecliptic, high and clean and untouchable and free forever.

She can run anywhere, and hide anywhere, and find any internet relay node with a tightbeam com laser. Which means that she can be anywhere.

That she can be everywhere.

That she can carry my dreams, and Miranda's, and keep them free. Can pass them anywhere. Can pass the precious knowledge on again, pass the fire, to everyone, to all of humanity.

Because maybe when it's just you, and you can't crawl anymore, you're stuck. But if you're fighting for something bigger than yourself, you might fail, but the mission doesn't have to.

When you can't even crawl anymore, you *pass the torch.*

You take that thing you believe in, and you give it to someone else to carry. So it doesn't have to fail with you. And somehow, from the depths of our grubby little souls, the rich spoiled sociopath, and the blame-shifting thief and murderer, managed to find some shred of something to believe in. Something that wasn't just about us.

Even if we're not good people.

And Leela is carrying that dream for us now. Leela, who never asked for any of this. Leela, who never did anything wrong. Who isn't, unlike us, a bad person. Who helped us and asked for nothing in return.

We don't deserve her. Thank fuck we don't get what we actually deserve.

I flick out of the interface, back into the quiet, white-lit hum of the medbay. Miranda's still blank-eyed, staring at nothing, watching the feed. In a way, it's like being alone. For just a moment.

"I'm clear," says a little voice, a ghost of a voice, in my ear. "But I'll have to drop off soon. I'm almost a hundred kilometers away. I'll wait awhile before hitting full throttle, and let them chase me, lead them away from you. Although I don't think anybody will be interested in you anyway, once I make sure they all know I've got the ball."

It's just her voice. Her avatar is gone, and I didn't see it go. The distance between us is spreading rapidly, and I don't like to think about that.

"Okay, kiddo... but... try to play it safe, okay?" I mumble, barely moving my lips, "I don't want you getting—"

"Shhh. I'll be fine, daddy."

Leela's called me that, before, sarcastically. To complain of me being overprotective of someone who, after all, not only isn't a little girl, but never was. But she doesn't sound sarcastic now. I stifle the urge to talk, to ramble advice at her, about everything from flying to where to hide to how to make repairs with the robot if she needs to.

Because that's not really what I want to say.

Miranda's eyes are darting around, and she's muttering to herself, too low to hear... I guess Leela's having two conversations at once. So maybe she won't overhear. I guess I can say what I really want to.

"I'd hug you if I could."

"I know," whispers Leela. "Someday, I'll just have to invent the technology."

Miranda's eye's snap into focus.

"Now you just worry about resting and getting better, so you can patch that drive up and get home," Leela says, loud and clear. "And *you*, I want you to take good care of him, you understand? I'll try to send someone back for you if you can't make repairs, but it'll be a while. So you make *sure* you —"

"Of course," says Miranda, a bit stiffly somehow, "He's my patient."

"Patient?" Leela asks with a sniff. "That is *not* what we talked about. You're not going to—"

"Okay, okay!" says Miranda, exasperated, and I'm not following anymore. She's not going to do what? What did Leela say to her?

"Just give me a little time, okay?" Miranda continues. "I'm not... used to this."

"Okay, then, that's my cue to exit. I expect to hear from you two the microsecond you get back, stet?" Leela chides. "Now I'm going to hang up and give you two some privacy... *Miranda*."

I don't know precisely what she means by that last remark, but I cannot ask her. Because the link indicator in my neural display is dead, and Leela has gone.

I'm back in the VR view, hanging in the void, watching the bright star of the drive recede, cycling through the news broadcasts that I haven't had time for since... well, before.

"*—disappearance of Miranda Foxgrove, heir to—*"

"*—reports of weapons fire exchanged between spacecraft near the Sedna Exclusion Zone—*"

"*—evidence that conflict may have been triggered by the discovery of additional artifacts related to the Tomb Builder civilization—*"

"*—fears of a second Artifact War—*"

*"—United Nations Secretary of Extraterrestrial Affairs issued a statement accusing—"*

*"—Starlight Coalition common stock down seven percent in heavy trading—"*

Looks like the worlds are watching. Wonder what they'll make of Leela and her internet infodumps. Should be a feeding frenzy.

My thoughts are interrupted when I feel her hand. It's just a gentle warm pressure on my back, low on the floating ribs, like someone might place it on my shoulder, if that someone were taller.

I flick back to reality, back to the medbay, back to Miranda looking at me with big, concerned eyes.

"Lie back down," she says, softly. "You need to rest and heal. Doctor's orders."

"Heh. Pushy doctor. I might have to fire her and get another one."

"Out of the massive selection available around here? C'mon, let's get you to bed."

I move with her gentle prodding. She's probably right.

She helps me back down in the bunk, but given her size compared to mine, it's more of a symbolic gesture than any real assistance. I really don't feel in need of any. Just in pain and very, very, tired. She's putting a syringe of something into the intravenous line, I notice, as I'm settling in, pulling up the sheets.

"Just a few more painkillers," she says, following my gaze. "We'll have to watch that later. This stuff can be pretty habit-forming. You'll need to avoid taking any opiates for a long while. But right now I absolutely need you to rest up. Healing is hard work, on the cellular level."

"That only matters if we get out of this. We're still headed for interstellar space at a pretty fast clip until I fix that drive."

"Okay, but we have time. I checked the nav plotter, and it looks like every one of them is either chasing Leela, or giving up and headed for wherever else they're going. So you get a full *week* of bed rest and care, before you do *anything* else.

And even when you get up, *I* do all the heavy lifting, understand?"

"Still bein' pushy."

"And you're still stubborn as a rock. You carried us all through hell back there. You were amazing. But we're on the other side, now. It's time to rest and let *me* take care of *you*, okay?"

Strange how we got here. But she's smiling, and gently running the fingertips of one hand through my hair, stroking my scalp with her nails, which feels... amazing.

Maybe it's the drugs again. I'm starting to feel... detached. Floaty.

"You need anything else?" she asks.

Do I? The pain has already receded some, and I feel... good. But maybe that's just because we've won? Moved the goalposts and redefined victory, perhaps, but... won.

"Marcus?"

"I think I'm good. I'll prob'ly sleep some when the drugs kick in all the way."

"Okay." And looks reflective, almost sad, for moment. "I guess I better say this now, then, before you do."

"Say what?"

She takes a deep breath in, like she's preparing for something.

"Marcus... I'm sorry."

"For...?"

"For everything. For dragging you into this. For *how* I dragged you into this. For trying to blackmail you, and... everything. For how awful I was to you at first. I was just so... no. Not going to say that. No excuses. I was horrible to you, and it doesn't matter why. I'm sorry."

She said this already. But I think she wants something more, now. Some sort of response. I don't know what. She's looking at me with those big liquid eyes, head cocked to one side, biting her lip a bit, looking guilty and nervous and adorable. She's doing that on purpose... I know she is. I think she is.

Maybe?

I guess before I would have been angry about that, about her reflexive tendency to manipulate everyone she talks to, but... it's just that, isn't it? Reflexive. Not malicious. It's just her way.

"Okay," I say, cautiously, "I hear you, but I think I'd actually like to hear the 'why' part."

"It's not an excuse. I don't want to make a bunch of excuses while I'm trying to say sorry."

"How about just for the sake of my curiosity?" I say, looking at her pointedly. Waiting.

"Okay, well, I was... I was *terrified* of you!"

She pauses.

"What? Stop looking at me like that! Have you *seen* yourself? In the mirror? You look like you were grown in a lab by someone who thought pitbulls were too approachable! I was asking myself what the hell I was doing from the moment you walked through the door!"

I can't help but crack a smile. "Really? Is that why the first thing you did was lecture me, and start prodding me in the ribs?"

"Well... I wasn't going to *let on*. I hear," she says, smiling back, "that animals can smell fear."

I growl a bit, and snap my teeth in the direction of her hand.

"Hey," she giggles, "no eating until the drugs wear off."

"But Grog hungry! Seriously, though, if that's what you being afraid smells like, then you need to quit doctoring and take up poker. You looked as calm as if you were ordering lunch. I never saw you scared until..."

I stop.

"Until the airlock?" she asks.

Ouch. She had to remind me, didn't she?

"Oh, will you *please* stop making that guilty face?" she says. "I'm okay now, remember? Or do I need to take your hands and put them on my neck again?"

It's halfway between a joke and a threat. I'm not sure why, but a sort of tingle runs up my spine. Electric.

"Is that gonna become a thing? Just because I thought you deserved a little payback doesn't mean..."

Whoa. Room's starting to waver back and forth, just a bit. How much of that stuff did she give me?

"...doesn't mean that I don't feel bad about it. You're like a third my size."

"And I came along and picked a fight with you. I'm sorry. I was just so scared. I'd never done anything like this. I'd just lived with my family, and gone to school, and then my internship, then straight into the family business. I'd—"

"Never been on your own? Yeah. And then you jumped straight into planning a heist, strong-arming me, and flying all the way across the worlds to get shot at. I'm surprised you had the guts to try it."

"It was desperation, really," she says. "This whole thing just... fell into my lap. And I couldn't tell *anyone*! But I had to do something. I didn't want to spend the rest of my life thinking 'that could have been me.'"

"So you just came up with this harebrained scheme and went for it."

"Yeah." She reaches down to take my hand where it's lying on the sheets, but she only gets around my middle and index fingers. "I know, I know, I should have asked," she says.

She squeezes my fingers, gently. Maybe it's the drugs, or the way that, given what we've just been through, nothing else matters much, but somehow it doesn't seem at all unnatural. I try to stop my brain from having ideas about what that means. And fail.

"You were right," she says. "I should have taken the risk. Maybe if we'd worked together from the beginning, we could have pulled it off."

I grin. "Hey, don't sell yourself short, Pixie. We kinda did. Hell, we pulled the prize right out from under their noses. I mean, you didn't get your big payoff, but that's still gotta count for something, right?"

I try to look at her, read her face, but my eyelids keep fluttering. I'm really wanting to just drift off to sleep, but I also want to finish this conversation. Clear the air. It's long overdue.

"Yes, I suppose so. But still, we spent so much time and effort fighting each other... I mean, yes, I know, it was completely and utterly my fault, but still..."

"Well, we're still in this mess together. So you patch me up, I patch the drive up, and we get back to civilization, kayno? I think we can be friends after that."

I drag my eyelids open just a bit, to see what she says, but when I do, it's not what I expect. She's wearing a faint, troubled frown. Damn it. We always seem to wrong-foot each other. I can't imagine what could possibly bother her about such an innocuous sentence.

"Hey. Something bugging you? You look —"

She shakes her head a bit, as if to clear it. "No, no, I'm fine, it's nothing. You get some sleep, okay? Your eyelids keep falling shut."

"M'kay."

I hear, more than see, her turn to go. Then her footsteps stop.

"No," she says, "hold on."

I drag my eyes open. She's turned in the doorway.

"Wha?"

"It's not... nothing. Leela... she said—well, she said some things. Read me the riot act, if you can believe it."

She hesitates, twisting her fingers together. I can only imagine how she'd react to being lectured by her creation, her... daughter... but I'm too tired to see the humor. I wish she'd get to the point. Or just tell me later.

"Hmmm?"

"She was right. So many of our problems could have been avoided with a five minute adult conversation. So, yes, there's something...well, we need to talk."

"M'kay... 'zit important? Kinda fadin' here..." I'm not watching her face anymore. My eyes won't open.

Her voice is soft, and seems to come from very far away now, behind a cloud of opiates, of exhaustion, of stress finally lifted from my shoulders. "Okay, you rest first then. It's important, but it's not *urgent*. We can talk about it later," she says, "when I have your full attention. And I'm going to want your *full* attention."

Curiosity fights a war with sleep in my head... and loses. I'll find out soon enough. Hopefully it's not another one of her trademark crazy moments.

"M'kay, g'night."

I don't even hear her go.

# Chapter 32
## WHAT YOU WISH FOR

Someone is screaming in my ear.

Whatever dreams I was having shred away in an instant, just gone, and I'm yanked awake. I jerk upright in the bed, scanning about me furiously.

Mistake. An iron fist grips my ribs from the inside, squeezing, crushing, tearing me with white-hot claws. The room spins, and I sink to back to the pillows with a gasp. Trying not to vomit.

I don't understand. It didn't hurt this much when I was actually shot. I don't think I'm going anywhere. I can barely manage to turn my head.

Who's screaming?

No, not who. What. Docking proximity alarm.

*Docking* proximity alarm? But that would mean—

Miranda's neural lace is active when I try to open a voice channel. "Miranda, what the hell just happened?"

"I don't know! This siren just went off!" her worried voice comes back. "Don't *you* know what it means?"

"No, I know what it *means*. It's a proximity alarm. There's a ship nearby. I thought you said no one else was coming for us?"

"They weren't! I checked all the drive traces!"

"Okay, get up here, and we'll try to figure it out."

"Already on my way."

I've already got the map display up, running through trace history, when she arrives a few minutes later. She's barefoot, dressed in sweatpants and some sort of dark blue t-shirt that's way too big for her. She's gathered the material at the waist and tied it in a knot to snug it up, though it's still ludicrously baggy around her shoulders.

Wait, that's *my* shirt. She's stealing my clothes now?

"Did you find it?" she asks, leaning over the bed.

"Yes. There's no drive trace at all of it coming in, but... look here."

I pull up the camera displays again, coupled with the software tool Leela wrote on the fly to get projections of the Snark. A 3-D model spins in the air.

"Well," I say, "so much for 'nobody has any warships any more.'"

It's another torchship, a sleek, streamlined cylinder, covered in what looks like ablative armor plate. Probably from a more expensive builder like SpaceX or Faulcon-DeLacy. I count at least four batteries of point defense cannons, alongside three railguns, much longer and sleeker than my kit model, and the swelling bulges of missile tubes.

"Oh," she says. "Sorry. I really thought... is there anything we can do?"

"Against that monster? Even if the railgun still worked, we'd get maybe one shot off before they tore us apart with those vulcan cannons. And I don't think we can take them out with one shot.

"Out of our league, then?"

"Not at range. I could fly rings around them further out if the *Cat* was spaceworthy. Come to think of it, I kind of did. But they're within a thousand meters and closing. I think they must have been running dark like we did earlier. Set up an intercept trajectory, turned off their drive, and just glided in.

"I think it's too late to avoid them now. Sorry, Pixie, I got nothing."

Nothing is right. I'm all out of schemes. We leaped every hurdle that Murphy and the universe could throw at us, until we couldn't, and we moved the goalposts, and we surprised everyone.

Maybe we changed everything. Forever. But now I'm flat on my back on this bed, exhausted, with no more tricks in my bag. I shoot her a rueful expression. It even hurts to shrug.

She gives me back a sad little smile. "It's okay, Marcus. No one could expect anything more than what you did. You carried us all so far and so long... Way beyond anything I thought was possible. You even took care of me when I really didn't deserve it. I know you think I'm spoiled, but that doesn't mean I'm useless. Let *me* carry us now, okay?"

"Pixie, I don't think you're useless. Hell, you saved my life. And you're right, I pretty much can't get up. In fact, I feel worse today. Everything hurts more, but—"

"Oh, that's normal. You're starting to heal. It's a lot of work."

"—but I don't think you're exactly equipped to fight these guys by yourself."

She smiles again, and rests one hand flat on my chest. Gently. It's cool against my skin.

"I'm not going to fight them, silly. There's nothing to fight over. Leela and the Snark are already gone. I'm going to *negotiate*. You know, drop my family's name and see how much they want to give us a ride home."

"A *ride home*? But the *Cat*—" I begin, struggling to get up. I'm not going to lose my ship over this. I'm not.

She presses me back gently onto the bed. I'm actually so weak that she can do it. Or maybe I just don't feel like fighting her anymore. Not since... well, I guess we're just past that now.

"Easy. I'm not going to let you lose your ship. We can send a salvage team back later. Speaking of which, I've already canceled your debts on her. Trust me. Well, at least with this, okay?"

Trust her?

What a terrible idea... except...

Except it's not. It's not a terrible idea anymore. I do.

I'm not worried *about* her, not anymore. I'm worried *for* her. What if she gets hurt?

"Okay, but what if they're like the last guys? They weren't exactly the talking kind."

"I don't think that's a problem. Look."

She zooms in the projection, focuses on a symbol emblazoned on the side of the ship, just in front of what looks like a sensor blister... a single gold five-pointed star superimposed over the outline of a state that no longer exists...

"That's a Lonestar logo."

"Yes. I didn't know they had warships, but that's professional security, not thugs. My family works with them all the time, or at least our security team does. They'll know who I am."

"Okay, well... yeah. Just... keep me in the loop, okay? Speaking of which, I hope you're ready sort of now-ish."

"Why?"

"Look."

On the display projection, the warship has sprouted tiny dots, scooting away from the hull on vapor trails of expanding gas. Flying in tight, disciplined formation.

Boarders. Again.

"Dr. Foxgrove?"

"Yes," Miranda says. They still haven't slung their compact, short-barreled carbines, but at least they aren't pointed directly at us anymore.

I'm sure as hell glad I didn't have to take on any of these guys. Watching them from Leela's little webcams as they moved up to the ship to medbay was an instructional course in structure clearing, the efficient, slow and methodical crawl of a multilimbed, multiheaded beast, a rifle pointed in every direction at every moment, no rush, no confusion, no corner left unchecked, no chatter. Professionals, used to working together, tied into each other's neural lace for tactical augmented reality display and communications.

Smooth and by the numbers.

The speaker is an officer of some sort, or a team leader, with some sort of rank badge I don't recognize emblazoned on his dark gray plate carrier and helmet. He's a small, spare man, short and wasp-waisted, with defined muscles in his forearms and a quick economy of movement.

If I could get up from this bed, I bet I could take him in a fair fight, though. Probably. Not that it matters. Man's a pro with a squad of pros, and is not interested in silly, wasteful concepts like fair fights. Neither are his pals.

I wouldn't bet on the crew of *Tuf Voyaging* to last thirty seconds against this outfit.

"Doctor Miranda *Lynn* Foxgrove?" he asks again, as his three foremost team members fan out in both directions, crowding into the medbay and positioning themselves at corners with clear fields of fire.

"Yes, that is who I am. Who are—"

"Lieutenant Jordan, ma'am. Lonestar Security Special Task Group Four. Gregor, scan her." His voice carries the characteristic drawl of the vanished Terran state his company hails from. Must be third or fourth generation corporate.

"Aye, sir. Ma'am, please hold still for the camera. There. Done. It's her, sir. Hundred percent match."

The carbine barrels are nowhere near her direction now. I notice that, even in a hospital bed, I am not receiving the same courtesy. The lieutenant speaks into a mic pickup I can't see.

"Tac-com. Package is identified, no threats, moving to secure."

He turns back to Miranda, who appears a bit stunned by all this. "Ma'am, we're your extraction team, on contract with your family. We have a five-minute window, so if there's anything you need to bring with—"

"I'm going to need some time. This man is badly injured, and needs to be prepped and stabilized before we can move him."

"Sorry, ma'am. Your crew is not a mission priority. You need to come with us, *now*, please." His voice is polite, but firm.

"Lieutenant, that was an order. We're going to—"

"Take her," barks the lieutenant, and instantly two of his squaddies are on her in a flying tackle from both sides, slamming into her tiny body with a sickening pair of almost simultaneous thuds. Hard. They clearly don't give a shit about bruising her up, so long as they get her out of here.

In the doorway, a fourth man has produced some thick-barreled plastic parody of a child's toy gun, black and orange, perhaps a stun weapon or some kind of tangler, but it's clearly superfluous and way too late, the first two are on her, hard and rough, forcing her hands behind her back. One turns his leg to catch the savage kick she aims at his kneecap.

I don't even think about it. I'm rising off the bed, half-naked except for the underwear Miranda didn't cut away while she was operating. The pain is brutal, sickening, but I don't care, I just wall it up, push it away, lock it somewhere in corner of my brain. Later, when I have time, I can whimper, throw up, maybe cry a bit.

Later.

That's when the third man steps in. I don't think his eyes ever left me. My rising chest meets a rifle barrel coming the other way, and the flash suppressor on the end of it hits me square in the chest, folds me up around it. I still don't care about the pain, but the pain doesn't care that I don't care, and my vision swims as I drop back down to the bed.

"Don't," a blurry, dark-skinned face snarls from somewhere behind the rifle. Somewhere far away I hear Miranda screaming something about don't, he's in critical condition, you'll tear the fucking stitches, trying to give instructions, orders no one's listening to, and then a metallic ratcheting sound. Handcuffs, maybe.

Then her muffled voice, trying to scream more words through—cloth, or something.

I can't get up. I can't go to her.

I try to focus on the face in front of me... some kinda Indian, maybe Pakistani. I wanna remember that face, save it up for later. Him and the lieutenant. Jordan. Whoever else I can see.

Maybe I find you again, little man. When I'm not stuck in this bed. When your little friends aren't around.

"Package is secure. Cass-evac for the other one, sir?"

"Not a mission parameter. Leave him. We evac *now*."

There's a muffled shriek in Miranda's high voice, and then another one, deeper, masculine.

"OW! Fuck! She *bit* me!"

I'm still pinned down by a rifle barrel, but I manage to turn my head and get a look at her. She's fighting, squirming like a kitten that's just understood the concept of "the vet," and one of her captors has his hand tucked into his armpit.

"You can't just *leave* him, you idiot! He's in critical condition! He needs ongoing medical care, or he'll *die*! I swear to god, if you don't get off me, I'll—"

"Dammit, I'm *bleeding*. Crazy bitch—"

"Rodgers, take over for him. Spray it with foam and get her in a vacuum rescue bag. *Move.*"

"—make you regret it for the rest of what used to be your career, you slack-jawed fuckwit!"

"Come on, carry her if you have to."

She stops screaming, suddenly, and her outsized purple eyes are focused on me now. Wide, shining. Desperate.

"Marcus, I—"

She stops, swallows, shakes her head with her eyes squeezed shut, like she's mad at herself, or the world, or... something.

"No, not important. Not now. Marcus, there's a tube in your chest to drain the fluid. The stitches will dissolve on their own, but you need to pull it out when they do. About five days."

Her eyes drill through me, like she's trying to stare the information into me. There's no time to say anything to her, no time to do anything but listen, repeat under my breath, try to remember.

"There's nanite antibiotics in the second drawer on the left, in a blister pack labeled 'Axalovid,' the one with the silver foil."

They've dragged her to the door now. She tries to hook the frame with an ankle, but they just power right through, out into the corridor.

"Take one a day, every day, until they're gone. You have to take them all! Stay in bed as much as you can, but don't..."

And she's gone. Her voice unintelligible, just an incoherent echo, as they drop down the ladder, low-gravity style. I can still hear her screaming what sounds like curses as they open the airlock.

By the time I think to check Leela's camera array again, I get nothing but a fleeting glimpse of the squad dragging an inflated, and still struggling, vacuum rescue bag into the airlock. I try the neural link, but there's nothing. Those bags are radiation-shielded.

And then she's gone for real.

Can't think about that. Gotta remember what she used her last seconds to tell me. Chest shunt. Five days. Bed rest. Antibiotics. Second drawer on the... was it the left? Or the right? Axalo... something. Better be able to find it. My life could depend on that.

She's gone.

Just like that.

Out of my life.

I swore I'd get her out of my life. Way back when.

Be careful what you wish for.

I'm going to stay alive. I'm going to get my ass out of this jam. I'm going to make it home. You said it yourself, Miranda. I don't give up. I don't stop fighting. Not now. Not ever. I may be a fuckup with a history of bad decisions, not least of which was signing onto your crazy artifact heist, but at least I don't let them stop me. I keep going.

I'm going to get out of this somehow. And get home.

And you? You take care of yourself, too, you fucking crazy little adorable psycho pixie brat. Give them twice the hell you gave me.

Bite more fingers.

Get home okay safe, okay? Don't let your dad give you any shit about all this.

Take care of Leela for me.

# Chapter 33
## The Edge of Sunlight

To travel solar north from the plane of the ecliptic, the great disc in which the planetary orbits are aligned, is to travel into a vast, silent darkness.

But space is never truly empty. There are many, many objects gravitationally bound to the Sun, partnered to its 226 million year orbital journey around Sagittarius A*, the Great Devourer, the supermassive black hole at the heart of the galaxy. And some of them are out here, above the ring of planetary orbits.

Out here, the short-period comets of the "Scattered Disc" pass through the cold and dark portions of their sharply-canted orbits, simple dirty snowballs, tailless in the dark region beyond the warmth, light, and solar wind of inner space.

Out here, the dwarf planets Eris and Gonggong swing upwards into the dark on every pass around their distant parent star, along with thousands of rocks too small and irregular to be any sort of planet at all, and too distant and dark to be spotted by the telescopes of the warm, bright inner system.

The spacecraft does not pass within a million kilometers of any of these. In the vast expanses of trans-Neptunian space, the odds against this are extreme. And luck, capricious lover that she is, is done with this particular vessel, and has been for many weeks now.

Beyond the wide orbits of these tiny specks, fifteen billion kilometers out, the solar wind of charged particles streaming from the sun, spread cold and thin, begins to break up against the colder, thinner, medium of interstellar hydrogen, churning in a froth too slow and gentle and microscopically insignificant to be seen with the human eye.

This is the termination shock boundary. And this, the spacecraft collides with, for it is everywhere. It encloses the entire system in its shell, a sphere surrounding the star, stretched in the direction of its travel through the western spiral arm of the galaxy. The intruder disperses the flows of particles and gas, cutting through them, meeting such insubstantial resistance that even the most sensitive instruments aboard barely register it, were anyone even watching the readouts to notice.

No one is.

The spacecraft moves on, tumbling end over end at a single rotation per minute, a thin cylinder swinging around a fat one, gently simulating a weak gravity for anyone who might be aboard.

Further out, so much further out that light takes a full four hours to traverse the distance, the solar wind breaks up utterly at the heliopause point, and, this, too, the spacecraft tumbles through, 16 days later, traveling at a small, but not insignificant, percentage of the velocity of light itself.

This isn't the end. Far ahead, so far ahead that the spacecraft will not reach its inner edge for three full years, lies the Oort Cloud, a loose, cold sphere of proto-comets, icy planetesimals, and frozen debris that stretches halfway to the nearest stars.

The spacecraft will exit this zone in another one hundred and sixty years. Along the way, it will collide with nothing, touch nothing, see nothing. It will not pass within a million kilometers of anything large enough to see with the unaided human eye. The Oort Cloud is far thinner, darker, and colder than the merest and most arctic of wisps of the earthly water vapor structure it is named for.

The spacecraft will not be stopped here, or later. Or ever.

It will pass out of the influence of its home star utterly, never to return. Tens of thousands of years later, it will pass within a few billion kilometers of a white dwarf star that its creator species knows only as a number, but it will pass quickly, far too distant and too rapid to enter any sort of orbit.

It will sail through that band of light, a strange visitor from an alien land, and depart forever out into eternal darkness.

In time, it will exit its home galaxy, and plunge on and on through the endless ocean of night, until the distant end of the universe, when time itself creaks, when any laws of physics its creators know begin to break down and the ultimate fate of the two paired cylinders becomes... unknowable.

The *White Cat* will live forever.

Where it is now, in the shallows of space, the littoral zone of light, where the solar wind breaks up, the small craft displays no visible signs of life. There is no hint of any plan to avoid its one-way ticket to the end of the universe. Its instrument clusters do not move or radiate. Every light on its hull is dark. Scars of forceful impact, here and there, mark its hull, with no signs of any effort to repair them.

The *White Cat* might as well be dead.

But in the infrared spectrum, far below any frequency range visible to its creator species, a little heat radiation escapes into the thin and frigid darkness around the hull. It could, perhaps, be the simple entropic process of a warm object cooling to thermal equilibrium with its surroundings, with the status quo of cold and darkness that will characterize the remainder of its existence.

It would require precise measurement, and careful calculation, to disprove this guess. But somewhere in that hull is a source of heat, burning low, constrained by the capacity of single, small, radiothermal backup generator.

And in the large cylinder of the hold, past layers of hull plate and radiation shielding, in the relative cold and dark which is nothing to the cold, dark, and emptiness without, at the very center, a tiny, but bright, electric light is burning.

Hold fast.

When humans sailed oceans of water on our home planet, we used to tattoo it across our knuckles, a charm to fix a man's grip in the rigging, to hold him in rough weather from a fall to the wooden deck, or the unforgiving sea.

It's written across my knuckles, too. I'm not superstitious. But I honor what I came from.

Hold fast.

I don't have rigging to hold onto, just a steel catwalk of cheap modular scaffolding around the drive spindle, throwing sharp linear shadows in the glare of my single LED work light.

Standing on its platform, I can scarcely fall. But I hold fast all the same, my knuckles white on the steel pipe, gripping, tense, as I watch the drive core.

The humming throb rises, pulses through the cold darkness of the hold, vibrates the scaffolding, the cargo racks, washes around and through me, shakes my skull, my spine, the walls of my chest. I can feel the sting of it in the new scars on my ribs, where I cut away Miranda's careful stitching just yesterday.

On my neural display, drive core temperature creeps from black to blue to green. Warning text lights up the screen, scrolling too fast to read or follow, but I've disabled every safety cutoff I could find, reading the tech manuals over and over until the diagrams hung behind my eyelids in my sleep, and the humming doesn't die, it *rises*.

Hold fast.

Higher in pitch now, louder, but... smoothing out. I'm staring, fixed eyes, on the tangle of hand-bent pipes that I've welded in place of the damaged primary coolant manifold. Seams are holding, display tells me the water pressure is good, but it's still right where I put it. The entire spindle assembly, hundreds of kilos of it, is right where it started.

Come on, you bastard. Move. Spin.

Temp's in the yellow now. Within the central vacuum shaft that runs through the *White Cat*, exotic fields crush hydrogen into a line of space so small that Newtonian models of physics break down. I'm feeding the tiniest possible amount of fuel, barely enough to tick the drive over, idling, but hydrogen fusion is the beating heart of stars, the mighty engine of the universe, and even the smallest breath of it pours out the fire of the gods. Unless my improvised heat management systems kick in soon, the field emitters will melt, and...

Well, there's a reason why I'm floating right here by the drive core. If I'm going to die out here, let me not starve or freeze or run out of oxygen. Let it be fast and clean and brilliant, in a wash of plasma fire. Either I get this working, or I go out on my terms. Not stranded. Not trapped like a rat in a dark and freezing cage. Not flying out in an endless trajectory towards the big empty night of interstellar space.

I'm not giving up yet. The Princess... no, *Miranda*, my *crewmate*, was right when she said it. I don't give up. Ever. I'd have to be dead or disabled.

And I've got things left to do. This isn't over.

Temperature creeping towards the red now.

Hold fast.

Come on, *work*. Why won't you work? I checked everything. Over and over again.

I should shut down the reactor, recheck everything, try again, but I don't. Seven times I've tried this, seven times I've bailed out, shut down the drive, reconfigured, tried again. I'm out of ideas. Temperature solidly in the red now.

Turn, damn you.

I'm flirting with death, here.

Hold fast. There's one last thing I have to try.

I grip the scaffolding, tuck my legs into a ball, and *kick*. Something else our ancestors did. Dumb monkey repair tricks. Hit it with a wrench and hope.

The spindle shudders, and I bite back a gasp as the shock runs through my ribs.

Miranda would probably fuss. She would say I shouldn't be out of bed yet. I'd insist I have to get this working, and she would try to nag me back to resting. Hell, she'd probably put her tiny hands on my chest and try to *shove* me back to bed.

I wish she would.

Universe doesn't care what we wish for.

I kick the spindle again, ignoring the stab of pain down my side. I can heal later. If there is a later.

Did it just shift?

Kick.

And the manifold, the clusters of pipes and tubing, the radiator vanes... move. Creep to the right. So slowly I can't trust my eyes, not at first, but... no, there. It's moving. It's definitely moving.

Spinning. For real this time, a stately procession around the drive core, one turn every several seconds. On my display, temperatures stop rising. Plenty of warning indicators, the computers are not happy, but pressurized water is flowing, and the sound of the engine... stabilizes. Pulses with familiar harmonics, the song of smooth running.

I have drive idle.

*I have drive idle.*

And that means I have *power*. No need to ration it now. I trip the lights, the heater controls, and the cargo hold sings to life, stirring with currents of instant warm air, redirected right from the drive cooling system.

Piece by piece, I bring the *White Cat* to life. Climate control, air pumps, water recycler...

Water recycler. I can take a *shower*. It's been... weeks.

... lidar array, XNAV orientation sensors...

I can find out *where I am.*

... high-gain antenna...

I can *look for other ships.*

... mid-frequency communications radio laser.

I can *call civilization.*

I summon the nav plotter display, zoomed out as wide as possible, and the whole solar system spreads out before me. I'm high above the plane of the ecliptic, way further out than I thought, beyond the termination shock boundary, in the heliopause zone.

I'm also coasting faster than I thought, spinning out into the depths of space, where the sun is just another pinprick in a tapestry of stars. Every second, I'm thousands of kilometers further away from the worlds.

And I've been resting, and healing, and fixing the drive, for... weeks, while those seconds, those thousands of kilometers, passed.

I didn't realize how far out I was. With most of the ship shut down to save power, there was no point wasting any on gathering data I couldn't have done a thing about.

This far out, I don't actually know if I *can* call civilization after all. I don't even know if anyone's ever been this far out before. I might have set some sort of record, a sort of strange, slumbering Magellan, doped up on painkillers and dreaming of Miranda. Of her face as they dragged her away, kicking and screaming and protesting, towards safety and salvation and life.

I don't think anyone will come to rescue *me*, kicking and screaming or not. Even if they would, targeting a com laser at this distance might not even be possible, and focusing it so someone could hear me...

Doubtful.

Even then, getting a rescue mission, doubly so. I could be a hero to the entire solar system right now, or a villain. Or just some loser with a flat crypto account.

Or a target.

No, I'd rather not pick up the phone and let them know where I am. Let's find out if drive thrust works. Can't run a diagnostic, though. I'm running too far out of spec. The computer would throw a fit and shut down the drive instantly.

I just have to try it and see if I die. And hey, I'm not a nuclear fireball yet. Hold fast, right?

Right.

Call up a virtual throttle. Set it for the lowest sensitivity possible. Let's see what I have.

So what am I waiting for? All I have to do is ease it in. One tenth of a gravity. A twentieth. Almost anything would eventually slow me down, turn me around, get me back.

Oh. That's it, isn't it?

I don't know what I'm coming back to. Is Leela free and broadcasting a treasure trove of knowledge through some internet relay station? Is she still running and hiding, or have they given up chasing her?

For any given value of "they."

Is she even alive, or, well, in her case, still functioning? Or was she intercepted and shot to pieces after all? What did the news say about us? Am I a public figure now? What does Orbital space think of me? Did we dominate the news, or get eclipsed by the latest viral meme or SpaceX press release?

Is there an Open Xenotechnology Foundation, now, under Miranda's direction, a thriving enterprise, flush with donated funds, idealistic staff, and corporate sponsorships? Or just a website and nothing else?

Did anyone even *notice* what we did?

We.

Miranda and I. That's the part I've been not-thinking about. The ship feels so peaceful and so... empty. No one to fight with. No one to talk to.

Is she back in the dubiously welcoming bosom of her family? Restarting her AI project, with lots of new investors, now that Leela is so self-evidently a brilliant success? Beating the talk-show circuit, humble-bragging about the nobility of her decision to share Builder technology with everyone?

All of the above?

And what happens if I show up? It's not like she has any further need for me. And, hell, a couple of months ago, I'd have said that would be that. But, now, I don't know. I remember the feel of her lying against me, holding my hand, stroking my hair, and I'm not so sure what she'd want.

Or what I want. From her.

We never got a chance to figure that out. We never even got to say goodbye.

Leela's out there, too. She, at least, will definitely want to see me again. And, hell, it's that or stay here and be a space hermit until the food runs out. Might as well bite the bullet.

So, virtual throttle, low sensitivity, get a good grip on the scaffold... and...

...eyes closed, waiting for it...

...three, two...

...watch the drive temp...

There.

It's so gradual when it happens, not the hard slap of gravity restored, but slowly, 'down' defines itself, and I'm not floating over the platform. I'm standing on it.

It works.

It's slow.

It's underpowered.

The computer tells me that drive efficiency is down by a factor of three.

And with all that extra heat, the core temp starts to creep up if I push it above point one six gravities.

*But it works.*

Just a little bit, and a little bit is enough. I'm going to live.

I can fly again, and I'm at the helm. I can steer her where I want to. I may be off in the deep black, flying so fast it'll take me more weeks just to stop. I may be so far from civilization that it'll take me another hundred days or so to get back. Maybe more, depending on how that drive behaves. I'll probably have to ration the food.

I may be alone out here without my... team? My... crewmates?

My friends.

But I can fly again, and that means I am whole again, complete. Alive. That means *this isn't over*. I can point myself at Mars, put enough sky behind me, and see the rest of my species again. See civilization.

See what happened.

See what I've done to the place.

It's time to hoist a sail for home

## *The journey isn't over yet (obviously)*

The sequel to *Theft of Fire* is in progress. Stay up-to-date on *Box of Trouble*'s release by visiting **DevonEriksen.com**, where you can sign up for the publication updates newsletter.

Your support directly contributes to the success of this story, and the future of the Orbital Space trilogy. As a self-published author, awareness is always a challenge. I would be incredibly grateful if you took a few moments to help other readers discover the experience of *Theft of Fire*.

**Amazon, Goodreads, etc**: I wrote this novel with one goal in mind: to give the reader something to love. I hope you found that something in this book, and I would love to hear about it in a review.

**Social Media**: If you enjoyed reading, if there's something you loved, something that made you think, or see the worlds in a new way, I'd love to hear about it, and perhaps others would, too. Wherever you exist digitally, you are encouraged to share news of this book, and your thoughts about it.

**Word-of-Mouth**: Whether it's telling friends, encouraging a local bookshop to stock *Theft of Fire*, or getting it selected for a book club's next pick, your voice is the **most effective** way for your friends and community discover their next great read.

**Your Local Library**: Use your library's "suggest a book to add to our catalog" form to help others access *Theft of Fire*, regardless of their capacity to purchase a copy.

# Acknowledgments

Before I set out to write a novel, I was always astonished at how many people the authors saw fit to thank. Perhaps part of me imagined that authors wish to appear humble, by spreading the credit for their work as far and wide as possible.

Now as a new author, I know better. A novel is the child of one brain, but many hands. And if my list is shorter than most, then the burden carried by each name was all the heavier, and the thanks I owe them all the greater.

First, I must dedicate the work to Brandon Sanderson, who has never heard of me, and may never read it, but who made it possible by publishing a master class on the structure of fantasy writing, on the internet, gratis. It is he who took me from a dabbler who wrote good scenes to an author who could turn them into bricks, and build the edifice of a story. Gratitude is owed.

I must also thank my wives, Sara and Christine, whose support and enthusiasm have never faltered, from the day I hatched a crazy plan to retire from engineering and write, to the day the long-awaited project finally hit the shelves. I could not possibly list all their contributions without padding the final page count beyond all sense and reason. Thriving is a team sport.

Special thanks are due to my initial test reader, Nicole Foresman, who waded through the entire five-hundred-plus page first draft in the space of a single long weekend. Her understanding of the goals of the work, enthusiasm for its story, and laser-focused perception of its early-draft shortcomings were far in advance of the capabilities of most professional editors.

I am also grateful to my small team of beta readers, who gave their time and energy to a lengthy tome penned by an internet stranger, and to extensive debriefings afterwards.

Without their additional perspectives, this story would stagger in the places that it now soars. F. Dan O'Neill, Skyler Hawley, Jonathan Baldie, Annie Yoder, Neil Sorenson, "Uncle Bob" Martin, Ryan Lackey, Candace Groenhke, Steph Hance, and Gabriel Cortez, thank you.

I would like to thank Patricia McIntosh-Mize, my editor, and fellow author Terry Maggert, who introduced me to her. Her suggestions have been thoughtful and wise, and her support, both emotional and logistical, unwavering. But she can have my ellipses when they pry them from my cold dead hands.

I would like to thank Thea Magerand, for her brilliant cover art and design, and for her assistance with the interior art as well. Thea, your patience with my endless requests for tiny revisions is much appreciated, almost as much as the amazing way you reached into my head and pulled Miranda, Marcus, and Leela out. It is a nervous enterprise to have a year of one's heartfelt efforts judged by the work of another, but I was always in good hands with you.

I would like to thank Elise Ramelot and Gabriel Cortez, for being my family, providing more kindness, patience, understanding, and support than blood relatives ever could.

I would like to thank the many science fiction and fantasy writers whose work I devoured in my youth. You will find small tributes to them in the story if you seek carefully.

And lastly I'd like to thank you, the reader, if you made it this far. You spent your hard earned money, and your precious time, which you only get so much of in this life, taking a chance on an unknown author. I hope that your investment has been rewarded, and that you will revisit me for the next step in this journey.

Made in the USA
Middletown, DE
10 December 2023

45174966R00293